PRAISE FOR *THE UNCLAIMED VICTIM*

"Thoroughly grounded in the sparse kno~~~~ ~~~~ ~~~~~~s, Pulley's well-paced and, at times, ~~~~~~~~~~~ ~~~~~~~~~~ ~~~cessfully portrays the gritty social and ~~~~~~~~~~~~~~~~~~~ ~~~veland. Her use of a parallel narrati~~~~~~~~~~~~~~~~~~~~~ .nd her plucky but beleaguered heroi~~~~~~~~~ ~~~~ 1990s Kris—will have readers rooting for them ~~~~ ~~st page to last. A genuine gothic treat, leading me to suspect that what the Torso Murders saga needed all along was a woman's touch."

—John Stark Bellamy II, historian and author of *They Died Crawling*

"Architecture speaks to D.M. Pulley, and it tells her the most wonderful stories. Her mysteries are as twisty and strange as the real-world buildings that inspire her. *The Unclaimed Victim* is a new exploration of Cleveland's most notorious unsolved mystery: Who was the Mad Butcher of Kingsbury Run? D.M. Pulley offers a chilling explanation that suggests the murders go on to this day. Has she cracked the case that drove Eliot Ness insane? I think maybe."

—James Renner, author of *True Crime Addict*

"A murder in the present intertwines with a set of killings from the past in D.M. Pulley's engaging, addictive thriller. Pulley is both a natural storyteller and a meticulous researcher, and her tale takes us into a fascinating, forgotten corner of 1930s Cleveland. *The Unclaimed Victim* is a haunting and unputdownable novel!"

—Dan Chaon, author of *Ill Will*

"D.M. Pulley dips from past to present with the touch of a master, squaring the bloody circle of two lives with an ending that's both shocking . . . and perfect."

—Matthew Iden, author of *The Winter Over*

THE
UNCLAIMED
VICTIM

ALSO BY D.M. PULLEY

The Dead Key

The Buried Book

THE UNCLAIMED VICTIM

D.M. PULLEY

Text copyright © 2017 by D.M. Pulley
All rights reserved.

Published by Thomas & Mercer, Seattle

www.apub.com

Amazon, the Amazon logo, and Thomas & Mercer are trademarks of Amazon.com, Inc., or its affiliates.

ISBN-13: 9781542046435
ISBN-10: 1542046432

Front cover design by PEPE *nymi*
Back cover design by Ray Lundgren

Printed in the United States of America

For Flo, Rose, and all the others

He who fights with monsters might take care

lest he thereby become a monster.

And when you gaze long into an abyss,

the abyss also gazes into you.

—Friedrich Nietzsche, *Beyond Good and Evil*, 1886

HACKED BODY OF WOMAN
FOUND ON E. SIDE BEACH

The naked torso of a woman's body, washed up today on the shore of Lake Erie at the foot of East 156th Street, provided police with the most gruesome and puzzling murder mystery of recent years.

—*Cleveland Press*, September 5, 1934, p. 1

CHAPTER 1

April 7, 1999

It wasn't him.

She stared at the clear plastic bags lying on the metal table and shook her head. A button-down denim shirt sat in one. A pair of jeans lay folded in another. A sock in a third. White labels had been stuck to each bag with handwritten notes. *Case #32-004-A,* one of them read. They were all dated April 6, 1999.

Yesterday, she thought.

Streaks of mud darkened the fabric. The white sweat sock looked like it had been pulled from a puddle. The stink of rotting leaves, dirt, and animal urine seeped out of the sealed bags.

"Do you recognize any of these items?" the man across from her asked.

The braided leather belt next to the jeans looked hauntingly familiar, but she shook her head. The clothes could be anyone's.

"We found this in one of the pockets." He opened a leather wallet and set it in front of her. Her father's face glared up at her through the yellowed plastic film holding his driver's license into the framed pocket. His salt-and-pepper hair was buzzed tight to his scalp as if he might still be in the armed forces. The permanent stubble of beard darkened his hard jaw and cleft chin as he glowered at the camera. He hated pictures. She could see it in the annoyed set of his eyes, pointing at her as though he'd lost his patience, as though she'd done something wrong.

She shook her head and whispered, "No. Someone must've taken it."

"These items were found in the same vicinity as the . . ." The man across the table paused, catching himself. "As the remains. I understand this is difficult, but the evidence strongly suggests the victim was Alfred Ray Wiley. When was the last time you spoke with him?"

The remains? A buzzing numbness spread down her arms and legs. A manila file folder sat closed on the table next to the evidence bags. The edge of a photograph peeked out from the side of it with a hint of blood. Her father's picture watched from behind the plastic as she tried to remember, to think at all. *The victim was Alfred Ray Wiley.* "Uh, I'm sorry, what was the question?"

"When did you last speak with your father?"

"I don't know. Maybe Christmas?" It sounded terrible coming out of her mouth. She was a terrible daughter.

"Did he mention anything to you? Anything he was worried about? Anything strange?"

She shook her head. "No. We just . . . we had an argument."

"What about?" He pulled her father's driver's license from its holder and handed it to her as though it would help her remember.

She held it between her shaking hands. It felt wrong to be holding something that was his, something that belonged in his back pocket. "School . . . He . . . he wanted me to move back home."

Her father's eyes drilled into her from the photograph. *This whole college thing was a mistake, Goddammit! I don't care about your grades. No daughter of mine has any business livin' in that city. Shacked up with a man no less . . . Don't you lie to me. The landlord told me . . . I don't care if he is just a friend. He could be as queer as a three-dollar bill, you're still livin' like a Goddamned prostitute . . . Lookit. If you can't afford the place, you don't belong there.*

"Is that all? Did he mention any problems at work? Any money trouble?"

"No . . . he just . . ." She wiped away a stray tear before it brought on a flood of them. The license fumbled between her fingers and fell to the table with an awkward clap. "He was mad about the money. School's expensive and uh . . . he didn't think I was getting good enough grades."

She didn't explain that she had gotten a roommate without his permission to help pay the bills. Or that he'd hung up on her in a rage and they hadn't talked since.

An arm wrapped around her shoulders and gave her limp limbs a squeeze. She felt herself collapsing inward under its weight.

Her interrogator pressed on. "Did he have any enemies? Anyone that might wish him harm?"

She shook her head. "No. I don't . . . This is crazy. It can't be him!"

"Show her the tattoo," the man holding her whispered.

The police officer opened the manila folder and flipped through several large glossy photographs. Fragments of pink skin, black hair, crusted blood, and white bone flashed between his fingers. He stopped and pulled out a large close-up image of a man's shoulder marked with a dark gray skull with wings. *Death from Above,* it said. Her father had one just like it from the war. He always kept it covered up by his shirtsleeves. A familiar scar and dark mole muddled the ink.

Dad?

"That's enough," the man next to her said.

"We're going to need a signed statement. Without prints or dental, it's going to be tough to make a positive ID any other way. There's DNA, but getting a match . . . Was he a blood donor?"

Without prints or dental. The photograph of the tattoo didn't show the rest of him. His hands. His mouth. Her eyes flitted between the lone sock and the closed folder in the officer's hand.

"Just give us a minute." The man gripping her shoulders held up a hand. It was her father's best friend, Ben.

The metal chair screeched against the floor as the officer pushed himself away from the table and stood up. "Take all the time you need."

He left with the file of photographs under his arm.

Kris Wiley blinked her eyes clear as though waking from a trance. She was sitting in the Auglaize County Sheriff's Office. Her shirt was inside out.

"I'm so sorry, Kritter. I know he'd never want you to see all of this, but there was nothing I could do." Ben let go of her shoulders and grabbed both her hands. Water welled in his eyes. His face had gone red. She'd known Ben all her life and had never once seen him cry, except from laughing too hard. He was wearing his deputy sheriff's uniform. Growing up, she knew Ben was a cop, but he never wore his uniform when he came over to watch the games with her dad. It felt like Halloween. He squeezed her palms. "We just have to get confirmation from the family. For the official records."

"What do you want me to say?" she heard herself ask in a small voice. It didn't even sound like her own. Her real voice wanted to scream *Stop!* so she could think, so she could make sense of it. So she could prove to everyone that none of this was really happening, that whatever they had found wasn't him. But time kept careening by as she sat there. It had all happened so fast—the phone call from the Auglaize County Sheriff's Office at 6:00 a.m., her waking her roommate, asking him to explain it to her professors. The words *family emergency* rattling through her head the entire drive from Cleveland back home.

She watched it all unfold like it was happening to somebody else. And she couldn't stop an evil voice in her head from whispering, *Does this mean I can stay in school? Does this mean I'm free?* She shook the thought away and pulled her hands back, digging her fingernails into her palms as penance. *I'm a terrible daughter. Ungrateful. Stupid. I deserve to be the one that's missing.*

Ben winced as though someone were squeezing his fingers in a vise. "We need you to confirm it's him."

She kept her eyes on the pile of clothes. "That *what's* him? These clothes? The wallet? Anybody could've stolen them, right? They don't prove anything."

"They found him, hon. And you don't want to see what they found, alright?"

She opened her mouth to protest but nothing came out. *He's not dead. He'd never let himself be dead.*

"I know it's hard, Kris. No one understands that better than me. Your dad was a like a brother to me . . . We're trying to make this as easy as we can."

"A tattoo doesn't make it him," she protested. *Oh my God. Did it? What would I even do?* "What if it's not him, Ben?"

"No one's seen him in four days, Kritter," Ben pushed back gently. "He's been missing at the train yard all week."

"Maybe . . . maybe he went hunting or . . ." She stared at the ugly gray speckled linoleum. *He would never leave me all alone like this. Would he?* The question swelled in her chest.

"They found his truck."

"What?" she heard herself ask. "Where?"

"Along the Auglaize River outside Fort Amanda."

He'd taken her there before, back when he was still trying to teach her to fish. Before she hit puberty and he started treating her like an alien. *What is that pink stuff on your face?* She felt herself falling off a cliff. "When did you find it?"

"Last night." Ben kneaded his hands together. "I talked to the boys at the canoe livery myself. He headed upstream Saturday afternoon and no one's seen 'im since. Kris, I need you to believe that if there was any chance in the world that he was still out there somewhere, I'd be the first one lookin' for him."

Kris watched him rub the tears back into his eyeballs as she plummeted further away. "There has to be some mistake."

"I know. But they found 'im, and . . ." He cleared his throat and shook his head.

"What?" All Ben had said on the phone was, *There's been an accident, Kritter. You have to come home. Can somebody give you a ride?* She'd said no. Her only friend at school was her roommate and he had to work. *Then take it nice and slow, girl. Be safe. Everything's going to be just fine.* He'd lied to her. Nothing was going to be fine. "What did they find?"

He breathed in a shaking breath and shook his head. "Fishermen pulled a piece of him out of the river. It was only a few miles from where they found the truck. Hunters found the clothes in the woods. It's him, Krit . . . We're still looking for the rest of him, but I'm afraid the facts don't lie."

"A piece of him?" Her stomach shrank at the thought of an arm or a leg floating in the water.

"Yeah. I know . . . Might've been a bear." He rubbed his face.

"No. That doesn't make any sense. A bear? In Ohio?"

"We're not ruling anything out just yet." Ben gently patted her knee like she was six years old again. He gave it a squeeze and shut his eyes to think a moment. When he opened them, he said, "We don't have to do this today, kiddo. I'll have them run the DNA. You give us a sample, just a swab of saliva, and we'll have something to work with. It'll take a while. A week or two even, but we'll do whatever we have to. Alright?"

She nodded. His tone of voice told her she was being ridiculous, refusing to make the ID, but she could picture her father storming into the room, furious with them both for giving up too easily. *Just couldn't wait to be rid of me, huh? Couldn't be bothered to even look?*

"You don't have to decide anything right now." Ben squeezed her shoulder and went to speak with the other officer out in the hallway. Their hushed voices drifted in through the open door.

"I don't think we're going to be able to get that ID today. We'll have to run the DNA."

"Against what? Alfred Wiley's not in the system."

"Yeah, but his daughter's sittin' right in there and she's willing to give a spit sample. That's gotta be good enough, right?"

The other officer didn't respond right away. "If we pull a positive, it works fine, but you know as well as I do that a negative doesn't mean . . . I really should get confirmation from the family. Once we begin the autopsy, it'll be harder to get an ID."

"Dammit," Ben hissed. "She's only nineteen years old. She needs some time to process all this. I'll take the heat if this comes back on you. Alright?"

"There's no other family?"

"Nope . . . Not unless you count me."

The quiet voices of the two men echoed off the cracked linoleum and yellowed ceiling panels of the tiny conference room. Kris picked her father's driver's license up off the table again. His unsmiling lips and impatient eyes daggered up at her from under the hard laminate. The fluorescent lights overhead cast a ghostly sheen over the evidence bags. She squinted at the spots of blood dotting the front of the button-down denim shirt. It didn't prove anything. From the smell of it, the clothes had been lying in the woods for weeks. She stared at his unyielding face and could hear him talking.

Don't be stupid, Kritter! You know damned well that there's another explanation for all of this. Do you really think I'd leave you to your own devices? That I'd just up and die and let you go off to some hippie art school *for Christ's sake?*

No. She didn't.

I'm always going to be your father.

She pressed his photo to her chest and forced herself to breathe.

A few moments later, Ben was back at her side with a vial and cotton swab. She let him scrape the insides of her cheeks, then watched him cap the sample and hand it off to the other officer. He turned back to her, wiping his hands on his trousers. "You hungry? You can't have eaten much."

She shook her head.

"Well, you can keep an old man company, can't ya?"

Ben led her out of the Auglaize County Sheriff's Office and into the small parking lot. She didn't notice she was still clutching the license against her shirt until they were halfway across the pavement. Her eyes darted back toward the interrogation room and the line of plastic bags. *No. I'm not going back there.* She slipped the thin piece of plastic into her pocket as Ben opened the passenger door to his sheriff's department cruiser. *If they ask, I'll give it back. They're the ones that gave it to me. I didn't steal it.* It still felt wrong, though.

Kris had loved riding with Officer Ben when she was a girl. He used to let her turn on the sirens. Sitting there, she felt nine years old again. She hugged her knees to her chest and wished herself small. They left her rusted-out Jeep in the lot and headed down the street.

Downtown Wapakoneta felt vacant compared to the streets of Cleveland as they headed east toward the Dixie Highway. The stores lining both sides of the street looked like a cardboard movie set—a contrived replica of small-town America. All the buildings had shrunk in the seven months she'd been away.

Out the window, the roller rink and high school rushed by. The band was practicing on the football field. Their disjointed, brassy music drifted in and then out of her window.

"How are things going at school?" Ben asked. She could hear him doing his best to keep his voice light.

"I don't know," she whispered and pressed her forehead to her knees. A severed arm floated through a dark stream of thought. A tattoo blurred in the water.

"Last I heard, you were thinking about transferring out to some art school?"

Kris tried to blink the flashes of torn flesh and bone from her mind, wishing she could unsee the photos. "Um. Yeah. I guess I was. Dad doesn't think it's such a good idea," she heard herself say.

They call them starving artists for a reason, Kris. He'd laughed, and for a moment she could hear the sound of it. She squeezed the armrest and forced in a breath.

"I'm sure he just wants what's best for you." Ben patted her knee again. "You got a good head on your shoulders. He always said that, you know."

Ben winced at the past tense. She winced too. *He never said that. Not to me.* They sat in silence for two traffic lights. The Lil' Chef diner was up on the next block, but the thought of food made her sick. The acrid smell of piss and rotting leaves seemed to cling to her shirt. It was still inside out.

"Ben?"

He gave her a weak smile. "What can I do for you, kiddo?"

"I want to go home."

CHAPTER 2

The mailbox at the edge of the driveway was overflowing with envelopes. Ben stopped the car and pulled them all out and picked up a cardboard box sitting on the curb. Without a word, he threw them all onto the backseat and pulled the rest of the way up the gravel drive.

Kris hadn't been home since Christmas. The snow that had covered the yard in a clean blanket had melted away, exposing the overgrown grass and weeds underneath. Brown and yellow paint was peeling off the siding and the window frames in tiny strips. The whole place needed a shave.

Ben stopped the cruiser in front of the windowless garage door. The low-slung ranch sat like a shoebox in a cornfield on the edge of the tiny nowhere village of Cridersville, Ohio. Kris got out of the car and forced her feet to the front door. Yellow crime scene tape stretched across it. Ben ripped it down, muttering, "I told 'em not to seal it, dammit! Sorry, Kritter. We had to come through this morning and check some things."

The front door stared blankly at her as she fumbled with her keys, fingers shaking.

"I got it." Ben pulled out his own key from a fat ring of them and turned the knob.

Inside, the house stood perfectly still as though the life had been snuffed out of it. It felt wrong, like a poorly made diorama of her childhood home, like the right parts and pieces had been carefully arranged in the correct locations for her benefit. All the curtains were drawn. Her father always closed up the house before leaving on a trip. *No sense giving the burglars a sneak preview,* he'd say.

She stepped past the entryway and was greeted by the unmistakable smell of her father left to his own devices. Stale cigars, day-old coffee, open beer cans, baked beans, barbecue, and gun oil.

Ben opened the front curtains to let some light into the tomb. Three sets of antlers hung above a flannel couch that was as old as Kris. The 1970s wood paneling was sparsely decorated with swap-meet paintings of ducks and pheasants and hunting dogs.

Dogs.

Kris's eyes shot to the empty bowls on the floor by the refrigerator then up to Ben. "Did they find Bogie and Gunner?"

"Hmm? Oh, not yet, but they were pretty far from town. Don't you worry about those mutts, Kritter. They'd go feral in about two hours." He forced a chuckle. "We're gonna have a hell of a time convincing them to come back."

Kris tried to smile but could only manage a grimace. Her father had spent years training them to retrieve ducks and run raccoons up trees. He loved those stupid dogs. She supposed she did too. Her eyes darted from the overflowing ashtray to the rifle pieced out on the coffee table to the picture of her he'd hung over his favorite chair. Her thirteen-year-old self grinned back with a mouth full of braces. She'd curled and fluffed her long brown hair out to full capacity and was wearing makeup she'd smuggled into the house in her backpack. Under the pink blush, her face was still as round as a little girl's.

He'd looked at her coming down the driveway like she'd grown three heads. *Wow. You look . . . very nice.* That night he'd taken her out to dinner, casting wary glances at her the entire evening like he didn't know her at all. Everything that came after that night seemed to widen the gap between them. Her first bra, her first period, her first kiss, she hid it all from him, hoping to erase the distance, but it was never the same again.

"I don't feel well," she whispered. "I think I need to sleep."

"I understand. How 'bout we have dinner tonight? I'll pick you up around five? Deal?"

The room was spinning. That ugly, flannel, duck-covered room. It was all she could do not to pick up the ashtray and throw it through the window. He wasn't there to stop her.

"You alright, kid? Here. Let's get you to bed." Ben put an arm around her shoulders and led her down the narrow hallway past the one bathroom to her old bedroom in the back. Her father had given her the biggest room not long after his terrible realization that she was a girl. *Lord knows I don't need all this closet space.* She didn't either. He hardly ever took her shopping, but she'd taken the room as a consolation prize. Her teen magazines and feminine products stayed carefully hidden under her bed.

Nothing had changed.

Soccer trophies and ribbons still lined the top of her dresser. Photos she'd taken of friends still hung from her bulletin board. Her teddy bear still sat on his shelf.

Ben laid her down onto the worn blue quilt. He took off her shoes. He patted her head and said, "We're going to get through this, girl. We will. Now get some rest. I'll see you at five."

She didn't even hear him close the door.

Kris woke four hours later to the sound of the phone ringing in the kitchen. She bolted upright in bed. It took her another ring to remember where she was . . . and why.

Ring.

She ran to the kitchen and snatched up the phone. *Dad? Where are you?* She cleared her throat and managed a broken "Hello?"

"Krissy? Is that you? It's Becky."

"Becky?" Her heart rate fell at the sound of the girl's voice. It wasn't him. Becky Calhoun had been her best friend in junior high school. She hadn't talked to the girl in over two years.

"Oh my God. Are you alright?"

"What?" Kris rubbed her eyes.

"Is it true? I mean about your dad?"

"I—I don't know." Words caught in the gray muck that had replaced her insides. "I really . . . Don't—"

Becky cut her off. "You poor thing! My uncle just called and said they found his truck up north. He said he saw you down at the sheriff's office. It's not true, is it? Is he really dead?"

Is he really dead? Her voice choked down to an inaudible whisper. "I can't . . ."

"Are you there? Krissy? Krissy?" The shrill voice pulled away from the phone. ". . . I don't know. I think she hung up. Do you think we should go over there and check on her?"

Kris hung up the phone. Becky didn't care if she was okay. They weren't even friends anymore. She took the phone off the hook and stumbled back to bed. The last small-town tragedy to hit Cridersville had been when Earl Coven and Calvin Dean ran a car off the Blackhoof Street Bridge when they were in high school. It had sent the entire town into an uproar for weeks. Village council members made vows to crack down on underage drinking. Her classmates held a candlelight vigil on the football field. Girls took senior pictures next to the shrine of teddy bears they'd tied to the bridge. Every stay-at-home mom in the county baked a casserole. Earl's baby sister was hounded like a celebrity by newfound friends that wanted to "help" her cope with the tragedy. Rooms would go quiet whenever the Coven or Dean families walked in. Earl's parents moved away the following semester. Kris didn't blame them. Her own mother had died in a car wreck when she was six years old, and people still treated her like a circus freak. *Step right up and see the motherless girl.*

And now the whole town thought her father was dead.

She glanced at the digital clock on her nightstand. It was only 2:00 p.m. She could be back in Cleveland before dinner. She got up, put her shoes back on, and threw her backpack over her shoulder.

Down the hallway, the door to her father's room stood open. The sight of it stopped her feet. He always kept it closed. The cops must have opened it during their search, she figured and crept closer, stealing a peek inside. The room was tiny, with only a twin bed, a narrow dresser, and a framed picture of her mother on the nightstand. The photo sent a tremor through her, a jolt of pain. It was the only picture of Rachael Wiley in the whole house. The rest were stashed in a photo album in the bottom of Kris's bookcase in Cleveland. Her dad didn't like to dwell on the past. That's what he always said.

Kris stepped into his room for the first time in years. The closet door stood open. His clothes hung neatly on the short iron bar—three good suits and two pairs of coveralls for work. His work boots were polished military style and set on the floor at the end of his badly jostled bed. *What were they looking for?*

An antique gold wristwatch sat on the nightstand next to the picture of her mother. He never used an alarm clock. *I tell myself when to wake up and that's what I do.* Old Spice and shoe polish and pipe tobacco hung in the air like a ghost. The smell of him reminded her of every bear hug, every piggyback ride, every little-girl moment they'd shared back when he still liked her. Back before everything changed. The urge to pick up his pillow and bury her face in it and cry nearly overwhelmed her, but she took a step back instead. He didn't like it when she touched his things.

The first time she'd seen him truly angry, she had been nine years old and he'd caught her taking the loose quarters off the top of his dresser. The memory of that day left its mark, so did his belt, and she hadn't set foot in his room since. He'd be furious to know she'd taken his driver's license. She pulled it out of her pocket and debated leaving it there in his room, but then she'd have to explain it.

The silver dish of loose change still sat on top of his dresser, but in the wrong spot. His collection of old keys and lost buttons and golf tees spilled haphazardly over the edge of the plate. The third drawer of the bureau hung open a half inch. Biting her lip, she glanced over her shoulder out into the empty hall and then pulled the drawer open the rest of the way. Carefully folded undershirts had been shoved to one side by the police officers in their search. Four hardcover books were piled up next to them. They didn't belong. Her father didn't read anything but *Field & Stream*.

Frowning, she picked them up one by one. *Whoever Fights Monsters* by Robert Ressler. *In the Wake of the Butcher* by James Jessen Badal. *Torso* by Steven Nickel. *Butcher's Dozen and Other Murders* by John Bartlow Martin. A library code marked the spine of each of them.

She flipped to the back cover of one and saw that it belonged to the Cleveland Public Library. She read the words again to be sure, then slammed the book shut. He hadn't visited her at college once— not to move her into her apartment, not to visit, nothing. She'd tried not to let it bother her. She'd told herself how much he hated the city.

Holding the books in her hand, she stared at the empty place in his undershirt drawer and debated what do. He'd kill her if he caught her snooping, but the books weren't even his. The library would want them back at some point, she reasoned. The cover of *Butcher's Dozen* featured ghostlike zombies wandering in the dark. *Torso* brandished a headless corpse.

Dread gnawed at her stomach as the plastic bags of clothes lined themselves up again in her mind. *We're still looking for the rest of him.*

The books spilled out of her trembling hands, and she sank to the floor. The glossy covers splayed onto the wood boards with their grotesque images of zombies, death, and murder. It wasn't a bear, she thought to herself as her eyes locked on the words *And Other Murders.*

She could feel black waters closing over her head as she sank past the surface of her grief. *No.* She clawed her way back up. *There has to be some other explanation.* She scanned the book covers again for some sort of answer. Blood-red letters shouted at her from one of the covers, *My Twenty Years Tracking Serial Killers for the FBI.* She gaped at it. It was a message. *FBI.*

The notion that her father was hiding something from her had crept into her head in high school as she started questioning the world around her while the distance between them grew. He had become like a stranger to her, disappearing on long hunting trips for days at a time. He did have a military background. *FBI?* She bit her lip. Her father had always been the smartest man in the room. Maybe he'd seen whatever happened to him coming. Maybe he left the books for her to find. *Maybe he trusted me after all.*

Half-ashamed at her hope and half-exhilarated by it, Kris stuffed the volumes into her backpack and closed the drawer. Occam's razor told her that the police were right, but she couldn't believe it. *He's not dead.*

A tiny voice inside warned her that she was just postponing the inevitable, but she didn't care. What mattered was keeping her heart beating and her lungs breathing and her brain from shutting down. If he was still out there, he needed her. Like Ben said, if he had any doubts, he'd be out there looking for him. She was the only one with doubts.

She forced herself down the short hallway to the kitchen. Clean dishes sat in the drying rack. A plate, a mug, and a fork. All she could find in the fridge was expired orange juice, a block of cheese, half a pack of sliced ham, three beers, and some mustard.

Her father hated to eat alone. Since she'd gone off to college, he spent most nights down at Shirlene's Diner, talking with the other regulars and the truckers that were always blowing through town on their way south. All sorts of things passed through the no-man's-land between Lima and Dayton—trains, tanker trucks, livestock, farm equipment. Nothing much stayed.

She gave the ham a whiff, then stuffed a few slices in her mouth. It tasted awful. She spat the half-chewed meat into the garbage and grabbed a can of beer from the door of the fridge. He'd have smacked it right out of her hand if he'd been standing there. She scanned the living room where he sat night after night, watching whatever game, and cracked open the can.

"I'm drinking your beer," she announced, daring him to come back and give her hell. The feeling that the room had been staged to look like home crept back into her head. *None of this is really happening.*

As she was closing the fridge, a knock shook the front door.

"Kris?" a familiar voice boomed. "Kris, you in there?"

Ben had left the curtains open. A familiar hulking shadow cupped its hands to the picture window. She ducked behind the kitchen counter and pressed her back to the cabinets. She took another long drink.

It was Troy.

The banging grew louder. She shrank back and considered her options. Everyone in town apparently knew about her trip to the sheriff's office and wanted to console her. The thought made her skin crawl. All her life, whenever anyone heard about her mother dying, they'd give her that look, that sad, pathetic, *oh poor little you* look as if it would somehow help. And now this.

The sound of her bedroom window sliding open brought her to her feet. Troy had broken the lock on it senior year when he'd started visiting her late at night, after her dad had gone to sleep. She grabbed her backpack off the counter and slipped out the side door and into the garage. The latch clicked softly closed. A moment later, his footsteps went creaking through the house.

"Kris?"

She skirted around her dad's "roadster." His pet project for the past year had been restoring a dusty 1971 Ford Mustang convertible. The engine was scattered over the rest of the garage. She picked her way as silently as she could to the back door. The footsteps approached from inside.

She ducked behind the fender as the door to the garage opened. It was ridiculous, she realized, crouching there, not breathing. But she didn't want to see him. The last time she'd seen Troy, they'd fought all over again about her moving to Cleveland, and he'd gotten angry enough to slap her. The act had shocked them both to the point of tears, but it had certainly removed all doubt from her mind. They were through.

The door closed a minute later. She listened as the footsteps went back through the house and out the front. A car engine started up at the end of the long driveway and finally pulled away.

Kris hauled herself up against the carcass of the Mustang and took a breath. *I've got to get the hell out of here.* As she grabbed her bag off the ground, one of her father's library books fell out. A crude painting of a severed head stared up at her from the dusty garage floor.

We're still looking for the rest of him.

CHAPTER 3

Kris wished she'd remembered to bring a coat. The wind still had the bite of winter, and she hugged her backpack to her side as she made her way down the train tracks toward Shirlene's. *Why the hell did I leave the car in Wapakoneta?* It was sweet of Ben to drive her, but *damn!*

The cornfields on either side of the tracks lay dormant, spiked with dried stalks, littered with dead leaves. The land flattened out for miles all around her, stretching to the horizon, lined by ditches and two-lane roads. A half mile ahead, a semi rumbled down the South Dixie Highway.

Thoughts she hadn't been able to articulate in the interrogation room stole through her head one by one. The evidence bags, the flashes of blood in the photographs, the grim set in the sheriff's eyes. Nobody said it, but the word *homicide* hung in the air like the stink of rotting leaves.

Did he mention anything to you? Anything he was worried about?

Kris shook her head at the thought. Her father had been fishing the Auglaize River for years. He knew just about every person in the county and seemed to get along with every single one of them just fine. He always carried a rifle in the truck. He'd been in the air force.

He knew how to defend himself. The dogs wouldn't have left his side. It wasn't him they found floating down the river. *But then who the hell was it? And where is he?*

Kris shut her eyes and was six years old again, waking up in the middle of the night, toddling into her parents' bedroom after a bad dream. The bed was empty. The sheets and blankets were mussed, but both her parents were gone. She found her father in the hallway with his chin to his chest and the telephone dangling from its cord.

Where's Mommy?

Stop it, her father snapped at her from a deeper part of her mind.

Shirlene's sat next to the train tracks right before they crossed under the South Dixie Highway, looking more like a gas station than a diner. The parking lot was half-full with a scattered assortment of pickup trucks and eighteen-wheelers, as usual. Mel was behind the counter when she walked in.

"Hey there, Kritter!"

She waved back and tried to smile. Obviously, he hadn't heard the buzz around town. She glanced at the truckers seated at the counter and the booths lining the three walls. None of the Auglaize County Sheriff's Department cruisers sat in the parking lot.

She found an empty stool at the counter.

"What you doin' here? In town visiting your pop?" he asked, setting a glass of ice water in front of her.

She nodded, not trusting her voice.

"What can I get ya?"

The beer she'd pounded gurgled in her empty stomach. Food sounded awful, but Mel was standing there with his pad. "Chicken soup?" she asked with a forced smile.

He clipped her order slip onto the kitchen wheel but not without giving her a thorough once-over first. She never just ordered soup. She was a cheeseburger and fries with extra ketchup, and they both knew it.

She turned to the window and scanned the road for Ben's cruiser.

Not a minute later, Mel set a steaming bowl in front of her and put his elbows on the counter. "Everything alright?"

Every friend of her father's treated her like a surrogate daughter. Every one of them had an opinion about where she should go to college, where she should live, whom she should marry. Not one of them approved of her moving to Cleveland.

"I'm fine," she said in a voice that wouldn't convince a stranger, let alone Mel.

He eased his elbows off the counter but kept talking. "I thought your pop was taking a fishing trip, said he planned to canoe all the way up to Cloverdale. When'd he get back?"

Kris swallowed hard. She couldn't bear to tell him that they thought he was lying in pieces in the morgue. The man would be heartbroken. It wasn't the sort of thing you just said. "I'm not sure. Say, Mel, can I use your phone?"

He frowned at her but said, "Sure. You know where it is."

She left her soup untouched and headed back behind the counter, past the kitchen, to Mel's storeroom. The short-order cook waved at her from the fryer. She gave him a nod, then rushed inside the back room and shut the door.

The oversized closet was lined with giant vats of ketchup and mustard and enormous bags of hamburger buns. She picked up the phone and dialed.

"Auglaize County Sheriff's Office," the receptionist said in her flat robot voice.

"Hi, Mary. Is Ben there?"

"Is this Kristin? Oh, my. You sweet, sweet girl. Are you alright? I just can't believe w—"

"Thanks," Kris interrupted. "I really need to talk with Ben."

"Of course, dear. I'll buzz him. I just want you to know if there is anything you need, anything at all—"

"Thanks, Mary. I really appreciate that, but . . ." What she needed was for everyone to just leave her the hell alone and find her father. "Can I just talk to him?"

"I'll go get him."

A minute later, Ben's voice came on the line. "Kris? Where are you? I just got a call from Troy."

"Did you tell him to come see me?" she asked, knowing full well the answer. *Of course he did.* All her father's friends liked Troy Reinhardt. All of them were upset when she broke off the engagement. He was a small-town football star. He came from money. None of them noticed how he'd hold on to the back of her neck when they went places like she was his dog. None of them knew about him sneaking through her window every night, pushing her further and further past her limits until they'd all been stripped away. No one said no to Troy, not even her, not even when she'd wanted to. No one knew about her lonely trips to the free clinic up in Lima to get birth control pills. Not even Troy.

"He's worried about you. We all are. Where are you?"

"I took a walk down to Shirlene's. I was hungry and . . . Listen, Ben. I need to get back to Cleveland."

"I don't think that's such a good idea, Kritter."

"You said it's going to take a few days for the lab to run the tests, right? What am I supposed to do until then? I can't just sit around the house and wait to find out the truth. I'll go crazy, Ben!"

"You're gonna go crazy in that city. That's what you're gonna do. It's not safe, Kris! You need your family around you right now."

Kris stiffened at the word *family*. Without her father, she didn't have a family. No brothers. No sisters. No mother. No grandparents. The air went out of the storeroom. She grabbed the edge of a shelf to keep from crumpling to the ground.

"I have finals," she croaked, forcing air in and out. "I have . . . work. I have friends. I have a life, Ben. I can't just let this eat me alive for the rest of the week. We don't even know if it's really . . ."

"Kris, honey, let us help you. This isn't healthy."

The thought of casseroles and concerned "friends" and Troy all pounding on her door was too much to stomach. More importantly, she needed to get to the Cleveland Public Library and see if anyone remembered her father. She needed to figure out why he'd left the books for her to find. She thought about saying as much to Ben, but it sounded ridiculous even to her. Instead, she squeezed her eyes shut and dug deep. "He wouldn't want me trapped in the house, Ben. He would want me to take my finals and finish out the semester. The semester he paid for, for Christ's sake . . . You know I'm right."

Dead air buzzed on the other end of the line.

She softened her voice. "It's only two hours away. I can always come back. I *will* come back as soon as we know something for sure. I promise."

"Putting this off isn't going to make it any easier, Kritter. You know that, right? You're going to have to deal with this one way or another."

"I know. And I will. I just need . . . I need to go for a little while. I need to think. And get my things in order and decide what to do next. I can't do that here. Do you understand? This isn't my home anymore."

"You know this will always be your home." Ben let out a sigh. "Alright, kiddo. You're a grown woman now and I can't stop you, but you have to promise me you'll stay in touch. Let us know how you're doing. You hear? We should have the DNA results back early next week."

She nodded at the phone. "Okay. Will you come pick me up?"

A minute later, Kris left the storeroom and returned to her bowl of soup.

"Everything alright?" Mel asked again. He took his time refilling her glass to study her face.

She nodded and ate a spoonful of sickly warm soup to prove it.

"Well, I don't know what's goin' on, but you tell your father that a fella from the city was in here lookin' for him the other day."

A piece of chicken caught in her throat. She coughed it out. "What man?"

"Looked like some sort of cop to me. He left me his card. Let me see if I can go find it." Mel lumbered back to the storeroom, limping to the right as he always did. The poor guy had a bum hip and had to stand there pouring coffee all day. He kept a bottle of whiskey under the counter. He'd sneak a pour into his coffee mug whenever he thought no one was looking.

A minute later, he hobbled back with a small rectangle of paper in his hand. "Here. Make sure he gets this and tell him the guy didn't seem all that friendly."

Photographs of blood and bone flashed in her head as she took the card. It read, *David Hohman—Private Investigator.* She frowned at the street address in Cleveland. Below it *www.torsokillers.com* was handwritten in blue pen. With numb hands, she stuffed the card in her pocket. "Thanks, Mel."

He nodded, then waved at something over her shoulder. Ben's cruiser had pulled up just outside the front window.

"I should get going." Kris stood up on buzzing legs. *Torso Killers.* "What do I owe you?"

Mel just waved at her. "Your money's no good here. Just tell your pop I said hello. Haven't seen him in a while."

Kris pressed her lips together and nodded.

She stared out the window the entire ride back to her car, debating whether to tell Ben about the card. His clenched teeth and hard grip on the wheel left no doubt that he was angry she was leaving. He'd be even angrier when he saw the card. He wouldn't let her leave. She could hear her father's voice yelling at her from inside her head.

Have you lost your Goddamned mind, Krit! You don't know this Hohman guy! He might've tried to kill me! No way in hell are you going back to your precious Cleveland! You're gonna march your butt home and do exactly what Ben tells you to do. Understand?

Ben stopped the cruiser alongside her Jeep. "So. You sure you wanna do this?"

She forced a thin smile. "Yeah. I'll be fine. It's just for a few days. Just so I can get my head together. Okay?"

"If you say so," Ben said, shaking his head in resignation. "Call me when you get there."

Kris nodded and got out of the car before she changed her mind. Keeping secrets wasn't a new thing to her. She'd hidden everything about herself that might incur her father's wrath or disapproval—tampons, makeup, dirty books, R-rated movies, beer bashes in the woods, Troy sneaking in through the window, birth control—all of it. Lying felt almost as natural as telling the truth. Besides, it was sort of the truth, wasn't it? She would come back soon, and she'd tell Ben about the card then. *What can he do? Ground me?*

It was a foolish and selfish and childish thought, she knew that and wasn't proud of it, but she just wanted to go home. She got into her car and headed east, not stopping until she'd reached the county line.

Once she was out of Ben's jurisdiction, she pulled the Jeep to the side of the highway and slid the piece of cardboard out of her pocket. The words *Torso Killers* sent her rifling through her father's library books at the bottom of her backpack, scanning the titles until she found it. *Torso: The Story of Eliot Ness and the Search for a Psychopathic Killer.* The image of a headless body floated on the cover of the book beneath it, and for a moment, the torso was her father's. Her eyes focused on the word *killer*, then flitted back to David Hohman's card.

Swallowing the lump lodged somewhere between her heart and her head, she opened the book.

FINDING OF TORSOS
REVEALS SLAYINGS

Headless and otherwise mutilated, the nude bodies of two men were found late yesterday afternoon in thick brush in a small ravine at the foot of Praha Avenue S.E. and E. 49th Street by two boys who summoned police to investigate the most bizarre double murder here in recent years.

—*Cleveland Plain Dealer*, September 24, 1935, p. 13

CHAPTER 4

March 27, 1938

"Do you know this woman?" The detective held up a black-and-white photograph.

Ethel blinked at the image, trying to clear the thick cloud of cheap wine and reefer and God knows what else from her head. It wasn't a woman at all. A nipple. A breast. A thigh. Parts and pieces were laid out on a metal table, all of them crusted in black at the edges. "What the hell is that?" Her words slurred despite her best efforts.

"Do you recognize her? The scar?" He pointed to the jagged mark puckering the pale skin stretched over blood and bone. "Any of your friends go missing in the last six months?"

Ethel shook her head and went to close her bedroom door.

The cop stuck his foot in the jamb and brandished another grisly photograph. This one was simply the head of a young man with a black collar of dried blood where a neck should be. The rest of him was gone. "What about him? You know him?"

Ethel nervously glanced over her shoulder at the naked man sprawled out on the bed behind her. Ma Pratchett would be furious if one of her customers got hauled down to Central Station. "Maybe. It's hard to tell."

"Take another look." The detective pressed and held up another picture showing the rest of the decapitated body and then an enlarged photograph of a tattoo. It was some sort of cartoon character.

Something twitched in the back of her mind that told her she'd seen it before. *One of Eddie's boys?* She tried to force her eyes to focus. "I'm not sure. I doubt it."

The detective gave her a hard look. She didn't catch his name, but his stocky body and thick fists told her he packed a hell of a punch. The cheap suit and porkpie hat said the rest. He wasn't crooked. He only drank on weekends. He liked his sex straight and Christian, and his poor wife would never even think to complain. He'd never bought a girl, and dropping to her knees wouldn't make him go away. He felt sorry for her standing there in her cheap stockings and flimsy robe. Repulsed even. If he had the energy to care, he'd probably try to help her, but he'd take hauling her off to the workhouse as a consolation prize.

"Think real hard," he warned and shot a look over her shoulder toward her occupied bed.

She'd have to give him something. "I might've seen him once or twice around here."

The detective raised an eyebrow. "Buying or selling?"

"Young kid like that? What do you think?"

The detective looked down at the severed head for a moment. "Anybody pimp for him?"

Ethel shifted her weight uncomfortably. Her eyes darted down the red painted hallway, scanning the row of shut doors. "I don't know the swish trade. Different customers, you know?"

"What about Eddie Andrassy?" The detective held up the mug shot that had circulated around all the papers three years earlier.

Eddie's hauntingly beautiful face hovered in front of her like a warning. "He pimp for him?"

"I don't know nothin' about him." It was a lie and they both knew it.

"We can discuss this here or back at the station. I'm sure your friend on the bed there should be getting home to his wife anyway."

"I don't know, alright?" she hissed under her breath. "Eddie knew a lot of boys."

"Did he know him?" The detective brandished the severed head at her again. Long lashes. Clear skin. Sad, really. "Were they romantically involved?"

The wine turned in her gut, bringing a wave of sickness with it. She'd managed to avoid the shakedowns the first time the cops came tossing beds in the vice district they all called the Roaring Third, but the detective had her cornered. The clock at her bedside pointed to 5:15 a.m. She should've kicked the john out hours ago, but she'd passed out instead. *Morphine?* She couldn't remember. "What was the question?"

"Were they lovers?"

"I doubt it, but that never stopped Eddie."

"Never stopped him from what?" The cop narrowed his eyes.

"From takin' a blind sale." Ethel waited a moment for the dumb dick to catch her meaning, but the look on his freshly shaved face told her he wouldn't. She rolled her eyes and dropped her voice to a whisper. "Pimps like to slip mickeys in a boy's drink, then sell him out to the highest bidder."

The detective didn't speak for a moment. "And then what?"

"And then nothin'. A boy might wake up in a gutter somewhere. He might never be seen again. You take your chances when you take a free drink." The grimace on the cop's face made her feel a bit calmer, more in control. In truth, she couldn't prove a thing about Eddie's habits, they were all just drunk rumors, but churchgoers were fun to shock. She tapped the photograph of the unfortunate young man's face. "This one looks a bit old for it, though."

"You ever take a drink from Eddie?"

She shot him a glare. "I buy my own drinks, okay? But you spend enough time around here, you get to know people."

"What about Flo Polillo? Did you know her?"

Fat, gray, black eyed, and brawling—Flo was the dead end Ethel knew she had coming. Flo was what happened to girls too stupid to get out of the game. Flo was what happened when you drank up all the money and forgot to make a plan. Pieces of Flo had been found behind a warehouse back in the freezing winter of 1936. Back before the Mad Butcher had a flashy name and anybody gave a damn.

"Everybody knew Flo. You had a nickel and some booze, you could've known her too."

"Was she friends with Eddie?"

Ethel shook her head. It weighed fifty pounds. "Nobody was friends with Eddie."

"We got lots of people on record saying they talked."

"That don't mean nothin'. Eddie liked to talk. He knew people. People with money. You needed to make a bunch of dough fast, you talked to Eddie."

"You know of anybody that wanted to kill him?"

Ethel breathed out a small laugh. "Yeah. Anybody that ever worked for him."

The detective furrowed his brow. "I thought you said he helped people get money."

"Yeah. You'd find out too late that no money's worth the sort of work he'd get you."

"So he specialized in rough trade?"

The stories she'd heard came back to her in an unwelcome wave. Rumor had it that a girl down the hall had overdosed herself the day after she'd turned one of Eddie's tricks. She was dead before anyone noticed. "You could say that."

"Flo ever work for him?"

Ethel shrugged. "I wouldn't be surprised if she had."

"What about Rose Wallace? She work for him too?"

The name tightened Ethel's jaw. "She might've."

Poor Rose. Born broke, black, and skinny, the old girl never had a chance. But man, she was funny. She'd have the whole bar rolling, mimicking the last pervert she'd met. *You wouldn't believe what this fool wanted.* Ethel'd be sitting there contemplating jumping off a bridge, when Rose would wander into the bar with some story that could even make Flo blush. Rose had been a rare friend right up until the day she'd vanished from her house a few blocks away. Her bones had been found in a burlap sack under the Lorain-Carnegie Bridge about a year ago. Quicklime had eaten the rest of her.

The detective pulled out a notebook and flipped through the pages, but his eyes didn't move. He was stalling. After a few drawn-out moments, he put the notes away, but his foot stayed wedged in her door frame.

The buzz of wine and weed in her ears dulled to a low hum. In the sobering silence left behind, an alarm began to clang. She'd said too much, and to a cop no less. "I gotta go."

"Just one more thing, Ethel."

She flinched at the sound of her real name. *Did I tell him that?* "What?"

"What can you tell me about Eddie's clients?"

"Nothin'. I didn't know 'em."

"You're going to have to do better than that." He leveled his eyes at her.

Ethel swallowed hard. "I really don't know."

"See, it's my job to know when someone's lying to me, and I'm very good at my job. Now you can answer my question or I can haul you, your naked friend in there, and Ma Pratchett all down to Central. Now try again. You said that Eddie knew people with money. Were any of his clients doctors?"

She didn't speak for a moment and squeezed her eyes shut, hoping as she often did that she would vanish into the shadows behind her lids, never to be seen again. But the red hallway, the electric-yellow light bulb hanging overhead, and the detective were all still there when she opened them.

He shoved another photo of hacked-up arms and legs under her nose. "This is Flo Polillo. See what happened to her? Now I want you to think real hard. Don't help me, help yourself. You could be next . . . Now who did this? Who was he?"

She closed her eyes to block out the bits of Flo. "I dunno."

"Was he made? Italian?" he prodded, knowing full well that the mob protected Ma Pratchett's house and got a heavy cut of all its earnings. Knowing full well that implicating Mayfield Road would be signing her own death warrant.

She bit her lips together and shook her head.

"Was he a devil worshiper?"

Ethel rubbed her forehead and shrugged. Rumors had been flying about witchcraft and the devil ever since Eddie's headless corpse had been found down in Kingsbury Run. Mutilated bodies kept turning up, and now the drunks and tramps were all convinced the Run was haunted.

"You don't get it, do you? A madman is loose on the streets of Cleveland. Some pervert is killing your friends." The detective brandished the pictures again. Flo's arms and legs. Eddie's tattooed boy. Now a new one of Eddie's severed head. Then Eddie's naked body. The Butcher had left nothing between his legs but a gash. "Now I know you know something, and I'm not leaving here empty-handed."

The look on Rose's face the day before she disappeared still haunted the darker corners of Ethel's mind. "Rose had some trouble before she went . . ."

"What sort of trouble?"

Ethel paused. She knew she was on dangerous ground and dropped her voice to a whisper. "I don't know, but it looked like somebody had messed her up pretty good."

The detective looked up from his notepad and eyeballed the doors down the hallway. "Did she go to the hospital?"

"No. She didn't," Ethel said flatly. A trip to the hospital was an invitation for arrest, and he knew it.

"Why didn't she report him?"

"Like you'd take a two-bit whore's word over some rich guy's," Ethel hissed. "Doesn't matter anyways. She never saw his face."

CHAPTER 5

The ragged pain between her legs jolted her out of a dream. Hot putrid breath steamed against her ear. Teeth on her neck. For a bleary moment, Ethel was fourteen years old again and back in the one-room apartment. Back before her father left them for good. *Billy,* she thought, bracing herself as the pain came again and again. *Don't let him see you, Billy. Stay under the bed.*

Ethel squeezed back tears and forced out a moan then an arch, knowing it would make it all end quicker. The hard buttons of her back crushed against the cold brick wall behind her. The fat man grinding himself into her pulled her hair and shuddered a low growl like a dying dog.

She opened her eyes to find herself twenty-four years old again and her brother dead for over five years. She scanned the unfamiliar fire escapes overhead and tried to remember how she had gotten there. And, more importantly, if the beast shrinking from her had already paid.

The tinkling of quarters hitting the ground was her answer as he hitched up his trousers and stumbled away, dead drunk. She steadied herself against the bricks as he left. Glancing at the coins, she quickly calculated how many drinks they would buy.

What day is it? Tuesday? The muted orange of the night sky told her nothing. At least it wasn't too cold. But the warm snap wouldn't last. The last solid memory she could conjure was Ma Pratchett throwing her things onto the brick street. *I'm sorry, honey. There ain't nothin' I can do about it.* The old wench had puffed on the end of her cigarette before slamming the door. *I can't have my girls snitchin' to the police about the clients. And what was all this bull about rich men, huh? Old quiff like you'd be lucky to fetch two bucks from a dockworker.*

The hunched old man lurched his way out of the alley, and she waited until he'd rounded the corner to collect her fee and straighten her skirt. She eased her grip off the steak knife she kept buried in her pocket and studied the half-moon imprints on her palm where her fingernails had dug in. The photographs the detective had shoved under her nose rifled through her mind again in their rotating wheel. *You could be next.*

She couldn't remember the last time she'd slept.

"Hey." The toe of an old shoe nudged Ethel's arm. "Get the hell outta my house."

Ethel opened her eyes to see the shadow of a large man hovering over her. The sun had dropped over the edge of the bluff, and the sky had turned sulfur yellow. As she pulled herself up, the dull ache in her head told her she'd slept the entire day away. The chill in her bones told her the temperature had dropped while she slept. She could barely feel her toes. The tin and cardboard roofs of hobo shanties dotted the steep hillside. The rusted steel web of the East 55th Street Bridge stretched out over her head. Kingsbury Run, she realized, looking down at the train tracks at the bottom of the gully. *What the hell am I doing down here?*

The face in front of her came into focus—dark skin and black sunken eyes bent into a permanent frown. A knit cap hid a mop of wiry hair and oversized ears. "Willie?"

"Amber? That you?" he crouched down to take a better look at her. Amber was the name she'd been using since her last stint in Mansfield. Like a guidepost, it told her where she was. *Cleveland, 1935 or later.*

The stump of a left arm peeked out of his torn shirt, ending abruptly above the elbow. Willie had lost it years ago, but the story of how it happened kept changing. The latest legend involved a knife fight with a mobster. "What the hell you doin' down here?"

"What the hell's it look like?" she spat back, sitting up. Her head pounded its hungover drum harder than usual. A vague memory circled her head. She'd picked her way down a steep hill into the Run to find a place to sleep. It wasn't a good sign. "Where you been?"

"Catched out on a freighter for a while. Been keepin' real low. Ever since they found Rose, cops been after me."

Ethel nodded. The police were looking to pin all those dead bodies on anybody they could. Not that any of them really cared about the likes of Flo or Rose or Eddie, but all the unsolved murders were making people nervous.

She scanned the empty shanties along the hillside while blowing warm air into her cold hands. None of the fires were burning. A heavy silence hung in the grass where voices should be. It was a ghost town. "Why'd you come back?"

Willie's frown creased deeper. "I'd promised Rose I'd keep an eye on her little girl. You know, last time she went out? And well . . ."

Ethel shook her head at him. "And you lost her." *If he'd even tried at all. If he hadn't sold her off to some pervert.*

"You could say that . . . You seen her?"

Rose's youngest couldn't have been more than eight years old. Ethel had only seen the girl once when she was hardly bigger than a baby. A little black girl would hardly last a day on her own. Ethel didn't want to imagine where she'd ended up. The shake playing in her hands told her it had been too long since her last drink. "No. I haven't heard nothin' about her either."

She studied his pained expression. *At least he feels guilty, the bastard.* Willie fell back onto his ass and hung his head between his knees. "I been lookin' for months. Shit just ain't right . . . Look, you can't stay here. Cops toss the Run twice a month lookin' for their Torso Butcher Man. I'm catching out again tonight."

Ethel nodded and stared out at the empty tracks, cursing the ham-fisted detective that had kicked in her door. *How many men had she been with since then? How many butchers?* "You know who they're lookin' for?"

"Nope. Alls I know is they lookin' in the wrong places."

"One of them dicks visited me the other day." *Yesterday? Last week?* "Askin' about Eddie's tricks. Son of a bitch got me thrown out on my ass."

Willie raised an eyebrow. "What'd you say?"

"What could I say? Nothin'." She lied and held up her hands in mock surrender. "I never met any of them rich perverts. Did you?"

He held out his hands and motioned to his lanky black frame. "What you think? I ain't their flavor."

Ethel fished the near-empty flask out of her hem and drained it so she could think. "Rose ever say anything to you? Anything strange happen before she disappeared?"

Willie slanted his eyes back at her. "She seemed sorta jumpy. Needed money. I think Eddie might've got her a bad gig or two."

Ethel didn't say anything for a moment, waiting for the liquor to do its job. The sky had gone from jaundice to fever pink, and the train tracks were slipping away into the lengthening shadows. They didn't have much time until the railroad bulls came through. Or worse.

"Any idea who got Eddie?" she asked, even though she knew the answer. Enough people wanted Eddie dead they could've filled a directory.

"Shit." Willie threw a rock down at the tracks. "Whoever it was made damn sure we all saw it, though, right? Laid him out like a warning to the rest of us trash down here. Like they was tryin' real hard to tell us somethin'. And it worked too. Can't find a dead drunk down here after dark. Only ones here anymore is cops made up like hobos . . . Now who's all this helpin'? That's what I wonder."

Ethel didn't respond. The flashlights of two Nickel Plate Railroad security guards traced along the tracks in the distance.

"I ain't waitin' around for some phantom killer to come and take my head, boy. I'm outta here." The rumble of a slow-moving train brought Willie to his feet. "You comin'?"

Ethel gazed out at the tracks. It was tempting, but she knew better than to jump a train to nowhere with Willie and his one feeble arm. The old pimp would run her ragged just for scraps. She curled her fingers around the knife hidden in her pocket and braced for a fight. You never could tell with Willie. "Not yet."

"Suit yourself. You best stay out the Run, though. If Ma kicked you out, it ain't just the Butcher that wants you dead. I'd lay real low if I was you." Willie headed down the embankment but stopped at the tracks. "Do me a favor?"

"Yeah?"

"Keep your eye out for Rose's girl."

CHAPTER 6

"Good morning, Sister. Have you accepted Jesus Christ as your Lord and Savior?"

Ethel turned toward the sunny voice that sounded just a little too pleased with itself. The girl attached to it walked over, holding a banjo in one hand and a piece of paper in the other. She couldn't have been more than sixteen years old. The odd thing wore a smile too big to be trusted, a straw boater hat, and an ugly blue dress.

Every day since she'd been thrown out of Ma's, someone had shooed her away from their storefront or threatened to call the police. Every day other women judged her with their eyes. She was going to hell, and everyone knew it. Ethel blew a cloud of cigarette smoke in her face. "What do you care? I ain't your sister."

"We are all sisters in the eyes of the Lord. The prophet Matthew said, 'For whoever does the will of my Father in heaven is my brother and sister and mother.'"

"Oh, really?" Ethel sucked on her smoke and gave the girl a slow and sleazy up and down just as thorough as all the appraisals she'd endured. Thin. Plain. Young. Stupid. *Five dollars a throw. Tops. Ten if she were younger.* "What's your name, sugar?"

The girl shifted her weight in the clunky black farmer's boots tied to her feet. "Mary Alice Eberly. And you?"

"Ambrosia," Ethel said. It was the name she used for the church-going johns. They ate it up.

"It's wonderful to meet you, Ambrosia." The girl beamed like they were now best friends. "Do you attend church?"

Ethel smirked at this. "Not regularly, but my knees are bruised from prayin'. What the hell are you supposed to be with the banjo and the clothes?"

The girl stiffened her chin and handed Ethel her leaflet. "I am here to spread the word of God to those that are seeking a better life. Do you want to be condemned to misery and suffering for all eternity? Do you want to go through life blind to His love? Or do you want something more?"

Ethel knew all about wanting more. Countless days of sleeping with her eyes open in burned-out buildings, trying not to freeze to death, had made her keenly aware of the emotion. "So what do you want? Money?"

"No, of course not. I want to help you find your way."

"Yeah. Sure you do. So who you out here hustlin' for, hon?"

"Who am I what?"

"I've seen you girls around. Someone dressed you girls up like this and turned you out. Who was it? And don't say, 'Jesus,' honey. Who's your boss?"

The girl smiled like she welcomed the question. "I answered a call from God himself. He came to me and commanded me to devote my life to serving—"

Ethel held up a hand. "Fine. If you don't want to tell me, don't tell me."

She puffed her cigarette down to the nub and turned her eyes down the redbrick road toward the factory chimneys and exhaust stacks. The workers would be getting out soon. In the distance, the bells of three Catholic churches began to chime.

Ethel could feel their clocks ticking every minute of every day. Every ten minutes she endured in the back of a car or in an alley was another few dollars. The minutes she stood alone, waiting and watching for the next dollar, were worse. Every day on the calendar brought her closer to the warmth of summer. Even in the April cold, she could feel it coming. That's what she told herself, standing there in the slush, trying to keep warm. Only a few more weeks left and the pain would end. She needed to find a roof, but none of the brothels would touch her. The Italians wouldn't have her in their cathouses, not after she'd sung to that cop. Not even on the west side of town.

"Answering the call is not easy. But it's better than this," the girl said softly.

Ethel leveled her eyes at Mary Alice. "What do you know about *this*?"

"I know you're not happy."

"Who is? You? If you're so damned happy, why are you out here botherin' me? Huh? You don't look happy. You look stupid."

"I am happier than you. If you let me, I can help." She put a soft hand on Ethel's arm.

Ethel jerked it away and raised her fist, but the girl just stood there smiling, welcoming the punch with open arms. It was more unnerving than the opening snap of a knife. "Are you nuts? I don't need your help, little girl. I don't need your Jesus, and I don't need your Goddamned pamphlets!" Ethel threw the leaflet in the girl's face.

Mary Alice didn't flinch. "What do you need, Sister?"

Ethel felt her guard slip for just a moment, exposing the raw skin beneath it for the first time in . . . months? Years? *What do I need?* She hadn't dared to even hope for anything she wanted or needed since—

Ethel shuddered despite herself.

The thought that the girl might have glimpsed the gesture sent a violent urge to claw the poor thing's eyes out down through Ethel's broken fingernails. She threw the spent cigarette to the ground and shook it off. It wasn't the girl's fault Ethel hadn't had any luck finding a roof to put over her head. She appraised this Mary Alice Eberly again. Clean gloves. Newer shoes. Full cheeks. Whoever he was, the boss was keeping her well. He couldn't be half as bad as some of the johns she'd had that day. Men with any real money spent it on younger girls with access to a soft mattress, not old whores like her. Without a proper house, she wouldn't last much longer. The photographs of Flo Polillo's hacked-up body hung over her like a warrant. The Butcher was still walking the streets. She might've serviced him that very day.

Ethel held the girl's eyes for several moments, searching for the hollowed shame and grim wisdom that came with being misused. They didn't have the wide glimmer of a happy child, but they weren't the worst she'd seen.

"You are searching for something. Aren't you?" Mary Alice prodded. "I can show you the way of the Lord."

Ethel weighed her meager options for a moment and decided that nothing the poor girl's boss might throw at her could be worse than the Cleveland winter still hanging on. She couldn't take another day walking through the snow in thin leather pumps, trading herself for a few meager hours in the heat of a pub. *People like little Mary Alice here think hell is a blazing inferno, but they're wrong. Hell is cold.*

Ethel let her eyes grow heavy with pain and fall to the ground. It wasn't much of a stretch. "Yeah. Maybe I am searching."

"Let the Lord into your heart, and you will have nothing to fear."

Ethel shook her head. "But I can't. He won't let me."

"Jesus doesn't judge. He died for your sins. He died for you."

"No. That's not what I meant." Ethel made a show of looking up and down the street.

The effect worked, and the girl's eyes darted around. "Who won't let you?"

"No one. Forget I said anything. He can't see me talking to you." Ethel prided herself on being a good judge of what people wanted, and Mary Alice was dying to save her from a devil.

"Who is he?"

"Nobody. I have to go."

The girl frowned. "Can we talk again sometime? The Lord has brought us together for a reason."

Ethel gave the poor thing a smile. It was almost too easy. "I don't know. I'm not supposed to talk to people. His punishments can be terrible."

The girl's eyes swelled as though she shared in the pain. "You must be brave. If the Lord is calling to you, you must answer."

"I don't know." Ethel bit her lip and looked up and down the street again, then said, "Maybe tomorrow. But not here. It can't be out here on the street."

Mary Alice nodded fervently. "Come to the Harmony Mission tomorrow evening at five o'clock."

The girl motioned down the block at the mammoth building towering over the street. Ethel blinked up at the structure, not quite believing that she hadn't noticed it all afternoon. All she'd seen was the wrought iron fence ringing the lot with its sharp points and the long brick walls blocking the sidewalk from whatever lay on the other side. *Go away,* it said. And it wasn't just one building, she realized, but many. A house here. A church there. A prison? No, a factory, but it didn't have the customary line of haggard men or desperate women clogging the sidewalk, begging for a job.

"There's a doorway hidden in the courtyard on the south side. Knock on the door twice. We'll keep you safe."

Ethel scanned the small windows lining the upper stories of the enormous brick compound. They were clean and unbroken and eerily empty. No drawings, no laundry lines, no little faces pressed to the glass. "Are you sure?"

The girl nodded. "Just don't be late. There's a strict schedule."

What happens if I'm late? But Ethel just nodded. "Alright. I'll see you tomorrow."

The girl pressed her paper pamphlet into Ethel's hand. "I'll be praying for you, Ambrosia."

Ethel stuffed the paper into her bodice next to her cash. She didn't look at it again until much later that evening when it spilled out onto the bar as she fumbled for enough money to pay for her drink. She frowned at the jumble of letters covering the back of the pamphlet, unable to read any of them. On the other side, a crudely drawn devil leered up at her with its pitchfork.

It was holding a severed head.

WOMAN SLAIN,
HEAD SOUGHT IN COAL BINS

Detectives combed the Central Avenue-E. 20th Street section today searching for the head and the remainder of the body of Mrs. Florence Genevieve Sawdey, 41, whose dismembered torso was found yesterday in an alley.

—*Cleveland Press,* January 27, 1936, p. 1

CHAPTER 7

April 7, 1999

Kris pulled her rusted Jeep into a free spot on Jefferson at six o'clock that evening. When she cut the engine, her veins kept humming with cortisol. Her backpack dug into her shoulder with the weight of her father's books. *Whoever Fights Monsters. Torso. Butcher's Dozen.* The blood she had glimpsed in the deputy's photographs hung over her head. *We're still looking for the rest of him.*

Thurman Avenue, stretching out in front of her for three dingy and run-down blocks, offered no comfort. The one-way street where she lived was more of an alley than a road, flanked by tiny bungalows on one side and the decaying mass of the abandoned Harmony Press factory on the other. Torn chain-link fences lined the postage stamp yards. Most of the asbestos-shingled houses served as cheap rentals for students and fatherless families. A few little old ladies still clung to their childhood homes. Kris saw one of them peeping out a window as she made her way down the narrow street.

A faded whirligig spun aimlessly in the yard as she passed by. The fat, polka-dot-painted ass of a cartoon woman bent over a bucket of wildflowers next to it. A cracked garden gnome held his pipe and grinned up at her. Bumper stickers had been slapped onto the peeling siding of the next house. One loudly proclaimed, *Smile! Jesus Loves You!*

"Does he?" she muttered to herself.

To her right, a twelve-foot-tall iron gate blocked the yawning arch of the old Harmony Press loading dock. She peered through the bars into the empty cavern. It extended deep into the shadows, a tunnel to nowhere. Closed doors dotted the walls on either side. Concrete porches stepped down to acres of brick pavement that stretched from the sidewalk below her feet back into another courtyard she couldn't quite see. There was no sign of life anywhere. The factory windows hovering over her head were all dark. The building had been empty for over fifty years according to her roommate, Pete. He'd heard they used to print Bibles inside. *Ironic, right? A Bible factory gone out of business?* He'd nudged her, trying to impress her with his depth of knowledge and humanity, back before he'd given up on sleeping with her. Their tiny bungalow sat across the narrow alley only a few houses up from the gate. The lights were out there too.

Up on the corner where Thurman hit College Avenue, a boarded-up storefront sat as a reminder of the urban squalor that the yuppies were rapidly renovating away. Thurman Avenue hadn't succumbed to the wave of gentrification just yet, and the crumbling factory proved it. Her father had managed to find the most dilapidated street in all of Tremont for her to live. She figured it was just another punishment for moving away. Another test he hoped she'd fail.

A small hunched figure was headed her way. It was wearing an orange bathrobe. Kris crossed the street to avoid it.

"Hello there!" a voice croaked and then let out a cough. "Can you help an old woman get something to eat?"

"I'm sorry," Kris called back without making eye contact. She fumbled with her keys. "I don't carry cash."

It was true, but it still felt like a lie. Kris had learned her first month in Cleveland that giving money to a derelict was inviting a conversation that would never end.

"I understand," the woman muttered in a phlegmy frog voice. She was almost to Kris's doorstep. "You lived here long?"

Kris rolled her eyes. She pulled the door open and gave the woman a wave without looking her in the face. "A few months. I really gotta get going. I'm sorry. Good luck to you."

"No. Good luck to you, honey. You seem like you need it more than m—"

The door shut before the woman could finish. Kris threw the dead bolt and the chain for good measure. She hated being rude, and the whole encounter left her feeling mean and dirty. And sad.

Kris flipped on her kitchen light to find the answering machine blinking on the kitchen counter. As she pressed the button, her heart contracted with the flailing hope it was him.

"Hello. This message is for Miss Kristin Anne Wiley. My name is Robert Weismann from the *Lima News*. I'm calling in regards to your father, Alfred Ray Wiley. We understand that you visited the Auglaize County Sheriff's Office this morning and are contesting the identity of a set of remains found in the northern part of—"

Kris slammed her hand onto the delete button. *Damn it, Ben! What did you do? Call a frigging press conference?*

The next message beeped.

"Krit? You there?" The deep voice crawled through the dusty speaker like it was her bedroom window. Troy wanted something. Ben must've given him her new number. She'd disconnected her old one when he wouldn't stop calling. "I know things have been weird between us, but you're goin' through a lot, babe. Call me. I can help if you'd just—"

She unplugged the answering machine before he could finish. She paced her kitchen back and forth several times, debating whether to call up Officer Ben and give him a piece of her mind. It wouldn't do any good, she realized that. It probably wasn't even his fault. Bad news spread through a small town like wildfire. There was nothing else to talk about. It would still feel good to yell at someone, though.

After five deep breaths, she pulled the rogue business card out of her pocket and studied it again. Why would a killer leave a business card? she wondered. He wouldn't, right? Biting her lip, she picked up the phone. *Don't be stupid, Kris,* her father warned her from his place in her brain stem. *You don't know a thing about this guy.*

Yeah, but this guy doesn't know me. I could be anyone. What could it hurt? After a few more rounds of debate, she dialed the number.

"Hello. You've reached the office of David Hohman and Associates," a reassuring voice spoke nice and slow, as though talking a jumper off a ledge. "We are a full-service, PISGS-licensed private investigation firm ready to help you with background checks, missing person cases, wrongful death claims, litigation support, or private security. Please leave your name and number, and we will get back to you as soon as possible."

After a long beep, she just stood there paralyzed, eyes watering, breathing into the phone, wanting to leave a message but too scared to do it. Finally, she just hung up. Rubbing her eyes dry again, she scolded herself for being a hysterical girl. *Keep it together, Kris.* She scanned David Hohman's street address embossed on the cardboard, then ran her finger across the indented blue ink that read, *www.torsokillers.com.*

Kris tossed the card onto the counter and spread her father's library books across the kitchen table. Each one was about the same killer. She picked up *Torso* again and thumbed through the black-and-white police photographs in the center of the book with disgust. The Torso Killer apparently got his name by cutting off his victims' heads and arms and legs. White cakey flesh ripped open at the seams covered each page along with images of men in suits and hats standing under bridges and sifting through the dirt. The dates below the photographs were all from the 1930s.

She snapped the book shut again and tossed it on top of the others. Who reads this horrible stuff? she wondered and tried to picture her dad sitting in his plaid easy chair with a book in his hand. She couldn't do it. All she could see were hacked-up pieces of him wrapped in plastic bags. A shudder ran down her limbs.

The crude sketch of a headless, armless torso taunted her from behind an acetate book cover. *Without prints or dental, it's going to be tough to make a positive ID.* She shook the police officer's voice from her head and turned away from the murder books, queasy. Whatever they'd found out in the woods didn't include a head or hands. The thought of him laid out on a metal table like the black-and-white photographs in the books—

She lurched up from her seat on shaky legs and felt the room spin. It had been hours since she'd eaten anything. A dusty bookshelf sagged against the wall with her dwindling supply of ramen noodles and boxed macaroni. Toast crumbs littered the cracked Formica counters. The fridge hummed from its corner of the kitchen, its avocado-green shell dulled by years of use. She staggered over to it. The light inside had burned out long before Kris moved in, and she had to squint to see that half of her food had gone missing.

"Pete," she muttered weakly. "Dammit. Stop eating my food!"

She glanced over her shoulder, down the narrow hallway to his room. It was empty. Pete had been spending nearly all his time at his girlfriend's place lately. Ever since he'd figured out that Kris wasn't interested in hooking up, he'd made himself scarce.

Not scarce enough, she mused, grabbing some turkey from his shelf in the fridge. Her food had a habit of going missing, but her constantly broke roommate swore up and down that he never touched it. Thankfully, he was moving out in May. But of course that meant she'd had to find another roommate—a task that had proved near impossible when she'd first tried it that fall. No other Cleveland State students had answered her ad to live all the way over in Tremont. Just Pete.

Maybe now I can move. The thought stole through her head like a thief.

Forcing down three pieces of processed meat, she grabbed David Hohman's card and padded across the matted gray carpet in the living room back to her bedroom on the opposite side of the house. She plopped down at her computer and flipped it on, wondering why this stranger was looking for her father and what any of it had to do with a bunch of murders that happened sixty years ago. The word *FBI* flashed through her head.

As the dial-up Internet connection chirped and whined, she scanned the photographs taped to her walls. Black-and-white portraits of old men at the bus stop mingled with crumbling brick buildings. None of her attempts at art were great, but great felt just an arm's length away. Tightening the aperture, adjusting the angle, framing the shot—there were just a few tweaks that might make the pictures special, but she couldn't quite grasp the secret. Instead, she forced herself to study her failures every day, hoping to figure it out.

Her father thought her photos were a waste of time. Anything she wanted to do was foolish as far as he was concerned. Moving to Cleveland, studying art. Not marrying Troy. He thought she should've stayed in Cridersville and gone to the local college.

I don't want to go to Rhodes! Kris had yelled, struggling to keep the tremor she felt out of her voice. One crack in her armor and she knew it would be over.

She could still see him glowering over her in the kitchen back home. She could feel the counter digging into her back.

"Of course you do," he growled. Debating anything with her made him furious. Rage flashed in his eyes like he was a caged beast.

"You could take your classes and live here rent-free. A school is a school, now dammit!"

She concealed her fear with a smirk and flopped the college ratings onto the kitchen table. It was her ace in the hole. "That's not exactly what *US News & World Report* says, Dad. Cleveland State was ranked one of the best values in the state of Ohio four years running. Rhodes didn't make that list. I mean, sure, staying close to home would be easier but . . ." She paused, choosing her words carefully. "Aren't you always telling me to make decisions with my head and not my emotions?"

What he'd actually told her was to stop thinking like a stupid girl. His pointed glance said as much, but he looked at the magazine in spite of himself.

"CSU costs the same as Rhodes, and it has so much more to offer. I could study business or law. There are work-study programs—"

He held up his hand to silence her. "That city is a cesspool. I'm not sending my only daughter up there. It'd be like sending a sheep to the slaughter!"

"Like hell." She crossed her arms defiantly and pressed the only button she had—his pride. "You taught me how to take care of myself, right? How to survive in the wilderness, how to shoot a coyote, how to field dress a buck. You did *not* raise a sheep!"

He gave her a cool appraisal as though debating how to take her down and eat her alive. She just stared back, willing herself not to squirm, holding on by a thread. Finally, he just shook his head. "You aren't going to let this go, are you?"

"No, I won't." The sound of steel in her voice surprised her, given the quaking emotions she felt inside. She'd won. She'd actually won.

"You're gonna have to earn your own room and board, understand me? You've taken that cost on yourself." He shook his head, and his shoulders slumped in resignation.

"Of course." She nodded eagerly but could feel him divorcing himself from her and the entire situation with each word. He hated to lose a game of cards, let alone an argument.

"And I get to choose where you live. I will not have you holed up in some crack house. Got it?"

"Well, okay . . . I mean, as long as I can afford it."

That was it. She'd pushed him one protest too far. His eyes went cold and drifted away.

"I mean, I get to have a say in it, right? We'll look for places together?" The scrambling backpedal in her voice made her cringe inside. She sounded like an anxious little girl—a thing her father had trained out of her since birth.

"I give it two months." He stood up from the table and headed to the garage, washing his hands of her. "Once you get a taste of the real world, you'll come running back with your tail between your legs. You'll see. You want to play this little game. Fine. Let's play."

He slammed the door to the garage behind him.

Kris flinched at the memory of it, then blinked up at her flickering computer screen. That was over a year ago, and the chill between them had only grown colder. The week after Christmas was the last straw. He'd hung up on her in the middle of their fight over her getting a roommate behind his back and him demanding that she move home. They hadn't talked since. She applied to art school without even discussing it with him.

Guilt gnawed at her empty stomach. Maybe he'd been right, she thought. Maybe if she'd moved back home . . . or never left.

Kris gazed at her worthless photographs. Maybe they'd both be sitting at Shirlene's laughing with Mel at that very moment. The photograph she'd taken of the old man behind the lunch counter hung on the wall over her computer. Mel grinned back at her with a haunted sadness in his eyes, or maybe it was just the ache in his hip. She wiped away a flood of tears and forced herself to look away.

One of her prints was missing.

With the computer still wheezing and whirring to life, she pulled herself up and walked over to the blank space on the wall where a photo should be. The torn tape still clinging to the plaster proved she wasn't crazy. She scanned the floor to see where the picture had fallen. She checked behind and under the bed, but it was gone.

"What the hell?" she muttered to herself. Pete had never shown any interest in her artwork, but she stormed through the house back to his room anyway. His walls were papered with concert posters for bands she'd never heard of. Giant black speakers sat on either side of a collection of plastic milk crates stuffed with vinyl records. His dresser was littered with receipts and sample-size bottles of cologne.

The picture wasn't there. A sharp pain squeezed her chest. It was a portrait of her father. She'd caught him smiling. And now it was gone.

She stopped in the kitchen next to her father's murder books and tried to remember if she'd taken the photograph down for some reason. Maybe their fight? Things don't just vanish, she told herself. Then again, fathers don't just go missing and wash up in pieces down the Auglaize River. The kitchen window rattled behind her as a car blew past along the narrow street outside, and an involuntary shudder ran through her.

The tiny bungalow was over a hundred years old. All the floors were crooked, and the basement was a nest of cobwebs too terrifying to enter. The landlord used the cellar as storage, filling it to the rafters with dead stoves, moldy cardboard boxes, broken storm windows, and doors that had come off their hinges. Pete liked to joke there was a ghost in the house every time the floor creaked all by itself or the wind blew a door shut, and they both agreed that the ghost must live down there. It was supposed to be funny, but she couldn't help but check the basement door at night. She glanced over at it as she walked back to her bedroom. It was shut.

Her father had insisted on renting the house despite the many better listings she presented. *I like the owner,* he'd said. *He's steady. We understand each other. Says the place has been in his family for generations.*

It was the cheapest of the lot, so she went along with it. Of course, he didn't mention that the old bastard was also spying on her. *What the hell is going on, Kris? The landlord tells me you have a man living there now . . .*

The argument still made her bitter. Who cared how expensive the utilities were or how many hours she had to pull at the bar just to buy food? All that mattered was whether the landlord thought she was a whore.

Back in her room, her dial-up connection had finally sputtered to life, and the Netscape Navigator home page shouted the day's biggest headlines. *Y2K ONLY 8 MONTHS AWAY!* Every week there was another story about the municipal power grids collapsing along with all of Western civilization when the date counter in all the computer programs flipped over to 2000 at midnight, January 1. Shortsighted programmers had coded the years as two digits, and those two digits were about to run out at the end of 99, thereby ending the world.

The headline below it read, *NOSTRADAMUS PREDICTS THE END IS NEAR.*

Kris ignored the news stories and typed in the web address from David Hohman's card. A huge photograph of a severed head greeted her along with the question, *WHO WAS THE TORSO KILLER?*

CHAPTER 8

Scrolling down the home page, Kris quickly realized the website was really just a series of message boards where strangers argued over which one of their favorite suspects was the true Torso Killer. A whole discussion group devoted themselves to a Dr. Francis Sweeney, another to Frank Dolezal, and still another to the county coroner, Dr. Samuel Gerber. As she scanned the boards, it became clear that the killer was never found.

One of the tabs along the top read, *VICTIMS.* She clicked on it.

A list of names and labels appeared under the heading *Official Canon of Victims.* The first, Victim 0, was given the name Lady of the Lake. Victim 4 was known as the Tattooed Man. Others were just labeled "Unknown." There were thirteen in all. Only three had actual names—Edward Andrassy, Flo Polillo, and Rose Wallace, although there was some debate whether Rose was actually Victim 8. All they'd found of Victim 8 was a bag of bones.

Kris swallowed hard.

The dates when pieces of each body were discovered sat tabulated next to each victim. They ranged from 1934 to 1938. Another time, another world, a million miles away from where she sat, but her hand trembled as she read. Names and dates set in neat rows like bags of evidence on a table. No family members. No next of kin. No obituar-ies. Just dates and gory details—whether the head was ever found and what parts had been dissected by the killer.

Kris clicked on a file link next to Victim 0. A photograph of an armless and legless torso slowly painted itself across her computer screen. She closed it before it could finish.

"Jesus," she breathed. She recognized the picture from one of her father's library books.

The list of "unofficial victims" was longer, with dates ranging from the 1920s to the 1950s. An entire discussion board devoted itself to an alleged victim called the Black Dahlia. Twenty different people argued back and forth whether a dead Hollywood starlet named Elizabeth Short had been murdered by the Torso Killer in 1947.

Kris tracked her way back to the beginning. *WHO WAS THE TORSO KILLER?*

She clicked the tab labeled "Dr. Francis Sweeney" and opened up an endless screed of debate as to whether this man was indeed the Torso Killer. Many believed he must be and presented detailed forensic analysis of the dissections of all thirteen bodies that indicate the killer must have been a doctor. Accusations flew about primary versus secondary sources and whether the Cleveland Police Museum files were still open to the public. Sweeney's connections to a certain politician were referenced again and again along with the secret sus-pect Eliot Ness had apparently kept prisoner in a hotel for several days for an unconstitutional interrogation. Kris's eyes flitted from one argument to the next until she found what she'd been looking for. Dr. Francis Sweeney died in a veteran's hospital in 1964.

Frank Dolezal's discussion board flooded her screen with heated arguments as to whether he knew the Torso Killer. Skimming through, Kris gathered that Frank had been arrested for the murder of Flo Polillo and coerced into giving a confession. He allegedly hung him-self in his jail cell before he could stand trial after changing his story multiple times. When the coroner finally performed the autopsy, he'd found a bunch of broken ribs. Dolezal's family and nearly all the website commentators agreed Frank had been murdered by a policeman or somebody with access that didn't want him to talk. Some theorized it was to keep him from ruining the state's case. Others believed it was because he knew the identity of the real killer.

Half-baked conspiracy theories bled over onto every page. A congressman protected the identity of the killer. The police flubbed the investigation at the urging of the governor. The press fanned hysteria over Cleveland's Jack the Ripper to sell papers. Eliot Ness and the rest of the police invented the killer to scare the railroad hobos and prostitutes out of the city. One adamant denier shouted, *"Ness just wanted an excuse to burn the hobo jungles to the ground!"* The irate man went on to berate Eliot Ness for being a drunk and a notorious union buster.

After over an hour of reading the threads, Kris blinked her eyes clear. She'd scanned the code names of all the commentators as she went, but the only one that looked remotely familiar was a DHOH. The name appeared over and over.

DHOH: What if the killings never stopped?

Kris read the words again. *David Hohman?*

The rest seemed like the musings of people with nothing better to do than obsess over a serial killer. Was this the sort of thing her father was into? she wondered, trying to picture him hunched over a computer at the Auglaize County Library, firing off his theories about a maniac from sixty years ago.

The books she'd found seemed to point to some sort of obsession, but everything she knew about the man begged to differ. Hunting, fishing, cars, guns—these were the things her father cared about. He was never any sort of history buff or crime fanatic. He didn't moon over Charles Manson. The man hardly even watched the news.

Then an unsettling thought occurred to her. *Maybe I don't know him at all.* She couldn't deny how far apart they'd drifted over the past several years. All she ever did now was disappoint him. Her once doting father and hero had become a closed book.

And now he's gone.

She shook the thought from her head and filled the empty space it left with facts:

Fact—her father was missing.

Fact—this David Hohman knew her father somehow and went looking for him at the diner.

Fact—her father had books about a serial killer from the 1930s.

Fact—David wrote the address for a chat room about the same killer on his card.

Fact—David claims to be a private investigator.

A series of scenarios flew through her head. Maybe her father had found a pile of old bones out hunting in the woods and figured he'd found another victim of this famed murderer. Maybe he'd hired David as a private investigator to help him prove his own pet theory about the killer. Maybe David Hohman was an old buddy from her dad's time in the war and they just shared this morbid hobby. Maybe her father had been working undercover with the FBI for years and Hohman was his contact. She shook her head. Maybe her father filled his lonely nights haunting chat rooms and fell in love with this David person. That one felt unlikely, but stranger things had happened. It's not as though her father would ever confide such a thing in her.

They probably met right here online, she thought as the cursor blinked in the text box. The little dash of hope flashed on and off as she held her breath. On and off. *Maybe David knows what happened.* It wasn't likely. *Maybe David knows where he is.* He probably didn't. *Maybe David killed him.* But no, he wasn't dead. *He can't be.*

After a moment's debate over whether she could bear knowing the truth, she exhaled a breath of prayer and created an account on torsokillers.com under the username Kritter. Once her registration processed, she opened the "Victims" page and scrolled down to the bottom. She posted a question under a new thread titled "Hello?"

KRITTER: David Hohman? Are you there?

After a few minutes, another user popped up.

LOWJACK: Who wants to know?

Kris wasn't eager to give out her personal information to some conspiracy theory wacko in a chat room, unless that wacko was David Hohman, and even that would be risky. She glanced at the card that some unfriendly man had left for her father. For all she knew, he was the last person to see him.

KRITTER: David? That you? You gave your card to a friend of mine in Cridersville?

After a protracted pause, the response came back.

LOWJACK: Cridersville?

Kris didn't respond. She just waited to see if her original question would get answered. A few minutes later, he came back with another one.

LOWJACK: Did somebody die?

CHAPTER 9

Kris recoiled from the question as her cursor blinked impatiently for an answer. She glanced out her window at the street. It wasn't like the person at the other end of the Internet could see her through the glass. She could be anyone. She could lie about it or confess her worst fears and it wouldn't matter.

LOWJACK: You there?

Kris bit her lip and forced air in and out through her nose. He could be anyone. He could be a killer. But if she didn't answer, she'd never know.

KRITTER: They found a body in the woods out there. In pieces.
LOWJACK: Auglaize County?
KRITTER: Yes.
LOWJACK: ID?
KRITTER: Not yet.
LOWJACK: Your friend?

Her hands trembled as she typed the answer.

KRITTER: They think it's him. I think/hope they're wrong. Why were you looking for him? How did you know him?

She waited a few minutes for a reply.

KRITTER: David? You there?

He didn't answer.

While she waited, she scrolled up into the acres of text she'd passed over. Missing persons flyers ran down her screen one after another along with dead-end threads.

Lost.

Missing.

Unsolved Death.

The phone rang next to her computer. She snatched it up. "Hello?"

"Kris?" It was Glen, her boss down at the Lincoln Tavern.

A held hope fell out of her lungs. It wasn't her father. It wasn't David Hohman.

"Oh. Hi, Glen." She scrolled back down to see if Lowjack had written back. The screen went blank. She tapped the space bar and wiggled her mouse. A text box appeared to inform her the dial-up connection had crapped out.

"I've been trying to call you for the past thirty minutes! Are we coming to work today or what? I've had you on the schedule for a week. Vin called in sick. I'm pouring drinks by myself down here."

She glanced at the clock. It was 7:36 p.m., and she was late for her shift. "Shoot, I'm sorry. It's just that . . ." There were no words for it. The pleas *Lost, Missing, Unsolved Death* hung like ghosts on her black monitor.

"You can tell me all about it when you punch in. Now get your buns down here." With that he hung up.

The dead tone hummed in her ear while she stared at the blank computer screen. The chat room went out with her crummy dial-up connection. She set the receiver back down and weighed her options. The thought of calling Glen back with her sob story made her stomach sour. She could just quit her job, she mused. She could stay in her room, chatting with strangers all night until she went crazy. Strangers that might be homicidal maniacs.

Kris flipped off the computer and headed out the door.

"Hey, sweetie. Can I get another Jäger?" The mullet-haired man at the end of the bar waved at her.

"Sure. Just one?" Kris tried to hide her quaking emotions with a smile. *Did somebody die?* She never should've gone in to work. She realized it the second she walked through the door, but now she was stuck. She grabbed the heavy green bottle and began to pour. She glanced at the door, half expecting David Hohman or some other Internet psycho to slip through. Or her father.

"Why don't you set yourself up with one too? Eh?" He lifted his chin at her in his best attempt at charm.

"I can't drink with the customers, sir," she muttered and handed him his shot. Technically, she wasn't even supposed to be behind the bar. She wasn't twenty-one, so Glen hired her as a "waitress" at a deep discount. If the police ever asked, she was just running drinks to the booths in the back.

A pair of frat boys came in and saddled up to three others at the end of the bar. A couple locked in deep conversation huddled together in one of the booths. Tracy Chapman sang from the jukebox in the corner, painting the air a smoky blue.

"Oh, come on now. One little shot isn't going to kill ya. Is it?"

"My boss might." Kris busied herself cleaning glasses below the bar.

She hated the blustering drunks that pestered you, spilled their drinks on the floor, and had to be dumped into a cab at the end of the night. Mullet Head worked construction from the looks of his boots, flannel shirt, and thick hands. Her father had the same hands from repairing railroad lines and engines. They used to pick her up when she was small. The ache in her chest made it hard to breathe.

Mullet Head didn't notice or care. He wasn't going to let up. The ring on his finger said he was married, but the way he looked at her said he liked to mess around. "The boss ain't here, is he? C'mon. I hate to drink alone."

Glen strictly forbid skimming drinks, especially by her, but he'd gone down to the basement storeroom. She was alone behind the counter with nothing but the terrible feeling she'd done everything wrong. It was her fault he'd gone fishing by himself. It was her fault for leaving home. It was her fault for not listening to him and leaving him alone. *Selfish. Ungrateful. Rotten.*

The door opened again. Two chatty girls stumbled in drunk.

"Sure," she heard herself say. "Why not?" She slapped a second shot glass onto the bar and filled it.

"Here's to our future. May our children be as gorgeous as you," the man slurred and clinked her glass.

Over my dead body. Kris threw back the shot, and the man whooped in approval. The sickly sweet liquor coated her throat like cough syrup and flushed her cheeks. She glanced up at the clock. *It's going to be a long night.*

"Can I get a thank you?"

"Thank you," she said flatly and went back to washing her glasses.

"How about a smile, girlie? I bet you'd be a real looker if you smiled." Mullet Head leered at her.

Kris caught her own reflection in the mirror over the bar. She looked as bad as she felt. The whites of her eyes were shot with red, and bags puffed out like she hadn't slept in days. Her hair was a mangled mess. *A real looker.* She shook her head. On a good day, she considered herself pleasantly average with her brown hair and narrow frame that she usually kept hidden under baggy clothes. The only remarkable thing about her at all was her eyes. They changed color from green to hazel to amber. When she was a little girl, her father used to call them her mood rings. In the dim light of the bar, they'd gone dark.

"I don't think she likes you, Sal," the balding man on the stool next to him taunted.

"Nah. You like me. Don't you, sweetie?" He grinned at her until she turned away. "Man, she's got a cute ass, doesn't she? Nice and tight. Kinda sporty."

"I seen better," Baldy chuckled.

"You're a runner, right? Played some volleyball? Which is it?"

"I'm guessing softball," Baldy said with a big laugh.

"Nah. She's a nice girl. Right? Tell it to us straight, sweetie. You're not a dyke, are you?"

Kris clamped her lips into a thin smile to keep the stream of curses in. "Sure am."

Baldy nearly fell over laughing. "I told you she played softball."

"Nah. Do you?"

She didn't answer. Instead she said, "Can I get you boys another round?"

"Well, that depends. You gonna have another drink with us?" Mullet Head slapped a twenty on the counter. "There's a big tip in it for you. Even if you are a dyke. Shit, that might be even better. Bring your girlfriends along, and we'll hit the town. They all as cute as you?"

Ugh. At this point she was ready to drink an entire bottle. "Me and the other dykes have plans."

"Oh, yeah? So what time y'all get off?" Mullet raised his eyebrows at her.

Why is everything out of this asshole's mouth a double entendre? Kris decided to ignore the question. "What'll it be, gentleman?"

"A shot for me. One for you. And another couple of beers."

Kris did her best to ignore the beady eyes roaming up and down her body as she poured two Miller Lites and two more shots of Jäger.

Mullet Head picked up his shot. "C'mon, girlie. Don't leave me hangin' over here."

Kris picked up the tiny glass and clinked with him. She waited until he knocked it back before slapping hers back down onto the bar, untouched.

"Damn. She just dissed you," Baldy laughed.

"Nah. You wouldn't dis me, would you, sweetie? Have the shot."

"Thank you, but I have to keep working." Kris could usually flirt her way out of a bad situation with a well-timed joke and a smile, but she had nothing for this idiot. She made her way down to the other end of the bar to check on her other customers. The frat boys stared slack-jawed at the Cavs game on the TVs over her head. Unfortunately, all of them had full beers.

She served the two drunk girls a couple of poorly mixed cosmos, all the while keeping her eye on the door. *There is no way any of those murder fanatics know where I work.* She hadn't even given him her name, but the nagging fear kept pulling its strings. It couldn't just be a coincidence—the books, the chat room, the killer that liked to chop up bodies. David Hohman may be an obsessed wacko, but he was also a private investigator. If he went looking for her father, he might find her too. He could be watching her at that moment.

Mullet and his friend tried waving her back down, but she ignored them as long as she could, restocking the condiments and checking the kegs. After a full five minutes, she decided she couldn't shun them any longer.

Her shot was still sitting at the end of the bar.

"Y'all doin' okay?" she asked, hoping for a fresh start.

"I have to apologize for my friend here." Mullet slurred his mea culpa. "We shouldn'ta called you a dyke. That was inappropriate. Meant no offense."

"None taken." And to prove their idiotic remarks hadn't bothered her in the slightest, she picked up the shot and downed it.

"Atta girl!" Mullet grinned. "So you got a boyfriend?"

Really?

"I do," Kris lied. She hadn't been with anybody but Troy in her entire life, a fact that he loved to throw in her face. *We're meant to be together, baby. You're mine.*

"Does he know you're down here, talking to me?" Mullet's eyes dropped to her tits. "Wearing that tight T-shirt?"

"Yep." Kris grabbed a rag and started wiping down the counter.

"I wouldn't let you out of the house lookin' like that. Would you, Donnie?"

Donnie didn't answer. He was looking up at the TV. The Cavs had a run going.

Mullet kept going. "So that's the game, isn't it? You put on these tight clothes and flirt with us to get better tips, right?"

She looked down despite herself. Glen insisted that she wear a tight T-shirt as her "uniform." She hadn't been thrilled, but she hadn't refused. *Man's got a point, Krit,* her father taunted from her subconscious.

Mullet laughed. "Well, c'mon then." He threw a five-dollar bill onto the counter. "Earn your tip, sweetie. Tease me."

"Why don't you shut the fuck up and go home to your wife?" The words were out of her mouth before her lips could catch them.

"Oh, shit!" Donnie let out a laugh and gave her an approving nod.

"What'd you just say to me?" Mullet straightened up in his seat, suddenly sober.

Kris threw her washrag onto the bar and shook her head. Glen still wasn't back. She couldn't leave the bar. All she could do was bite her lips together and count to ten to keep from saying more.

"Didn't anybody ever teach you manners? Shit. If I was your daddy . . ." The bastard leaned over the bar, closing the distance between them, his lips curling into a sneer. "I'd put you over my knee right here. What do you think of that? Huh? You lookin' for a daddy tonight, honey?"

Without thought or warning, Kris punched the son of a bitch dead in the face. Ten years of hauling logs to her father's woodstove had apparently paid off, much to her horror and utter satisfaction. His stunned expression before he hit the ground was almost worth it.

Next came a blur of shouts and threats and profuse apologies as the shock of what she'd done reverberated from one end of the bar to the other. Minutes later, Glen was shoving her out the door and into the alley.

"What the hell's the matter with you, Kris! You'll be lucky if they don't press charges!" he shouted.

"I'm the one who should be pressing charges! You wouldn't believe the shit he was saying to me. He said he liked my ass and offered to be my daddy!" The words *And my daddy might be fucking dead right now!* nearly slipped out, but she'd be damned if she was going to break down sobbing in front of Glen.

"I'm running a business here. I can't have bartenders belting the customers. He could sue!"

"He was wearing a fucking wedding ring. You really think he's going to drag you to court to discuss his right to grab my ass? This is sexual harassment!"

"Grow up, Kris. You want to work in a bar, that's the business. You're fired!"

The words hit her like a slap. "F-fine . . . That's. That's fine."

Shaking, Kris staggered across the gravel lot to her car. Panic swept up and down her body. *Fired. I'm fired.* As she sank behind the wheel, a single thought skittered through the empty dark outside her windshield.

My dad's gonna kill me. Then she broke into tears.

HUNT FIEND IN 4 DECAPITATIONS

Head Found in Kingsbury Run

Somewhere in the countless byways of the crowded Southeast Side, detectives believed today is the grisly workshop of a human butcher who in the last 10 months has carved up and decapitated four persons.

—*Cleveland Press*, June 6, 1936, p. 1

CHAPTER 10

April 5, 1938

"You're late. Quick. Come inside."

Mary Alice grabbed Ethel by the arm and dragged her through the loading dock door and down a narrow corridor. They passed the doorway to a sweaty kitchen where three women in matching blue dresses stood toiling over steaming pots. None of them looked up.

"Wait," Ethel protested, her feet nearly stumbling over themselves. "Where are we going?"

"Shh!" Mary Alice hissed and dragged her into a tight broom closet at the end of the hall. "Sister Frances can't see you. Not like this."

"Like what?" Ethel looked down at her low-cut bodice and torn stockings. She'd been with five men that afternoon and had eight dollars stuffed between her tits to prove it. It was enough to buy a room for the night, but finding a hotel that would have a woman like her was another story.

"Take off those clothes," she demanded and started undoing the buttons herself.

"Hey! Hands off!" Ethel shoved her into the wall. The whiskey she'd drunk that afternoon still sloshed in her veins. The terrified look on the poor girl's face amused her enough to laugh. She pushed up against her for effect. "You want to touch, you gotta pay. You got three dollars, Sister?"

Mary Alice's eyes bulged from her head in utter shock. "I have no idea what it is you're suggesting, but we do not keep money here. Not ever. The Lord's work is its own—"

"Well, then no titties for you. Now get me out this damned closet."

"They will not let you stay! I've tried to let in strangers before, but if you aren't one of us, they won't let you in. Not unless . . ." Her voice trailed off as her eyes circled the tiny room.

Ethel looked down and saw the poor thing was carrying a plain blue dress just like the one she was wearing. It was the same frumpy smock the maids in the kitchen sported. "So. You want me to put on this ugly dress and pretend to be what exactly?"

Mary Alice smiled weakly. "My cousin Hattie from Mount Airy?"

"Hattie? Jesus. You couldn't think of an uglier name? Or find an uglier dress?" Ethel snatched the wool monstrosity out of the poor girl's hands. "You really think this'll work?"

"Hattie's family has drifted badly from the faith. The corruptions of modern life have overtaken you all. But you've been writing me for months about your call to the Lord."

Ethel arched an eyebrow. *My call to the Lord?* "Sure. Why the hell not?" She fished the eight dollars out from her cleavage along with her knife and handed them to the bewildered girl. "Hold these." Then she stripped down to her corset with the efficiency of a professional.

"You can't wear . . . we don't do that with our . . ." Mary Alice pointed to the lace and bone holding in Ethel's gut and pushing up her breasts.

"With your what? Tits? You girls just let 'em swing?" Ethel reached up and squeezed one of Mary Alice's breasts. The girl stumbled into the corner, aghast. "Well, shit. I guess you do."

Ethel slapped her corset on top of the pile. Her own breasts flopped onto her ribcage, bruised and bitten, and she pretended not to notice the concern in the girl's eyes. She threw the ugly blue sack over her head and covered up all her sins. "How's that?"

"Better." Mary Alice forced a smile. "But we have to cover your hair and . . ." Her voice trailed off as she noticed Ethel's high heels sticking out of the bottom of the hem.

"You don't like 'em? Fine." Ethel kicked off her heels. Her feet fell to the ground like broken bedsprings.

"Good." Mary Alice started stuffing the harlot's hair under a ridiculous white tea cozy of a hat.

It all reminded Ethel of the time she'd dressed up as a nun to titillate some perverted priest, or maybe he was just some regular pervert pretending to be a priest. She chuckled to herself and was tempted to share the story, but she was fairly certain it'd make the poor girl currently fussing with her hair faint.

"Now. If you want to stay here, you need to keep a vow of silence. I told Sister Frances that to atone for your sins, you have taken the vow. It's the only way anyone might believe you're one of us. Do you understand?" Mary Alice grabbed Ethel's hands for emphasis. "No talking."

"No talking." Ethel forced a smile and a nod. "For how long?"

"As long as it takes."

"What the hell is that supposed to mean?"

"Do not curse. It is not our way."

"Your way? Who the hell are you people?"

"Do not speak so lightly of hell." Mary Alice's eyes flashed with anger for a fleeting second. "Our people lead a simple, modest, plain life. We live for the Lord. We follow His teachings. We keep His customs. When we come of age, we are baptized and born again in the Lord and keep His faith. And cursing is not our way."

"Well, it sure as shit is *my* way."

"Do you want to go back out there? Back in the cold? Back to *him*?" Mary Alice's voice was developing a bit of a bite. "If you want to stay here and eat and bask in the warmth and love of the Lord, no talking. Not a word. I am risking everything to bring you here."

"Risking everything? Why? What will happen if they find out?"

Mary Alice just shook her head. "The Lord has brought us together. He has sent a message with you, and I will do His bidding."

Ethel almost felt the need to correct the poor girl but thought better of it. If Mary Alice thought saving a washed-up whore was her mission in life, so be it. As long as there was a roof over her head and the food was hot and the wine was . . . *Wait.* "Will there be drinks with dinner? Wine? Beer?"

"Goodness no. Never! Liquor corrupts the spirit. Our bodies are our temples and—"

"No hooch? Jesus, Mary, and Joseph." Ethel nearly tore the stupid hat right off her head and marched right out to the nearest tavern. *What was the longest I've ever gone without a drink? Two days? Three?* She could already feel the hollow itch that would creep under her skin once the buzz wore thin. She would leave tomorrow. Or later tonight. She'd just sneak out when the urge struck and . . .

The girl stood there pleading with her doe eyes.

"Right." Ethel gave the moppet a smile. *Warm bed. Hot food. Warm bed. Hot food.* "I understand. It's not our way."

Mary Alice pressed a finger to her lips to shush the woman. "Vow of silence."

"Right." Ethel mimed locking her lips and throwing away the key.

Satisfied, the girl opened the closet door. "Welcome to the Harmony Mission, Hattie."

It was the best meal Ethel had eaten in years. Pork roast, potatoes, carrots, cabbage, fresh baked bread, and sweet fried corn. She was on her third helping before she noticed it.

None of the women were talking.

The din of forks and knives and bowls being picked up, passed, and set down again filled the enormous cavern below the wood-plank ceiling hanging high overhead, but that was it. Her eyes circled the ten tables in the center of a large room. They were set in five orderly rows with six to eight women at each table. Ethel glanced over at the dour women on either side of her, at Mary Alice across the table, then at the table next to theirs and the next.

Not a word.

Ethel chewed her corn in amazement. She'd never seen so many women in one place without a single thing to say. Not even in prison.

Mary Alice caught her staring and almost imperceptibly shook her head in disapproval. She raised her eyebrows and demonstratively clasped her hands together and bowed her head. They were praying, Ethel realized. Her eyes rounded the room once again at the rows of silent women. Some had closed their eyes. Some were nodding their heads in some secret rhythm. She was pretty sure the fat one in the corner was snoring, but they were all making like they were deep in meditation.

Good Lord.

After a solid five minutes, she realized she'd forgotten to ask about cigarettes. With her head held low, her eyes wandered the sides of the room, searching for an ashtray. The walls were red brick. The floor was fresh varnished wood. There wasn't a speck of dust or a cigarette butt in sight.

Ethel shut her eyes and silently cursed. *Damn it!*

She'd never considered herself much of a talker. Never had much to say, really. Her story was just another hard-luck sob nobody wanted to hear. Her mother died too soon. Her father drank too much. Her brother was far too young to take care of himself. And the landlord knocked on the door every day. There weren't many ways to make money after the crash of '29, but Ethel was sitting on one of them. She learned that hard lesson when she was a mere fifteen years old, but she was hardly the youngest she'd seen dragged into the trade. There wasn't much else for a girl like her to do. Not when the landlord wanted the rent. Not when her little brother wanted food.

"Good evening, Sisters." A deep voice boomed from the end of the room. The man attached to it held his hands up like one of the soapbox preachers that prowled Public Square.

"Good evening, Brother Milton," the ladies all answered in unison, all except Ethel. He wasn't particularly tall, maybe a bit fat, but in that room full of silent, simpering women, he was a giant.

"I'd like to take a few moments to commend the work of a few outstanding servants among you," he announced, then grabbed a slip of paper from a pale girl standing beside him.

A soft murmur swept through the room. The silence settled back in its place with a disapproving arch of his brow. He continued, "Sister Helen typeset more pages today than three of our youngest sisters combined. The Lord is at work in those nimble hands. Praise be to God."

"Praise be," the sisters repeated, nodding together.

Ethel searched the room out of the corner of her eye until she found one woman blushing and stifling a smile. *Helen, I presume?*

"Sister Mavis distributed more pamphlets and reached more lost souls today than ever before. May we all see the glory of Christ in her mission. Praise be to God."

"Praise be."

The man called out the names of a few more needy women and praised God for working their hands like a puppeteer. Then the tone changed. "Finally, it has come to my attention that the devil has been walking among us, Sisters. Lucifer has been whispering in our ears. Complaints, idle gossip, and foul humors have been winding themselves like a serpent around us and between us."

The man's reproachful gaze scanned every face in the room for emphasis. Ethel rolled her eyes. She'd met enough horrible men to know the devil didn't whisper. Brother Milton paused an instant too long on Ethel's bored expression, and she felt the room shrink. She dropped her head as if in prayer, but she suspected it was too late. She'd been spotted.

The man continued with his hellfire and damnation, but now she was certain he was talking only to her. "If you dare not speak the words out loud to Sister Frances or to me, you must not utter them in dark corners. Satan is listening, my sisters. Satan hears the betrayals in your hearts and in your minds and takes root there. Would you let the serpent enter these halls?"

"No, Brother," the sisters chanted.

Brother Milton looked right at Ethel and said, "I see we have a new face among us. Welcome, Sister, welcome. Come and let us meet you."

Shit. Ethel kept her head down but forced herself to stand. A cold hand grabbed hers. It belonged to the pale girl that stood sentry next to the only man in the room. She pulled Ethel in her bare feet with the eight dollars still stuffed in her drawers to the front of the room. *Shit. Shit. Shit.*

"Tell us your name, Sister."

Ethel bit her lip and debated answering the question by giving the tiny priest in his pants a nice squeeze.

Mary Alice sprang up and called weakly, "Forgive her, Brother Milton. She has taken a vow of silence. She won't speak again until the Lord speaks to her."

"Ah." The fat man gave her a nod of approval, his eyes bent with sympathy. "And do you speak for her, Sister Mary Alice?"

"Yes, Brother. She is my cousin Hattie. Her family has strayed from the faith." Mary Alice pressed her lips together and hung her head.

Apparently that was all the explanation needed. Ethel looked out at the ten tables of women now gazing up at her as one of their own and wondered how many had run away and how many had been cast out. Most of them were too old to marry and too old for whoring. They looked like orphans, every last one of them.

"I see." Brother Milton put a heavy hand on Ethel's shoulder. "Welcome to our family, Hattie."

Then he did the unthinkable. He pulled her into his arms and gave her a warm hug. Her own arms just hung limply in astonishment. It was far more startling than if he'd stripped her naked right there. A well of emotions she didn't even remember rose up inside her, and it took all her strength not to shove him away and run for the door.

He released her just in time. "There is no greater calling than a call to the Lord. Hattie, may you hear His song in your soul, and may you sing again with God in your heart. Sisters, let us pray . . ."

The room bowed its collective head and began pleading with Jesus the Savior to rescue poor Hattie. Ethel feigned prayer and scanned the roomful of ugly dresses until they fell on a face that wasn't bowed and praying.

A young man stood in the far corner by the kitchen door. He wore a plain suit and wide-brimmed hat much like Brother Milton's. He gazed right into Ethel's eyes and gave her a smile. She'd seen that sort of smile before. The landlord had on the same smile the first time he'd caught her alone in the apartment.

Time to pay the rent, it said.

CHAPTER 11

Somewhere deep inside the monstrous Harmony Mission, a pair of footsteps creaked across the ceiling above Ethel's bed. She opened her swollen eyes and stared into the darkness of her cell. Trying to sleep was useless. Night sweats prickled her skin as the alcohol evaporated out of her pores. Her heart hammered her ribs while her brain beat against her skull in rhythm. Her trembling hands rubbed her legs to soothe the screaming nerve endings and scatter the phantom spiders crawling over her skin. The sheets were damp and shivering along with her.

This was a horrible mistake.

The faint glow of the moon trickled in through the window high above her pillow, casting a ghostly patch of light on the far wall. Her room in the ladies' dormitory was only slightly wider than the narrow bed they'd given her. The dark wood wall panels and ceiling seemed to draw closer as the unseen stranger walked overhead.

Ethel sat up and listened.

All the women had gone to bed directly after dinner. They'd cleared the table and done the dishes in short order, then filed down the hallway two by two. Mary Alice had grabbed her arm and led her down one corridor and then another. A right turn, then a left, then down a set of stairs so narrow they had to walk single file, then several more turns, through a door, across a breezeway, down another narrow brick tunnel, then up three flights of stairs. There were so many twists and turns Ethel was thoroughly lost by the time they'd reached the dormitory.

The long narrow hallway just outside her cell was lined on both sides with identical dark wood doors. It reminded her of the Mansfield workhouse. She rolled over onto her side at the thought.

"This will be your room, Hattie. Mine is just across the hall." Mary Alice had grinned as though this was some great relief.

The tiny room was only big enough for a bed, a bedside table, and two hooks on the wall where she could hang her ugly blue dress. A Bible had leaned against the stiff straw pillow as a welcome. It was now lying somewhere on the floor.

"Good night, Hattie. I'm so glad you decided to join us," Mary Alice had beamed at her before closing the door. She didn't bother to wait for an answer. Hattie's vow of silence wouldn't allow a single word, but Ethel felt a dozen choice ones boiling up in her chest.

Glancing out the one window set high above the thin mattress, she'd seen that the sun hadn't even set yet. *I'm getting myself the hell out of here. Thanks for the grub, but I ain't joining the likes of you Bible-thump—*

The sound of a dead bolt sliding home had snapped her head back around to the door. She'd gone over to the door and tried the handle. It didn't budge. The little bitch had actually locked her in there.

Ethel had knocked on the wood. Her sweaty eyes fell on the bolted door looming there in the dark.

There was no answer.

"Mary Alice!" she'd hissed. "This wasn't the deal!"

Nothing.

Ethel had pounded her fist. *Bang. Bang. Bang.*

The door had swung open on the fourth punch, and Ethel had found herself face to face with a stern-looking schoolmarm.

"Can we help you with something, dear?" the stone-faced woman demanded. Her thin lips and wrinkled skin were set in a permanent frown, her gray hair pulled tight into a knot. Her tone had made it clear she was not in the business of helping anyone.

Ethel's eyes had darted past the old crone into the empty hallway. Mary Alice was nowhere to be seen.

"If you're looking for a privy, you'll find a chamber pot under your bed. Next time, I suggest you finish your toilet before the nightly reading begins. You have twenty minutes to commune with the Lord before lights out. Good evening, Sister."

With that, schoolmarm had closed the door in Ethel's face and thrown the bolt before she could think to knock the old broad on her ass and make a run for it. She was trapped.

Ethel climbed up onto the thin mattress with shaking legs and gazed out the window, pressing her nose to the cold glass. The window looked out into a narrow courtyard. A bank of identical windows gazed back at her twenty feet away. A few hours earlier, yellow lights had glowed in each one. In the lower windows across the light well she'd seen the backs of five heads all sitting in bed, bent over their Bibles before bed. Now they were empty.

Ethel counted thirty lined up in three rows. Hers was on the third floor. Cold air hissed through the window seams in urgent whispers. A light rain was falling from the piece of sky above. The setting sun had cast a golden glow onto the walls at the far end, leaving long shadows over everything else. Down in the courtyard, she'd seen four bicycles lined up against the far wall. A small potted garden sat somewhere on the stone floor. Now it was all hidden in the dark.

A flicker of light down at the far end caught her eye. Two figures were walking with a flashlight and bowed heads. They were both men.

I see how it is. The women stay locked up in their prison cells while the men are free to wander.

What she wouldn't give for a drink and a smoke. She studied the windows across the courtyard. They were all small and set high above the ground. There were no ladders or drainpipes to shimmy down. The Mansfield workhouse wasn't this secure, she mused. The only things missing were the armed guards.

Ethel drew the knife out of the hem of her dress and slid it between the door and the jamb to see if she could move the bolt. It didn't budge.

Feeling the familiar itch crawling under her skin, Ethel unlocked the latch of her window and slid open the sash. Raindrops hit her face as she stuck her head out. Looking up, she could see two more stories of windows sitting over her room. They'd put her in a taller tower than the gals across the courtyard. Her path up to the roof looked hopeless. Freedom was a forty-foot drop down onto hard stone.

Defeated, Ethel closed the window and plopped down onto the shivering mattress. Like it or not, she was stuck there for the night. The naked lightbulb over her head was out without a string or a switch on any of the walls. Just like prison.

She'd been in worse places, she told herself. At least she was out of the rain. She was safe. She was fed. There had been nights she might've killed someone for a dry room and a warm bed. It had been days since Ma had thrown her out onto the street. *How many?*

Night was too dangerous and busy for her to sleep, and there weren't too many places she could curl up in the light of day. The empty buildings she drifted between had been badly burned in insurance schemes or vandalized, and they housed nothing but jittery vagrants and gangs of street toughs. It was hard to tell which was worse, the arson-scorched buildings or the hobo jungles lining the shores of the river.

The casualties of the Depression littered the banks of the Cuyahoga with their shanties. Starving children huddled with battered women alongside homeless men in the grips of a blackout. Fear hung over the river shantytown in a hushed silence that had ridden the rails in from Kingsbury Run.

How many bodies had they found in the Run? Four? Five? Ethel scratched at her clammy skin and couldn't remember. All she could see were the detective's photographs of what the killer had done.

Ethel pulled the ugly sack of a dress over her head and hung it on a nail. *I should take Mary Alice down to the jungles. Show her what hell really looks like.*

As she curled up on the thin mattress, the thought of Rose's little girl drifted unbidden into her head. Ethel couldn't bear to imagine where the poor thing might be, helpless and alone. Willie had asked her to keep an eye out, but she didn't even know the girl's name. There was no saving her. There was no saving anyone. Now more footsteps creaked across the ceiling.

In the thin light of the moon, Ethel got up out of bed and felt around blindly under it until she found the edge of the bucket she'd been promised. She hauled it out and crouched over it, gazing up at the sliver of sky out her window.

A muffled voice came from somewhere outside her room. *The hallway? The room next door? Somewhere upstairs?*

A softer voice answered, but Ethel strained to make out the words. *Was that a laugh?* It sounded like a woman's voice.

She climbed back into bed, wondering what woman was allowed to laugh at that hour. Frankly, she hadn't heard any of the sisters laugh once all evening.

The lower voice said something else. *Or was that a grunt?* The next sound left no doubt about it, and under it was the familiar squeak of bedsprings. The softer voice was laughing again. *Or crying?*

Ethel sat up as the squeaking grew louder. Somewhere upstairs one of the sisters was getting the business, and from what she'd seen of the sisters, it was a good bet it wasn't her idea. She hugged her trembling knees to her chest.

Every creak of the bed was a reminder of the first time it had happened to her. She held the sides of her pounding head and shut her eyes. Every man was the same man. Breathing hot breath in her ear. Sweating his stink into her. Grunting faster and faster. Until he finished with her.

The squeaking over her head finally stopped. A few more muffled words filtered down through the wood slats of her ceiling, followed by the click of a door.

Ethel listened to the light tap of the raindrops against her window, waiting for the footsteps to return. Waiting for the knock to fall on her door. She pulled her knife out from under her pillow and gripped it tightly in the dark.

CHAPTER 12

Sometime after dawn, Mary Alice opened her door with a cheery smile. "Good morning, Sister Hattie! It's going to be a beautiful day!"

Breakfast assaulted Ethel's senses with the steaming smell of meat, the jarring clang of forks, the screeching scrape of knives. The food made her nauseous, lying on her plate like the arms and thighs in one of the detective's autopsy pictures. She pushed it away and gripped the edge of the table to steady her head. Faces of the girls came in and out of focus with wet chewing sounds and whispered prayers. She searched their eyes for telltale tears or buried shame. It could have been any of them and none of them at the same time.

"Good morning, Sisters," a familiar voice boomed from the front of the room. The reverend walked across the floor with the stern schoolmarm who had slammed the door in Ethel's face the night before.

"Good morning, Brother Milton," they all answered at once like a multiheaded beast. Another wave of nausea swept through Ethel, and she buried her face in her hands. *I have to get out of here.* But her legs felt too jittery to stand.

"Today may God's grace be with you as we go about His work. Let us pray."

Was it him? Was he the one that violated a girl the night before?
There he was, standing like a king before a hundred spinsters, all
ready to get down on their knees at his command. He had them all
locked up in a tower at his disposal every night. His voice washed its
deep bass over her into a drowning ocean.

The answering chorus faded away. Then Mary Alice was pulling
her down the hallway to God knows where.

What happened next happened in pieces. Riding on a rattling bench
in some sort of railcar. The sisters singing hymns like a spinning car-
ousel. Heaving her stomach up onto the frozen dirt. A barn reeling
against the ice gray sky. Cold water down her throat, on her face. The
cool hard edge of a sink against her forehead. A thin cot at the end of
a long hall. Lace curtains fluttering near the window. Crackers dry as
sawdust. A couple of drops of sharp bitter oil on her tongue, burning
her mouth, poisoning her throat. Mary Alice's hushed whisper, "A
little laudanum should calm the shaking."

Then the frantic bees swarming under her skin went still.

A squealing sound snapped Ethel out of her stupor. She was standing
in a barn stall. She dropped the shovel in her hand and made her way
across the dirt and straw toward the sound. Dread bled into her gut
as the brutal screams grew louder.

Outside the barn, two men were wrestling a writhing naked body
onto the ground with ropes in their hands. Ethel's mouth gaped in
horror at the sight until she realized the creature was a large pig and
not one of the sisters.

They strung the screaming animal up by its hind feet, hanging
it from a giant iron hook where it thrashed and spun. One of them
placed a metal bucket under the pig's furious snout. The taller one

pulled a large knife from the black apron he was wearing and without warning stuck it right in the pig's jugular. Ethel recognized him from the dining hall the night before, standing in the back with the landlord's grin. The short one held the beast as it bucked and fought. Hot blood steamed in the frigid air, splashing into the bucket and out over the dirt.

"Hattie. Are you alright?" Mary Alice came up behind her and nudged her shoulder. "I've finished five stalls in the time you've taken to do one."

Ignoring her, Ethel stared as the fight bled out of the pig.

Mary Alice gazed up at the two men and waved. "Good morning, Brother Bertram, Brother Wenger."

The man holding the pig steady waved. "Good morning, Sisters." He was maybe twenty-five years old with a spotty beard.

The tall one took a step toward them, bloody knife still in his hand. There was that smile again. "Do you need something, Sister Hattie?"

Ethel shook her head, keeping her eyes on the limp animal. It was dead. Brother Bertram slid the blood bucket aside and positioned a larger trough below the carcass.

"No, we're just fine, Brother Wenger. Thank you," Mary Alice sang and pulled Ethel away from the slaughter and back toward the barn.

Wenger went back to the carcass. With one clean motion, his knife split the pig's stomach from neck to tail, and its entrails came spilling out.

Ethel's jaw dropped.

"Good Lord, Hattie!" Mary Alice scolded, dragging her back to her stall. "You act as though you've never seen meat before."

Ethel picked her shovel back up with the image of steaming intestines and entrails still fresh in her mind. She'd seen lots of things, but she'd never seen anything get disemboweled before. The terrible photographs the detective had shown her rifled through her head again.

They called the killer a butcher, she thought, sick to her stomach. *The Mad Butcher of Kingsbury Run.*

"The Lord frowns upon the idle, Hattie."

Ethel managed to choke down lunch, watching Brothers Wenger and Bertram out of the corner of her eye. No policeman would ever question them, she realized. Not Bible lovers like them. They could be cutting people to pieces out here and no one would ever know.

After they cleared the plates, Mary Alice led Ethel to the sprawling fields that surrounded the barn and a homely farmhouse, dragging a leather harness with a big metal blade behind them.

"What the hell is that?" Ethel asked when they stopped at the far end of an empty stretch of dirt and dried stalks.

"Shh! Remember your vow, Hattie!" Mary Alice stepped between Ethel and the barn, putting her back to the other workers so none would see her talking. "This is a plow. We use it to till the fields. We need to turn the soil over for planting."

"Oh, stuff my vow. I didn't sign up to be a pack mule or to be locked in a cell all night while the brothers raid the henhouse."

"What?" Mary Alice gaped at her.

"One of the brothers was buggering someone last night in the room above mine," Ethel whispered back. "What the hell is going on here? You got Brother Wenger with his knife. You got your reverend and his whispering devil. Which one of 'em sleeps in the room upstairs?"

After a long blank stare, Mary Alice muttered almost to herself, "But there's no one that sleeps on the fourth floor. It's storage."

"Well, somebody was up there, and I'm not sticking around to find out who. This is ridiculous! I quit!"

"You can't just quit," she hissed back. "It doesn't work that way. Do you know what they'll do if you . . ."

"If I what? If I leave?"

"If they find out I've deceived them?" Mary Alice's face went pale. Her eyes flooded as they searched the field for eavesdroppers.

"What will they do?"

Mary Alice just shook her head.

"Beat you? Whip you? Make you pull a plow with your bare hands? What?" Ethel joked, but a nagging feeling bored its way into her gut. She didn't want to see Mary Alice hurt. Not when the poor thing had only wanted to help her.

"They will test my humility, and if they aren't satisfied, I will be . . . I'll be shunned."

"Shunned?" Ethel mocked the word. "Like all those spinsters will refuse to sit with you at dinner? So what? People been shunnin' the likes of me my whole life."

"No." Mary Alice's eyes pleaded with her. "They will cast me out, and I will have nothing. No home. No food . . ."

Ethel stared at her for a beat. *This fool wouldn't last a night in the Run. Or anywhere else. They'd turn her out. They'd . . .* It was unthinkable. Like it or not, she was stuck with Mary Alice. "Goddammit!"

Mary Alice's eyes bulged at Ethel's outburst. She shook her head, but it was too late. The three sisters that had been clearing brush at the next field stood up with loud gasps.

"Hattie? Was that you?"

Ethel sat next to Mary Alice on a bench in a rattling horse trailer the entire trip back to the city. It was the sort of thing they used to cart livestock to the slaughterhouses. She let her head fall back against the clattering metal wall. Tops of naked trees and banks of frigid clouds rolled past the airholes. A blood red barn passed by the cattle wagon. Ethel watched it through the tiny holes, debating whether she should make a run for it.

When they got back to the Harmony Mission, the trailer pulled back into the loading dock, and the ladies poured out. Wenger climbed down from behind the wheel of the truck and sauntered past them all, stopping to give Ethel an appraisal. "You feeling alright, Sister Hattie? I hope the ride back was kinder to you." He put a hand on her shoulder and gave it a far too familiar squeeze. It was as though they were old lovers, and Ethel couldn't help but grimace as she surrendered a polite nod.

"Thank you for your concern, Brother Wenger," Mary Alice said with a bow of her head and then ushered Ethel out of the loading dock and up the stairs. They were both covered head to toe in dirt and sweat.

As Mary Alice pulled her down the narrow hall to the dormitory washroom, Ethel whispered, "What's his story anyway?"

"Shh!" she whispered back and pushed her through the door. They were alone. "We only have a few minutes. Brother Milton will question you, and if you don't answer well . . ." She just shook her head.

Ethel couldn't believe she was bound to this simpering fool. "Don't you have a family you could go to, if, you know, if you get 'shunned'?"

Mary Alice shook her head violently. "You don't understand. If you're shunned by the faith, you're shunned by everyone. It doesn't matter anyway. They washed their hands of me when I left."

"Why? Aren't they proud of your . . . whatever it is you do here?"

"Not everyone believes in Brother Milton's mission. They fear he has strayed from the fold. He heeds none of the Brethren and answers only to God. But there's no time. You must listen. You grew up in Mount Airy. Your parents never joined a church or received Jesus into their hearts. You felt a calling and found an excuse to come see me."

"Okay. But what does that matter. I can't speak, right?"

"No. You can't."

"Right. So wh—"

Mary Alice screwed up her face as a group of three ladies came through the door.

"Bless you, Sisters," the interlopers murmured. Then they pulled off their dirty dresses and set about washing their hands and feet in a trough set along the far wall.

Mary Alice and Ethel followed suit and scrubbed away the mud ground into their hands and faces in total silence. Ethel scanned the arms and legs and backs and bellies of the women out of the corner of her eye, looking for signs one of them had fought off the man she'd heard the night before. She counted a few scattered bruises and scrapes but no bite marks. Their breasts looked unmolested. Mary Alice nudged her shoulder and shot her a pointed look. Ethel dropped her eyes for a moment.

Bending to soap her feet, Ethel caught a glimpse of Mary Alice's back. It was covered in long, thin scars and several fresh welts. Ethel gaped at them a moment and went back to scrubbing her toes, wondering what sort of flogger or whip had left the marks. There were at least twenty of them. Each one a frozen scream. A cold feeling crept down her spine.

Finally, the other women wrapped themselves in the clean rags hanging from nails on the far wall and left the room. Mary Alice shut off the water.

"Your vow of silence has helped you hear God's voice," she continued in a rush. "His voice is everywhere, and you've been listening. But you've heard the devil speak to you as well. Lucifer urges you to break your vow and reject God's will. This battle has been raging inside of you, and today Lucifer won. You must beg for God's grace to overcome your weakness. Understand?"

"So the devil made me do it?" Ethel couldn't help but smirk.

"You don't believe in the devil?" Mary Alice raised her eyebrows.

Ethel shrugged.

"Make no mistake, Ambrosia. I've seen the devil. He is quite real." The look in the young woman's eye gave Ethel pause. Mary Alice turned and grabbed a towel of her own. Her welts shrieked across her back in raised purples and thin silver.

Ethel looked down at the various marks the world had left on her own body. Cigarette burns, two stab wounds, long slash marks on her forearms, the stretch marks on her belly, and the long scar that ran through them. If there is a devil, she mused, he's a drunk looking for a girl.

Glancing up at her friend's tortured back, Ethel wondered what sort of devil Mary Alice had seen.

SEEK NAME OF 5TH
HEADLESS CORPSE

Police Hunt Maniac Killer

Seeking to establish the identity of the fifth victim of supposed decapitation murder in Greater Cleveland in less than a year, police last night took fingerprints of a 40-year-old man in the county morgue and searched missing person files of the last six months for his description.

—*Cleveland Plain Dealer*, July 23, 1936, p. 3

CHAPTER 13

April 7, 1999

The Elvis clock on the kitchen wall shimmied out the seconds as a phone rang 150 miles away. A voice Kris didn't recognize answered the call.

"Auglaize County Sheriff's Office."

She nearly hung up, but the urge to hear a friendly voice kept her on the line. Between everything that had happened—the sheriff's office, losing her job, and the unnerving chat with Lowjack—she could barely stand the feel of her own skin. *Did somebody die?* "Yeah, hi. Can I speak with Deputy Weber please?"

"He's gone home for the day. Can I leave him a message for you?"

The dancing clock read 11:08 p.m. Ben would be asleep by now. She should've called him earlier to tell him about David Hohman and his strange website. "Can you tell him to give Kris Wiley a call?"

"As in Al Wiley's girl?"

Breathe. "Yep."

"Shoot. I was so sorry to hear ab—"

Kris cut him off. "I appreciate it. Please just let him know I called."

She hung up and debated trying Ben's place, even though it was late. A stiff wind rattled the plastic siding outside her thin walls. Pete hadn't come home and probably wouldn't. An unnerving silence settled over the tiny house as the breeze died.

The basement door was still shut. She scanned every room, opened the closet doors, and turned on all the lights. Outside, a drunk stumbled past her door, mumbling to himself. It was a relief to just hear another person, if only for a moment.

She picked up the phone again, then set it back down. *I'm being ridiculous.*

Ben would be worried sick if she called. Kris was the closest thing to a daughter he had. He didn't have kids of his own to fuss over. He was the odd sort that never got married. It was probably why he and her father were such good friends. She used to joke that they were married to each other. Her father had dated a few women over the years, but he always said there was only one lady for him. And she was dead.

Mom. It was a thought she rarely allowed herself. Pressing her head against the cupboards behind her, she could see the crunched metal of her car. When she was small, she'd been too scared to ask about the accident, scared her father might yell or cry or fly apart and blow away. As she got bigger, the questions just seemed cruel, like twisting a knife in the poor man's side. He wasn't really much of a talker anyway, and now she might never have the chance again.

"Oh, God. Dad." Kris squeezed the tears from her eyes.

A knocking sound snapped her head off the cupboard. Her eyes darted around the empty kitchen, and she hoped Pete might pop up to explain the noise. She held her breath and listened. Another thump came from down in the basement like a can of paint hitting concrete.

She grabbed a kitchen knife and took a tentative step toward the basement door with her eyes on her exits. The floorboards creaked under her feet. She pulled open the door and flipped on the light. The bare bulb dangling from the center of the room below cast a yellow glow through a curtain of dust and spiderwebs.

"Hello?" she called out in a weak voice that made her cringe. "Anybody there?"

Nothing moved.

She crouched there for a solid minute, scanning the wreckage the landlord had stashed. The place was a fire hazard. Boxes and trunks piled up next to the furnace. Wood doors stacked against the walls. A rusted stove nearly blocked the foot of the stairs. After she was satisfied that the boogeyman wasn't lurking down there, she turned off the light and closed the door. There was no way to bolt it shut, so Kris grabbed a kitchen knife and locked her own bedroom door instead.

Her tired bones collapsed onto her bed in a heap. But the prickly feeling that someone else was there listening kept her muscles tensed to run. Her ears strained to hear another thump, another creak in the floorboards . . . another person breathing.

She finally passed out with the lights on around 3:00 a.m. In her dreams, she fell into the black waters of a river over and over, fighting to breathe as the current carried her farther and farther from shore.

The sun broke through her swollen eyelids around noon. Stretching out her arms, she knocked her hand into the dried wood of the knife handle. Kris pulled the crude weapon out from under her pillow and examined the dull blade before tossing it onto the bed and shaking her head at herself. A little bump in the night had scared her half to death. *What a nutcase.*

Her blank computer screen seemed to agree with her. She hadn't had the guts to log back in to the chat room in the dark. She still didn't have any answers about David Hohman or her father. Disgusted with herself, she flipped the machine on and went back to torsokillers.com, determined not to let Lowjack push her around.

A ridiculous cartoon of a construction worker popped up on the screen. *Site under construction?* Someone had taken the chat room down. She typed it again but got the same roadblock. *Damn it!*

She snatched David Hohman's card off her desk and read the address. Ten minutes later, she was in her car. It was horribly irresponsible, she realized, chasing after some lunatic stranger that may or may not know her father and that may or may not have had something to do with his disappearance. The spring sun shining overhead gave her courage as she weighed her options. She didn't have to go inside. She'd just drive past and try to get a look at him. She didn't even have to get out of the car.

A minivan full of kids sat idle at a green light. Kris laid on the horn. "Wake up!" she shouted at the soccer mom and buzzed past her on the right.

At the next light, she picked up the business card and checked the address again. According to the map in the back of her phone book, Franklin Boulevard sat north of Tremont in Ohio City. Out her passenger window, the downtown Cleveland skyline sprawled out on the other side of the Cuyahoga River. The towering statues of the Lorain-Carnegie Bridge watched her as she turned down Lorain Avenue toward West 25th.

As she approached the address, doubt crept into her head. She should have been calling Ben or going to class or figuring out how to pay the next tuition bill. Forget paying for school, she didn't even know how she was going to pay rent. It was due in two weeks and she'd just gotten herself fired. A scolding voice inside told her this entire infatuation with David Hohman was just a distraction to keep cold reality from creeping in. It sounded a lot like her father.

She stepped on the gas.

Ben hadn't called her back that morning, and a part of her was glad. She didn't want to know if they'd found more evidence . . . more pieces of the body. *It can't be him.* But the thought had grown less convincing.

Her Jeep rolled to a stop outside 2905 Franklin Boulevard. There was no office building or seedy strip mall at that address. Instead, she found herself outside an imposing redbrick Victorian mansion with a matching extension. The sign out front read, *Cuyahoga County Archives.* She double-checked the business card, figuring there had been some sort of mistake.

The smell of old books and the hush of a library greeted Kris at the door. A tweedy receptionist behind a table in the foyer flashed an expectant smile. "Good morning!"

"Yeah, hi." Kris approached the desk sheepishly. "This might be a weird question, but is there a David Hohman here?"

"A who?" the woman asked, her smile folding into a frown.

"David Hohman? He's some sort of private investigator?" Kris held up the business card as proof.

The woman took the card, studied it, and gave it back to her. "I'm sorry, but there's no one here with that name. This is the county archives."

"Yeah. I know. It's pretty strange, right? I mean, why would some-one put this address on their business card?" Her eyes circled the foyer that opened up into large, dusty rooms on either side. It was an old mansion, she realized. They'd taken an enormous house and stuffed it with old records and cast-off furniture.

The fallen look on Kris's face must've pulled a heartstring. The librarian stood up. "Let me go ask our director, Terri. She might know this man."

The bird of a woman flitted away down the hall to a hidden room in the back, leaving Kris alone in the grand entrance of the repur-posed Victorian. A frayed topographic map of Cleveland hung from the far wall of what must've once been the drawing room. A collection of black-and-white photographs of mansions flanked the adjoining wall under a yellowed paper sign that read, *Millionaire's Row*. Nearly all the old houses had been torn down.

On the other side of the foyer, a beat-up wooden desk sat in what used to be a dining room, now piled high with file boxes and ancient bound books. Edging closer, Kris studied the spine of one. It read, *Criminal Docket 9 Cuyahoga County*. In another stack of documents, a file box read, *Coroner Case Files—Torso Murders*. She started at the words and took another step toward it, but the woman was on her way back down the center hallway.

"Terri says there was a David that spent a lot of time here a few years back. He was a bit of an oddball. I guess he had a thing for old coroner reports. She'd sometimes find him asleep in the stacks. But she hasn't seen him in quite a while. I wish there was something more we could do." The receptionist clasped her hands and returned to her seat behind the makeshift desk.

Kris nodded and stole another glance at the box marked *Torso Murders*. "You have quite a collection here."

"Well, we do what we can."

"Can anyone just come in here and go through the archives?"

"Of course. That's why we're here. All these records are public. Most people who come in are interested in property records or family history. Can I help you find something?"

"I'm curious about that box over there. The one about the Torso Murders. Is that public?"

"Yes, it's one of our more requested records. But we do ask that you wear gloves. So many people have gone through them, they've taken quite a beating over the years."

"Really? Why? I mean . . . something called the Torso Murders sounds pretty terrible to me."

"If I had to guess, I'd say it's the most famous unsolved crime in Cleveland's history. Amateur detectives are always trying to crack the case. They've written books about it, you know."

Kris bit her lip. Four of those books were sitting in her backpack on the backseat of her Jeep. "Was anyone in here lately to read them?"

She nodded. "That's why the files are out. A gentleman came in the other day to look through the coroner's reports and several other things. We left it all there for him because he said he planned to come back. They've been sitting there for over a week."

"Did he give you a name?"

"Yes, he did. Now what was it? Something common like John or James. You'll have to forgive me, I'm terrible with names."

"What did he look like?"

"I don't quite remember. He was older. Tall. He had a nice suit, but he wasn't too friendly, now that I think about it. Help yourself. I'm about ready to file all that away again. I don't think he's coming back."

Kris was only half listening as she walked over to the table and sat down. She pulled open the file box to find a loose collection of handwritten notes on standard forms. The tight, narrow cursive lettering had been smudged and the white paper smeared with a million fingerprints.

The tweedy woman appeared behind her with a pair of thin white gloves loosely sewn and clearly disposable. "You can see why we ask you to wear these."

Kris nodded and pulled on the ill-fitting hand socks. She waited until the librarian had gone back to her desk, then squinted to decipher the smeared ink.

Body found at mouth of sewer outlet.

No sign of skin abr—ions.

Multiple hesitation marks, inconsistent with pr—s victims . . .

The date for the medical examination was listed as April something, 1938. Kris squinted to make out any other details. She remembered from her reading that the first Torso victim was found in 1934, so she flipped through the pages in the file to find it. There was nothing there dated before 1937. She opened a second cardboard file holder marked *Suspected Torso Victims* and found a thick pile of records dated between 1939 and 1941. They were all for murders that were later ruled out as potential Torso victims for one reason or another.

Decapitation too crude.

Inconsistent disarticulation of the limbs.

Crime of passion.

Gangland hit.

Kris leafed through one dead end after another, and there was still no sign of the earlier murder victims. No sign of Flo Polillo or Edward Andrassy or the unidentified young vagrant the books and discussion boards called the Tattooed Man.

"Excuse me," Kris said, scanning the table for another box or two. "Is this all of the coroner's files?"

The librarian looked up from her pile of paper. "That's everything we have for the Torso Murders."

"But some of the files are missing." Kris leafed through the stack of papers dated 1937 and 1938. All of them were nearly illegible and at most covered only three of the thirteen victims.

The young woman gave her a pained smile. "I'm afraid documents related to that case have a tendency to walk away."

"You mean people steal them? But why?"

"Hobbyists take them. Collectors buy them, I guess. I don't really know. I've heard there's a whole cottage industry around the buying and selling of murder memorabilia."

"But . . ." Kris gaped at the worn papers. "Isn't that illegal? Stealing from the archives?"

The woman shrugged. "I suppose it is, but the Cleveland police don't really have the time to deal with it, and we're not staffed here for security. There's just three of us most days."

"Aren't the files digitized somewhere?"

The woman shook her head and laughed. "We have over three million documents under this roof. The county just approved funds to scan five percent of them, and even that's going to take us several years. I'm sorry, but welcome to the archives."

"What about the man that was here the other day? Did he take something?"

The thin face of the woman pinched into a frown. "Goodness, I hope not, but I can't say for sure . . . He was here for hours, and I'm sure there were times he would've had the chance. We provide access to the photocopier for free for just this reason, but people will do what they will."

She stood up to look over Kris's shoulder at the papers still left in the file.

Kris watched the woman carefully leaf through the pages while her head raced with questions. *Had her father come all the way to Cleveland to search the records himself? Had he found something?*

"You know, it does seem a few papers short. I wish I could tell you for sure." The librarian puckered her lips around an imagined lemon as she strained to remember. "If you want to know more about the murders, go visit the *Cleveland Press* archives over at Cleveland State. They should have all the newspaper clippings from back then."

It was her cue to leave. Kris stood up and headed to the door, but her feet stopped halfway there. She pulled her father's driver's license from her pocket. "Excuse me? I'm sorry, but can I ask you one more question?"

The woman looked up from her filing with raised eyebrows.

Kris set the ID down on the woman's desk. "Do you recognize this man? Has he been here before?"

She picked up the license and studied his face. "That's him. He's the one that asked for the files."

"It is?" A chorus sang in her ears. "When was he here?"

"Oh. At least a week ago. Maybe two?" The clerk didn't notice the blood drain from Kris's face as her hopes went silent.

He'd been there and she hadn't even known. He'd been there looking for a killer.

CHAPTER 14

Kris stepped off the elevator in CSU's Rhodes Tower and pushed herself through the door marked *Special Collections*. The enormous room housed its own library in a humidity-controlled chill. Floor-to-ceiling shelves stuffed with metal shoeboxes lined the two walls to her left. Microfilm readers and computers lined two tables to her right, and the center was a maze of bookshelves and microfilm storages.

The only other person in the room looked up from behind her computer in the center. "Can I help you?"

"Uh, I'm not sure." Kris bit her lip and stifled a shiver. She'd passed the building where her art history professor was giving a lecture at that very moment. That's where she should've been that morning. "I'm looking for information about the Torso Murders?"

The woman's plump cheeks dimpled with an apologetic smile. "Good luck finding anything."

Kris frowned. "What do you mean?"

"All of the *Cleveland Press* clippings on the Torso Killer walked off years ago. Half of them never even made it into the archive in the first place." The woman noticed the confused look on Kris's face and explained, "Staffers at the *Press* got wind of the paper's shutdown and made off with anything they could sell. Photos of the Beatles.

Clippings from the first Ramones concert. Torso Murder photos. You name it. You're not the first one to come looking, and I know for a fact those clippings were picked clean."

"This is crazy. Aren't there any records left on these murders?"

"You could try the microfilm." The woman's heavy arm gestured toward an enormous wood flat file.

Kris walked over and opened a drawer. It was full of identical cardboard boxes, each the size of a Rubik's Cube. She picked one up marked *May 1934*.

The large woman followed her over and tapped on a box in the drawer. "It might take you a while. There's no index to these. You'll just have to read through each daily paper, unless you have a specific date you're looking for . . . It might be easier to search the *Plain Dealer* records. You can access their database through CLEVNET at the public library."

"I might be able to come up with a date. Here." Kris pulled out James Badal's book and flipped through the pages until she found it. *Victim 0—the Lady of the Lake.* "Let's try September 5, 1934."

The woman ran an orange-painted fingertip over the boxes until it stopped on September. She pulled the box out from its place. "That's strange." She frowned, shaking it. She popped the lid open, and the box was empty.

The librarian pulled the drawer out as far as it would go and began shoving boxes back and forth, searching for the lost film. Kris watched as the nagging feeling that it wasn't a coincidence strummed her nerves. She flipped through the pages of the book in her hand until she found the next victim.

"What about September 23, 1935?" she asked in a small voice.

"Hmm?" The librarian, in her frenzy to find the film, seemed to have forgotten she was standing there.

"September 23, 1935. It's when the next two victims were found."

The woman pushed the drawer shut and pulled open the one beneath it, scanning the labels until she'd found the right one. She lifted the box marked *September 1935* out and her face dropped even further. "I'll be damned."

"Someone took it," Kris whispered.

The librarian slowly shook her head, her chin trembling. "I can't believe this. People just have absolutely no respect at all. Those films were irreplaceable!"

There were over fifty drawers, each one filled with microfilm, and Kris was willing to bet at least ten more were missing. "I'm so sorry. I had no idea. I just . . . I'm gonna go. I'll check out the county library like you said . . . I have to go there anyway. Thanks. I mean, thank you for your time."

Kris scuttled out of special collections, leaving the poor woman gaping into an open drawer. She hauled her backpack onto her shoulder and took the stairs two at a time down the tower and out into the crisp morning sun.

During the entire fifteen-minute walk from Rhodes Tower up to the public library on Superior Avenue, Kris turned it all over in her mind. Someone was systematically removing all record of the Torso Murders from the archives. *Why?*

The computers at the county library were no help at all. Kris sat down at a terminal and logged in only to find that the *Plain Dealer* archives were still in the process of being digitized. Whole decades hadn't been uploaded to the system yet, and the records were currently off-site, being scanned. She typed in the key words *Torso, Andrassy, Polillo, Dolezal* and got nothing but a blinking cursor.

Defeated, she decided to renew her father's books, wondering if they might be the only surviving records of the crimes. The line at the checkout counter took nearly ten minutes to wade through. When she finally reached one of the clerks, Kris dumped all four books onto the counter in a heap.

"You don't have to wait in line for returns. Just shove 'em down the chute." The woman behind the counter pointed to the silver slot on the opposite wall.

"No. I, uh, I wanted to renew them. Or rather, I'm renewing them for my dad. He's . . . he's not feelin' well and couldn't make the trip." Kris pressed her lips into what she hoped looked like a smile.

The woman rolled her eyes ever so slightly, clearly annoyed. Her name tag read, *Simone*. "You got his library card?"

"No, I—"

"No library card, no service," Simone interrupted. "There's nothin' I can do. Why don't you just go return the books, and when he's well, he can come back and get 'em."

"He can't. I don't know when he'll be able to . . . Look, he needs these books."

Simone was already looking past Kris to the next customer. "All's you can do is bring in his library card, ma'am. Next!"

"No. Not next." Kris glanced back at the woman behind her in line and pleaded, "I'm sorry. I just need a minute. Listen, I really would appreciate your help. I don't have his library card, but could you look him up in the system? Please . . . Alfred Wiley. Here. I have his driver's license."

The look of utter desperation on Kris's face must've struck a nerve somewhere inside the clerk's heart. Simone took the driver's license from Kris and slapped it down on the counter next to her computer and started typing. "We don't usually do this," she muttered, shaking her head, and then announced to the growing line, "I'm sorry for the delay, folks. This will take just a minute."

"Thank you, Simone." Kris wiped away a tear she hadn't even felt escape. They were just leaking out now for no reason, it seemed. "It means a lot to me."

Simone stopped typing, picked up a book, and scanned it into the system. After a minute, she picked up the driver's license and checked it again. "Huh. Your pops move recently?"

Kris blinked at her. "Uh. No."

"These are checked out under a different address, so I can't renew these. Besides . . ." The woman handed Kris her father's driver's license back and dropped her voice so Kris would lean in. "You need to tell your daddy or whoever that these books is three years overdue. That's a fine of over a hundred dollars . . . You hear what I'm sayin'? Don't mean nothin' to me, but I'd just drop 'em in a box if I was you. Or just don't come back."

Kris nodded and picked the books back up again, eying the security guard in the corner. "Thanks. I understand. But could you . . . could you tell me what address was used?"

Simone gave her a hard look, as if weighing her need, then pressed a button on her keyboard and grabbed a piece of paper from the printer behind her. "Here. We gonna forget we ever discussed this, alright?" She handed Kris the sheet and then said loudly, "You enjoy those books now. Next!"

Kris stepped away from the counter with the slip of paper in her hands. She waited until she was past the security guard and out into the street to read the computer-printed profile.

Alfred Wiley
Harmony Mission Press Building
710 Jefferson Avenue
Cleveland, OH 44113

CHAPTER 15

The abandoned Harmony Mission Press complex sprawled over an entire city block. It wasn't just one building but fifteen slammed together at odd angles as though the builder had suffered a schizophrenic fit during construction. French baroque met medieval Gothic and art deco in a crash of building styles and materials. Brick, stone, and peeling wood siding spread out in discreet wings over a fenced-in courtyard. The grounds were littered with garbage and cigarette butts. Shadows lurked behind the stone and brick arches of the tiered balconies overhead.

Her father might be hiding somewhere inside the empty complex, according to the thin computer printout in her hand. Kris read the address again and shivered. The house she rented sat farther down the block, directly across the street from the loading docks of the old factory. *Has he been across the street this entire time? Watching me?*

Kris stuffed the paper back into one of her father's stolen library books. He'd checked them out three years ago. Long before she lived across the street from the old factory. Long before she'd even dreamed of moving to Cleveland. The headless corpse on the cover of the book told her nothing, except that her father was obsessed with a killer. A killer who would be elderly by then, if not dead himself. A killer no one cared about anymore . . . except her father apparently. And David Hohman. And all the other wackos in the Torso Killer chat room. And whoever was stealing from the archives.

A falling-down shack sat in the middle of the gravel courtyard across from the corner of Jefferson and Thurman where she stood. The windows of the place hung crooked and cracked, with faded curtains blocking the view. A portion of the roof had caved in. A plank of loose siding hung from a bent nail.

"Hello?" she called at the little building that must've been a caretaker's house years ago. She picked up a golf ball of a rock and pelted it at the siding. *Thunk.* "Hello?"

There was no answer or sign of movement. The multistory factory loomed darkly at its back. Kris gauged the height of the pointed iron fence that lined the lot, scanning the length for gaps, debating whether she should climb it.

She headed down Thurman to the loading dock. "Hello?" she called into the cavern. "Anybody home?"

No one answered. The enormous gate was chained shut.

Kris rounded the corner and headed down College Avenue to West 7th Street. The brick face of the factory presented a more unified front to this side of the block. The building was several stories taller there as well. The words *Harmony Press* had been carved into the stone arch above the first doorway where another iron gate blocked her way. She kept walking past the building, its empty windows set high above the sidewalk so that she couldn't see inside.

Farther up the block, an iron gate hung open. She stopped in front of it and peered into the dark, narrow corridor and back out again. Up and down the street, cars began their slow crawl back home at the end of the workday. The sun had dipped below the rooftops of the houses lining the other side of West 7th. A few straggling residents made their way along the sidewalk to their vehicles or their apartments. The temperature dropped as she stood there debating the wisdom of stepping inside the empty building alone. At night.

Shit. A few scattered snowflakes began to fall.

"Hey there," a voice said.

She jumped at the sound and turned to see a young guy heading toward her. He was holding a grocery bag. Dreadlocks hung down past his shoulders, and his smile shone brilliant white against his dark tan skin. "Uh, hi."

"What are you doin' out here all alone, girl?" He winked at her. His eyes were warm and friendly as she searched them for bad intentions. He looked to be about twenty, twenty-five tops. From the backpack on his shoulder and the Rasta knit cap on his head, she guessed he was a student.

She forced out an awkward laugh. "Nothing really. I'm just looking for someone."

"Here?" He lifted his eyebrows and motioned toward the open gate.

"I'm not sure. Maybe. It's . . . it's kind of a long story."

"I'd love to hear it. Wanna come in?"

It was Kris's turn to raise her eyebrows. "In there? Is that . . . where you're going?"

"Yup. Havin' a little party. You should come."

Kris eyed the bag in his hand and then glanced down the dark, chilly corridor again. "You live in there?"

"You could say that. Been here a couple of years now, I guess. You live nearby?"

She nodded her head as she calculated the risk of going into the building with a total stranger. "Yeah, sort of."

"Well look at that, we're neighbors." He propped up the grocery bag on his hip and held out his hand. "I'm Jimmy."

She made a quick study of his clean hands and clear, kind eyes before offering hers back. "I'm Kris. So you, uh, really live here?"

He shrugged. "Yeah."

"But how does that work exactly? Doesn't somebody own it?"

"Sure."

"What's the rent like?"

"You could say we have an arrangement."

"An arrangement?"

"Yeah." He grinned. "If they kick me out, I'll leave."

She nodded her head and looked up at the peeling paint of the window frames. "So they let you live here rent-free. Why?"

"You'll have to ask the owner."

"Who's that?" She frowned. *Dad?*

"Some old hippie chick. I don't know her too well, but I really don't think she minds. I'm not the only one livin' up in here. There's at least twenty more. Most of 'em keep to themselves."

Her jaw fell slack in disappointment at the word *her* and then at the thought of a pack of homeless people holed up inside. She'd lived across the street for nearly a year and had never seen a soul. *Is my dad here too?* She couldn't picture him there. "It doesn't make sense. Why would the owner just let people live here for free?"

"She might be crazy," Jimmy laughed. "What do I care? She considers this an *artists' colony*. There's a few painters hangin' around, I guess. It's a sweet deal for me. You wanna come in?"

"I've never seen this gate open before," she said, hoping to extend their conversation instead. "I must've passed by it a million times. It was always chained shut and padlocked."

"Jill opens the gate whenever she feels like having company."

"Jill?"

"Yeah. You ever see her? Weird old lady, about so tall." Jimmy put his hand out at his shoulder to a height at least six inches shorter than her father.

She shook her head. *Old lady. It doesn't make sense.*

"She doesn't like people. She's not mean really, she just keeps to herself and does her art. She made all these gates, you know."

Kris stopped to look at the twisted iron bars. "Really?"

"She's good, right? Gotta love a girl that welds. I talked to her once or twice about it, but she doesn't say much. She opens the gate up every once in a while. We've decided it's her way of inviting us to have a little party, so that's what we do."

"Maybe she's just having something big worked on or delivered," Kris speculated out loud, then clenched her teeth.

"Maybe. Who cares? You comin'?" Jimmy held out his arm like an old-fashioned gentleman.

Kris glanced up at the darkening sky. *Don't be stupid, Kritter.* "I probably shouldn't. I'm not really in the partying mood. This has been a really . . . really bad week."

"Hey, chin up." Jimmy reached out and brushed her chin with his fingertips. "Come and have a beer. I promise I won't bite."

You don't know this guy, her father warned from his perch in her mind. *Sure, he seems nice, but he could be a rapist.* She tried to stall. "So, how do you get inside when the gate's not unlocked?"

"Shit. There's a hundred ways into a building." He waved his hand at her silly question. "Here you just have to know which fence to hop. Which window's open."

She scanned the bank of windows high above the street, then eyed the wrought iron fence wrapping around the corner. "If you say so."

"What? You never broke a rule? You one of those good girls, does everything they're told?" He cocked an eyebrow at her.

"No. I wouldn't say that." But every time she broke a rule, she'd be terrified her father would find out.

Kris realized she was running out of time to decide. Jimmy would get sick of teasing her and leave her standing there in the cold. She tried to convince herself to go home, but the thought of going back to her creepy haunted house all alone was unbearable. She hated to admit it, but she'd never felt so lonely in her life. Besides, she reasoned, if her father was hiding inside somewhere, this was her best chance to find him. "Okay. Just one beer."

"Deal." He flashed a sincere smile and ushered her inside.

A fat candle left burning on the first landing was the only light to be had once they passed through the gate and into the shadow of the factory. Jimmy led her up the concrete steps past the candle and around a corner to the next set of stairs. They passed through another iron gate into a narrow courtyard flanked by dead potted plants. Snowflakes fell onto the floor of the garden from the narrow rectangle of sky framed by three stories of red bricks and dark windows towering overhead. Buttressed balconies looked down at them from the tallest tower. Through the black iron gate straight ahead, she could just see into a larger courtyard.

Jimmy led her under a brick arch that formed a second-story breezeway between two separate wings of the complex and then around a tight corner. "Watch your head," he warned and then ducked into a narrow tunnel that led out of the snow and down a corridor that ended in a half-sized door. It sat propped open, and the glow of another candle burned somewhere just inside. Jimmy crouched through the low door and jumped down onto the floor on the other side. "Here, let me give you a hand."

Kris took it and had to sit down on the edge of the door frame to touch the floor inside. "Who designed this place, Willy Wonka?" she asked, staring back at the half-height door set three feet above the floor.

"We call it the hobbit door," Jimmy laughed. "Isn't it great? This place is a funhouse. When the old factory closed back in 1959, it never reopened. Lucky for us." He picked up his bag of groceries and continued down a long hallway lined with dark wood panels and glazed bricks.

The hall grew darker as they went. "How do you keep track of where you're going?" she asked, glancing out a window onto a street she didn't quite recognize. *College Avenue?* Jimmy didn't slow down long enough for her to figure it out.

"You get used to it." He turned into another stairwell.

She scrambled after him. "Why aren't there any lights on?"

"Jill only pays to keep part of the building running. We have electricity and running water, at least some of the time. The rest is supposed to be sealed off."

"Why?"

"It's falling apart, in case you hadn't noticed. I doubt she can afford to keep up with all of it. You gotta just let some things go, you know?"

"So she let this part of the building go," Kris repeated and stared up at the cracked and missing concrete under the stairs directly above her. Chunks had fallen away, scattering gravel on the treads below her feet. Water stains dripped down the slanted ceiling. Rusting bars peeked out from the broken surfaces that resembled parts of the moon. "Is it . . . is this safe?"

"Probably not." He stopped and smiled up at her stricken face. "Scared?"

She shook her head, but they both knew she was lying.

"I like to think of myself as an urban explorer," he continued.

"An explorer?" she laughed awkwardly. *Is that code for squatter?*

"Yeah. Like a discoverer of forgotten places. I take nothing but pictures. That's the rule." Jimmy opened a door that led through a narrow courtyard. "They built the Harmony Mission Press in phases, just adding on to what was there. No one has a full set of blueprints for any of it, I've looked. This place is full of doorways to nowhere." He opened a door coated in cracking paint and showed her the walled-up opening directly behind it. "Nuts, right? I could spend a lifetime in here."

Kris stopped and gazed back out into the courtyard behind her. None of the windows were lit. There was no sign of her father or anyone else. Jimmy kept walking farther and farther into the darkness as she debated turning back. *Do I even remember the way?*

"Jimmy?" she turned and called after him. "Jimmy, wait."

He didn't answer.

Kris passed by a window and looked out at the piles of bricks and windows stacked above her for any sign of where they were. There was only a puzzle piece of sky. She nearly went sprawling on her ass as she stumbled down a step set in the middle of the corridor.

There was no sign of Jimmy anywhere. Kris passed by one door and then another. Then the hallway forked in three separate directions. A dull glow fell through a bank of transom windows along the top of the wall. They were too high up to see out and get her bearings.

The seeds of panic took root as she turned around, trying to choose a way to go or remember the way they'd come in.

"Jimmy!" she hissed.

Somewhere down the hall, a door clicked open.

Kris sucked in a breath and backed herself down the adjacent corridor away from the noise. Jimmy didn't live alone. Other people inhabited in the building. Homeless people. Footsteps padded across the floor ahead of her. With her heart pounding her ears, she inched her way farther down the hall until her back pressed up against a door. *Shit.*

Reaching behind, she felt for the handle. There wasn't one.

"Who's there?" a voice whispered from the darkness ahead. "I told you mothafuckas to stay out of my hallway."

Smells of cigarette smoke and garbage wafted down the corridor to where she stood. Kris put a hand over her mouth and debated whether to scream or run or both.

A flashlight clicked on and shined right in her face, blinding her. She held up her hands on instinct.

"Who da hell is you?" the voice demanded.

"Hey, Maurice! What's happenin'!" Jimmy came trotting down the adjoining hallway. Kris had never been so relieved to see another person in her life. "Where'd you go, girl?"

"I told you mothafuckers to stay out my hallway!" Maurice said again. "And she don't even live here."

"Take it easy, man. This is a friend of mine. Here." Jimmy pulled a beer out of the grocery bag and handed it to the disheveled man wielding the flashlight. "My deepest apologies."

Maurice snatched the beer like a hermit crab and scuttled back down the hall.

Jimmy nudged her shoulder. "You alright?"

"Yeah. Sure." She wasn't even close to all right, but she didn't want to be rude.

"C'mon." He led her through the doorway into a concrete stair tower. The steady thump of music greeted them as they climbed up a set of stairs to a blank door. "You ready to have some fun?" Jimmy gave her a slow smile and looked her up and down.

Her pulse had slowed down from fight-or-flight to a mild panic. She forced a smile and nodded.

Jimmy swung open the door. "Welcome to my house."

SIXTH HACKED BODY
FOUND IN KINGSBURY RUN

Head, Legs and Arms Missing

The two legs, from knee to foot, of the decapitated murder victim were found in Kingsbury Run a few yards from the spot the torso members were found. Detective Orley May ordered the run searched in a hunt for the head and the missing arms.

—*Cleveland Press*, September 10, 1936, p. 1

CHAPTER 16

April 6, 1938

Dinner at the Harmony Mission proceeded much as it had the night before. When the time came for Brother Milton to address the dining hall after the usual prayers, all the sisters dropped their forks in anticipation.

"The Good Lord smiled on our work today, Sisters."

A low murmur of approval swept through the tables.

The reverend lifted his eyes to silence them. "Brother Noah Wenger tells me God has smiled on our gardens this year. They survived the winter in good stead, and with hard work we should expect an abundant crop of corn, carrots, potatoes, and beets."

Wenger stood up next to Brother Milton and took the slightest bow as though he had anything to do with it. All he had done that afternoon was walk around and supervise the women as they slaved in the dirt. That and butcher a pig. Bloody entrails fell out again in a dark corner of Ethel's mind.

"And Brother Wenger also tells me we suffered a lapse of faith in the fields today."

Dozens of eyes turned to Ethel, and she felt a wave of blood rush to her face.

"Sisters, be mindful as we do God's work that we must hold on to our faith as a life raft in a stormy sea. Temptation lurks all around us." He held up a hand as though he were some sort of wizard casting a spell on them all. "Hold fast to the Lord, Sisters, lest you give in to the lesser voices in our lives. The voices that tempt us to lay down our labors and seek out our own pleasures."

He opened his arms to Ethel and continued the sermon. "Voices that lure us away from the Lord to decadence, to vice, and to sin. They are all around us, Sisters. We must not listen. Only the Lord can guide us through the storm. Only the Lord can answer the questions in our hearts. Only the Lord holds the answers . . . Sister Hattie, come and join me."

Ethel stole a glance at Mary Alice across the table. The girl had gone pale, but she nodded back. A wave of whispers followed Ethel as she approached the front of the dining hall. The numbing effects of the laudanum had faded, and she could barely hide the tremble in her limbs.

Brother Milton wrapped a heavy arm around her shoulder and gave it a squeeze. "Sisters, let us pray," he bowed his head. "Our Lord, who art in heaven, grant us your wisdom and your grace as we seek to redeem our good sister. May your judgment and her penance cleanse her of her irreverent pride. Cleanse her of all her sins as she repents in your name. Amen."

"Amen," murmured the crowd.

Ethel caught sight of Brother Wenger out of the corner of her eye. He said "amen" the loudest.

The reverend turned to her and grabbed her by both shoulders and said, "Sister Hattie, do you take Jesus Christ as your Lord and Savior?"

She wiped all expression from her face, forcing herself to lower her eyes in deference and nod.

"Do you reject Satan in all his forms from within and without?"
She nodded again.

"Do you agree to repent your sins to the Lord until you are able
to bring Him freely into your heart?"

She bit her lips and nodded. The angry welts on Mary Alice's
back flashed their warning in her mind. *Run,* they said, but her feet
wouldn't move.

The reverend released her and turned to the congregation.
"Sisters, let us pray that through penance and prayer, our lost sister
Hattie finds her home."

"Amen," they agreed.

"Brother Wenger, please show Sister Hattie the way," the reverend
said and put Ethel's hand in his. The naked pig thrashed and spun on
its hook somewhere deep inside her.

In the sea of staring faces, all Ethel could see was Mary Alice. She
looked terrified.

Brother Wenger led Ethel away from the dining hall and down a
corridor she hadn't seen before. He released her hand to open a narrow door. It led outside into a rectangular courtyard. Brick walls and
heavy stones towered overhead, framing the gray sky. A cold dusting
of rain fell on her shoulders as he pulled her down a narrow stairway
and through another door.

As he led her down a maze of hallways and through unmarked
doors, Ethel mused that whoever had constructed the building
couldn't seem to make up their minds—up, down, inside, outside.
Then a more sinister thought occurred to her as they passed a bank
of windows looking out into another hidden light well. Maybe it was
deliberately built to trap people like her.

She wanted to ask where they were going and what would happen
to her when they got there, but she'd promised Mary Alice her silence.
Her fingers itched for her knife, buried in the mattress of her room
somewhere above them.

Wenger didn't speak. His firm grip on her arm left no doubt—she was his prisoner. The instinct to kick him in the groin and run gathered its springs inside her, but he kept moving them onward, deeper into the building until she lost all sense of where they were.

He pushed open a door only tall enough for a dwarf and pulled her inside. The stair landing behind the door wasn't wide enough to fit them both, and he pushed her off balance onto the first step down.

"After you, Sister," he said in a low voice.

She strained to hear in his tone what would happen next. He didn't sound angry or violent. There was no whip in his hand. It was too dark in the stairwell to check his face for that smug grin of his, but she could hear a sense of satisfaction in his voice. He enjoyed his role as disciplinarian and the power he held over her. She wondered again as he manhandled her down the stairs if it was his voice she'd heard grunting and panting in the room above hers the night before. It would work in her favor, she decided, if that was the sort of punishment he had in mind.

Better me than poor little Mary Alice.

Ethel decided to play the part of the terrified virgin for him as though he were a proper paying customer. Rapists wanted to hear their girls whimper and cry and cower. They liked the taking more than the sex. If she cried and pleaded for him to stop, he might not hurt her much. She let him push her down the steps one at a time in front of him. The glow of a window somewhere far overhead left only enough light to see a few feet in front of her as they went. Twenty-two steep concrete steps wound down deeper into the dark. She gripped the cold stone wall to her right and the thin metal-plated guardrail to her left while Wenger stayed close behind her, gripping her shoulder, steering her forward.

The bottom of the stairs ended in another door. He nudged her to the side and unlocked it with a key. Cold, damp air wafted up from the dirt floor on the other side as he swung the door open. It was some sort of cellar. He flipped on a light switch, and a single bulb flickered to life down a long, narrow corridor. Wooden doors set into the damp stone walls lined either side.

He picked up her hand in his and led her down the hallway to the third door on the left. She counted twelve in all as he fumbled with another key, his hands trembling in his excitement. Finally, the thick wood swung open. *This is it.* She peeked into the tiny dark closet on the other side. *This is our destination.*

"Do you know where we are?" Brother Wenger asked in a soft voice, backing her into the room.

She didn't have to pretend to be terrified. He had the hungry look of a predator pinning down his prey.

"This is where they kept prisoners during the Civil War. This whole place was once a hospital. They treated Lincoln's soldiers upstairs and kept his prisoners right here."

There was no window, no bed. Just a round drain in the dirt floor. Metal shackles hung from the far wall.

"I've been watching you, Hattie. You mock your sisters at prayer. You mock Brother Milton. You mock me. I can see the devil looking through your eyes." He smiled at her and brushed her cheek gently with the back of his hand. "You are not a true Christian, are you?"

Her blood froze in her veins. *Mary Alice.* If Wenger knew the truth about her, the poor girl's fate rested in his hands. The terrified look on her face pleased him.

"It's okay. Mary Alice did the right thing bringing you to us. We will help you, Hattie. We will help you believe. We will release you from the beast. But first, you need to remove all of your false notions of God. You need to be born again in the light of Jesus to accept Him fully into your heart." He put his hands on her shoulders and gave them a squeeze. Then his fingers drifted to the buttons of her dress.

Here we go, she thought and let the fear already twisting its way through her veins show in her widening eyes.

He chuckled, thrilling at her reaction as he unhooked one button after another. "I'm not going to hurt you, Sister. I am bound by my faith, but we are all exposed in the eyes of God. We must all cast aside our armor and lie naked before Him to fully receive His salvation."

She didn't fight as his fingers guided her dress off her shoulders and onto the floor. Each touch sent a shudder through her, and she let her eyes well up with tears, remembering the first time she'd been helpless at the hands of a man. Her fear fed his enjoyment just as she intended. He smiled as he gazed over the terrain of her body. She willed herself to blush.

Wenger lowered himself to his knees and pulled one stocking down her leg. She was truly naked without her knife. "There is no shame in showing yourself to God. He sees through all the lies you might tell me or tell yourself. Only He sees the real you."

His finger traced her scars and paused at the marks on her belly. "You've been through quite a lot, haven't you?" There was no hiding the truth from the bare lightbulb hanging in the corridor behind him. She wasn't the virgin she was pretending to be. Ethel bit her lip and braced herself for him to lash out and punish her for what someone else had taken before he'd had the chance. He removed her second stocking as gently as the first.

He stood up, blocking the light in the hall completely, swallowing her in his shadow. "Do not be afraid, Hattie. We are all sinners before God in thought and word and deed. We must all be born again into the body of Christ, but first we must leave our sinful ways behind us. First we must repent."

The clammy cold air fondled her bare skin as he spoke. She began to shiver.

"Adam's sin is imputed to the whole of mankind," he continued, bent on delivering a sermon he'd obviously spent some time perfecting in his own mind. "We will all die in body and in spirit, separated from God for all eternity, unless we take Jesus into our hearts. For He will be resurrected, and He will call the saved to His side. If I don't help you find Him in your heart, you will be condemned to eternal suffering and will spend your days on earth as a beast. You must open your heart and mind. Let me help you, Hattie."

He gazed at her with the same lust she'd seen in the eyes of her clients. She suspected that if she pressed herself against him, she'd find him hard with anticipation.

"Moses spent forty years in the desert until he found his way. I'm going to help you find your way home to the Lord, Sister. I don't think it will take forty years, but we shall see." He smiled again.

His plan started to take shape in her mind as he stepped into the doorway. Terror shot up her spine. *No.*

"Anyone who watched you at dinner can see you don't know your prayers, Hattie. If I had to guess, I'd say you've never even read the Bible."

She didn't protest or argue. Her eyes were too busy darting around the tiny room as Wenger stood there blocking the exit. Her clothes were gathered in his left arm. *This isn't happening. I can't let this happen.* He outweighed her by more than fifty pounds. His eyes seemed to read hers and challenged her to charge.

"Let us begin your journey to salvation, dear Hattie." His voice rose with a frightening fervor. "We will start from the beginning. Genesis, chapter one, verse one. To understand the power of God, you must first imagine the world without God."

Does anyone even know I'm here? He took a step outside the room as her eyes widened in protest.

"In the beginning . . . it was dark."

A scream escaped her throat as he shut the door.

CHAPTER 17

Ethel pushed against the door to her prison cell with all her strength. Her hands fumbled in the blackness for the handle, but there wasn't one. The dead bolt slid home with the metallic ring of a death knell. She pounded on the wood with her fists until she was sure they were bleeding.

"Let me outta here!" she shrieked. Vow of silence be damned.

The sliver of light below the door went out.

She yelled for all she was worth. "Come back! . . . Please! . . . You can't just keep me in here like a prisoner! This isn't Christian, Goddammit! . . . Help! Mary Alice? Somebody?"

After tortured minutes of pounding and screaming, her voice was cracked and her fists were raw. She fell to her knees and stared into the darkness. The dirt floor was cold under her bare shins. She shivered in the dank basement air. *What the hell was I thinking? I just stood there like an idiot while the son of a bitch stripped me.*

It had never occurred to her that he'd go to the trouble of getting her naked and just leave her to rot. She'd never considered he'd just turn away from a willing victim. Quivering lips and wide eyes had never failed her before.

If he'd gotten down to business, she would've had a chance. With him fully distracted by her body, she could lie there and wait for the perfect moment to pounce. Thumbs in the eyes or a stiff punch in the throat would've at least been options. If he wasn't too mean, she might've just waited it out to see if he fell asleep. *But this.*

She should've begged to hear more of his Jesus talk instead.

Ethel pulled herself to her feet and felt the walls all the way around her cell. Large blocks of stone stacked and set in mortar surrounded her, far too heavy and thick to move. Two paces to the side. Three paces deep. The room was barely large enough to lie down. It was a tomb. It smelled of moss and dirt, the air was thick with it. She couldn't breathe. *Oh, God, I'm going to die in here. I can't breathe. There's not enough air.*

She backed into the door as a wave of panic crashed over her. Her fingers traced the seams, searching for a latch, a hinge, a handle. There was nothing but rough-hewn wood. She pressed her nose to the joint between the door and jamb and breathed in slightly fresher air from the corridor. Her eye strained to see through it into the world outside, but there was nothing but black.

He's coming back, she told herself. *He said this was just the beginning.*

She shuddered to think what might come next and curled up into a ball next to the door. Hugging her knees in a vain attempt to stay warm, she sat there rocking back and forth, dreaming up a plan to escape.

Mary Alice will have to fend for herself. I ain't no saint and there is no way in hell I'm letting that rat bastard play his games with me. The second that door opens again, I'm gettin' the hell out of here.

Her options were limited. Wenger was far bigger and stronger, and in a tight space like this, she wouldn't have a chance. What she needed was a weapon. Her knife was safely tucked away in her mattress. *What a dummy!*

Ethel let go of her knees and stood up again. Eyes wide in the dark, she forced herself to picture the room the way it had looked in the light. There had been nothing in there but the chains hanging from the walls. With her arms held out in front to protect her face, she inched her way to the far wall and began to feel around for the shackles. They weren't where she remembered them. Her hands swept the stone side to side. Dust fell to the floor with the dappled sound of rain. A nest of cobwebs tangled in her fingers, and she shook them from her hand. *They were here. I saw them,* she told herself as the panic of blindness rose back up again. She squeezed her eyes shut, raising her arms to the next row of stone.

Cold metal slammed into her fingers. A creak and rattle followed as the thick steel links clamored against the stone. Her fingers grabbed at them, the rough burrs digging into her skin as she pulled with all her might. The chains didn't budge. She traced the clinking metal up to the wall and down to wrist cuffs, searching for a weakness. She tugged and pulled and tested, hoping for something to give. The wrist cuffs were too stiff with rust to move. Her hands hurt too much to continue yanking on them, so she drew back a chain from the wall and hurled it against the stones.

Clank.

More dust rained down onto the dirt floor. Loose mortar and sand puffed into her mouth as she reared back and threw the chain against the wall again.

Clank.

The metal links wouldn't budge. The crumbled mortar crunched under her feet. She felt through the rubble, hoping to find a sharp fragment of stone, fantasizing about shoving it right through Wenger's throat.

She knew how that story would end. Blood spurting up from the severed arteries, the bulging eyes, the gurgling breath as his lungs flooded, the sirens, the screams, the running, the cops. She'd spent two years in the workhouse for manslaughter. *Am I ready to go back?*

She sat back on her bare ass and thought about it. Odds were good she wouldn't even find her way out of the maze of the building without being caught by someone. *What would they do to me then? They could kill me down here. They could beat and torture me. They could just leave me here to starve, and no one would ever know.*

As she rocked herself back and forth, the fact that Mary Alice feared being shunned more than anything else worried her. *Does she know about these rooms? Has she ever been down here? Would she even know where to look for me?*

The seconds stretched into hours as Ethel sat there listening to her own breathing. The dust and dirt caked her mouth as a nagging thirst set in. Tiny cuts lined her throat from screaming. Bizarre colors and fleeting images pulsed in the dark. She'd shake them from her field of vision only to have them return a moment later. Waves of nausea came one after another as restless shakes tremored up and down her bones. Whether it was the cold or the urgent screams of her liver for more booze, she couldn't quite tell anymore. The last time she'd dried out, she'd had fits of nightmares as the things she'd buried with booze came back to haunt her.

The photograph of the dead girl flashed in the dark. The arms and legs missing. She'd had the thought that the stumps looked as though they'd been chewed by wild dogs, as the detective pummeled her with questions.

Do you know this woman?

The head had been lopped off. How the hell was she supposed to tell, she wondered, trying like hell not to let the picture bother her. Assuring herself it was no one she knew.

Any of your friends go missing?

An image of Wenger with a knife loomed its shadow over her along with the way the guts of that pig had spilled out of its body. She hugged her knees to her chest. They couldn't even identify seven of the victims. They were nobodies that no one missed. No one would report her missing either.

Please, God. She found herself praying inside her head. She tried to stop herself, determined not to give that bastard Wenger the sick satisfaction. *Get me out of here.*

"Shh." A whisper in the dark jolted Ethel out of her thoughts.

"Hello?" she whispered back in a hoarse voice.

"Shh," the voice said again.

"Who's there?" she hissed and snapped her head toward the empty black space behind her where the door should be. "Hello? Can you hear me? Help!"

"Shh," the voice came from over her other shoulder.

She jerked away from it and banged her arm into the stone wall. "Ow!"

"Shh," it said again, only this time it seemed to come from right in front of her.

She swung her arms wildly into the darkness, desperate to clock the shit out of whoever was hissing at her. "Stop it!" she rasped.

"Shhh."

Ethel leapt up and turned side to side, certain she'd make contact with something or someone. But she was alone. Her foot grazed something cold and hard on the ground. She knelt down to feel it with her hands. It was the floor drain. A round metal grate the size of a small dinner plate covered the hole.

"Shh," it said.

"What?" Ethel pressed her ear to the grate, then spoke down into the hole. "Is someone there?"

The sound of running water answered her. *Shhhhhh.*

Ethel slapped herself in the head for being afraid of the dark. She listened again as water rushed past the hole in the ground and then stopped. Someone was taking a shower or using the toilet, she realized and recoiled a bit from the sound. But the air wafting up from the pipe wasn't any more foul than the stink of the cellar. She laced her fingers through the drain slots and pulled up on the grate. It lifted freely. The round slotted plate weighed about fifteen pounds, she guessed, pulling it onto her lap and testing its heft with both hands.

It would do the job nicely.

CHAPTER 18

Ethel crouched by the door, clutching the metal plate in her hand, waiting for her chance to escape her purgatory. Her fingers went numb. Her arms ached. After what could have been an hour, she let the plate rest on her legs and her head loll back against the wall.

The hole in the center of the floor shushed her with the distant sound of rushing water. She blinked her eyes to reassure herself that they still existed, to remind her whether they were open or closed. She rubbed her invisible hands together and set them on the dirt floor gritty with disintegrated mortar. The hard masonry wall behind her dug into the knobs of her spine. She rocked her head back and forth on the uneven stone behind it as the chill in her bones worked its way deep into the marrow.

How long does he plan to keep me here?

She imagined driving the steel plate through his skull, crunching through that smug smile of his, breaking his teeth. The rough pitted edges of the drain cover dug into her thighs as it balanced there, waiting.

Afraid to let her mind wander, she recounted every minute she'd spent with the Harmony Mission, searching for a clue. *Do they know where I am? Have others here been locked away for hours and hours too?* The lash marks down Mary Alice's back worried her skin. She rubbed her shaking arms to reassure it.

Wenger saw from the start that she wasn't one of them. Ethel rifled through the faces of the spinster women in her mind and wondered if any of them suspected the same. Mary Alice had been crazy to try to smuggle an old whore like her inside. *Is she down here too or in some other torture chamber in this rat's maze?*

Ethel closed her eyes and pictured the poor girl tied to a bed somewhere on the fourth floor while Wenger or Bertram or Milton grunted on top of her. She gaped into the darkness and found herself hoping, praying even, that Mary Alice would be all right. She never should have accepted the fool's offer. She should've just stayed on her corner and in the pub down the street. She deserved to be cold and alone. At least she'd be drunk and Mary Alice would be safe. All the poor girl had wanted to do was help.

No one ever tried to help her. Not really. Not even when she was nine months pregnant. Ma Pratchett still wanted her cut, same as always. The perverts that had picked her out of the line with her swollen belly sent a shiver of revulsion through her all over again as she curled up into herself on the floor, cradling the heavy plate in her arms. The fiends itching to hurt their own mothers slapped her around. The infantile begged to be babied and diapered and shat in her bed. Some demanded to suckle. None of the beasts that took her upstairs offered to help.

The day she went into her labor, Ma Pratchett dropped her on the doorstep of the orphanage where all the girls delivered their bastards. A sniff of sickly sweet ether and she woke up the next day empty with a scar across her belly. The doctor had taken the baby out along with the offending organ responsible. None of Ma's girls came back to the brothel intact. The doctors always had a medical reason for taking pieces out. A complication, a hemorrhage, something to write on their form. But the girls knew the truth. They were unfit mothers in the eyes of the hospital, and orphans cost too much. So did illegal abortions.

Ethel felt the vertical scar running from her navel to her quick. She didn't even know if it had been a boy or a girl. Not that it mattered. After they took the baby, she wouldn't stop bleeding. They kept her two weeks in a bed with twenty other nameless girls rotating in and out. All of them had the same sad story. None of them looked each other in the eye.

She couldn't let Mary Alice end up like that.

The memory twisted in her. Ethel swallowed a wad of dried spit and wished like hell for a stiff drink. Bourbon was her favorite, but any booze would do. Even the swill the hobos down in the Run drank until they went blind would be better than sitting there in the dark with nothing but her nightmares to keep her company. A hard drink and a laugh would fix almost anything for a little while, and that's all that mattered. Just a little while.

If we're going to hell anyway, might as well go happy! The room would roar with drunken laughter at the toast, clink glasses, and stagger around overjoyed to be damned. She laid her throbbing head on the dirt floor and tried to imagine the faces of her so-called friends. Slow Tony, Mabel, One-Armed Willie, Flo, Rose. They'd all gone. Tony and Willie had hopped trains heading out of town. Mabel got sent up to Mansfield.

Flo and Rose were dead.

Ethel dug her fingernails into her thighs to cut through the bleak madness in her head. If she was going to get out of there, she had to focus. She had to stay awake and be ready. But her arms felt too heavy to lift off the ground. They ached from her day of shoveling shit at the farm, but it was worse than that. A black hopelessness weighed down each of her bones. There was nothing waiting for her outside the stone walls of this prison. Just booze and cigarettes, but it wasn't enough.

She lifted her wrists and traced a finger down the scars running the length of her forearms. If only she'd gone a little deeper. Tears burned in the backs of her eyes. She deserved to rot down there in the dark. Maybe it was all finally over and she could disappear. Every time she lifted her skirt, she wished herself away to a place where no one would find her.

And now here she was.

She curled into a ball and shut her eyes. Someone still knew how to find her, and she couldn't begin to guess what he planned to do with her.

The sounds of someone befouling one of the nuns upstairs the night before echoed in her ears. *If it wasn't Brother Wenger, who was it?* The crying grew louder in her mind until it felt as though the girl were there in the room with her. Her eyes flew open, not that it helped. It was just as dark in the room as in her head.

Somewhere outside the room, a woman was weeping. The longer she listened, the more convinced she became it was real. It sounded like a bird fallen from its nest, wailing and injured on the ground. Ethel sat up and pressed her ear to the seam between the wall and the door.

"Hello?" she hissed through the gap. "Who's out there? Are you okay?"

The crying grew louder.

"Hello!" Ethel raised her voice, then pounded on the door. "Where are you?"

Ethel pulled away from the door and pressed her ear to the wall and then the dirt floor, trying to locate the voice. *Mary Alice? Oh, God, what are they doing to you?*

A high-pitched scream pierced the air. Ethel's head snapped up at the sound. Another scream tore through dark. Clutching her ears, Ethel shrank against the wall, desperate to block it out. "Stop! Stop it!" she pleaded.

Another gutted scream rose up. It was coming from the sewer drain, she realized. Ethel felt her way to the spot in the floor.

A low, muffled voice greeted her at the drain. The words she strained to hear sounded like ". . . the curse of the Lord is on the house of the wicked, but He blesses the habitation of the just."

"Ple—ease," a woman wept.

The low voice got lost in the pipe. Ethel cupped her ear to it. "You . . . for forgiveness . . . absolved . . . your sins."

"For-forgive me. God. Please. I'm sorry. I'm so sorry. Please let me go. *Let me go!*" she shrieked.

"That is what we are here to do, my child . . . We're here to set you free."

The beginnings of another scream echoed up from the ground but died in an unnatural gurgle. Ethel sucked in her own scream and stopped up her mouth with both hands. *They killed her.*

She leapt to her feet, colliding into a wall. Her lungs collapsed as she sipped the thinning air faster and faster. *They killed her.*

Purple spots clouded her vision. The silence that followed terrified her more than the screams. It stretched out for an eternity. She sank down to her knees, waiting for some sign of life besides her own labored breath and the distant sound of water. There was nothing.

A rush of fresh air swept her bare skin as the door behind her creaked open.

BABY FARM IS TORSO DEATH CLEW

Unwed Girls' Clinic Traced

The mystery of the headless dead turned today to a hunt by detectives for a baby farm and abortion clinic known to have been operated in Cleveland's Northeast Side.

Detective Sergeant James T. Hogan ordered his men today to inquire for such a place in the belief that the young woman whose dismembered torso washed ashore yesterday on Lake Erie's beach at E. 165th street may have been the victim of an illegal operation or may have died after childbirth.

—*Cleveland Press*, February 24, 1937, p. 1

CHAPTER 19

April 8, 1999

A wall of smoke and music greeted them. Kris walked into the fog of a two-story great room flanked on two sides by rows of brick arches with a gallery of balconies overhead and a giant window at the far end.

"What is this?" she asked, gazing up at the vaulted ceiling overhead. Her voice was drowned out by the bass thumping through four-foot speakers. Jimmy led her by the arm onto the dance floor.

No one was dancing. Ratty couches lined the edges of the gallery. The seats were occupied by a throng of slovenly dressed guys and girls with punk hairdos and Dr. Martens shoes. They all appeared to be Kris's age but came from a different planet where tattoos and piercings and dyed hair were the norm. Nearly everyone was smoking something. A cloud of nicotine and marijuana hung above the gallery, shimmering under the red and yellow Christmas lights strung between the balconies.

Kris scanned the twenty or so faces dotted around the room and recognized none of them. None looked old enough to be friends with her father. He would have hated the lot of them. A girl in the corner shrieked out a laugh. She had a safety pin threaded through the skin over her eyebrow and a hoop ring sticking out of her lower lip. A guy with spiked black hair passed her a four-foot glass bong. He had a hole in his earlobe big enough to see through.

A few of the couch people waved to Jimmy. He threw them a nod and set his grocery bag on top of an enormous speaker in the corner. "You want something to drink?" he shouted over the music.

"Uh. Sure." She turned and scanned the upper balconies. Groups of heads with various knit hats and odd hairdos sat chatting in clusters above them. Her father wouldn't be caught dead anywhere near them.

Jimmy handed her a J. Ruppert's, undoubtedly the cheapest beer in all of Cleveland. "Thanks." Kris cracked it open. *Blech.* "So, uh, who are all these people?"

"Who, them?" he waved a hand at the disjointed crowd. "I have no idea." He winked at her and led her to the nearest pair of couches.

They sat down next to a guy wearing a ski cap and a *Frampton Comes Alive!* T-shirt. He handed Jimmy a joint. He had a poem tattooed on the side of his neck. Kris squinted to read the words but then worried she was being rude. Next to all these heavily styled stoners, she realized she must look like a Mormon. She wasn't even wearing lip gloss.

"Thanks, man." Jimmy took a long drag and said in a hitched voice, "What's up, party people?" then blew out an enormous cloud of smoke. He handed the tarry bundle of paper to Kris.

She took it out of courtesy and held it for a moment, debating whether to just pass the joint to the girl with the braided pigtails. Jimmy kept talking to Frampton, but Kris felt the eyes of the entire room on her, waiting to see what she would do. Her father would've had a fit if he could see her sitting there. His absence opened a gully beneath her feet, a canyon without a floor. Nothing was there to stop her or catch her. Nothing but air.

"You gonna hit that?" the girl next to her asked.

"Oh, sorry." She passed the joint over.

Jimmy grinned at her, clearly amused. "Everybody, this is Kris."

She waved at them weakly. Her eyes burned with the clouds of smoke and the red lights glowing over her head. The grimy fabric of the couch cushions sucked her down to the broken springs.

"Kris, this is Tommy, Bruno, Ansel, Scully, and Jane."

They each gave her a smile or a nod as the joint made its way back to Jimmy. He took another hit and passed it to her.

She waved him off and took a swig of beer instead. The thumping electronic music switched over to reggae. All the heads in the smoky room started bobbing together in rhythm. *Jesus, what the hell am I doing here?*

Jimmy shouted in her direction, "You alright?"

She gazed into his sleepy stoned eyes, weighing whether to bother even asking Jimmy about her father or just leave.

"You look like you got something on your mind."

"I'm sort of looking for someone," she shouted back. Against her better judgment, she pulled her father's driver's license from her back pocket and handed it to him. "Have you seen this guy?"

Jimmy squinted at the license through the smoke and waved off the joint being passed in his direction. Then he looked up at her, troubled. Or maybe just stoned. He handed it back to her and said, "Let's take a walk."

Jimmy pulled her through a cloud of bobbing music and smoke, past the couches to a staircase on the right. At the top of the stairs and around the corner, the music grew fainter, and she could start to hear herself think again. "Where are we going?"

"Who is this Alfred Wiley guy?" Jimmy asked as he pulled her down a narrow hall toward a closed door. "Boyfriend?"

She glanced at his broad shoulders, becoming uncomfortably aware how easily he could overpower her. The room full of drunk and stoned people behind them didn't give her much comfort. "No. He's . . . he's my dad."

"Oh . . . Shit. I'm sorry." Jimmy stared at her a beat then went to open the door to what she was certain must be his bedroom.

"Wait." She pulled her hand back from his, a panic building inside her. The room buzzed with all the secondhand smoke she'd inhaled. She couldn't remember how to get out, and she didn't know this guy from Adam. "Have you seen him? Is he around here? In the building, I mean."

His deep brown eyes bent with sympathy. "I'm sorry. I haven't seen an old dude like that in here. It's mostly old drunks like Maurice or, you know." He waved his hand toward the party.

"Oh." Disappointment flooded her body along with a wave of exhaustion. For a moment, she'd seen a glimmer of recognition in Jimmy's face, but this whole thing was a dead end. *But why did he list this place as his address? Where is he?* The unanswered questions reeled past her. She slumped against the wall.

Two warm hands cupped her face. Deep brown eyes poured into hers. "I'm sorry you can't find him. I really am."

For a terrible second, she was certain he was going to kiss her, and she felt herself lean in. He seemed nice enough, inviting her in out of the cold, offering her beer. His full lips and lean build made him more than a little attractive. She hadn't been kissed in . . .

Kris stiffened and shook her head. "I can't."

"Relax. I'm not gonna hurt you," he whispered, but instead of driving her into the floor with a kiss, he let go. "I want you to meet someone."

She blinked her eyes clear. "You do?"

On the other side of the door, six people sat on the floor circled around six candles. They were holding hands and swaying back and forth. All of them looked like different versions of the stoners they'd sat with on the couches. All except one.

A heavyset woman with pale wrinkled skin and long gray hair tied into a braid sat at the head of the circle. She looked old enough to have mothered all of them.

"Good evening, Madame Mimi. Can we join you?" Jimmy asked.

The woman glanced up at Jimmy and whispered to the others, "Widen the circle for our friends."

The students shifted to make two more seats around the tiny bonfire of candles. Madame Mimi pulled two more red votives out of her bag and lit their wicks.

"What are we doing?" Kris whispered, then immediately wished she hadn't. Every eye in the room turned to her. She shrank in apology and stared into the candlelight. The room reeked of patchouli and sandalwood.

"We are communing with the dead," Madame Mimi answered gently.

Kris lifted her eyes and frowned at the old woman. *What?*

"We are in a place full of ghosts. A girl was held prisoner right here, in this very room."

Kris shot Jimmy a look that said, *Is this lady nuts?* She didn't want to commune with the dead. She wanted to find her father and prove that all of it had been a terrible mistake.

Jimmy tilted his head and threw her a side-eye that said, *Shut up and listen.*

"You are a skeptic. You want to know why," Madame Mimi said softy. "Some of us are searching for answers. Some of us are looking for meaning."

The older woman studied her a moment and added, "Some of us have unfinished business with the dead."

Kris sat there stunned for a moment in the fog of incense and candle wax, certain the crazy hippie lady had somehow seen right into her soul. Then her inner cynic spoke up. *The woman's a con artist.* It was her job to read people's expressions, and Kris realized she must've looked like she'd seen a ghost at the mere mention of the word *dead*.

"We must all clear our minds. The dead will speak to us if we listen," Mimi announced.

They sat in silence with their eyes closed while Jim Morrison shared his drunken musings about dead Indians from the gallery below. All except Kris. She let her gaze wander over the group deep in prayer or meditation or whatever it was they thought they were doing. Jimmy was stooped over at the waist with his eyes closed. The blond with a crocheted Rasta tam rocked back and forth. One of the girls had dreadlocks so thick and heavy Kris wondered how she lifted her head. Beads and metal amulets had been woven through the sticky twigs of her hair.

"Relax your mind," Mimi said in a low, soothing voice.

Kris told herself it would be rude to upset the whole séance. She watched the candle flames dance and weave. *This thing will be over soon, and I'll go home. Maybe Ben called to tell me it's all just been a mistake. He's fine. He's coming back. Breathe, Kris. It's going to be all right.* The weariness of the last twenty-four hours sank deep into her bones.

"We are safe here. Let yourself go. Let the candles light your way."

Kris felt herself drifting in and out of consciousness as the fortune-teller kept muttering about peace and relaxation in that soothing slow voice. Her mind wandered down the narrow corridors of the building, through the hobbit door.

The throbbing drumbeats below her began to quicken their pace as the music shifted. Instead of drifting lazily down the brick pathway, she was now running down a long, narrow hallway. She took a wrong turn and got lost in the courtyard. The iron gate was closed. Panic shot through her as she scanned a hundred doors and windows looking down at her. They were all locked.

He's coming.

Kris's eyes startled open. She was back in the room with the hippie lady. Madame Mimi was looking right at her. The feeling that someone was behind her still pulled at the nerves in her back, but there was no one there.

"Who has a question for the dead?" she asked the group, but her eyes stayed on Kris.

A guy with a goatee answered with his eyes still closed, "How many ghosts are living here?"

The rest of the stoners kept their heads down and waited for the answer. Madame Mimi made a study of Kris's face, then answered, "They drift in and out, but over three hundred people died in this building."

"Whoa," Goatee answered and bobbed his head in agreement.

"How'd they die?" Beaded Dreadlocks whispered as though it might happen to her next.

"Many died in the hospital in the old wing. During the war." Madame Mimi kept her voice low and even, a hypnotist at work. Kris found herself staring at the long necklaces dangling from the old woman's neck. One looked like an eye. One looked like an owl.

"Which war?" a voice asked.

"It was the Civil War. Lincoln's men camped two blocks away. Many wounded were treated here. Some lost their legs. Some lost their lives."

"No shit."

"Who else died here?" It might've been Jimmy asking, but Kris kept her eyes on Madame Mimi.

"Many infants and children. This was an orphanage for many years before it became a Bible press and mission."

Kris recoiled at the idea of dead children but then figured the words were specifically chosen for effect. The more horror the better if you're staging a séance. The bits of history lent some real intrigue, but Kris told herself that anyone with a library card could have sussed all that out.

"Do they see us?" another girl asked.

Kris scanned the room for drifting specters despite herself. The candles threw shadows all over the room. Severed heads and broken torsos lurked in all of them.

"They see us as often as we see them," Madame Mimi answered.

"Why are they still here? What do they want?" a small girl with a garden of tattoos up and down her arms asked.

"What do *you* want?" Madame Mimi asked in response.

Kris wanted to get the hell out of there.

"It's different for all of us," the old fortune-teller continued. "Some are angry. Some are lost. Some like to watch. Some are too frightened to move on."

"What about the girl that was a prisoner here, in this room?" Jimmy asked. "What does she want?"

Mimi directed her red-rimmed eyes right at Kris. "A way out."

Kris decided she'd had enough of the charade. "So she's trapped here? Doesn't she know she's dead? Or is it like that movie, you know the one with Bruce Willis?"

A few pairs of eyes glared up at Kris's irreverence, but Madame Mimi wasn't fazed. "This girl was murdered many floors below us."

Kris stiffened.

"When death comes suddenly and violently, the shock can render the dead immobile. Petrified. The victim is frozen in those final living moments and can't break free."

Kris's heart tightened. Her father's face peered out from behind the plastic of his driver's license in her back pocket. *Trapped.*

"Isn't there anything we can do to help her, you know, find peace?" someone asked.

"We can try. For this, I'll need total silence." The fortune-teller shot Kris a look and then pulled a bundle of dried twigs from a fold in her caftan and lit one end with a candle. She blew out the flame and then waved the smoldering ember around until the room hazed over with smoke.

Kris inhaled deeply and tried to block out the idea of a petrified soul hanging over her, of her father trapped under the surface of the Auglaize River. Something in the smoke tugged at the corners of her memory. It reminded her of her childhood back home.

"Lost soul," Madame Mimi whispered. "If you can hear my voice, come. Come and sit by the fire. You are safe here with us."

Kris blocked out the woman's voice and focused on the memory straining to come back to her. *Her father's pipe? A campfire?* Every time she came close to placing it, it slipped away from her. *Her father's garage? The smell of gunpowder? The discharge of her father's rifle that time they'd gone pheasant hunting?*

The smoke cleared for a moment, and Kris swore she smelled rain. She cracked her eyes open at the hazy circle of faces all bent with concentration.

Madame Mimi had her eyes closed and whispered, "She's here." She waved the smoldering bundle of twigs around some more.

Kris shook her head and ignored the woman. The nagging smell pulled her in deeper. *Birthday candles being blown out? Her grandmother's living room? Her mother's cigarette?* The thought was startling since Kris had hardly any memory of the woman before she died.

"It's alright. We're here to help. He can't hurt you anymore," Madame Mimi whispered. "You can stop running now. It's over, Rachael. You're safe . . . He's not coming back."

Kris's eyes flew open at the mention of her mother's name.

"It's time to rest. Go to sleep. Everyone be still, be at peace with the departed. Show her it is safe to close her eyes."

Kris covered her face with her hands, staring into her palms in disbelief. *It's just a coincidence. Rachael is a common name.* The group sat in silence for several moments. Kris dropped her hands. They were all in various poses of sleep. Beaded Dreadlocks was hugging her knees. Goatee was stooped over his lap. Madame Mimi had her head tipped back and her hands folded.

A cool wisp of air fluttered across her cheek. That instant, all eight candles went out.

Kris sucked in a gasp. She'd been staring right at them and *poof*.

"Good night, Rachael. Travel safe," Madame Mimi whispered into the dark room.

A quiet chorus of *whoas* and *wows* circled the room. Several voices agreed, "Travel safe."

Jimmy pulled himself to his feet, and a moment later, a string of purple holiday lights lit up overhead. The circle broke up and stood to leave. "Thank you, Madame Mimi," several voices chorused as they wandered out.

One added, "That was super trippy."

Mimi began packing up her bag of tricks. Kris considered asking about the ghost's name but talked herself out of it. Her mother had died in a car wreck, not in a creepy building 180 miles from home, and she didn't want to give the con artist any more grist for her mill.

Kris stood up. The walls pulsed different shades of purple. A futon mattress sat in one corner on a low frame of wooden warehouse pallets. The floor was littered with large pillows. A glass bong sat in the other corner next to a large bongo drum.

The far wall was covered in a web of pencil, marker, and pen lines all written in different hands. Kris walked over to it. Lovingly drawn pot leaves grew next to scribbled graffiti.

Let go of the umbrella and let in the rain.

I'm frosting this couch with my head!

Alice just fell down the wrong hole. Silly rabbit!

The bizarre statements were mixed with random song lyrics by Jimi Hendrix, Johnny Cash, and Tom Waits. Girlie doodles filled in blank spaces with ladybugs eating flowers and caterpillars crawling on mushrooms.

A set of words stood out from the others in dark red ink.

I will go into Thy house with burnt offerings. I will pay thee my vows.

She frowned as she read it and scanned the wall. Another odd sentence in the same writing sat a few feet away next to a penciled butterfly smoking a joint.

He shall cover thee with his feathers, and under his wings shalt thou trust.

She squinted at the words and took a step back. *Feathers?* More red letters were set high off the floor.

For the life of the flesh is in the blood . . .

and it is the blood that makes atonement

"What the hell?" she whispered. It sounded like a Bible verse. The red ink looked like blood against the dark purple. She reached up a hand to touch the grooves left by a small brush. They'd been painted on. She turned to ask Jimmy about them but he was talking with Mimi.

"Thank you for having me, Jimmy," she said and gave him a warm hug, during which he slipped a rolled-up plastic bag into her pocket. Kris had no doubt what it was filled with.

On her way to the door, the fortune-teller stopped and motioned Kris over. She reluctantly obeyed. Mimi picked up Kris's hand, turned it over, and studied her palm a moment before she said, "You won't find him here."

"What?" Kris pulled her hand back as though it had just been infected with crazy. "Find who?"

"The one you're looking for."

"Wait." Kris shook her head clear and focused. Of all the people she'd met in the building, Mimi was the only one old enough to know her father, even if she was a nut. She pulled his license out of her pocket. "Have you seen him? He—uh . . . He was telling people he lived here a few years ago?"

Mimi furrowed her brow at the card and glanced over Kris's shoulder at Jimmy, then shook her head. *No.* She studied Kris's face another moment and said, "You need to be careful. They're watching you."

CHAPTER 20

"What the hell was that all about?" Kris demanded after the old woman left.

"What do you mean?" Jimmy smirked. He pulled another joint out of his pocket and offered it to her.

"You know what I mean." Kris waved him off angrily. *He's not here. After all that, she's never even seen him.* "The ghosts? The palm reading? 'They're watching you.' Does she think if she scares the shit out of me, I'll pay her money or something?"

Jimmy thought about it for a moment, then shrugged. "She didn't ask for money, did she? I'm sure she didn't mean any harm. You alright?"

Kris had spent the previous night holding a knife, convinced someone was indeed watching and stalking her. "Yeah, I'm fine. It's just . . ." *I'll never find him.*

"Hey." He gently squeezed her shoulders, his eyes soft. "I'm sorry. I thought she'd be able to help."

Kris shrugged him off but took the bite out of her voice. "You don't buy all her mother earth psychic stuff, do you? It's just parlor tricks."

"Call it what you want. Parlor tricks, intuition, hocus-pocus, I don't care. Mimi sees things that other people can't see. She's told me some things I hadn't even admitted to myself. She's cool if you give her a chance. She lives across the hall if you ever want to talk to her. You never know. It might help."

"Help what, exactly? It's a scam."

Even as she said it, Kris couldn't help but wonder what Madame Mimi would say about the human remains lying somewhere inside the Auglaize County Sheriff's Office. *She'd probably say whatever would keep me coming back.*

"I hope you don't give her all your money."

"Nah. Mimi and I have an arrangement." Jimmy winked at her in the most enticing sort of way. He was flirting with her, she realized, and she still didn't know her way out of the building. And now they were alone. In his bedroom.

She shifted her weight uneasily. "You give her weed, don't you?"

He smirked at her like, *So what?*

"So what does that make you exactly, besides a total sucker?"

He laughed. "A good friend to have. Speakin' a which, you want another beer? You look like you could use it."

Kris nodded despite the red flags waving in her head. *He's a drug dealer. My father would kill me. If he was here.* She let out a helpless laugh to keep from crying.

"Shit. You don't have to be a psychic to see somethin's bothering you." He lifted her chin. "It's written all over your face."

She gazed up into his deep brown eyes. The lids were heavy with thick, long lashes. They drifted from her irises down to her mouth and lingered there.

She bit her lips together in self-defense as the thought of kissing him rushed through her. He looked like an amazing kisser. He was the exact opposite of Troy. And she longed to feel anything but this . . . His lips curled into an amused grin that told her he'd seen the temptation all over her face.

"I should get going." She pulled away before it was too late and stumbled toward the wall of scribbled artwork and bizarre quotes. "I like the mural, by the way. Who drew all these?"

Jimmy stuffed his hands in his pockets. "Friends. Strangers. Some of them were already here when I moved in."

"Which ones?"

"Those trippy Bible verses. There were tons of them all over the walls. I painted over most of them, but a few were just . . . too good to let go."

Kris scanned the painted red letters again. *It is the blood that makes atonement.* "Do you think a girl was really trapped in here? You know, like Mimi said?"

Jimmy gave her a grim nod. "Yeah. I do. At night, sometimes I feel like I hear her crying."

Kris raised an eyebrow at him. "Are you sure it's not just the wind or something?"

"Could be. It's not that hard to believe, though. I mean, these buildings have been vacant since the old Harmony Mission Press closed down in the '50s. A lot of shady things happened here."

The music in the gallery below downshifted into a slow throbbing bass line. Jimmy's slow gaze wandered over her with the music. Kris inched closer to the door. "Doesn't that, uh, make you nervous?"

"Not really. It's sort of fun living in a haunted house, right? You wouldn't believe our Halloween parties. Mimi told me once that she could sense that more murders had been committed in this place than in any other building she's investigated. A serial killer may have even lived here at one time."

Everything that had come loose inside her tightened back up at the words *serial killer.* "I'm sorry, Jimmy. I have to go home. Thanks for having me."

His eyes bent into a puzzled frown. "You don't find this murder stuff amusing, do you?"

"Amusing? No. I don't find it amusing." Her pent-up emotions beat against their cages. "I mean, what the hell is wrong with people? They treat serial killers like rock stars, stealing pictures and coroner's reports like they're freaking autographs. People died! They fucking *died*! And it's like a big joke or a carnival ride to you and your stoner friends. I just . . . I need to get the hell out of here!"

"Whoa." He held up his hands in self-defense. "I don't think it's a joke, Kris. I don't. I care about the girl stuck in this room. I've spent the last year trying to figure out who she was and trying to find her family. I swear."

She caught herself midrant and studied his face. He looked sincere. "You have?" She squeezed her eyes shut. "I'm sorry. It's not you."

"Hey. It's okay . . . Do you want to tell me what happened?"

"No. I just . . ." She blinked the tears away and headed out of the room. "I have to go."

"Okay, but I can't let you walk home all by yourself at this hour." He stopped her in the doorway. "C'mon. It's the least I can do."

Kris couldn't tell if he just wanted to keep working her or if he wanted to make sure she made it home safe. "What about your party?"

"The party isn't going anywhere. I'll probably be kicking those fools out three days from now." He held her gaze a moment too long.

She forced herself to look away. For all she knew, he was some sort of lunatic serial killer himself. "I'm fine."

He took a step back like he could read her mind. "Listen. I get it. You just need a friend right now. I can be a friend. Okay? But you shouldn't be walking around here alone, and you know it."

It was moments like these that Kris most hated being female. If she were a guy, she could walk wherever she damn well pleased. She could wander the building, searching for her father all by herself.

Then what Jimmy said finally registered. *A serial killer may have even lived here. Her father may have tracked him to this very building.*

"C'mon. Let me walk you home."

Kris felt herself nod.

Jimmy led her, numb and stumbling, down the hallway to a different set of stairs, down three flights, and out into a large courtyard. It was surrounded on all sides by the walls of the factory. It would've been an atrium for the factory workers—a place to smoke cigarettes and see the sun—but it felt more like a gallows. Dark windows glared down in judgment as though waiting for the executioner to appear. She scanned them all for her father's face.

They crossed the pavement and under the next wing of the complex into a dark covered loading dock that resembled a cave. The yellow lights of Thurman Avenue streamed in through the enormous iron gate, and she realized she was inside the loading dock across from her house.

Jimmy led her to a small man-size gate cut into the iron bars. A rusty chain hung from the rails, padlocked shut, keeping the city out and the murdered ghosts of the factory in. Jimmy produced a thin awl and miniature tweezers from his pocket. Kris watched with detached fascination as he picked at the padlock with his tools until it clicked open.

"Nice trick," she said. "Are you a burglar too?"

The twinkle of affection playing on his face went out. The offense registered in his raised eyebrows and flat stare.

"That sounded terrible. I'm sorry." And she was. She'd tried hard to shed her lily-white, small-town ignorance when she'd moved to Cleveland, and the shame of having said something possibly racist made her cringe. "No, really. I didn't mean it like that."

"Hey. Occupational hazard." He flashed a smile, but it wasn't the same. He swung the door open for her with a flourish. "After you."

The tiny house she rented sat three doors down. She could see by the dark windows that Pete wasn't home, and her stomach sank. She'd have to brave another night in the creepy house by herself. "I can make it from here."

"I know," Jimmy said and took her arm anyway.

They walked together in silence under the glow of the streetlamps to her door. No one on Thurman left their curtains open, and only faint halos of light escaped through the edges as they passed by.

"Seriously, how did you learn to do that?" she finally dared ask.

He shrugged. "You pick up things here and there. What, they didn't teach you that in high school?"

She let out an awkward laugh. "Nope. They taught me to gut a fish and shoot a deer, but nothing useful."

He gave her a side-eye. "You killed a deer?"

"No," she admitted. "I always made sure to miss. My dad thought I was the most miserable shot in the world."

A car sputtered past, splattering slush onto the back of her jeans as she fumbled with her keys. She didn't want him to come in. She didn't have anything to drink. There were dirty dishes in the sink and ants in the kitchen and laundry on her unmade bed. But she didn't want him to leave with her inappropriate accusation still hanging between them.

She blocked the doorway and gave him a plaintive smile that she hoped said everything she wanted to say. "Thanks for the walk."

"It was the least I could do." He studied her face and the hard edges in his softened. She was forgiven. "You sure you want to be all alone?"

No, she thought, but she didn't want to be tempted to sleep with him either. All she really knew about Jimmy was that he hung out with fortune-tellers, dealt drugs, picked locks, and lived in an abandoned building where a girl had been murdered. But he'd been kind to her. He'd had plenty of chances to take advantage of her and had walked her home instead. "I'll be fine. Thanks for everything, Jimmy. For the party. For the talk. Really."

"Hey, anytime. We're neighbors, right?" His eyes offered a standing invitation.

She held his gaze too long. She forced herself to look away and nod.

"Hey, I hope you find your dad. If you ever need anything, come find me. Okay?"

"Okay," she said and forced an *I'm fine* smile.

The relaxed slouch in Jimmy's step as he strolled away left little doubt that he played with women like her all the time and was quite good at it. He had twenty stoned hippie chicks back in his squatter's den in the Harmony Mission waiting for him to come home.

Kris scanned both sides of the street, looking for anything out of place. The same three cars were parked in their usual spots. Overflowing trash cans lined the gutters. Thurman was utterly deserted, but as Kris scanned the dark windows of the Harmony Mission across the street, she couldn't shake the feeling that someone was looking back at her.

They're watching you.

CHAPTER 21

The silence of the tiny house vibrated in her ears under the low hum of the refrigerator and the slow drip of the kitchen sink. The answering machine sat on the counter, dead and unplugged where she'd left it. The creeping feeling that someone, somewhere, was looking back at her stayed with her even as she shut the blinds.

"Stop being so dramatic. Jesus, Krit," she said out loud to break the spell. "You're just tired. It's been a long, horrible day, and you just need to go to sleep."

Kris staggered down the hall to her bedroom and stripped off her clothes. She threw on her favorite flannel pajamas. The chill of the cold snap outside clung to the walls and floorboards, freezing the bottoms of her feet. Spring never seemed to arrive in Cleveland, not in April anyway.

In the bathroom, the sight of her reflection startled her. She'd gone white as a ghost. Even her lips were blue. She'd been worried she'd have to beat Jimmy off with a stick if she let him in to her house when he probably just wanted to make sure she didn't collapse and hit her head. The deep purple bags under her eyes were about as fetching as the tangles in her hair. *Did I even brush my teeth this morning?*

Her mouth felt sticky with beer. She brushed her teeth twice and flossed for good measure, but the uneasy sense that she no longer fit in her own skin deepened as she went about her routine. She'd become a stranger to herself, cleaning someone else's mouth in someone else's bathroom. She didn't punch strangers and get fired. She didn't go to abandoned buildings or flirt with drug dealers. She had a job and responsibilities and a father. *This isn't my life.*

Kris floated in her exhausted trance back down the hall and into her bed. Her head hit the pillow and she waited for sleep to put her out of her misery. But she just lay there. A pair of voices passed by her window.

"Can you believe she did that?"

"What a slut!"

"Right? Do you think you're sober enough to drive?"

A car door slammed. An engine started up and the car pulled away. Kris pulled the covers over her head. A minute later, a gust of wind rattled the single-pane windows. She shivered and rolled over.

She didn't know how long she lay there wishing for sleep when a set of footsteps crunched the broken glass and road slush that collected in the gutters along Thurman Avenue outside her house. It was just another drunk wandering home from the bar, she told herself. But she listened anyway. The sound of hard-soled shoes hitting the pavement grew louder, then stopped abruptly not far from her front door.

Kris sat up in bed. She waited for the sound of a car door. But there was nothing. She pressed her ear to the paper-thin wall. A car rushed past on the next street. A pack of girls chattered like seabirds a block away. But the feet outside her house stayed still. She listened for twenty breaths, until she wondered whether she'd imagined the whole thing. She forced her head back onto the pillow.

Then another footstep fell. Then another. The sound of sand on concrete ground the sidewalk just outside her room.

Don't turn on the light, she told herself. *You're not home.*

A shadow passed by her closed blinds.

Kris slipped out of her bed and crawled silently to her closet. Her heart pounded in her throat as she reached for the shotgun her father had insisted she bring to Cleveland, propped in the far corner. At the time, she'd been furious. *I can't bring a gun to college, Dad!*

It wasn't loaded, she realized as she slipped it out of its felt sleeve. The shells were under her bed in a sealed box. She could hear her father's mocking her lack of foresight. *They're about as useful under there as tits on a chicken.*

Shut up! she wanted to scream. *You can't keep a loaded gun in the house. It's not safe!*

The footsteps seemed to be pacing outside her room now.

Holding the gun under her right arm, she crawled back to her bed and began feeling around for the heavy cardboard box. Handfuls of dust bunnies. An odd sock. A photo album Troy's mother had made her.

The footsteps headed back toward her front door.

Kris shoved her entire arm under the bed and swung it wildly until she smashed her finger into the hard corner of a box. It weighed a good ten pounds. She clawed at it and dragged it out from under the bed.

It was sealed shut with thick reinforced packing tape. Her fingers ripped at the edges and pried the corners, but it was useless in the dark. She debated turning on her bedside lamp but didn't dare draw the attention.

Just as she was about to use her teeth, the footsteps crunched away from her front door. They faded back down the street they'd come from. Kris's arms went slack. She collapsed against the side of her bed. It was probably just some guy waiting for a ride. It happened all the time down in Tremont after the bars let out.

"What if I'm having some sort of breakdown?" she asked the dark room. The cold metal of the shotgun lay across her legs and the box of shells sat heavy in her lap.

She flipped on the lamp. Her fingernails had ripped through the outer paper of the cardboard like the teeth of a wild dog. She grabbed the nail file from her nightstand and cut through the tape. Twenty shells of buckshot sat in two red-and-copper rows.

She popped the barrel of the gun, loaded two shells, and snapped it closed. Her heart settled down to an almost normal pace, but her chest cavity ached from the pounding. She shoved the loaded gun under her bed along with the rest of the shells and climbed back into bed.

After snapping off the light, she lay there staring at the shadows on her ceiling. More voices walked past on Thurman as 2:00 a.m. came and went. It was a Thursday night, and the weekend was already in full swing in Tremont.

Lying there, she catalogued all the things she still needed to get done the next day. She had a paper due. Finals would begin in two weeks, a prospect that would normally cause her stomach to cramp with worry. Would she get good enough grades to keep her father happy? Would she flunk out? Would he stop paying tuition and insist she move back home?

None of it mattered anymore.

Kris sat up and turned on her light. "To hell with this," she muttered to herself and got out of bed. She padded over to her desk and turned her computer on.

The torsokillers.com chat room was back up. She clicked over to the "Victims" page and scrolled through to see if Lowjack had ever written back. Their earlier conversation finally rolled up on her screen, frozen in time. She skimmed the lines again.

LOWJACK: Did somebody die?

. . .

KRITTER: They found a body in the woods out there. In pieces.

. . .

KRITTER: David? You there?

New lines of text followed. Kris's eyes widened as she read what appeared to be excerpts of the police report.

> LOWJACK: Alfred Ray Wiley, White Male, Age 55. Last seen March 28, 1999, at Fort Amanda Canoe Livery by proprietor Stuart Wallings . . . Remains recovered April 6, 1999. Disarticulated limbs severed at the primary joints . . . Head, hands, and left leg not found. Strong indications of homicide . . . Positive ID of remains still pending confirmation by next of kin, Kristin Anne Wiley, Age 19 . . . DNA samples still under analysis by the Ohio BCI. On rush. (Typical wait times exceed 30 days.)

The words ran together on the screen as she scrolled down. Kris sat stricken. Seeing it laid out in black and white stripped her of any illusions. Seeing her name right there for the whole discussion board to leer at stripped her naked.

Lowjack posted a file link at the end of his brutal summary. A copy of the full police report painted across her screen. Her father's name sat at the top of page after page of clinical details surrounding the investigation. The license plate of his car. A schematic map of the county with floating markers to show where evidence had been collected. A diagram of a human body marked up with red ink to indicate the extent of the injuries and the parts of him still missing.

Kris lurched up from her chair and into the bathroom, certain she was going to be sick. She sank to the floor next to the toilet and heaved, but nothing came up. There was nothing left inside her, no food, no stomach, no blood. She gaped at the veins standing up on her hands as they gripped the toilet and debated opening them up to see if they'd actually run dry. Needing to feel something, even if it hurt.

Instead, she punched the sink vanity hard enough to crack the wood. A brilliant starburst of pain flashed up her arm. As she sat there clutching her hand, a thought emerged. *How the hell did Lowjack get the report?*

Holding her bruised hand, she stormed back to her computer and wiped the horrific diagrams from her screen. A trail of follow-up questions followed Lowjack's callous data.

MERYLO3: Type of blade indicated?

LOWJACK: Unknown. No mention of hesitation marks.

REN: Signs of preservatives or sedatives?

LOWJACK: Toxicology report not in. No mention of skin discoloration.

MERYLO3: Blood?

LOWJACK: None found on the scene.

REN: Possible candidate but DB does not fit profile. Employed. Rural. WASP.

LOWJACK: I have a feeling about this one. Keep an eye out for more.

Kris read the thread of discussion with growing rage. They were rating her father's case as though it were a game show. "What the hell is wrong with these people?" she seethed and pounded the keyboard.

KRITTER: How did you get the file?

Her cursor sat there blinking for a minute until the filthy voyeur wrote back.

LOWJACK: County records aren't hard to get. Not secured.

KRITTER: So you stole them?

LOWJACK: Borrowed.

KRITTER: Why?

LOWJACK: The county sheriff's office is in over their heads. They will never find the killer.

KRITTER: But you will?

He didn't respond. She sucked in a breath, realizing that she might be chatting with the killer at that very moment.

KRITTER: David, why did you go to Cridersville? What does this have to do with the Torso Kill—

Her screen froze. She tapped her mouse and pounded on the keyboard. A second later a dialog box appeared on the screen, informing her of a processing error. She picked up her keyboard and slammed it back down again, then navigated out of the crashed screen. When she attempted to log back in, the chat room was down. The cartoon construction worker grinned at her from behind the glass.

After trying two more times, Kris finally relented and turned the machine off. Curling up into a ball on her bed, she felt more than defeated. She felt scared. They knew everything about her and her father, and she was alone in the dark.

They're watching you.

Sometime before dawn, Kris finally closed her eyes and fell into a fitful dream. She was lost inside the Harmony Mission, running down the narrow corridors and up and down crumbling staircases. Every window she rushed past held the face of someone who had died there. The last face she passed was her own.

Kris jerked herself awake and sucked in a lungful of air. The morning sun painted her walls yellow. Her bedside clock read 9:29 a.m. Thirty seconds later her alarm went off. She had class in an hour. Falling back to the pillows, she considered not going. The blank screen of her computer watching from the corner convinced her otherwise. She threw her nightshirt over it. If she stayed there another second, she'd go insane.

The shower couldn't get hot enough. She stood under the scalding stream until her skin was bright red. She combed her hair back and forced down her oatmeal. Car keys, backpack, purse—she loaded up and opened her front door.

A shock of dark red startled the thoughts out of her. She lurched back from the mark dripping down her front door, slamming her shoulder into the jamb. *Blood. Oh my God, it's blood.* Her door was bleeding. Streaks of red paint trailed down the dented white steel to the ground, pooling on the concrete sidewalk at her feet. Her eyes darted up and down Thurman Avenue, expecting to see a killer holding a knife. Nothing but trash cans and old cars.

Paint, she told herself, looking back at the door. *It's only paint. Graffiti.* She forced herself to breathe and stared at the mark someone had left on her house. It felt like an accusation—a scarlet letter, but it wasn't a letter at all.

It was an eight-pointed star.

WOMAN, 35, IS 9TH VICTIM OF TORSO SLAYER

Examination of Skeleton Found Under Bridge Reveals Age and Sex

Ninth victim of the mad butcher of Kingsbury Run was a woman about 35. This was the assertion today of Dr. T. Wingate Todd, professor of anatomy at Western Reserve University.

—*Cleveland Press*, June 7, 1937, p. 1

CHAPTER 22

April 7, 1938

A burst of white light shined right into her face. Ethel shielded her eyes with both hands, recoiling from the beam and whoever held it. Her heavy steel grate was lost somewhere on the ground. She forced her blinded eyes open against the glare to find her bludgeon sitting by the open doorway at the feet of a hulking shadow.

"Are you alright, Sister?" It was Brother Wenger. "I heard crying."

"You killed her," Ethel croaked in a frayed voice. Her strained pupils slowly adjusted to the light. All she could see was his silhouette. She searched the dirt floor for drops of blood, the girl's screams keening up from the drain still fresh in her ears. *Mary Alice.*

"Good Lord. What did you say?"

"You killed her." Ethel staggered to her feet, her rage eclipsing her fear. "You're a monster! How could you do it? How? She was just a stupid girl. I hope you rot in hell, you sick son of a bitch!" She lunged at him, knocking him slightly off balance. She raised her fist and swung at his face. He just stood there with his hands by his sides. Her punch landed feebly on his cheek, barely even turning his head.

Growling, she struck him again only this time in the neck just shy of his windpipe. Then a wide slap into the side of his head. She lunged again, ready to tear that head off with her teeth.

"That's enough, Sister," he said in a deathly calm voice and grabbed both her hands in his. He lowered himself to his knees and dragged her down to the dirt with him. "I will not strike one of God's creatures. But you are a woman possessed."

She strained her arms, wrenching her back. "Let me go. You murderer! Help! Somebody, *help me!*"

He pulled her into his chest and wrapped her thrashing frame in a suffocating bear hug. "Dear Lord," he began in his minister's cadence. "Cast out this demon. Cast out Satan's legions invading this poor soul. Deliver Sister Hattie back into Your arms as You delivered Mary Magdalene."

"Stop it!" Ethel shrieked and strained to wrestle herself free. "Let me go, you lunatic! Goddammit!"

"She is but a girl, O Lord! Free her from Satan's grasp!" He forced her onto her back with his bulk and pinned both her arms down to the ground.

"You're Satan! Let me go! Murderer!" Her shrieks became incoherent as he continued his sadistic prayer.

He pinned both her shoulders down with his knees and drew a cross on her forehead with his thumb. "In the name and by the virtue of our Lord Jesus Christ, I drive you from us, whoever you may be, unclean spirit."

Ethel thrashed her head back and forth as her screams dried into hoarse whispers. Wenger reached inside his suit coat, and she kicked her legs against the ground, certain he was reaching for a pistol or knife. *This is it. This is the end.* Her body seized, and she stopped breathing.

A small leather Bible appeared in his hand.

He pressed it to her forehead. "May you be snatched away and driven from the souls redeemed by the precious blood of the divine lamb. Be gone, demon!"

Her eyes bulged up at him. He was clearly insane. His eyes were clenched shut and his face lifted to the ceiling. He seemed convinced he was performing some sort of magic spell on her. He thinks he's Jesus Christ in the flesh, she realized as his words finally sank into her frantic head. *Be gone, demon?* And judging from the look of him hovering over her naked breasts, he was enjoying his role as her exorcist immensely.

She drew in a careful breath and let her arms go limp under his knees. She let the tears already leaking out of her eyes flow in a torrent. "Help me," she whimpered as helplessly as she could manage. "Brother Wenger? God, please. Help."

This seemed to please him, and he lifted the bulk of his weight off her shoulders. He lifted the leather book from her forehead. "Sister Hattie? Have you come back to us?"

Ethel struggled to sit herself up, mostly because he was still on top of her, but her helpless dance worked. He pulled her up and into his arms.

"What happened?" she sobbed and let her eyes go on a wild search around the room.

"Shh. Be still. You're going to be alright." He pressed her head into his chest and rocked her back and forth. His hands were warm on her bare back, reminding Ethel of her nudity and everything he had tried to strip from her. *Had he stripped Mary Alice too?*

"I heard . . . terrible things," she whispered and pulled away, checking his shirt and hands for blood in the light. There wasn't any. *Had he been wearing gloves? Had he just strangled the girl until she stopped kicking?*

"Sometimes we see and hear things in the dark. Sometimes the darkness swallows us whole. By the grace of God, you've come back,

Hattie. Let us pray." He grabbed both of her hands and clenched them hard between his and his Bible and bowed his head. "Our Father, who art in heaven . . ."

She bowed her head and scanned the floor. Her steel plate was lying in the dirt not two feet away.

"Thou art the Creator of all things."

The screams of the dying girl had echoed up as though from the bottom of a well. As Ethel strained to hear them again, doubt crept into her mind. *What if it was just a night terror? What if I imagined all of it?*

"'Deliver us from all the tyranny of the infernal spirits, from their snares, their lies, and their furious wickedness.'"

He squeezed her hands against the Bible until they hurt. Wenger meant to have her soul whether she liked it or not.

"'Deign, O Lord, to protect us by Thy power and to preserve us safe and sound.'"

He was going to lock her up in the dark again until he was ready to snuff out her furious wickedness once and for all.

"'We beseech thee through Jesus Christ our Lord. Amen.'"

"Amen," she murmured in agreement. She didn't have much time.

He released her hands and stood up. "The fight is not over, Sister. Until you accept Jesus Christ as your Lord and take Him into your body, they will find you."

"Who will find me?" She pushed herself up onto the balls of her feet. Her eyes stayed focused on the steel plate twenty inches away.

"Satan's legions. The devil comes in many forms. Temptation. Sin."

"Murder?" she whispered, glancing back at the drain. If she wasn't crazy now, she would be soon if Wenger had his way.

"Don't be afraid, dear sister." Brother Wenger tried to keep the authority in his voice, but Ethel could hear it soften at the edges. "We will not leave you to face the demons alone."

Gazing down at her, he almost looked like he was in love. Not with her but with the idea of saving her.

"I'm scared." She crumpled her face into her hands, feeding his fetish as only a professional could.

He fell silent.

For a moment, she panicked that she'd gone too far and he'd seen through her ruse. He would slam the door shut and leave her to rot. Or worse. She made a show of stifling her tears, only letting them out in a few tortured wails as though struggling to be strong for him.

"You must learn to pray, Sister." He bent down and brushed her cheek.

She had him.

She turned away from him as though ashamed, shifting her knees toward her target. "I don't know how to pray. You were right about me. You were right about everything."

He put a hand on her shoulder. "I can teach you. That's why I'm here—to help. Let us start with the most simple prayer of all, the Lord's Prayer. Repeat after me, our Father."

"Our Father." She bowed her head all the way down to her knees and grabbed the edges of the plate with both hands.

"You can just bow your head to your chest," he said and gently tapped her shoulder. "Who art in heaven."

"Who art in heaven." She lifted the plate and heaved it with all of her strength into the side of his head. It hit his skull with a *clunk*, and he went sprawling. Ethel leapt to her feet and went careening out the open door without looking back.

CHAPTER 23

Ethel ran down the narrow corridor past doorway after doorway. How many more women were locked inside? She didn't stop to check. The bare bulb in the ceiling threw long shadows after her. As her eyes scrambled for the exit, she realized she'd run the wrong way. Brother Wenger had brought her into the hellhole dungeon from the other end of the corridor.

She glanced back to see his lantern light spilling out the open door to her cell. It was moving.

A low grunt bellowed out into the hall. She had slammed a piece of iron into his head. There would be hell to pay, and he wouldn't go to the police for justice. He'd take a pound of flesh and more.

She quickened her pace, not knowing where she was heading. The corridor ended in a low-set door, no taller than her waist. Her hand grasped at the knob, frantically turning, praying it wasn't locked.

"Hattie! Stop!" a dazed voice called from behind her. "You need help."

The handle gave, and she fell through the opening onto a landing two feet below. She hit the other side with a grunt.

"It's not your fault, Hattie." The voice was getting closer. The soft even tone of it sent a shudder through her bones.

Ethel scrambled to her feet and took off running down a low hallway into the dark, hoping the shadows would shield her. The wretched smell of sewage seared her nostrils as she gulped the swampy air. Vomit, feces, rotting meat. It smelled like the Run. Her head clouded with it.

Brother Wenger's voice called from the doorway behind her. "The demon has you in its clutches, Hattie. Let me help you."

A light shone in, lighting the brick walls and the low vaulted ceiling. She kept running. The shadow of a door stood open ten feet ahead. She lunged through it and plunged back into blindness.

"This isn't the way out, Hattie," the voice called from behind her.

She felt her way forward along a wall, running one hand along the cold flat stones and holding the other out in front of her. The wall turned a corner and her arm followed but the rest of her hit more stone. She'd found some sort of hole in the wall. Maybe a window well, but there was no light. Her arm dragged through the thick dust and rubble littering the sill. She kept going past the first window to another one, feeling for a way out. Eight openings down the wall, until it finally turned a corner. She slipped behind it.

A glow lit the wall in front of her. It was punctuated by three rows of windows stacked one on top of the other between the heavy stones, but they weren't windows at all. She turned her head to the opening next to her. Crumbling cloth and bones lay inches from her nose. It was a crypt.

She covered her mouth to hold in a gasp.

"You shouldn't be in here, Hattie," Brother Wenger said softly from the doorway around the corner. "Dear Lord, help me find my lost sister. Help me deliver her from Satan's grasp."

Ethel searched the rows of open tombs for a place to hide. They were all full. A skull with missing teeth gazed out at her from its shelf. Down at the far end, the wall turned again. She took off running for the next cavern, her bare feet only a whisper across the dirt floor.

"The Lord has spoken, Hattie. He has spoken to me just now in the ringing in my ears. You have helped me to hear." He let out a soft laugh that chilled the air. "Praise God."

She pressed her back to the stone wall and peeked out into the dimly lit corridor at the light. It had stopped moving closer.

"I cannot find you, Hattie. Not until you want to be found. You must find your own way back into the light. We must starve the demon out. The Lord commands it."

The shadows swelled on the walls, growing longer and darker as the light receded.

He's leaving me here.

"May God have mercy on your soul, Hattie," he whispered.

The sound of the door creaking shut careened past the open graves to where she stood crouched against the wall. The light went out.

Ethel released an exhausted breath as the tension holding her muscles together collapsed. She crumpled to her knees and struggled to think. He hadn't let her go. He'd locked her in another dark room, only this one was full of dried corpses.

Starve the demon out.

That was his plan. That's what his Lord told him to do. He was going to let her starve and rot until she went stark raving mad. He would torture her until she believed she'd been possessed by demons. He'd break her until she swallowed up any Jesus story he fed her.

Unless he killed her first.

She rested her head on her knees and let out a helpless laugh. The perfect silence of the tomb swallowed the sound of it. There was no doubt in her mind that she would go insane if she didn't find a way out. But she couldn't bring herself to move.

Her body sat there suspended in the dark, floating in an ocean. She could feel her arms and legs disappearing into it as though she'd never existed at all. They'd find her in a few years, just a pile of bones like the others. Ethel drew in another breath. The dust of a hundred dead bodies filled her lungs. Under the smell of sewage and rot lurked the darker scent of a dead fire. The ashes of it settled in a blanket over her bare skin, coating the inside of her mouth, matting her wet eyelashes in mud. *I'm being buried alive. Is this what happened to the screaming girl? Is she stuffed into one of these holes?*

Ethel clawed the thought from her head with both hands and forced herself to sit up and focus. Her eyes could do nothing in the dark, so she strained her ears to hear anything that might show her a way out. Under the unsteady rasp of her own breath, the sound of water running through pipes rushed somewhere overhead. She focused on the steady *shh* with all her might, trying to locate the direction it was coming from, hoping that if she followed the sound, it would lead her out. Sitting up, she turned her head in each direction, but it seemed to be coming from one place and then another and then nowhere at all. It was hopeless.

A voice whispered from several feet away. "Is he gone?"

CHAPTER 24

The feeling of another person hovering somewhere next to her sent Ethel scrambling back into the wall. Rubble scattered under her feet. A shower of dust hit the ground. One of the dead bodies had surely risen to swallow her soul.

"Is it safe?" The whisper drew closer. A warm hand fell on Ethel's shoulder.

"Ahh!" she shrieked and shoved its owner away. The body attached went tumbling, light and frail. It was surprisingly small, Ethel realized too late. It was the body of a child.

"Shh! They'll hear you!" the voice hissed from where it had fallen.

"He wants to hear me," Ethel hissed back. She was probably talking to herself, but she kept going. "He wants to hear me scream and beg and grovel. He wants to hear me break."

The voice rose up from the ground and floated over her. "We have to go. Before they come back."

"Before who comes back? Wait." Ethel peered blindly into the dark. "Who are you?"

"It don't matter." The soft voice sounded like it belonged to a little girl.

"Of course it matters," Ethel argued with the ghost. "Where did you come from? Did Wenger lock you up in here too?"

"No one knows I'm here."

"How old are you?" Ethel reached out a hand to the tiny thing but caught nothing.

"I dunno." Her voice had turned away and slipped farther into the dark.

Ethel had met thrown-away girls down in the Run. Girls without parents. They didn't last long. She'd seen them sold back and forth for less than a pack of cigarettes. Supposed do-gooders scooped them up and carted them off to "homes." She'd run away from a home for way-ward girls at the age of sixteen. At least on the street she had a fighting chance. The eerie feeling that she was talking to some younger version of herself lilted through her mind. *Maybe I really am crazy.*

Ethel pulled herself to her feet and held her hands out into the blackness toward the tiny voice. "Let's get a look at you. Come here, sweetie. I won't bite."

Her hand found a shoulder, then a head full of snarled hair sitting just below the height of Ethel's shoulder. Then it darted away.

"You must be about nine, I'd think," Ethel thought out loud. "You remember your parents?"

"We have to go," the voice insisted, trailing away from her.

"Wait." Ethel started after her with her arms out to guard her face. "How did you get down here?"

"I stay here," the faraway voice answered. "When I can."

"All by yourself?" Ethel considered which answer would be more horrifying. She certainly didn't want to run into the little urchin's "daddy."

"Sometimes." The girl had turned a corner.

Ethel tried to keep up, stumbling over rubble on the ground. *Bones,* she thought with a shudder. The smell of the sewer grew stronger as

they went. Bile. Feces. Fermenting leaves. Her hand found the rough
stone of a wall and traced it to a corner. The chill in the air deepened
as they went. Ethel shivered and cursed that bastard Wenger for taking
her clothes. The darkness undulated blue and black, growing thicker
with each step.

"You still there?" she whispered, trying hard to keep the panic
out of her voice. "I still don't know your name."

"Johnnie." The girl's voice made Ethel jump. She was only a few
feet away, waiting for her.

The name rang a distant bell. She sucked in a breath and steadied
herself. "Treat to meet you, Johnnie. I'm Ethel."

The girl didn't seem to care for pleasantries. Her voice slipped
away again "We have to go. They'll be back."

"They?" Ethel kept her arms out and dragged her feet carefully
across the sandy ground. "Who are *they*?"

"I don't know. I don't like them. They're bad."

"What kind of bad?"

"The hurting kind."

"Hurting how? What do they do?" Echoes of the screams she'd
heard earlier hung in the darkness behind her.

"They yell about devils and demons. They make them pray for
forgiveness." The girl's tiny voice sounded eerily unaffected, like she
was merely talking about a strange dream. "They make them scream."

Ethel swallowed hard. *Mary Alice.* "Did one of them look like the
man that locked me up in here? Did they sound like him?"

"I dunno. Maybe. They don't have faces."

Ethel frowned into the dark. "How many of them did you see?"

The girl didn't answer.

"Was there a woman? Did a woman get hurt?"

"Yes."

Ethel fought to keep the quavering out of her voice for the sake
of her little guide. "Didn't they see you?"

"I don't let people see me . . ."

The deadened tone of the girl's voice left Ethel unnerved. Johnnie had stayed alive in the city all by herself for God knows how long, living like a sewer rat from the sounds of it. That sort of life could break a child and twist together a monster; Ethel had seen it happen. The girl could easily stab her right there in the dark, and no one would ever know.

"You must've been scared to death. Why, uh . . . why did you decide to help me?"

"So God will forgive me." Her voice sounded farther away.

"Forgive you for what?"

There was no answer.

"Johnnie?" Ethel found another stone wall with her hand and traced it toward the voice.

"You'll have to climb through." The girl was suddenly beside her, hovering at her waist as though she were somehow inside the wall.

"Through what?" Ethel groped the dusty stone to her right where she'd heard the voice until she felt the edges and flat ledge of an opening in the wall. Another crypt. She felt around for bones and drew in a breath before climbing inside.

The opening was too narrow to crawl on her hands and knees, so Ethel was forced to wriggle into it until her entire body was swallowed by the stones. She inched her way along on her elbows, half expecting Johnnie to smash her head in with a rock, bracing herself for impact. The child was feral and clearly damaged. There was no telling what she might do now that Ethel lay there trapped in the wall.

Her eyes scanned the blackness warily as she went, blind but wide open all the same. A dim light registered far ahead. A shadow crossed in front of her.

"Hurry!" Johnnie hissed into the narrow portal. "Follow the ladder."

"Wait." Ethel wriggled faster until her hands reached the end of the stone slab beneath her and fell six inches onto a dirt floor. She pulled the rest of her body out and found herself in some sort of root cellar not quite tall enough to stand in. The faint light streamed down from a small trapdoor in the ceiling. The shadow of a wooden ladder fell against the stacked stone wall beneath it.

As Ethel's eyes adjusted to the filtered light, her body reappeared out of thin air. Her hands and knees were scraped and bleeding. A thick layer of dust clung to her naked skin. She hugged herself and scanned the tiny cellar for the girl. A tunnel punctured the wall where she'd climbed through. A pile of loose stones sat strewn next to it that matched the others in the wall. Johnnie was nowhere to be seen.

Ethel poked her head up through the trapdoor. "Johnnie?"

It was a basement. She scanned the block walls and wood floor joists stretched over her head. The room was the size of a small tavern. Coal furnace. Empty shelves. Water pipes laced overhead. The dull yellow light streamed down from the top of a slapped-together set of wood planks and stringers that formed the stairs. The realization that she'd just crawled inside someone's house struck her. On instinct, she covered her naked, filthy body with her hands.

"Hello?" she whispered.

Ethel scanned the walls and canning shelves and corners for a wild creature of a girl and saw nothing. *I don't let people see me.* She climbed the rest of the way out of the ground. The house was silent. There were no telltale footsteps or clinks of dishes. Whoever lived there was either gone or asleep. Ethel approached the stairs with her ears perked, waiting for the bark of a dog. Waiting for someone to shout for the police. Waiting for the crack of a gun. A train blew its whistle somewhere in the distance. At the foot of the stairwell, she could see the yellow streetlights streaming in through the window of the door on the landing above. The glass was cracked.

Standing in the light, she glanced down at her naked breasts swinging freely. It wouldn't do at all, not if she was going to go to the police for help. She turned and searched the basement again.

There was nothing but a pile of torn burlap sacks, none of them large enough to cover her. The sting of the cold still fresh in her mind, she tied two sacks over her feet, knotting them the best she could. She wrapped the largest one around her middle and climbed the stairs one creaking tread at a time. A dog barked a block away.

At the top of the landing, she saw the back door had been pried away from its jamb and hung loose in the opening. Gazing into the kitchen left no doubt. The house had been abandoned. A rat rummaged through debris scattered across the wood counter. The window over the sink had been smashed in. She glanced the other direction into the living room. A tattered couch. A torn chair. A scattering of newspapers.

The stink of feces and unwashed sweat registered as she stood there scanning the wreckage. Abandoned houses were rarely empty. Any number of squatters might be holed up in there, blind drunk and hostile.

"Johnnie?" she whispered again, knowing full well she wouldn't get an answer. She bit her lip and debated the futility of trying to locate the child. She could be anywhere, and there wasn't much good she could do for the poor thing even if she found her. Ethel was nothing but a homeless old whore. "Thank you, sweet girl," she whispered, "I won't forget it."

With that, she swung open the broken door and slipped away. Glancing back at the house, Ethel saw the door had been marked. Someone had painted a crooked eight-pointed star on the cracked wood. It looked like it had been painted in blood.

FIND TORSO SLAYER'S
10TH VICTIM IN RIVER

Police Seek Head of Mad Knifer's Prey

Parts of the body of the 10th victim of Cleveland's torso murderer were found cleanly dismembered in the Cuyahoga River today at the W. Third Street Bridge.

—*Cleveland Press*, July 6, 1937, p. 1

CHAPTER 25

April 9, 1999

"Can you describe the prowler?"

"No, I didn't see him," Kris sighed and rubbed her forehead. "I told you. Last night around one thirty. I heard footsteps pacing outside my house. When I woke up this morning, this strange symbol was there."

The uniformed officer the Cleveland police had dispatched didn't seem all that impressed. The name on his shirt read, *Thompson*. The impatient look in his eye told her this would be the least urgent call he'd get all day. "Any broken windows? Any evidence of attempted entry?"

"Well, no. But isn't this harassment?"

"Vandalism's illegal, but it's not exactly a capital offense. We'll fill out a report to make sure your landlord doesn't ding you for the deposit. Besides that . . . there's not much else we can do."

"Are you kidding? What if there's some lunatic serial killer out there?"

The man was busy filling out a form on his clipboard. He didn't even look up. "Do you know how many unsolved homicides are on the books this week? How many stolen cars and physical assaults? I'm sorry for your plight, miss, but the department doesn't have time to follow up on pranks."

"This wasn't a prank!" she yelled in his face. "A dead man is lying in pieces in a morgue! They think it's my father! And now these Internet freaks are stealing police files and harassing me!"

"Well I'm sorry to hear that, but that's a matter for the, uh . . ." He checked his clipboard. "Auglaize County Sheriff's Office. Understand? I don't have the access or jurisdiction to confirm any of that. All we've got here is some paint. I can't go around and arrest every kid with a can of paint."

"What about the website? What about my father? He may have tracked a killer to a spot right over there!" She motioned to the Harmony Press Building. "That building is full of vagrants! Did you know that?"

The officer glanced toward the old factory. "We have an ongoing concern over there. Jill Simon's been cited multiple times for zoning violations and building code violations. They giving you trouble?"

"No . . ." She bit her lip and thought of Jimmy. He'd been nice enough to walk her home the night before. She studied the red star on her door. Jimmy would never have done it. If he'd wanted to scare her or kill her or whatever, he would've done it the night before. She could still feel his warm hand on her face. She gazed up at the dark windows down the street. "But anybody could be in there . . . There's this crazy fortune-teller lady, Madame something. Maybe she did this to scare me. She said a bunch of weird stuff last night about how people are watching me."

The officer seemed to consider for a fleeting second the possibility that she might be in danger. "We can't spare the people right now to go chasing this down, but we'll start a file. If anything else happens, call it in."

"That's it?" Her mouth hung open. He wasn't going to help her.

"Here." He tore the yellow duplicate from his incident report and offered it to her. "Give this to your landlord and have him call that number if he has any questions."

"What am I supposed to do? Just sit here and wait for the crazy person to come back and kill me?" She ripped the piece of paper from his hand, no longer caring if she pissed him off.

"All I can tell you is what we tell every woman in these situations." He leveled his eyes at her to deliver a full shot of contempt at her lack of composure. "And there are hundreds of women in this city right now in worse straits than this. You get me?"

Her rage deflated at his shaming. No doubt there were legions of women in Cleveland stranded in their homes, waiting for a deranged boyfriend or husband or stalker to come back and beat their brains in. "What do you tell them?"

"Vary your routine. If you have another place to stay, go there. Avoid being home alone. Avoid walking in the neighborhood after dark. Keep your eyes and ears open. If he's lurking around here, try to get a look at the guy but keep your distance. That's all you can do."

It was a prison sentence. All her freedoms, all her peace of mind forfeited with just a few words. "For how long?"

The officer just shrugged and shook his head. His eyes sagged like he'd seen too much injustice, too much heartbreak, too much hopelessness to empathize with anyone, let alone some spoiled little white girl.

She glanced down at the scribbled form and then back at the red star bleeding down the front of her door. Lowjack taunted her from the computer screen in her head. *They will never find the killer.* "Thanks for your time, Officer," she muttered softly.

Thompson tipped his hat and shuffled back to his squad car, leaving her standing by herself on the narrow one-way street. He hadn't even taken a picture of it, she realized, staring at the dried drips of paint.

Kris shoved herself back through the door. The notion that she should call Ben passed in and out of her mind as she rifled through the drawers of her desk. She knew exactly what he'd tell her. *Come home, Kritter. Let us help you.* And he'd be right, but she'd be damned if she was going to let some graffiti-painting stalker ruin her life.

She yanked her camera off her desk and checked the film. The clunky Nikon had been a birthday gift from her father, and the memory of him holding it in his hands as he explained the user's manual in irritating detail hovered over her.

She steadied her hand and snapped two pictures—one close-up and one of the entire south face of the little house.

The sound of a car door slamming half a block away made her jump. She brandished her camera at the noise and caught a glimpse of a little old lady hobbling down the sidewalk in front of one of the houses. The camera film advanced with gunfire clicks before she released her finger from the trigger. *I'm going insane!*

Kris dragged herself back into the house. She'd already missed her class. Any more absences and she'd be forced to withdraw. Pete's door stood open and empty at the end of the hall as usual. She couldn't very well ask him to come home and babysit her. He had a life and a girlfriend and would be moving out soon anyway.

She didn't have any other friends.

She didn't have enough money for a hotel.

Back home, Ben and Troy and everyone else would smother her with concern and questions and advice and demands. She could feel Troy's hot breath whispering in her ear, *Let me help you, baby. You don't have to worry about a thing.* It wouldn't be long before he was climbing in through her window in the middle of the night again. The thought made her stomach contract. She'd barely escaped becoming Mrs. Troy Reinhardt the first time around. She couldn't face crying herself to sleep again, worried he'd gotten her pregnant and trapped her there.

A terrible idea skittered through her head. She pulled open the blinds and looked out at the fortress of brick across the road. Jimmy's smile resurfaced in her mind. *If you ever need anything, come find me.*

"That's crazy," she told herself and picked up the phone to call Ben. She didn't know Jimmy. She didn't know Jill the owner or any of the other derelicts holed up inside the old Bible factory. Although a part of her did want to confront the old fortune-teller and find out if she'd put a hex on her house.

The phone rang in her ear, and Kris nearly hung up. If David Hohman or Lowjack or whoever it was that had marked her door knew where she lived in Tremont, they certainly knew where her father lived. Her father's house wouldn't be any safer.

"Auglaize County Sheriff's Office," a woman droned in her ear.

"Yeah. Hi. Is Deputy Weber available?"

"One minute please."

Soft rock strummed in her ear as she sifted through what she should tell him.

His voice cut in before she was ready. "Weber here."

"Uh, hi, Ben."

"Kritter! How you holdin' up, girl?"

"Um. Okay." Her eyes drifted over the police report she'd printed off the chat room on her kitchen table. "Have you . . . found anything new?"

"Nothing definitive just yet. We're still waiting on that DNA. How you feelin'? Given any more thought to signing off? I know it's hard, kiddo, believe me, but the longer we drag this out, the longer it's gonna take to pull yourself together and move on."

"I'm just not . . ." She sucked in a breath. "Ben, have you ever heard of the Torso Killer?"

There was a long pause. "No. Can't say I have. Why you askin'?"

"Did Dad ever say anything about it to you?"

"No."

"Did he ever mention a guy named David Hohman?"

"No. Now lookit, Kris. I don't have time for games. Is there somethin' you want to tell me?"

Now was the time to confess about the business card left at Shirlene's and all the odd things she found. She bit her lip hard, imagining what he'd say. *Now dammit! That's interfering with a police investigation! This is serious business. And you've just been chatting with these sons of bitches? I want you to unplug that damned computer and get your butt home! You hear me?* It's what her father would say. "Uh. No. Everything's fine. I'm just catching up on school work and stuff."

Ben let out a loud stream of air into the receiver. "When you plannin' on coming back?"

"I can't just yet. I have . . . work and school." The work part was a lie, and the school part was quickly crumbling, but the overbearing tone of his voice forced her to dig in her heels.

"I don't think you understand, Kritter. We are dealing with a homicide investigation. The killer is still at large. Now you can either come back here on your own power, or I might just come out there and drag you back myself. I owe your dad at least that much."

Her jaw dropped in protest. Her first instinct was to do whatever he said, but then the rest of her instincts kicked in. And they were furious. "You can't force me to do anything. You're not my father, Ben. I haven't broken the law. You can't just come here and arrest me! I haven't done anything wrong."

His voice softened. "I know this is tough to understand, kiddo, and I know you've been through hell. But it's for you own good. Come home."

"I will. As soon as I can get away. I promise, Ben." She hung up the phone before he could argue with her anymore.

She grabbed a duffle bag from her closet and shoved several changes of clothes inside along with her toothbrush and her camera just in case she actually saw the bastard that marked her door. She grabbed a pen and a scrap of paper and left a note next to the police report on the kitchen table.

Pete, Went home to deal with some stuff. Told the police about the door, and they are investigating. Don't know when I'll be back. Will call soon.—K

As she jotted the words, she realized she wasn't writing them for Pete. She was writing them for the creep who'd marked the door. She was writing them for Ben in case he made good on his promise to try and drag her back to Cridersville.

Outside, Thurman Avenue was empty. The yuppies had gone to work hours earlier. The students were either in class or inside somewhere sleeping it off. The older residents lurked behind yellowed curtains, watching their game shows.

The dark windows of the Harmony Press loomed overhead without the faintest sign of life. She stopped at the giant iron prison bars and gazed into the empty loading dock.

The gate Jimmy had opened for her the night before stood with its rusted chain wrapped tight around the latch. She glanced nervously up the street toward her car, knowing she should just follow Ben's advice and head home. But the thought of her father's empty house and Troy at her window stopped her.

She eyed the gate again. The padlock had been left hanging open.

CHAPTER 26

Kris closed the gate behind her. She carefully wound the chain back around the bars and left the padlock hanging open just in case she changed her mind. She wandered in through the darkness of the loading dock with its brick ceiling towering over her head, eying the row of closed doors for movement, retracing her steps from the night before into a courtyard and up a narrow set of stairs.

It all looked different in the light of day. Dead plants clustered together in pots over a bed of mud and fallen leaves. An antique bicycle leaned up against the wrought iron fence lining the stairwell. She spun herself around to get her bearings.

A fluttering curtain in one of the windows overhead caught her eye.

Up on the second floor, a tiny face peered down from behind a broken pane of glass. Black hair puffed out in a halo around the head of a little girl. Her dark skin looked ashen and sallow. Kris gave her a small wave.

With a nervous glance behind her, the little face disappeared.

"Hey!" she called up after her. She scanned the rest of the windows nervously, but they were all empty. What sort of monster would bring a little girl to a place like this? she wondered. Does her family know she's here?

The door below the little girl's window didn't look familiar. She turned around, trying to find the door Jimmy had used, certain it had been a different one. She bit her lip and debated whether she had the nerve to wander through strange parts of the building alone, not knowing how many drunks and dope fiends were passed out inside. A little voice whispered inside her ear, *What if he's here?*

After a moment's hesitation, she went looking for the little girl.

The entrance opened into a long hallway that led away from the girl's window. Kris scanned the rows of closed doors lining the corridor. At the far end, a narrow window looked out over Thurman Avenue. Around the corner stretched another row of doors.

One was standing open.

Kris glanced over her shoulder at her escape route and took a tentative step forward. A puddle of light collected on the floor of the dark hallway at the foot of the open door. She watched for moving shadows. "Hello?" she whispered.

Footsteps creaked across the ceiling over her head, and she froze as if they could see her. People lived here, she reminded herself. *Little girls, artists, drug dealers . . . serial killers.* The hall went quiet again.

She inched her way forward until her shoulder was at the edge of the doorjamb and she could partly see inside through a dark, narrow foyer the size of a cramped closet into a larger room.

At first glance, it looked like a normal living room. A plastic-covered sofa with an ugly plaid print sat along the wall to her left. There was a flowered chair next to a round end table covered in old newspapers to her right. Kris stepped into the tiny foyer and peeked around the corner. A beer cooler sat propped near the door. The plaster under a broken window on the far wall was bubbled and water-stained shades of brown and yellow. The window looked out into the courtyard with the rusted bicycle.

"Norma? Is that you?" a shriveled voice called through a doorway in the far corner. A shrunken woman hobbled in behind it, wearing a fuzzy orange bathrobe. Her back was hunched into a question mark, and the remaining wiry strands of her hair were set in curlers. She startled at the sight of Kris in her doorway. "What are *you* doing here?"

For a second, Kris saw a flash of recognition in the woman's watery eyes that left her unnerved. Then she realized it was the beggar she'd seen the other night down on Thurman. "Oh, uh . . . sorry," she stammered. "I didn't mean to disturb you."

A pleasant smile spread over the old woman's face, and her eyes drifted until she didn't seem to be looking at Kris but rather through her. "Have you seen Norma?"

"Uh . . . no. I haven't," Kris answered slowly, playing along.

"Why are you here? Where's Norma?" the woman demanded and seemed to be searching the wall behind Kris for the answer.

"Uh—I'm sorry. I'm looking for someone."

"If you're looking for money or drugs, I don't have a thing for you, honey." The woman's voice rattled with phlegm. "Try the others across the way."

"No. I'm not. I was . . ." Kris studied the woman whose eyes flitted around the room but didn't seem to register a thing. Cataracts maybe. A large cat wound its way around the old woman's ankle and mewed at the intruder. "I was looking for a little girl. She lives upstairs. Do you know her?"

"Oh, my. A little girl?" The woman raised her eyebrows in surprise for a moment before they fell as though reminded of something sad. "We haven't had a little girl here in ages . . . What's her name?"

"I don't know. I was worried that she might . . . need help."

"We all need help, don't we?" She seemed to be asking the cat. The woman hobbled to the flowered chair. "I hope you don't mind if I sit. These old bones can't hardly hold me anymore."

"No. That's alright." Kris surveyed the room more closely. It smelled of cat litter and spilled milk mixed with traces of urine and mildew. The old woman was nothing but eighty pounds of sagging skin and brittle bone. Her sunken eyes and gaunt cheeks pulled at the frayed nerves in Kris's chest. The poor thing had probably been surviving on cat food. "Do you want me to call someone for you?"

"Call someone? Like who?" The old woman's lungs rattled with a cough.

Kris grimaced. "I don't know. Social services?"

"Why? So they can take me from my home?" She pointed a gnarled finger at the sofa. "Did that bitch put you up to this? I've lived here for twenty years, dammit. This is my home."

"Wow. That's . . . that's amazing. Did you, uh . . . used to work here?" The math didn't add up, but Kris didn't know what else to say.

The woman hacked again and waved away the question. "You tell Jill I ain't leavin'! Me and her, we had a deal. I ain't goin' anywhere!"

"Okay." Kris nodded and backed her way toward the tiny entryway. "I'll—uh—I'll go see if I can find Norma."

As she turned to head back out the door, she stopped dead in her tracks. An eight-pointed star had been carved into the wood of the innermost door. It looked almost identical to the one that had been painted on hers, only smaller. She blinked at the grapefruit-sized carving for a moment, then turned back to the woman slumped in her chair.

"I'm sorry, but . . ."

"What are you sorry about now?" the old woman rasped.

"Um. Why do you have this star on your door?"

"That? You don't want to know about that." She waved her hand, dismissing the thing and turned away to the window.

Kris took a plaintive step toward the flowered chair. "No. I really do."

"It's just a sign best forgotten. Leave it alone."

"Why? What sort of sign is it?" Kris frowned, staring at the thing.

"The old Mennonites would call it a hex sign . . . not that they'd admit to believing in such things."

"What does it mean?" Kris lowered herself onto the couch, making it clear that she wasn't leaving without an answer.

"Nothing. Everything." The crone laughed a stream of hot phlegmy air. "Just depends on who you ask."

"Did *you* carve that on your door?"

"Hell no. I've got nothing to do with them anymore. I'm old and I'm tired and I don't want to go diggin' up all this."

"But who did then?" Kris pressed, turning the word *hex* over in her mind and eyeing the points of the star. "Is it supposed to be some sort of curse?"

"A curse? You can't go believin' that nonsense. Some fools used to say it keeps the devil away, but from what I seen of the devil, huh . . . good luck to you."

"Mind if I take a picture of it?" Kris stood up and headed toward the duffel bag she'd left on the floor.

"Why on earth would you want to do that?" The way she laughed almost made Kris turn back around, but she was too busy digging out her camera.

Kris lifted the lens and centered the carved star in the frame before answering, "Someone painted one of these on my front door. They painted it in bright red. What the heck do you think that means?"

As she snapped the photo, a hand fell on her arm. The star lurched out of the frame as Kris startled, finding the old woman standing right beside her. The lady looked her dead in the eye, and Kris could see that, for the moment, she was still all there despite the coughing and shuffling routine.

"It means you shouldn't go home."

CHAPTER 27

Kris lurched back from the bony claw on her arm. "I—I'll go see if I can find Norma," she sputtered.

Out in the hallway, she brushed the woman's creepy touch off her arm and shook her words out of her ear. *It means you shouldn't go home.*

"What the hell?" she muttered to herself and then began calling out in an overly loud voice, "Norma?" until she reached the end of the hallway.

She glanced back at the open door behind her, expecting to find it gone, hoping the senile lady and her cat were nothing but an apparition. As though on cue, a shriveled face crowned with pink curlers poked out of the door and into the hall.

"Be careful out there," the woman said in her cracked voice.

Kris stumbled over her own feet. "Uh—thanks . . ."

"It's not curses you should be worrying about, little girl . . . It's the people that are scary. Remember that." The head disappeared back into the bright room. Her orange cat escaped out into the hallway and mewed plaintively at Kris.

Sorry, kitty, she thought to herself, turning the corner at a brisk pace. *You're on your own.*

Closed doors lined the hallway, and there was no telling how many crazy folks were living behind them. Kris slipped past each one, holding her breath. Her instincts told her to march straight out of there and call social services. Or the police. Little old women shouldn't be left to eat cat food in an abandoned building like homeless squatters. Little girls shouldn't be trapped with the rats.

Footsteps creaked on the floorboards behind her. Kris spun around, expecting to see the little old lady hobbling up with a knife in her hand, but there was no one there. A cold chill swept past her, sending goose bumps up her arms.

"I gotta get the hell out of here," she muttered and promised herself that she'd call proper authorities the minute she got out. It wasn't safe to go storming around the abandoned building on a crusade to find a little girl. Or her father. Not with crazy people and God knew who else waiting behind closed doors.

Kris retraced her steps back out into the courtyard. The window from where the little girl had waved down to her stood empty. She gazed up at it, half wondering whether she'd even seen the girl at all. Ten other windows looked down into the open space between the brick walls. Two broken sashes hung open on the upper floors, letting fresh air and sunlight and any number of odd creatures inside.

Eyeing the windows with growing certainty that someone was watching her, Kris tripped over a dead potted plant. She stumbled back and nearly fell into an open hole in the brick floor of the courtyard. "Jesus!" she breathed, regaining her feet. A round manhole cover had been lifted up and pushed aside. She peered down into the two-foot-wide opening and saw the rungs of a ladder leading down.

"It's an old access point." A woman's voice came up behind her.

Kris stumbled back from it in surprise. "Oh, God!"

"Sorry. I didn't mean to scare you." The woman gave her an appraising look before reaching down and dragging the manhole cover back into place. "Be glad you didn't fall in. It's a twelve-foot drop down into the old cisterns. I should've had it filled in years ago. I keep putting the cover back down, but they keep lifting it up."

She wore coveralls, a tool belt, and a frown. She looked to be in her mid-fifties from the weathered creases of her face and the gray in her cropped hair. She straightened herself up and extended a work glove. "I'm Jill. Who the hell are you?"

The name sent a jolt of anxiety through her. Jill owned the old Bible factory, and Kris was trespassing. She straightened herself and shook her gloved hand. The woman looked strong enough to beat her ass twice. "I'm Kris. I was just . . . looking for someone. I'm sorry. I should've—"

"You a photographer?" She motioned to the camera still hanging from her neck.

"Not really." Kris lifted it off her ribs self-consciously. "I guess I'd like to be. It just doesn't seem practical . . . my father thinks I won't be able to get a job . . ." She bit her lips together to make them stop flapping.

"Getting a job is overrated." Jill waved a hand in mild disgust, then grabbed a heavy piece of metalwork leaning against the brick wall behind her. "So what are you doin' in here? You lookin' for somebody?" The iron railing dropped down onto the top of her work boot, and Jill waited for her to say something.

The name *Norma* ran through her head as all her other thoughts seemed to scatter for cover. "Um . . ."

"Don't know anyone named Um. But who knows? This place is full of characters, maybe I just haven't met 'im yet." She shook her head as if to say, *Junkies,* and picked up her hunk of metal.

Jill had walked halfway across the courtyard when a name finally came to Kris. "Jimmy. I'm sorry, I'm looking for Jimmy."

Jill didn't bother to stop. She just called over her shoulder, "Top of the stairs to the left . . . and please tell your friend Jimmy to keep his dealin' out on the streets, okay? I don't need more trouble with the police. I swear I got half a mind to just clear these bums out . . ."

"But I'm not g—" The slam of a door cut off her words. The owner was gone.

Kris crouched down and picked up her duffle bag where she'd dropped it by the manhole cover. She paused to look down at the heavy metal plate. *I keep putting the cover back down, but they keep lifting it up,* she said. *They . . .*

She hauled her bag back onto her shoulder and hurried out of the courtyard without looking up.

Once she found the right stairwell, the rest was easy to remember. She headed down a hallway she recognized and through an open doorway into Jimmy's place. The stale smell of full ashtrays and spilled beer hung in the air. The couches lining the two walls sat empty and dejected. Sunlight streamed in through the huge window overhead. Motes of dust and ash shimmered under the glass, making the whole room feel like a sunken ship under ten feet of water.

"Jimmy?" Her voice bounced off the high ceiling and into the second-floor gallery. The giant speakers sat silent at the far end. Empty beer cans rattled across the floorboards as she crept inside.

She climbed up the stairs toward the bedroom where they had all gathered by candlelight to hear Madame Whatshername spin her bullshit. Wood spindle coffee tables overflowed with food wrappers and refuse. The stale air buzzed with silence.

"Jimmy?"

No one answered. Somewhere outside, a heavy truck rumbled down the street. It screeched to a stop and started beeping as it backed up into some tight spot. Kris wandered down the hallway toward the séance room. From what she'd seen the night before, it was also Jimmy's bedroom.

The door was closed.

Kris's stomach tightened as she debated whether to knock. The damn truck outside kept braying. *Beep. Beep. Beep.* If he was still asleep, he might be furious at being woken up. Or worse. He might pull her down into bed with him.

Beep. Beep.

She should just find a couch and wait for him to wake up, she told herself. She should just sit and get her head together. Too much had happened for her to keep straight. Somewhere outside, a crazy person was leaving her hex signs and stealing police reports. At that moment, Ben might be speeding down the highway, hell-bent on finding her and dragging her home. Somewhere inside the building, a little girl and a senile old woman were sitting and waiting for something or someone to come, and her father was nowhere to be found.

The beeping outside stopped. The truck outside cranked back into gear and roared down the road.

Kris grabbed the doorknob and cracked open the door. "Jimmy?" she whispered. "Are you there?"

He didn't answer.

She gave the door a couple of knocks. "Anybody home?"

He clearly wasn't, but she stood there listening for several more seconds before pushing the door open. The room lost all its mystery in the dull light filtering in through the cheap Indian batik prints hanging over his windows. The dark purple walls that had pulsed heat by the glow of the candles showed garish cracks and pockmarks in the light of day.

The quotes about altars and sacrifices standing out amid the hippie drivel looked even creepier than they had the night before. *For the life of the flesh is in the blood . . .*

She surveyed the room for pentagrams and upside-down crosses. A cheap statue of a praying Buddha sat in the corner, holding a cone of half-burnt incense. A low coffee table by the bedside was covered in red and purple candle-wax drippings of five or six melted votives.

The entire room smelled like him. Incense and sandalwood and smoke. She glanced back at the odd testimonials scrawled across his wall. *It is the blood that makes atonement.*

Atonement for what?

Kris stepped back out into the hall and listened to the silence. At least she hadn't woken him up, she reasoned, shifting uncomfortably on her feet. She set her bag down next to his door and stretched. It could be hours until he was back.

Down the hall another door stood open. She puzzled at it for a moment. Jimmy hadn't said anything about a roommate, but then again, they hadn't really talked much about anything besides ghosts and her father. She hardly knew a thing about him, and here she was snooping through his home.

A door slammed a floor below where she stood, making her jump. She stumbled back down the hall, tripping over a beanbag chair and landing on her ass with a thud.

"Hey! Who's up there?" Jimmy's voice boomed. Footsteps pounded furiously up the stairs toward her.

She scrambled back to her feet, eyes darting, but there was nowhere to go. "Uh. Hi." She gave him a little wave as he reached the top of the stairs.

He lowered his fist and raised his eyebrows in surprise. "Oh. Hey."

"I'm sorry, I just . . . let myself in." She took a step back, positioning herself in front of her duffle bag, wondering if coming there had been a terrible idea. "I—uh—ran into Jill, you know, the owner. She said you'd be here."

"Hey. No problem. I told you you're welcome anytime." He gave her a slow grin.

She felt herself smiling back. His light brown eyes were too soft and sweet to be a rapist's or a killer's, she told herself. "I guess I just had to see all this in the daylight . . . um, did you know that there's a decrepit old woman living in the next wing?"

"You met her? Isn't she a trip?" He picked an unopened beer up off the nearest coffee table and offered it to her "Hair of the dog?"

"Oh. No, thanks."

He gave her an almost-shrug and cracked the beer for himself. He plopped down onto a couch and patted the seat next to him.

She took a chair by the stairs instead. "Doesn't, uh, anyone worry? A little old lady living all by herself *here*? I mean, her window's broken. Her apartment reeks of mold and cat urine. Does anyone check on her?"

"I think she's got a friend or two."

"Who? Norma? Have you ever actually seen this person or anyone else visit her?"

"I figure people have a right to live their lives. Don't they? She seem unhappy to you?"

"Well, no. But she didn't seem exactly right in the head either."

"You a doctor?" He cocked an eyebrow at her, amused.

"Okay, no. Fine. But what about the little girl that lives above her?"

"What about her?"

"Well, is she alright? Where are her parents? Did somebody bring her here, like, against her will?"

"Wow. You don't even know the girl, and you're just ready to swoop in and save the world, huh?" He chuckled and took a long swig of beer.

"No . . . I don't know." She shifted in her chair uncomfortably. Here she came to ask for a favor and now she was lecturing him. "Don't you worry about the other people here?"

He took another long drink of beer and considered her a moment. "Yeah. I guess I do. But I'm sure as shit *not* gonna run to the cops or child services. That's sometimes the worst thing you can do to somebody you're trying to 'help.'"

"What do you mean?"

"Take Old Girl in her flowered apartment. Where's she gonna go? She's got no money. She's got no family. You ever seen a state-run nursing home before? You ever see what they do to old ladies like her? Strap 'em to their beds. Dope 'em up when they start cryin'. Maybe she's better off here where she's happy."

Kris frowned, trying to weigh whether or not he was right. The old lady could fall and break a hip. *What then?* she wanted to ask. "What about the little girl?"

"Don't know much about her yet, but I've seen her in here with a lady that looks to be her mom, and her mom's beat up pretty good. I'm guessing the dad could be the problem."

"How do you know?"

"Because the two of them are hidin' out here from *somebody*, right? Do you know the first thing a cop'll do?"

Kris shook her head.

"The cops will arrest Mom for kidnapping and return the little girl back to her lovin' daddy. You think that's the best thing for her?"

"You don't know that. They might . . ."

"Might what? Put her in a foster home while her mama serves time? You ever been in a group home?"

Kris shook her head.

"This is the reason you should mind your own business. How you gonna help people when you don't even know what the real problem is? How can you know if your solution will be any better?"

"But . . ." She shook her head, not ready to concede. "They can't stay here forever, can they? They need food and running water. The little girl needs to go to school."

"Hey. I get it. Your heart's in the right place, but don't worry so much. Nobody stays here long. I'm guessin' Mom's just getting a plan together. She'll go stay with family somewhere else. Hopefully somewhere out of state." He downed the beer and leaned in to take a closer look at her. "I know you didn't come here to spy for social services."

She dropped her eyes and shook her head.

"So why are you back?"

Kris bit the inside of her cheek, debating what to tell him. "Something happened. Last night."

The smile pulling at the corners of his mouth dropped. "What happened?"

"I heard someone walking outside my house in the middle of the night. When I got up this morning, they'd left me a message." She studied his face as she talked. *Was it you? Was it your fortune-teller friend?*

"What'd it say?"

"It didn't say anything. It was just this giant star." His eyes betrayed nothing but concern as the story came spilling out. "They painted it on my door in red. The old lady over there has one on her door too. She says it's a hex sign or something, whatever the hell *that* means. I called the cops, and they didn't do a thing about it. They filled out a report and told me to 'vary' my 'routine.'"

He nodded. "They're not going to do shit about it. Not until it's too late anyway."

"What do you mean 'too late'?" She couldn't help but think of the black-and-white photos of hacked-up bodies in her father's books.

"Cops are there to *solve* crimes, not prevent 'em. It's kinda stupid really when you think about it. So what are you gonna do?"

Kris shook her head. "I don't know."

"You're welcome to stay here." Jimmy offered a half smile. "Got plenty of room."

"Oh. That's really nice, but . . . I wouldn't want to be in your way." Her eyes circled the giant two-story gallery. There were enough couches for ten people to sleep comfortably, but that wasn't the point. It was a big favor to ask. A favor she couldn't repay with anything but . . .

"Hey. Mi casa, su casa." He reached over and patted her knee like it was settled. "It'll be fun having a roommate again. This place can sort of get to you after a while."

"Yeah. I'm sure it can." This was her last chance to leave gracefully. She would just get into her car and go back home to Cridersville and Troy and the cavernous void left by her missing father.

"So why do you think somebody marked your door like that?" he prodded gently.

"I don't know. I thought for a minute it might've been your friend the fortune-teller," she admitted. "You know, trying to scare me into getting a reading or something. Or putting some sort of spell on the house. It *is* called a 'hex sign,' right?"

"Mimi?" He shot her a look that said she was nuts. "Nah, man. She wouldn't do somethin' like that. Not for free anyway. I'm tellin' you, she's cool."

"Well, then I don't know." Kris studied Jimmy's face again, debating how much she could tell him without really sounding like a crazy person. "Have you, um . . . have you ever heard of the Torso Killer?"

"Sure." Jimmy's eyes seemed to darken ever so slightly. "It's Cleveland's most famous criminal. All those people getting cut up like that? And they never found the guy."

"Right." Kris drew in a breath. "So my father had all these books about it in his room. And then there's this chat room where people steal police reports and trade their conspiracy theories about the killer. It's like some kind of sick obsession with these people."

Jimmy's brows knit themselves into a frown. "I wouldn't call wanting to solve a murder a 'sick obsession.' Not to the folks that lost somebody."

"Okay. Fine. Sure. But I'm talking about the people obsessed with the killer, like he's a celebrity or something." She backpedaled, a little surprised at his reaction. "It's just . . . Some guy went looking for my dad right before he disappeared, and he left a bogus business card with torsokillers.com written on it. You know the website?"

"Yeah, you could say that." Jimmy replied slowly and studied his hands. "Mimi says there's a connection between this building and the killer. So of course I've poked around online."

Kris paused to digest this revelation.

"Your dad's still missing, huh?" He looked over at her with sympathy.

"Yeah." She dropped her eyes to the floor, not wanting him to see the pain in them, not wanting his pity. "So I went looking for this David Hohman in the chat room. Someone started asking questions about . . . what happened. Then David or some other psycho stole the police report . . . And he threw it up there for all the other psychos to see. It wasn't just my dad's information either. My name was listed too."

"Wow. So you think that's how the guy that marked your door found you?" He bent his head, looking physically pained for her.

"Maybe. I don't know. Mimi said someone was watching me. I mean, if you're gonna believe what she says. God only knows who goes to those websites."

Jimmy ran a hand over his face. "Mostly its families of the missing and history buffs, but . . . I suppose there could be lurkers out there."

"Lurkers?"

"People watching and reading and . . . shit, I don't know."

"Why the hell would anyone want to do that?" She gaped at him, too frustrated to think, then blurted out, "I mean some sick bastard reads that my father might be dead and decides to come and harass me?"

The words *might be dead* weren't lost on Jimmy, she could tell, but he didn't dwell on it. "Could be just some bored asshole preying on somebody like you for kicks."

Kris put her head in her hands. "I just . . . I don't understand what any of this has to do with my dad. He never talked about this murder stuff. I'd never even heard of the Torso Killer until two days ago. All I know is that someone's dead. Someone was hacked to pieces just like in those awful pictures, and they think it's him . . ." Dashed red lines cutting through the police schematic of a human body still lurked on a web server somewhere. Legs and arms segmented into hunks of meat. And the words kept spilling out of her. "He got mixed up in this murder case somehow. He had the books. He was at the archives . . . What if someone decided to resurrect the infamous Torso Killer? What if he decided to copy one of his crimes? They do that, right? Killers copycat all the time, don't they?"

"I guess so." He put his hands on her shoulders as if to brace her. His face had creased into a deep frown. "But the Torso Killer isn't like Jack the Ripper or Jeffrey Dahmer."

Kris wiped her face and stiffened until his hands fell away. "Why not? I mean, he's a serial killer. He has all these demented fans. What if my father stumbled into that chat room . . . or somewhere else and saw something he wasn't supposed to? What if he had something on this Hohman guy?" Kris shook her head, not wanting to believe the wild theory that had been percolating in her head ever since she'd logged in to the website. Her father's best friend was a cop. Surely he would've told Ben if he had some evidence of a crime, but Ben didn't seem to know a thing about it. Besides, if she was right—

"No, I don't think you understand." Jimmy cut through her yammering thoughts. "You need to show me this thing they left on your door. You need to show Mimi."

Kris rolled her eyes. The fortune-teller gave her the creeps, and she wasn't entirely convinced the old lady hadn't painted the thing just to freak her out. "I don't know. I mean, I know she's your friend but . . . Don't you have to believe in fortune-telling or whatever for it to work?"

"Hey, you don't have to believe in the power of that weird star, but somebody else out there does, right? Don't you want to know what they think it means?"

"What makes you think Mimi will know?"

"Trust me. She knows things. Weird symbols are her business."

"Sure. She knows how to tell people what they want to hear. For a nice price."

Jimmy stopped and leveled his eyes at her. "She's not gonna charge you, alright? She's a friend. Besides . . . I'm pretty sure you're not gonna want to hear what she's got to say."

SEARCH RIVER FOR PARTS OF TORSO VICTIM

Dr. Gerber Refuses to Permit W.R.U. Experts to Check Gruesome Find

As detectives searched vainly today for additional portions of Cleveland's latest torso murder victim, they pondered whether the mad butcher who has baffled them for four years is the owner of a stream-lined, expensive car that stopped on the Jefferson Street Bridge the night of March 3.

—*Cleveland Press*, April 9, 1938, p. 1

CHAPTER 28

April 7, 1938

Thankfully, it was the middle of the night and the street was empty. Ethel picked her way across littered lawns until she hit pavement. She glanced up and down the road and saw she was at the corner of a larger brick street and an alley. The giant shadow of the Harmony Mission loomed behind her. The windows were all dark. Inside, the sisters were sleeping soundly, no doubt comforted knowing that their dear Hattie and Mary Alice were paying penance to their god.

Ethel darted up the narrow alley, clutching the torn burlap sack to her chest, searching for a clothesline. Freezing air bit at her bare skin. One tiny house after another flew past. Fences lined the street. She peeked over them all, searching for laundry. A dog pounced up at her from behind its gate, barking like a fiend.

"Shut up!" she hissed at it and kept running. A light flipped on in a window behind her. On the next block up ahead, sets of linen sheets hung in the dark. It was a laundry house, she realized, and her heart leapt. She pressed her bare back to the side of an old stone church and waited in the shadow there for several moments before streaking across a larger street toward the specters of pale fabric fluttering in the cold night air. She would have to act fast. There would surely be a dog out guarding a whole day's work.

Ethel reached over the chest-high fence and snatched the first linen she could reach. The dog on the other side wasted no time sounding the alarm. It slammed itself into the wood slats at top speed, snarling and snapping. Ethel reeled back on her heels with the bedsheet in her hand. The racket echoed up and down the alley. Lights snapped on in the windows.

Clutching the sheet around her naked shoulders, Ethel took off running for the river. Down an empty brick street, she dashed between the houses. Voices shouted in the distance behind her, but the dog had gone quiet. How far would they chase her for one measly sheet? she wondered, crossing West 5th Street and flying down the hill into the scrub brush.

Once she'd crossed West 3rd Street, she knew she was safe. Nobody respectable dared cross over into the wastelands down by the river known as the hobo jungles. She wrapped the sheet tighter around herself and picked her way in her burlap socks between the broken bottles and strewn garbage.

Makeshift huts of corrugated tin and slapped-together cardboard dotted the ridge. Some contained families clinging to each other by the thinnest of threads, but most were home to drunken derelicts. She didn't know a soul down there, and she was worse off than usual. No clothes. No shoes. Freezing wind. The white sheet around her shone like a beacon in the shadows around the river. It was only a matter of time.

"Are you an angel?" a gruff voice slurred behind her.

She turned to see a shortish man lumbering toward her. He was missing all but two of his front teeth. An unnatural gleam lit up his eyes, a light that said his mind had come completely unsprung. Ethel breathed a sigh of relief that he was alone.

"I sure am, sugar." She flashed him a winning smile. "Have you seen God?"

He let out an unnerving giggle. "Every day. You wanna see 'im too?"

"Oh, I do, baby." She threw him a wink. The smell of him accosted her from three paces away. It was the worst thing about her work. The smell. "You got a place around here? I'm feeling so cold."

Sparks flew from his eyes. He'd clearly been prepared to drag her into the bushes, but this was much better. "I got a place. You wanna see it?"

"I sure do. It's been so long since I've seen a real man like you. Can you make a fire, sweetie?" she cooed, wide-eyed. "I don't know how."

He wrapped an arm around her and squeezed her hard enough to break a rib. "I like fire," he breathed. His breath could peel paint. The reek of body sweat, rotgut, and a rotting tooth almost made her faint.

"Will you hold my hand," she purred into his ear. "I've just been so lonely for a real man like you."

Befuddled surprise, anger, pride, and finally shame played across his face as he released his grip. For a moment, she panicked he might just strangle her to death right there for letting those ghosts out of his bag. He managed to stuff them back in again and grabbed her wrist.

"Thanks, darlin'," she murmured, letting him drag her toward his hovel somewhere in the long grass. He was surprisingly strong for his size. She scanned the area while he pulled her along. Across the river, the city lights twinkled yellow and blue. Gratitude swelled inside her that she could still see after hours of blindness, but it was quickly eclipsed by a familiar fear. There was no sign of any roving gangs, but from the tint of the sky, it was still early. She'd have to work fast. "What's your name?" she asked her captor.

"We don't have names down here," he growled back.

She wanted to argue that point but thought better of it. The last thing she needed was to antagonize the man. "What would you like me to call you, sugar?"

He stopped and gave her a broken grin. "You can call me Papa."
Typical. "Oh, I like Papa. Can I ask you a question?"

"You can try." He chuckled and then yanked her down a narrow
pathway toward the water. Ten shanties were lined up along the river.
The breath caught in her throat as she wondered how many belonged
to friends of his.

She waited until he'd led her to a pile of tin and corrugated sheet
metal. It was the third from the right. He pulled her through the open
end facing the water. Under the roof sat a broken chair and a pile of
dirty laundry cobbled together into a sort of bed. The rags smelled
just as terrible as he did, but she let him push her down onto them.
"Do you know a guy named Slow Tony?" she asked.

Slow Tony was an Armenian pimp and supplier of all manner
of illegal thrills. He was rumored to have killed twenty men and was
somewhat of a legend on the West Side. She'd met him sitting with
Eddie in some tavern, back before they found Eddie headless down
in the Run. Slow Tony had offered her some unappetizing work.

"Nope." He took off his coat and eyed the tops of her tits, swelling
out over the edge of the bedsheet.

"Papa, honey." She let the linen fall ever so slightly. "I'm so cold.
Can you make us a fire?"

The words seemed to cast some sort of spell over him. His
unhinged eyes clouded for a moment. He gave her a small nod and
scooted himself a foot outside the roof and began to gather up the
kindling and scraps from his last fire. A can of industrial lubricant
sat on the ground next to him. He threw a few drops on the wood
and then threw a gulp of it down his throat. He offered the can to her.

"Oh, I shouldn't, Papa." As bad as she wanted a drink—bad
enough that her skin itched—she knew better than to try it. The bums
called it white lightning, the industrial juice they'd throw back when
even rotgut cost too much. She'd heard it made some of them mad

and turned others blind. She gave him a shy smile and wondered how many more drinks he could take before he went black. Large rocks lined the makeshift hearth. She could use one if need be.

While "Papa" struck a match, Ethel listened. The other shacks lining the river were quiet. Odds were good they were mostly empty and kept up by one or two bums to make it look like there were more of them. Ever since the Mad Butcher started taking heads and cops started their raids, the tramps had thinned out.

It might be best to wait until morning, she decided. She liked her odds with "Papa" a hell of a lot better than with a gang of toughs or the cold. He at least seemed somewhat controllable. As her brain debated the places she'd go in the morning, "Papa" sidled back up to her. He was still holding the can of lubricant in his hand.

She held her hands out to the fire and made a show of warming up. "Thanks, Papa. That's real nice."

He threw back another gulp of madness. "What . . . why did it brings you . . . these parts?"

"I got lost looking for my daddy." She played along with his sick little fantasy while racking her brain for other folks she knew on the west side of the river. If she was going to get the cops to listen, she needed clothes. She'd met a few working girls from that side of town, but none stuck out in her memory. She couldn't help but wonder how many of them were dead now. The black-and-white images of Flo's severed arms and legs flashed in her head, sending Ethel's gaze darting up and down the river.

"Lucky you found me. Did you—urp—did you know there's a killer? A killer out there huntin' all us."

Ethel clutched her sheet and made her eyes go wide like a little girl's. "A killer?"

Her tits all pushed up like that distracted him. "Why—ah—you so naked?"

"Someone took my clothes and shoes and left me here." She eyed the hazy drunk and wondered if he'd ever actually seen the killer. "Her name was Flo Polillo. Do you know her?"

A warped recognition lit up his eyes again as the words she'd said slowly processed. "Sounds like . . . a whore."

Terrified he might figure her for one as well, she rushed to say, "I thought she'd give me some help and then . . ." Fat tears rolled down her cheeks on command. "She robbed me."

"Fuckin' . . . whore." His words mashed together in his rotting mouth. "I can . . . new clothes . . . there's a guy. Pervert under the bridge."

She picked his words out of the slurred mess. "You can find me new clothes?"

He nodded and took another big drink. His eyelids went heavy and the crazed light grew dim. Like so many other drunks she'd known, this one suffered mostly from loneliness and craved a friend more than a whore. Being a friend was easier.

She wrapped an arm around him. "There's a man under the bridge?"

"Likes him the girlie . . . shoes and clothes."

"Papa, which bridge has the clothes?" She let her sheet fall to expose more of her breasts to keep him from passing out.

He turned toward her tits. A thin line of drool hung from his bottom lip. "Huh?"

"Which bridge?" She lifted his drooping chin with her finger.

"Lorain to Carn—egie," he drooled. "He hides up . . . under there. Mean som' bitch too . . . sold me some panties. Pretty . . . pretty pink panties . . ."

The empty windows of his eyes told her he'd gone to a full black-out. Ethel laid his head down into her lap and kept talking. "That's real nice, Papa." She ran her fingertips through his greasy, snarled hair, petting him like a child. "You're such a big man, Papa. Such a good man. Thank you."

Ten minutes of cooing and stroking his back and "Papa" was out. Ethel breathed a sigh of relief. If experience were any guide in the jungle, he'd be out for the better part of the next day. She laid his head down onto his pile of rags and eased herself away from him and his smell. The fire was warm. She hiked her stolen sheet up over her shoulders and watched the city lights dance off the brown water of the Cuyahoga.

It wasn't much of a river anymore—the human waste of the hobo jungle mixed with the industrial chemicals of the factories lining the river flats and the blood of the slaughterhouses to the north. Thankfully, the hard chill in the air was enough to keep the stink down.

She glanced downstream toward the Lorain-Carnegie Bridge where they'd found Rose's corroded bones in a burlap sack. All she could do was wait until morning.

CHAPTER 29

The sound of voices woke Ethel before dawn. She sat up and listened, scarcely daring to breathe. If a gang came to toss the camp, she'd be trapped. Her hands felt the dirt floor of the shanty for something sharp. There was nothing but a tin fork and that half-empty can of white lightning. "Papa" kept on snoring in his dead stupor. She was on her own.

"What'd he say?" one of the voices asked. She guessed it was about a hundred paces to her right. A low splash sent ripples down the river.

"Who cares?" Another splash disturbed the water. "It's twenty dollars. Shit, I'd kill *you* for ten."

"Do you think it was . . . you know?" The first voice rattled with whiskey and fear.

"Who? The scary headhunter? Nah. Probably it was a wop hit. What's it matter?"

"You see his face?" Another splash.

"Course I saw it." The other man laughed. "He gave me the money, didn't he?"

"What'd he look like?"

"I don't know. He sort of had a funny look about 'im. He said, 'Bless you, son,' when I took the sacks from 'im. 'Bless you.' How you like that?" This revelation was followed by another splash.

Ethel clamped her mouth shut with her hand.

"How'd he know we wouldn't just go to the cops? There's that reward for anyone that finds the killer."

"The cops would sooner hang the two of us as give us a listen. He said, 'If I were you, I'd throw these into the river and disappear, but the choice is yours.' You wanna go roll the dice with the cops? You wanna explain how we came to have a bunch of burlap sacks of chopped meat? You think they wouldn't hang us for the whole lot?"

"Nope. Just askin'."

"Well quit runnin' your yap and help me." There was one last splash.

"He threw a little somethin' extra in. When was the last time you had some honest-to-God whiskey?" There was a prolonged silence. "Ah. That's the stuff. Here."

"That the good shit from over the lake?" the other voice asked.

"Whooeee! That's the juice, boy."

"Shut your trap. You wanna fight off the bums? C'mon . . ."

Their voices drifted back up the hill.

Ethel bolted up and stared into the dark after them, debating whether to follow the two drunks and demand to know who had given them those sacks. She had no doubt what sort of meat they were holding. The screams she'd heard through the floor drain rang through her head. But she locked them away.

It wouldn't do any good to find the bastards, she decided, picking her way toward the water. They'd be blind drunk in no time and liable to slit her throat or worse. The hobo jungles were full of vagabonds like them, willing to do anything for a bottle of decent whiskey, let alone twenty dollars. None of them were ever sober enough to remember much of anything. A killer could give them whatever he pleased.

The riverbank sat silent. The black water slipped past the shore, carrying its secrets along with the filth of the world. There was no sign of the burlap sacks anywhere.

The sun finally rose above the factory smokestacks. Back in Papa's shanty, the embers of the fire were slowly dying. Ethel pulled the twine belt from the snoring drunk's pants and secured her stolen bedsheet into a makeshift dress. Papa snorted and rolled over.

She found her way up the hill toward the spot she'd last heard the voices of the two men. Behind her, the river ran the sludge and sewage out into Lake Erie, indifferent as the sky over her head.

Working her way up to the street, she saw a pair of depressions in the tall grass. She made her way over to them to find two men lying facedown a few feet apart. It wasn't that odd of a sight. Nearly all the inhabitants of the shantytown were sleeping it off at that hour. She approached the men slowly, not wanting to rouse them, but as she stepped closer, a queer feeling twisted her gut. They weren't lying right. She stopped at the misaligned feet of the closest one and knelt down. The air reeked of urine and feces. A brown bottle locked in the other man's hand had spilled out onto the ground. The feeling that something was wrong tightened its springs until she realized what it was.

They weren't breathing.

Frost covered their backs and the scraggly hairs on their heads. She lurched up and scanned the surrounding hillside. It was empty. She surveyed the ground for the weapon that had done them both in, but there was nothing. No blood. She circled the bodies until one of their faces appeared through the long grass. His blue eyes bulged out at the road. His mouth hung open over a pool of drying vomit. She glanced again at the bottle still lodged in the other one's hand, and it wasn't hard to guess what had happened. From the tattered clothing and unshaved faces of the men, she could see what the police would see. A couple of bums had drunk themselves into a stupor and frozen to death. It happened every day in the jungles. No one would know that a killer had given them the bottle. No one but her.

Ethel stood there and debated what to do about it. It was bad luck to be found with a dead body. At best, she could count on being taken into police custody for at least a week. At worst, they'd send her back to the workhouse. She gazed down at their bloated faces and couldn't muster a single emotion but disgust. *This is the price of doing a killer's dirty work,* she thought to herself. She eyed the pockets of the two dead men, thinking of that twenty dollars, wondering what price she'd pay one day.

She worried over the two dead bodies the whole way to the Lorain-Carnegie Bridge. It sat a mile to the north along the twisting river. She climbed up the ridge to West 3rd Street and headed toward it, weighing her options. The detective that ruined her life had instructed her to call if she had any information about the murders. But what information did she really have? She hadn't seen the killer. She'd only heard screams, which could be attributed to anything. Johnnie was just a deranged child living underground. The girl might've been lying or distorting what she'd seen and heard, and odds were good Ethel would never find her again. She didn't even know what Johnnie looked like.

Her makeshift dress dragged on the ground as she walked. The burlap rags on her feet were black with dirt. She smelled of hobo and had a criminal record for solicitation and manslaughter. No one would listen to the likes of her. She'd been raped and beaten more times than she cared to remember and had never filed a single police report in her life. *What good would it do?*

The photographs the detective had shoved under her chin flashed in front of her. A nameless, dismembered girl lying in pieces on the slab. Eddie's tattooed boy. Then Flo Polillo's hacked-up arms and legs. *You could be next.*

"Jesus, I need a drink," she muttered to herself. The taverns wouldn't open until eleven.

Over her shoulder, the Harmony Mission sat five blocks away. Brother Wenger would have discovered her escape by now, she figured. He'd be wondering how she had managed it. Maybe he'd decide God had set her free or that the devil had swallowed her whole, but she doubted it. He would eventually come looking for her. Maybe he'd bring her a nice bottle of whiskey to keep her quiet too.

The Lorain-Carnegie Bridge rose high above the river, high enough to kill a person if they ever decided to jump. It flew over the industrial wastelands and shantytowns below, connecting downtown Cleveland to Ohio City, separating the city above from the city below. At the base of the bridge, under the abutments, she found him.

"What in the world is a beautiful thing like you doing in a place like this, sweetheart?" he asked in a lilting drawl to match the long dress he was wearing. He was perched on top of the enormous abutment, high-heeled feet dangling over the gravel pits. "Come to see my view?"

"Hi," Ethel breathed, winded from climbing up the steep hill to his little home. She stood up on the concrete platform under the enormous steel girders of the bridge and gazed out over half of Cleveland. The frost had already melted as the temperature climbed mercifully above freezing. "It's impressive."

"Isn't it?" He looked up at her expectantly. He was an enormous man with dark Mediterranean skin and even darker eyes. It was a wonder he'd found a dress to fit him.

"Yeah, but I came here to see *you*, honey. A friend of mine said you might have some clothes."

"Oh, really?" He crossed his legs coyly and eyed her bedsheet dress. "Who's your friend?"

Ethel forced a wry grin. "Papa? You know him?"

The man twittered. "I've known a lot of Papas."

She didn't doubt it. Up under the bridge bearings between the steel trusses, over fifty women's shoes were set in a line. She could only guess how he'd collected them. "Well, do you think we could make some sort of trade?"

"It don't look like you have much to bargain with, sugar. And hate to tell you, but you're not my type." He flashed her the gold tooth set in the corner of his grin. "You got any money?"

"Will this do?" she asked and pulled out the twenty dollars she'd taken from the dead man's pocket.

The man's eyes grew wide. They were almost pretty the way he'd lined them with coal, but the shadow of a beard ruined the effect. "That'll do nicely. What can I help you with?"

"Dress, coat, shoes, makeup, and a hairbrush."

"Done, darling."

"And I'll need ten back."

His smile twitched at the corners.

Ethel shrugged. "A girl's gotta eat."

"Ain't that the truth, honey." The man pursed his lips and calculated the numbers in his head. "Five back, and I'll give you your pick of the litter. I'll even throw in a pair of leather gloves."

"Eight."

"Seven."

"Fine." Ethel held out her hand and they shook on it. His hand was the size of a dinner plate—a fact that he tried to hide with gaudy bracelets.

"So." He looked over her shoulder as she perused his three trunks of ladies' undergarments and frocks. "What brings you up here, sugar?"

"Let's just say I made the wrong friends." Ethel picked out a new slip and a dress and began trying on shoes.

"Haven't we all?"

"What's your name?"

"People call me Rickey, like the drink." He didn't bother asking Ethel hers.

"Say, Rickey." She turned to him. "You like to sit up here and watch the city, right?"

"Oh, I do."

"Have you seen anything strange lately?" She scanned the banks leading down to the river, wondering where they'd found Rose. "Anything you wouldn't want to tell the police?"

"As if I'd ever speak to those boys about a damn thing. They just love me." He rolled his eyes in disdain. "They come to arrest me every time they find one of those poor girls or lost boys all cut up. Haven't caught me yet. Seems they think us perverts are the same thing as killers."

She gazed up at his olive skin painted with rouge. "I think they're wrong."

"Of course they're wrong. I wouldn't hurt a fly . . . unless that fly was seriously messin' with me, and I sure as hell wouldn't be littering the town with body parts for people to find."

Ethel nodded. She'd seen plenty of street fights end in blood, but no pimp or hustler would take the time to cut up the body the way Flo had been cut. They'd just dump it in a swamp.

"But still they come lookin' for me 'cause I'm the devil in a dress. Now, you wouldn't believe how many of those police boys come down here lookin' for a little gin Rickey after it gets dark, but no one wants to talk about that."

"Do you know who the killer might be?"

"I might know somethin'."

Ethel stopped browsing shoes. "Who is he?"

"It isn't a he, sweetheart. It's a them."

CHAPTER 30

"State your name."

"Ethel Ann Hoffman." It wasn't her real name, but the Ethel part was true enough.

"What would you like to report?" The clerk behind the window hardly looked up from her notepad, which was a good thing. Even with the new dress and secondhand shoes she'd bought off the pervert, she looked a fright. Her hair was an unwashed mess, and the dirt of Brother Wenger's dungeon had found its way under her fingernails and into the callouses of her elbows and knees.

"I have information on the Torso Killer," Ethel announced, half expecting the room to go still with anticipation.

No one even batted an eye. The intake room at the Second District sat half-full of drunks waiting to file their own reports. The clerk didn't look up; she just repeated the question. "What would you like to report?"

It wasn't the reception she'd been hoping for, but she lowered her voice anyway. "I saw two men dumping burlap sacks into the Cuyahoga last night."

"And?"

"They were talking about some other fella that had given them the sacks full of meat and paid 'em a bottle of whiskey for their trouble." She kept the payment of twenty dollars to herself. "This morning both of them fellas were dead."

"So you're reporting a homicide." It wasn't a question. The clerk's pen just kept moving. "Where did you spot the bodies?"

"Shantytown near the West 3rd Street Bridge."

This made the clerk raise her eyebrows at least. Ethel had heard through the local taverns that one of the Torso victims had been found near that exact spot. "Take a seat. I'll see if we can free up somebody."

"Wait." Ethel stopped the glass window from closing. "I have an important message for the detective. The one investigating the Mad Butcher."

The clerk lifted her tired eyes to the window. "You and everybody else, toots."

"There isn't just one Torso Killer."

The clerk didn't seem impressed. "Is that all?"

Ethel searched her brain for anything else useful Rickey had told her under the bridge. "Some of the bodies were meant to be found— they were set up on a stage for all to see. The others were different. And there were more, maybe hundreds, that will never be found." She repeated the man's cryptic words, laying each one out for the clerk to write down, trying not to think of the girl she'd heard screaming through the floor drain. *Mary Alice.*

"Do you have information regarding other victims?" The clerk's pen kept moving, but she didn't look up.

Ethel had asked the man in high heels the same thing. *No, I don't and I seriously doubt anyone ever will. That's the joy of killing hobos and whores, honey. Nobody ever misses us. We're strangers even to each other.*

For a fleeting moment, she'd wondered if she was talking with the killer himself. He just laughed and waved a limp hand. *If those police boys weren't so obsessed with naked bodies and dirty, deviant sex, they wouldn't be lookin' at me.* When pressed, he went on to say, *You know perverts just as well as I do, sugar. They like what they like. They don't vary their routine. Not like this so-called Butcher. If a man wants to see you kill a chicken, you better kill it for him the same way every time, am I right? This Butcher swaps women for boys, boys for men, then back to women. And old women too. It makes no sense. These killings aren't about sex or perverts like little ol' me . . .*

"Do you know of other victims?" the clerk repeated, clearly losing patience.

"No." Ethel decided to keep Rickey's colorful remarks to herself. She could tell the woman on the other side of the glass didn't believe a thing she'd said. "But I heard some things. Tell the detectives to check below the Harmony Mission. There are rooms, hidden rooms down there. I heard a woman screaming."

"You mean the place where they print the Bibles?" The clerk finally looked up at Ethel with withering eyes. Apparently, she hadn't heard *this* today.

"Yes." Ethel ignored her. "They've got a hundred women holed up in there, women without families, and there are rooms below the basement. I was there. I saw them."

"Uh-huh."

Ethel squinted through the glass at the clerk scribbling down words in tightly packed lines, cursing herself that she couldn't read any of it. For all she knew, the woman was writing out a detailed description of the old whore at her window so the cops could arrest her and throw her into an insane asylum.

When the pen stopped moving, the clerk muttered, "Take a seat. I'll see who I can find," and closed the window.

It was Ethel's cue to leave. She'd done her bit filing the report, now it was the cops' turn to do theirs. Odds were good they would spend more time investigating her than her claims, and she'd be damned if she was going to spend the next three days in lockup or send another pack of detectives to bother Rickey. She could only hope the right man got the message.

The rumble in her stomach echoed the dryness of her throat. Down West 25th Street, taverns were just setting out their signboards. She staggered over to McGinty's and pushed her way through the door.

It was always midnight inside. The windows had been blackened with paint, only letting slivers of cloudy light into the smoky bar. She pulled up a stool.

"Jesus, Amber." Mags behind the bar slapped a worn hand on the counter. "What the hell happened to you? You look like you've been taken out wet. You want the usual?"

She nodded and let her shoulders slump into the bar.

"You got cash this time?" The grizzled barmaid arched an eyebrow. In Ethel's miserable days on Rowdy Row, she and Mags had reached an understanding. Mags would let her work the room as long as she had cash.

Ethel tossed two dollars onto the counter.

Mags slipped the bills into her register and filled up a glass with cheap wine, then barked, "Bangers and mash" through the narrow window to the kitchen in the back.

Ethel downed the drink in one go. Within a few seconds, warmth returned to her hands and feet, and the knots tying her up loosened. She tapped the counter and Mags refilled the glass.

Once the second glass was half-drunk, she could begin to contemplate what she'd do next. The situation felt all too familiar. No money. No home. No options. Her best bet would be to clean herself up in McGinty's washroom and go out looking for a paying man. She downed the wine and surveyed the room. Half the time she could find one right there. At the moment, there was nothing but drunks and men dead below the waist, but it was still early.

"Mags?"

"Yeah?" The barmaid glanced up from the sink. From the worried look in the crone's eye, Ethel could tell she was looking rough, and looking rough guaranteed that she'd only catch the worst sort of paying man. The sort that wouldn't pay much for even the most despicable sort of thing. Her age kept her from the best money, but she hadn't fallen to the bottom just yet.

"Can I use the washroom?"

"Help yourself."

The sight of herself in the bathroom mirror knocked Ethel back. The shape she was in, she'd be lucky to catch a railroad tramp. There were cuts on her knees and the palms of her hands. Dirt and dried blood were smeared across her hairline. She locked the door and stripped off her dress only to see bruises on her arms and back from where Wenger had thrown her down. She scrubbed the grime from her elbows and face and shook the dirt out of her hair. She wiped her teeth with the inside fabric of the dress and doused herself with the cheap perfume Mags kept handy for the working girls.

Even with all her efforts, odds were good she'd be sleeping under the bridge with the pervert that night.

Back at the bar, more of the stools had filled up with the lunchtime crowd. A pack of union organizers sat at the round table in the back with steins of beer. Steelworkers from the foundry and longshoremen from the loading docks bellied up to the bar. After years in the game, Ethel could guess which of the men were faithfully married and which of them liked whores. An off-duty policeman nursed a beer in the back of the room, but even in plain clothes, he was easy to spot.

Ethel sidled up next to a man wearing a clean suit and reached for another glass of wine. She could tell by his hands and the cut of his jaw he worked in one of the factories. Maybe a foreman. "Excuse me," she murmured and flashed him a smile.

He grunted and turned back to his friend.

Not one to give up that easily, she slid back onto her stool and waited for another opening.

". . . and the son of a bitch turned me down. Can you believe that? I been banking there for fifteen years and can't get a Goddamned loan."

"You can't trust the Jews, Hansel. I keep telling you this," his friend answered in a thick accent. Maybe Russian. "They are driving this country into the ground! They won't stop until we're all in the poorhouse. It's part of their plan, you know. That's how they took over Russia. Starved the people, ran them out of business until they were like dogs willing to obey. You think the stock market crash was an accident?"

"I don't know, Karl. You just work all your life, right? And what've you got to show for it?" Hansel downed his beer in one angry swig. "It's Goddamn criminal is what it is."

"Criminal is exactly right. Hitler saw this and he arrested them. Finally, some justice in this world."

"I don't know about all that." Hansel shook his head and tapped the bar for another beer.

"You just wait," Karl pressed. "Wait until those dregs down by the river rise up and start burning our houses and killing our children and then tell me Hitler was wrong. I saw what happened when the Bolsheviks started rioting. I was there. That labor strike was just the beginning. An entire army is just sitting down there in camps, waiting for their orders. The poor are organizing against us. And what are we doing? We are sitting here drinking beer and waiting for them to come and slit our throats!"

Karl slipped a folded pamphlet across the counter toward his hesitant friend. A drawing of the devil danced through a six-pointed Star of David. Ethel frowned at the jumble of letters shouting along the top, *Beware the 12 Signs of the Jewish Revolution!* She couldn't read them, but she recognized the devil and the Jewish star.

Hansel studied the cover and shot his friend a frown.

"Be careful where you read that," Karl warned. "And lock the doors or else you might be tempted to go out and shoot every last Jew you see. Keep your eyes open, my friend. The revolution is coming, and it will start along the river."

Ethel stared into her wine, seeing the murky brown waters of the Cuyahoga at the bottom of her glass. The sound of heavy burlap sacks being tossed into the depths by two bumbling drunks was still fresh in her ears. The idea that those two idiots were the seeds of a revolution was utterly laughable. They'd been too stupid to suspect the free hooch they'd been given by a killer might be laced.

Out of the corner of her eye, she saw Hansel stuff the bedeviled leaflet into his pocket. His hateful friend was right about one thing. The shantytowns along the rivers were drowning in misery. No one down in the jungles trusted the politicians, the landlords, the bosses, or the police to save them. Not from their poverty or the slashing knife of the Mad Butcher.

Ethel studied the two angry men downing their beers, and Rickey's gold tooth gleamed at her from the corner of her mind. *It isn't a he, sweetheart. It's a them.*

EIGHTH CITY TORSO VICTIM IDENTIFIED

East Side Woman Traced by Bridgework in Skeleton

... As Cleveland detectives worked for a clew which might direct them to Cleveland's latest torso death, Detective Peter Merylo yesterday disclosed that the bridgework of a woman's skeleton found under the Lorain-Carnegie Bridge in June, 1937, the eighth torso victim, had been positively identified as that of Mrs. Rose Wallace, 40, of 2027 Scoville Avenue S. E.

—*Cleveland Plain Dealer*, April 11, 1938, p. 5

CHAPTER 31

April 9, 1999

Kris, Jimmy, and Madame Mimi all stood on Thurman Avenue, studying the bizarre eight-pointed star painted on Kris's front door. A light rain drizzled down as they stood there in the cold April morning.

"Have you ever seen one of these before?" Madame Mimi turned her bloodshot eyes to Kris. They looked stoned and it wasn't even noon. "Growing up maybe?"

Kris puzzled at it for a minute. "I don't know. Maybe . . . ?" Then the image came to her—lying in bed, tracing the stitching in her blanket with her finger, feeling the tiny holes for loose threads, pulling one apart so she could feel the batting underneath. "I had a quilt with stars like that. They were like flowers in all different colors. My grandma made it, I think."

Madame Mimi nodded. "It was your father's mother."

Kris frowned. She hated parlor tricks. "Yeah. It was."

"She was German?"

"Pennsylvania Dutch. My dad said something once about going to visit the old country someday. I think my great-grandparents were from Austria."

Madame Mimi studied Kris's dark hair and amber eyes. "But your mother wasn't. What was she? Greek? Italian?"

"I'm not sure." Kris shifted her weight nervously. "I don't see what that has to do with anything."

Madame Mimi's eyes shifted from Kris to Jimmy and then back to the door. "Let's go inside."

Kris unlocked the door and let them both in. There was no sign that Pete had been back. The police report sat in the same spot on the kitchen counter. The dirty dishes were still in the sink. If Madame Mimi had been anyone else, Kris would've been embarrassed.

"Where's the basement?" Mimi asked.

"Uh . . . over here." Kris led them both behind the kitchen to the back door and the door to the stairs.

"Have you checked this?" Jimmy tapped the back door.

Kris shook her head.

"Let's take a look." He unhooked the security chain and dead bolt and forced the door open. The overgrown backyard was a postage stamp that backed into the patio of Edison's Pub. Another red star dripped down the back door—two squares superimposed and shifted forty-five degrees. Kris lifted the camera hanging from her neck and snapped another picture.

Mimi studied the star for a moment, then shut the back door and opened the slimmer one on the opposite wall that led down to the basement. A damp, earthy smell greeted them as they headed down the rickety wooden staircase and into the wreckage of old house parts her slumlord was keeping for a rainy day. The floor joists hung between the rough stone walls were so low they had to duck.

Madame Mimi batted away the strings of cobwebs as she made her way around the broken stove at the foot of the steps and across the dirt floor between the boxes to the nearest wooden support post. She grabbed it with her left hand and closed her eyes.

Kris shot Jimmy a glance.

He held up a finger that told her to wait.

The basement reeked of mildew and old age. Boxes and wood crates were stacked together under at least ten years of dust, utterly forgotten. They were probably full of the cast-off baby pictures and photo albums of whatever sad, lonely person had lived there thirty years ago.

Mimi's voice broke the silence. "One of them died here."

"One of who?" Kris whispered, but Jimmy grabbed her arm and shook his head.

"They killed some of them in these houses." Mimi continued as though talking to herself. "It was an open house. Open and empty. The mark was on the door . . . it lured them in."

Kris shot Jimmy another look, but he didn't notice. His eyes circled the floorboards overhead. A dark stain spread out over the underside of the planks not far from where Mimi stood. It darkened the wood with radiating lines where liquid had pooled and dried. It collected in the joints between the boards and ran to the lowest point in the floor. The marks stretched out across an area over five feet in diameter, far too large to be a pet stain.

A large dog could've done it, Kris argued with herself. Revulsion crept into her gut as she counted the number of times she'd sat on the kitchen floor in that exact same spot, talking on the phone, twirling the springy cord between her fingers. It never smelled of urine. The dark crust between the floorboards tinged the wood black and purple.

"It was the gypsies they wanted. The nonbelievers. The sinners," Mimi continued. "The next day they came back with buckets to wash the wood."

For a fleeting moment, Kris could see how the water would have dripped down between the boards. She could hear the brushes shushing back and forth.

The old stoned woman opened her eyes. She put a hand on a locked trunk sitting on the ground. "There was more than one. This place isn't safe. We should go . . . Kris?" She turned to her. "Don't leave the gun here."

Kris's mouth fell open to protest, but Madame Mimi was already heading up the stairs. Logical explanations fired off in her head. The old bat had broken into her house. She was probably the one who'd marked up her doors in the first place. And stolen her father's photograph from her room.

When she reached the kitchen, she shot a glance through the living room and saw the shotgun lying out plain as day on the floor next to her bed for all to see. It didn't take a psychic to figure out that the gun was hers.

"You got a permit for that?" Jimmy asked, waving toward it.

"Not exactly." She flushed and scurried down the hall to snatch it up off the floor. Didn't she leave it under the bed? she wondered, shoving it back into its felt sleeve. "It's my dad's. He's a hunter and has a bunch of them, and he thought . . ."

"He thought his sweet little girl could use some protection in the big, bad city." Jimmy nodded and she couldn't tell if he agreed with her dad or thought she'd been spawned by rednecks.

"I had to humor him." She shrugged apologetically and stuffed the gun into her old softball bag.

"You know how to use it?" Jimmy raised an eyebrow at her.

"Well . . . yeah."

"Good. Let's get out of here." Jimmy pulled her toward the front door. Madame Mimi was already outside, looking up and down Thurman Avenue.

"Wait." Kris stopped in the open door. "I still don't understand any of this. You're saying somebody was killed in here?"

"Is that so hard to believe?" Jimmy laughed and pulled her through the door and onto the curb. "You saw the stain. I mean, look around you, this neighborhood wasn't always this nice."

"Yeah but . . ." The boarded-up hardware store stood on the corner, looking like a crack den. The entire conversation was giving her the willies. She strained to focus as the cold rain dotted her face. "I don't mean to be crass, but don't people die all the time? It's an old house. An old lady could've just keeled over. It might've taken weeks for someone to find her. That would've left a big mess, right? It could happen to anybody."

Madame Mimi just stared at her with those stoned eyes until Kris was convinced she'd just put a curse on herself for speaking the awful words out loud.

"I mean, God forbid." Kris knocked on the wood frame around the door to undo the jinx.

Mimi cracked a smile. "Don't worry about saying the wrong thing. It doesn't work that way."

"I still don't understand what the heck this star is supposed to mean or why someone would put it on my door."

"The octogram has been used for centuries," Madame Mimi explained and pulled the door shut. "It was used by the pagans, then the Christians to demark different things. Rebirth, renewal, some considered it a hex sign and a shield against the devil . . . most famously it was a symbol of baptism."

"So what are you saying? Someone wants to baptize me?" Kris was fairly certain it had been done already, back when she was small. Not that she'd remember. Her father kept a Bible in the house, but they never really discussed it.

"No. The person that left this doesn't understand the Bible or history enough to understand the ritual of baptism. The practice started centuries before Jesus when the Jews would immerse themselves in water to cleanse their souls before praying. No. The person that left this was thinking of the first baptism discussed in the Christian Bible. Do you know the story?"

"Uh . . . no. I didn't really go to Sunday school." Her father had avoided church altogether. *God and I have an understanding,* he'd say.

"John the Baptist cleansed Jesus of his sins in the River Jordan. John sought to rid all the Jews of their sins by baptizing them in preparation for the coming kingdom of heaven."

"Okay?" *This is ridiculous.* Kris shook her head and locked the vandalized door. "What in the world is the 'coming kingdom of heaven'?"

"The end of the world." Madame Mimi smiled as if this explained everything.

"So?"

"Do you know what happened to John the Baptist?"

"What the hell is this? Religious *Jeopardy*?" Kris threw up her hands. "No, okay? I don't know what happened to John the Baptist."

It was Jimmy who answered. He nodded at Mimi like he'd just found a missing piece to a puzzle. "They cut off his head."

CHAPTER 32

"So what are you saying? Someone wants to cut off *my* head?"

"I'm not saying nothin'." Jimmy held up his hands and shot Mimi a look. "But every single one of the Torso Killer's victims had their head cut clean off."

The stolen police schematic Lowjack had posted online had shown the victim's neck cut in a broken red line and his head crossed out. Kris felt an uncontrollable rage rising up in her chest. "So whoever did this is trying to intimidate me with a biblical threat? Announce the second coming of the holy Torso Killer? *What?*"

"We should get off the street." Madame Mimi pulled Kris gently by the arm. "Whoever did this is sending a message . . . and not just to you."

Kris hauled the softball bag stuffed with her father's shotgun all the way back to Jimmy's apartment in silence, trying to process every horrifically ridiculous thing she'd heard. A person had died in her house. That was the only part that seemed clear. Whether the poor sap had just keeled over watching *Wheel of Fortune* or had been hacked up and memorialized in the Torso Killer hall of fame was a question she didn't even want to entertain.

Back in Jimmy's apartment, Madame Mimi climbed the steps and went directly down the hall, past Jimmy's bedroom, and through the next open door, with Kris and Jimmy trailing behind.

At the doorway, he stopped and turned to her. "I should probably tell you that . . ." He hesitated as though picking his words with care. "We've been trying to map how the Torso Killer is connected to this building and the Harmony Mission ever since Mimi felt it. It's sort of a hobby . . . like the séances. I just don't want you to be . . . freaked out."

Frowning, Kris peeked over his shoulder into the room. Black-and-white photographs of severed body parts were taped to the walls. Names and dates were written under each one. A map of Cleveland dotted with colored thumbtacks hung next to a broken window.

"Are you fucking kidding me?" she whispered, stepping into the room despite herself. It looked like the serial killer's crime lab in a Hollywood slasher movie. Her horrified eyes fell to Jimmy and she took a step back. *Liar.* "What the . . ."

He held up his hands in self-defense. "Hey. It's not what you think. We're not 'murder groupies,' alright? We're here for the victims."

Mimi's back hovered near a grainy photograph of a chewed-up section of an arm and a leg. The writing on the wall labeled it *July 6, 1937, John Doe VII, Dismembered Body Pulled Out of the River, Head Never Found.*

"It might have been him," Mimi murmured. "He was a hobo. He rode the rails in from somewhere near . . . St. Louis, looking for work. He could've seen the mark and thought he'd found an open safe house."

"A what?" Kris snapped. Her thoughts were spinning too fast to have patience with Mimi's bullshit.

"Hobos left signs. Little pictographs for each other. Get bread here. Talk about Jesus for a free meal there. That sort of thing. Safe houses were empty spots where they could bed down for the night.

Hex signs mean different things to different people. It might've been a sign of welcome."

"So you're saying that . . ." The black-and-white severed body parts were hard to imagine as a living, breathing man. "That guy there slept in my house?"

"Maybe." Mimi stood for another minute, then shook her head. She moved past the photo to another one—a photograph of blackened bones. A photograph of a woman's face was taped next to them. "No. It was a woman."

Kris rolled her eyes. "And you think this Torso Killer came in and killed her."

"That's assuming there was just one of them," Jimmy said. He walked over to the photograph of the woman. The name Rose Wallace was written on the wall below it. "If you look at the forensics—or what passed for forensics back then—the odds are good there was more than one killer."

Kris turned to him, his earlier words buzzing in her ear. *The Torso Killer isn't like Jack the Ripper or Jeffrey Dahmer.*

He pointed to the pictures on the far wall. "See Victims 1 and 2? They were decapitated, emasculated, and left out in the middle of Kingsbury Run, right on the edge of a shantytown for those poor folks to find. That's a totally different MO than Victims 7 through 12, who were hacked up into pieces and hidden or thrown in the river."

Her frowning eyes darted from one set of photographs to the next.

"There are inconsistencies all over the place. The cut marks on Victim 10 are totally different than most of the others. The knife work on Victim 6 points to two different styles of cutting, and detectives initially suspected an apprentice was involved. Why were some burnt? Why were some preserved?"

The way he talked made it seem like a game. Kris tilted her head, sickened. Mimi's head rested on the wall next to the photograph of Rose Wallace. Eyes closed. The fever dream kept going.

"Why was Victim 11 embalmed? Did the city's best suspect, the deranged Dr. Francis Sweeney, exact a revenge on Eliot Ness for kidnapping him and holding him prisoner in a hotel for questioning? Ness kept him for days, trying to extract a confession. Victims 11 and 12 were left under Ness's office window a few months after they let Sweeney go and might've been stolen from a funeral home just to mess with the guy . . . How could all these belong to just one killer? These are the questions that have been buggin' investigators for years . . ."

The words blurred together as Kris scanned the photographs again, trying to see what he saw, trying to find a way out. Coroners' reports were plastered below some of the photographs. She focused on one to keep the room from spinning. "How did you get these? I thought the reports were lost."

Jimmy turned to her with a frown. "What?"

"I went down to the county archives, and most of the coroner's files are missing. The *Cleveland Press* archives have been scattered too. Someone even walked off with the microfilm."

"It must've been fairly recent." Jimmy's eyes circled his macabre collection. "I got copies of some of those files just last year."

"But why would someone take them?" It was just one of the questions that had been plaguing her ever since she left the library, and the suspicion it had something to do with her father twisted in her stomach.

"I dunno. It could be some asshole with no respect for public records. Some collector or tourist." Jimmy turned back to Rose Wallace and looked at her with heavy-lidded eyes. "Or maybe it's deliberate. Maybe somebody's trying to destroy what little evidence of the killer we have left."

"But that makes no sense. There are books and books on the subject," Kris protested.

"Books aren't the same as police reports and the coroner's files. Details are selected and edited by the writers. Important details that might make a difference if the case is reopened are now missing."

"But I thought the case was closed years ago."

"There's no statute of limitations on murder. Maybe someone is trying to make sure they never open it back up again. Maybe someone got too close to the truth."

Dad. Her voice drifted as she pictured her father hunched over the records in the archives. "But it was so many years ago. Why would someone go to all that trouble to hide evidence?"

Madame Mimi lifted her heavy eyes from the photograph of Rose and leveled them at Kris. "Because the killings never stopped."

"What?" Kris shook her head, but the photographs of severed body parts Ben had tried so hard to hide from her eyes back in Cridersville would've fit in perfectly with the ones lining Jimmy's walls. The red dotted lines cut through ankles, knees, hips, elbows, and wrists. "No. It has to be a copycat. Right? There's no way . . ."

"No. She's right." Jimmy pointed to his collection. "Thirteen official victims were attributed to the Torso Killer, but this all happened before the national crime database. Cities didn't share information on homicides. Dismembered bodies turned up all over—in Pennsylvania, in New York, shit, in other parts of Ohio—and nobody put them together. Detective Peter Merylo was assigned to the case in the 1930s and he tried. From what I've read, his death count went up to over fifty."

Kris shook her head. "But don't serial killers travel around? This isn't the first time a killer has struck in other places, right?" She forced herself to do the math. The Torso Killer would have to be at least eighty years old by now. *That's assuming there's just one of them.*

Mimi went back to studying the photos of poor Rose, oblivious to them both.

Jimmy kept going. "But the victims keep turning up. There were three bodies found in the '40s in Pennsylvania. All naked. All decapitated and dismembered. One of them had the word *Nazi* carved into his chest." Jimmy pointed to a photograph on the far wall. "In 1950 a headless body was found in a steelyard in town. There were several more in the '60s and '70s . . . and that's just the bodies that were found."

"But." Kris waved a hand at the photos. "If the serial killer's still around, wouldn't they have found him by now? He'd be an old man!"

"Exactly." Jimmy announced like he'd just won his case. "It isn't a 'him,' it's a 'them.' Did you know there are over ten thousand murders in this country every year and over a third go unsolved? Police just don't have the manpower or the budgets to solve them, especially when the killing is random."

Kris's head began to reel as she struggled to figure out whether Jimmy was crazy or right.

"See, the most common way to solve a murder is by identifying the victim. Once the victim is known, they look for suspects among their family and associates. We're usually lucky enough to get killed by people we know. That's why the Torso Killers were so successful. Shit, that's why Jack the Ripper was so successful. These guys didn't know their victims, and better yet, they chose victims that nobody would miss."

Jimmy looked up again at the picture of Rose Wallace with inexplicable remorse. Kris puzzled at him a moment. "Did you know her or something?"

"No. But she doesn't fit. She was the only black victim, you know."

Mimi woke from her trance and looked over at him. "It wasn't her fault, Jimmy. You have to forgive her."

"Forgive her for what?" Kris demanded sharply. She felt herself coming unhinged.

"For getting killed, of course." Mimi admonished Kris with her eyes. "Rose would've been a better mother to Jimmy's grandmother if she'd lived."

"So you're related to her?" Kris stared at Rose's smiling face, searching for a family resemblance. They both had the same light brown skin and similar African features, but her eyes weren't as pretty. Below her smile, a photograph of two police detectives in hats pointed to a spot under a bridge.

Jimmy just shrugged. "Can't really prove it. Birth records were real sketchy back then, especially for the homeless."

Mimi patted Jimmy's shoulder like he was her own son and went back to mooning over the cut-off body parts of Victim 9. Suddenly, it all made sense. Jimmy's obsession with both the murders and the crazy fortune-teller must've started the minute Madame Mimi convinced him he was the great-grandson of one of the victims. *Jesus, this is sick.* Her suspicions that Mimi was the one who'd painted a star on her door deepened.

"So who do you think *they*—these killers—are?" Kris demanded, refusing to get sucked into the fortune-teller's lies. "And what the hell does any of this have to do with the graffiti on my door?"

Mimi sat down in the middle of the floor and pulled a large scrapbook out of her crocheted handbag. It was a collection of tattoo designs, both hand drawn and photographed. She glanced up at the confusion on Kris's face and simply said, "Understanding tattoos is critical in my line of work. When someone walks in for a reading covered in marks, you'll find the answers to their questions are written all over them. Now . . . do you recognize any of these?"

She flipped through page after page of images. Crosses, Celtic symbols, ankhs.

"Yeah. Sure."

"What about these?" Mimi flipped the page to a collection of swastikas.

"Of course. Nazis."

"After what Hitler did, we all came to hate the bent cross. It's a shame really. Do you know what it meant for centuries before he stole it?"

Kris shook her head, wanting to storm out of the room but sitting down anyway.

"To the ancient Hindus, it meant good fortune and well-being. These days, our Nazis have to be clever to hide their hate from the rest of the world. They use numbers and secret symbols. Like here." She flipped another page. "'88' stands for 'HH' or 'Heil Hitler.'"

"Do people really wear these?" Kris frowned at the black numbers tattooed across a skinhead's neck. "You know, outside of prison?"

"The Aryan Brotherhood and the KKK have more associates and supporters than you might think."

Kris glanced up at Jimmy standing over them. His face registered no emotion. Tattooed evidence of racial hatred didn't seem to shock him at all.

Mimi turned another page to show an eight-pointed star with a swastika ghosted over the top. "They've hidden their mark in all sorts of other symbols."

Kris drew in a breath. "Wait. I thought you said the star on my door stood for baptisms or beheadings or something."

"It does. The Nazis were praying for a rebirth or baptism of their nation. Religion and Hitler go hand in hand."

Kris was losing patience fast, but Mimi didn't seem to give a damn.

"Hitler removed all the parts of the German Bible that included the Jews, except how they killed Jesus of course, and he aligned the faith to his cause. He told his followers they were on a mission from God to defeat the devil. Hell and the devil were real things to these people, and the Jews were the devil's minions here on earth. It would be Christian to help the heathens find Jesus, even if that meant killing them. And more importantly, ethnic cleansing was imperative to saving the souls of their countrymen."

Kris just gaped at her.

"Don't be so surprised. Horrible things have been carried out in the name of the church."

"So what are you saying? That some Nazi left that star on my door?"

"Maybe." Mimi sighed and gathered her thoughts. "The octogram has been used by Nazi groups in the past. They loved mixing religion with old-world superstition and fear, and they twisted people's faith to justify a genocide. It's easier to cut someone up or kill them in a gas chamber if you convince yourself that you're doing God's work. People like to believe they're fighting a noble battle against evil."

Mimi turned to another collection of drawings, and a tattoo design jumped off the page. Kris recoiled in surprise. It was a red letter *L*.

"You recognize this one." Mimi decided, gauging her reaction. "Your father had one of these."

Kris didn't answer. She grabbed the book off Mimi's lap and flipped to another page. More red *L*s appeared, some surrounded by wreaths, some flanked by wings. "What the hell is this?" she breathed.

"The Silver Shirt Legion was an American Nazi movement in the 1930s. They were quite active in Cleveland around the time of the Torso Killings." Mimi flipped another page covered in photographs of raised branding scars all showing the letter *L*. "They considered themselves the cultural and social elite. Titans of industry and science. They had nothing but contempt for the poor uneducated masses huddled together in the shanties across the country. They were convinced the Jews would lead the destitute in a Communist uprising.

They were also convinced President Roosevelt was a puppet for Communists."

"What?" Kris tore her eyes off the pictures. The history lesson just careened off the rails into crazy town.

"Try to remember, after the stock market crashed in 1929, the country was in shambles. Labor unions were going on strike every other week and gaining strength. The Russians had just suffered through their own Communist revolution where the rich were either driven from their homes or killed. Many feared that the world as they knew it was coming to an end. Many in the Russian aristocracy and military fled to America. Several even landed here in Cleveland and joined the Legion."

A black-and-white photograph of a naked, headless corpse with the word *Nazi* carved into the chest hovered on the far wall. The Z was backward. Kris stared at it a minute, then turned to Jimmy. "So you think they were the Torso Killers? That they started killing poor people and dumping their bodies?"

"I don't know for sure. Maybe."

"But why? For what?" Kris protested, her eyes circling the collection of severed arms and legs pasted up all around her.

"To scare people to death. To stop the poor from organizing. To drive the homeless hordes out of Cleveland. Eliot Ness burned the hobo jungles to the ground in the name of catching the killer." Jimmy paused a moment, then shrugged. "And who knows? Maybe they just liked killing them."

"I need a minute," Kris whispered and shoved Madame Mimi's tattoo book off her lap. "Where's the bathroom?"

"Out the door and down the hall." Jimmy pointed her in the right direction and then fell into a hushed discussion with Madame Mimi.

Kris's head felt like it was floating somewhere above her body as she wandered out of Jimmy's room, down the steps, and out into the

THE UNCLAIMED VICTIM

245

hallway. The sun streamed in through the high windows overhead, leaving long streaks of light and shadow on the opposite wall.

The air force tattoo on her father's shoulder had been etched on top of a raised scar. The skin was bumpy and at the same time smooth. She used to trace the raised skin under the ink when she'd sit on his lap. *What happened, Daddy?* He'd kiss the top of her head and pull the sleeve of his shirt back down. *Oh, Daddy had an accident when he was young.* She frowned at this. She was only five or six years old at the time but was smart enough to know he was hiding something. *Did it hurt?* He shook his head. *It was a long time ago. It doesn't hurt anymore.*

It didn't look like an accident.

She could tell he didn't like talking about it but couldn't stop herself from asking, *Why does it look like a letter* L? He'd smiled at her, but it was a sad sort of smile. He tussled her hair and said, L *is for love, sweetie. It reminds me how much I love you.* She pulled up his shirt and looked at it again and frowned. He had drawn an army tattoo on top of his love. Like he was trying to hide it.

Now she knew what it stood for. *Legion.*

Kris splashed cold water on her face and looked at herself in the clouded mirror. Her skin had always been a shade darker than her father's. Her hazel eyes were a far cry from his light blue. Mimi was right. Her mother wasn't German or Austrian or particularly Aryan at all. She sifted through all the family photographs in her head. Her mother's parents had died in a house fire before Kris was born. Their wedding picture had sat on her mother's dresser. They both had thick black hair. Her grandmother's hair was curly.

There were no pictures of her father's parents. Kris had only seen them once or twice in her entire life. They moved to Florida when she was a baby and never came to visit. Whenever she asked about them, her father would explain how expensive it was to travel, and change the subject. When her grandfather died of a heart attack, her father went alone to the funeral while Kris stayed home with a neighbor. She'd been too young to think anything of it. Her grandmother had died of cancer her senior year of high school. This time her father offered to take her down with him to her burial, but she could tell he didn't want her to come. There weren't any aunts or uncles or cousins to meet, and her grandmother was a stranger. The woman never even sent her birthday cards. The quilt on her bed had been her father's only memento of his childhood.

All the suspicions she'd harbored in the back of her mind about her grandparents no longer seemed ridiculous. They didn't like her. They didn't like her mother. Her father always managed to explain away their permanent absence, making her feel silly and childish for wondering, but maybe she'd been right all along.

The last time she'd seen her father's parents was at her mother's funeral. They didn't speak to anyone, not that she could remember. They sat together in the corner with thin-lipped frowns and rigid backs. There was no purse candy or hugs or smiles for their grand-daughter. As Kris pictured them in her mind's eye, she could imagine angry, red *L*s cut into both of their shoulders.

Kris took off running down the hall. She rounded the corner into Jimmy's bedroom and grabbed her bags off the floor.

"Hey." He sauntered out of his murder room as she ran back down the steps. "You okay?"

Kris shook her head. "I have to go."

"Go where?"

"I have to go home. I have to see him, his arm. I have to see it . . ." She couldn't put the rest into words.

"That's not a good idea." Jimmy climbed down the steps after her. "If we're right, there's somebody out there looking for you. Somebody that wanted to silence your dad. It's not safe, Kris."

Kris kept walking. "And it's safe here? What am I supposed to do? Just hide and wait for them to come for me? I have to see the body. I have to see if it's him. I have to see for myself."

"Okay. Okay." Jimmy grabbed her by the shoulder out in the hall. "Just let me go with you."

Her mouth dropped open in protest. "Why? Why would you want to do that? We hardly know each other. And . . ." His murder room still fresh in her mind, she wasn't sure he was sane.

His eyes seemed sane. Kind even. "I got nothin' better to do. I'm not gonna just sit around here and smoke dope and wonder if they got you too. I'm sick of looking at photographs of dead people. Let me help you."

Mimi climbed down the steps in agreement. "He's right, Kris. They like their victims alone and vulnerable, drunk or asleep. All of the poor souls were alone when they found them. They prey on the weak. They believe they are culling the herd by cutting out the inferior and diseased. Don't let them find you alone."

"This is crazy." She backed away from both of them as if their mania might be contagious. "I mean, what if this whole theory of yours about the killers is bullshit? What if the paint on my door was a just prank like the police officer said? What if . . . what if my father is sitting in his easy chair right now back home, wondering why I haven't called? Isn't that the most likely scenario here? I mean, stuff like this doesn't happen except for in bad movies. What if you're just obsessed with this killer because . . . because you're bored?"

"What if? Shit, that'd be great!" Jimmy grinned. "Let's just treat this whole thing like a road trip, alright? I been stuck in this town without a car for fuckin' ever. So you gonna take me for a ride or what?"

CHAPTER 33

Three hours later, Kris pulled her Jeep into her father's driveway. Jimmy let out a low whistle. "So this is where you grew up?"

"Yep, right smack in the middle of BFE, surrounded by rednecks. Impressed?" Kris hated the defensive bite of her voice, but the long drive had done nothing to settle her nerves.

The sun had set over the cornfields, leaving nothing but a pale gray sky. There weren't any streetlights, and the nearest neighbor's house sat dark near the horizon a quarter mile away. She had grown up assuming her father just enjoyed the small-town quiet, but the house at the edge of the field looked like a deserted island. He'd been all alone.

A train blew its whistle in the distance, and the rumble of the freight cars hummed through the chill over the fields. She cranked open the car door and wondered if it would've been smarter to park it farther down the road. She dismissed the idea as utter paranoia and grabbed her bags. The softball bag swung from her shoulder as she walked up to the front door, her shotgun like a bone inside it.

The windows were dark.

"Anybody home?" Jimmy whispered behind her.

She held her breath as she slid her key into the knob, but the door wasn't locked. The police tape was gone. She glanced up at Jimmy and took a step back. Paranoid or not, it didn't feel right. She set her bags down and pulled the shotgun from its case and double-checked the shells in the barrel. It was loaded. She snapped it closed and pointed it at the door.

Jimmy lifted his eyebrows in a manner both amused and impressed. He pushed the door open for her with a flourish that belied the worry hidden in his eyes.

Inside, the house was exactly as she had left it two days before. The smell of the dirty dishes had grown slightly stronger, but that was it. Jimmy flipped on the light switch. It was all still there. The flannel couch. The deer heads. The rifle laid out in pieces on the coffee table.

"Damn. Who decorated this place? The NRA?" He motioned up to her awkward thirteen-year-old portrait. "Nice picture!"

Kris didn't smile. She scanned the living room and kitchen for any sign her father had been back. Not even his half-burnt cigar had moved from its perch in the ashtray. The clock on the stove blinked 8:18 p.m. as she moved past the kitchen toward the bedrooms. His bed was still rumpled from the police search. His boots hadn't budged from their spot on the floor. The photograph of her mother still sat on the bedside table, her dark eyes and dark curly hair framed in silver.

The bathroom was empty.

Her bedroom was just as she had left it. Except for the window. It stood open a half inch, with its broken lock dangling. *Troy.* Her ex-fiancé had climbed in the window, looking for her again. He'd stormed out the front door and forgotten to lock it. She set the gun down and closed the window. *Damn it.*

"Everything alright?" Jimmy asked.

"It's fine. Nobody was here. Nobody to worry about anyway." She sat down on the bed and put her head in her hands. Her father hadn't been there.

Jimmy sat down next to her and slung an arm around her shoulders. "What now?"

"I don't know," she said into her palms. "I need to see the body . . . or whatever they found of it. It's going to be horrible, but I need to see it. I just . . ." She sat up and looked at the clock next to her bed. "It's too late. They won't let us in tonight."

Jimmy didn't say a word, but she felt the question hanging in the air. *Do you still think it isn't him?*

She picked up the phone by her bedside and dialed.

"Auglaize County Sheriff's Office."

"Yes. Hi. Can I please speak with Deputy Ben Weber?"

"Kris Wiley? That you?"

"Hi, Mary," Kris muttered reluctantly.

"Ah, sweetie, I'm so sorry . . ." A heavy pause buzzed over the line.

"Thanks, can I talk to Ben?" Kris tried hard not to sound annoyed but didn't really succeed.

"I think he's gone home for the day. Can I leave him a message?"

"Yeah. Please tell him I called, and I want to go down to the morgue tomorrow."

"Oh, hon. To see your father? Are you sure? I don't think you oughtta do that to yourself. You have no idea wh—"

Kris cut her off. "Thanks, Mary. Just tell him I'll meet him there." She slammed the phone down before the woman could say another word and muttered, "I don't know what I was thinking coming back here."

She stormed out of her bedroom and down the hall to her father's room and stopped in the doorway. The walls were bare except for a picture she'd drawn of a baby deer back in junior high school. The dresser and nightstand held only the barest essentials. There wasn't a swastika or a red *L* to be found.

Jimmy looked in over her shoulder at the only photograph in the room. "That your mom?"

Kris crossed the threshold and pulled the picture from its spot on the nightstand. Holding it, she sank down onto her father's bed. "Yeah."

"She looks a lot like you." Jimmy sat next to her on the narrow mattress. "Mind if I ask what happened to her?"

Kris ignored the question. Rachael Wiley's ears and nose and chin were all subtle variations of her own. They could've been sisters except for the curls. She looked back at the blank spot on the nightstand and picked up his wristwatch. It was still ticking. She turned it over to check for any strange markings before holding it to her ear. *Tick. Tick. Tick.*

"You okay?" Jimmy's voice sounded like it was coming through a tunnel.

No! I'm not okay! she wanted to scream. Instead, she threw the watch against the wall. Its metal links went jingling to the floor. Jimmy shot her a look and went to retrieve it. She bolted up from the bed and stormed over to her father's closet and began pulling shirts and pants from the hangers, checking the pockets as she went. Loose change and scraps of receipts scattered across the floor as the clothes piled up next to her. There wasn't one strange thing in the lot. She pushed the piles of clothes out of the way and squatted down to check all the shoes lined up on the floor of the closet. They were all empty.

She spun around and tore the blanket from the bed, then lifted the mattress. Crouching down, she checked under the bed and didn't find so much as a dust bunny. Next she checked the drawers, tossing undershirts and boxers and socks and handkerchiefs and running shorts and T-shirts all onto the ground. By the time she'd reached the last drawer, she realized she was crying.

Kris sank to her knees and surveyed the mess she'd just made. *Oh, God. He's going to kill me.* The thought only made her cry harder because she knew it wasn't true. He'd never yell at her or shake her by the shoulders or give her the silent treatment again.

Jimmy hunkered down beside her, putting a gentle hand on her shoulder. "Hey. We'll figure it out. It's gonna be okay," his voice cooed softly, not because it was true but because there was nothing else to say.

"No. It's not," she muttered, wiping her face dry. She brushed off his arm and pulled herself up. "There has to be something here, right? Some clue or piece of evidence he was hiding."

"Did he have a place in the house? You know, besides in here, where he kept things? Like a place where he'd hide a porno tape or a dirty magazine?"

"No. He didn't have stuff like that."

Jimmy shook his head. "Girl, *all* dudes got stuff like that."

"Wait." Kris lurched up and staggered out into the hall toward the basement, with Jimmy close behind.

The door to her father's workroom sat behind an avalanche of duck decoys and other hunting equipment that lay piled against the cinder-block walls. She pushed her way through the barricade and opened it. A full collection of tools hung from the cobwebbed pegboards lining two walls. She flipped on the two long fluorescent lights. The dusty workbench sat crowded with cardboard boxes of ammo and neatly wound extension cords. The entire room smelled of mildew and gunstock oil.

"Jesus," Jimmy said, flipping the top of one of the boxes of rifle rounds. "Your dad prepping for a war?"

"No. He just likes to hunt," Kris muttered and turned her attention to the locked cabinets above and below the shotgun shell press to her left. It was where he kept his gunpowder and lead pellets.

"Is that why he's got all the knives?" Jimmy waved to the display shelves her father had mounted next to the door. Over twenty blades of various lengths and styles were lovingly arranged in orderly rows.

"I dunno. He just collects them from swap meets and things." She pulled at the steel padlock holding the upper cabinets shut, then opened the metal drawers below the press, searching for a key.

"It's not a fancy lock. I got it." Jimmy nudged past her and pulled his metal picks out of the thrift-store army jacket he was wearing. The name stitched over the breast pocket read, *Smith*. After a minute of rattling and jiggling, the shackle popped open. Jimmy set the lock on the counter next to the press. "What the hell is this thing anyway?"

The shell press looked like a filthy juicer.

"It fills shotgun shells." She didn't listen to his next question. Her heart thudded in her ears as she unfastened the clasp and opened the cupboard doors.

HUNT FOR MORE TORSO EVIDENCE

Police Seek Clews From Severed Leg

Following the discovery of a human leg in the Cuyahoga River at Superior Avenue N.W., believed to be part of the tenth and latest victim of Cleveland's mad torso slayer, six detectives under Detective Lieutenant Albert Smith last night searched both banks of the swollen river in hopes of finding other parts that might lead to identification of the victim.

—*Cleveland Plain Dealer*, April 9, 1938, p. 1

CHAPTER 34

April 8, 1938

The late-afternoon sun shocked her eyes as Ethel stepped out of McGinty's and onto West 25th Street. The road hummed with street traffic as men in caps headed back down to the river to fill the second shift. Women dragged screaming children in and out of the West Side Market, and derelicts shuffled between them, begging for work, for bread, and most of all for booze. The smell of rotting vegetables mixed with the smoke from the mills. She followed the stink down Lorain Avenue back to the river.

A small crowd had gathered at the water's edge. Idle kids mixed with businessmen and housewives straining to catch a peek of the collection of uniformed police officers milling about at the water's edge.

"I heard it was a woman's leg they found," one well-kept woman murmured to another. They each had a toddler on their hip.

"I can't believe they haven't caught him yet. Ness should be run out on a rail! How are we supposed to let our children out to play with a madman running around this city with a knife?"

"I'm sure they're doing all they can," the first one whispered. Ethel glimpsed a pair of divers jumping into the frigid water. "How are they supposed to catch the man when they can't even figure out who the victims are?"

"I wonder if they'll find a head this time."

Both women seemed to hold their breath as the divers disappeared below the polluted brown muck of the Cuyahoga River. Ethel scanned the base of the bridge for her shoe-collecting friend. There was no sign of Rickey or his trunks of clothes. She pushed her way through the packed shoulders to the edge of the bluff.

Two plainclothes policemen were standing ten feet away in deep discussion. "Two divers aren't gonna be enough. We need to drag the river again."

"Yeah, but Merylo got a tip earlier today about some sacks being dumped here last night."

"Excuse me, Detective?" Ethel approached the men.

"I'm sorry, ma'am." A uniformed officer intercepted her before she reached the detectives. "This isn't a cocktail party. You're gonna have to stay back with the others right now."

"I have some information about the murders," she insisted, raising her voice louder, hoping to catch the detective's attention. "Please. I'm the one that filed the report this morning."

A stocky detective looked up from his notes. "It's alright, Charlie. Let her through. Fellas! Let's finish the perimeter sweep like before. Got it?"

Several heads down by the river nodded up at the detective, and the clump of officers dispersed.

"Now. How can I help you, miss?" The man adjusted his hat and studied her face. She didn't recognize him, but she could tell by the flush of his cheeks that he'd started the day with a belt of whiskey.

"I—uh—filed a report today at the Second District station. I was worried no one would get it, but then I saw the crowd here. Where did you find the body?"

He led her closer to the river and away from the ears of the crowd. "We didn't find a body. We found a leg."

She felt his eyes on her as she digested the news.

"Alright. So what was in this report?"

Ethel recounted what she'd seen the night before. The detective took notes the entire time, hardly registering any emotion whatsoever.

"Could you take me to the spot you found the bodies?"

"I think so."

"Let's go take a look." He then shouted over her shoulder, "Grotowski! I got a bit of a leader. Take charge of the search for a bit."

A taller man in a gray suit gave the detective a nod.

He turned back to Ethel and said, "Lead the way."

The unlikely pair passed a hundred curious spectators and headed toward the West 3rd Street Bridge. Ethel scanned the crowd for a familiar face. None of the nuns from the Harmony Mission would be allowed to gawk at such a scene, but she looked anyway. There was no sign of Mary Alice or Brother Wenger among the morbidly curious faces. "I think I see something," one shouted.

Ethel turned away from them in disgust. Some poor girl was dead and these folks treated it like the oddities tent at the world's fair.

"You live around here?" the detective asked, eyeing her dress and the state of her hands. No doubt he'd pegged her for a working girl the instant she walked up.

"No. I got thrown out of my house after talkin' with one of you coppers about the Butcher."

"Don't that just beat all?" He shook his head. "It's the reason we haven't caught this son of a bitch, you know. Everybody's lookin' to protect their own little enterprises, meanwhile a killer's runnin' free."

"I guess folks are worried they'll get hauled in for somethin' silly," Ethel said, testing the waters.

"I ain't vice. Your business down at the river is your own, but if you have something that can help us catch this bastard, I won't forget it. I promise you that."

They rounded the top of the bluff, and Ethel struggled to regain her bearings. The three glasses of wine didn't help. She sighted up the hill to the end of West 5th Street where she'd run naked in nothing but a sheet. She trudged into the tall grass where she'd met up with "Papa."

The detective fell silent as she retraced her steps back to "Papa's" shanty. The old fool was still passed out cold in his tin hut.

"This is where I was when I heard them," she told him in a quiet voice.

The detective peeked in at the passed-out vagrant and then into the other empty huts along the river.

"The voices came from over there, and I heard four splashes as they threw something into the water."

The detective walked a few hundred feet to the north toward where she was pointing. He crouched down onto his haunches and scanned the ground. He took several more notes, then stood back up. "So where did you say the two of them fell?"

Ethel scanned the hill above them and did her best to pick the path that would lead to the bodies. Step by agonizing step, she felt the detective's interest in her story waning and began to worry she'd imagined the whole thing. She wove her way up and down the hill, searching the tall grass for two corpses.

She finally stopped when she found the bottle one of them had been holding. The bodies were nowhere to be seen. "They were right here!" she protested out loud.

The detective picked up the bottle with a handkerchief.

"That was the bottle they got for dumpin' the body," she insisted, sounding more and more like a crackpot.

The detective sniffed the bottle and recoiled. "We'll take this back and see if we can't get an analysis. Anything else?"

Ethel bit her lip and debated explaining how she came to be in the field in the first place. She finally settled on "I think my friend might be missin.'"

The detective flipped over another page in his notebook. "Name?"

"Mary Alice."

"Age?"

"I dunno. Eighteen?"

"Race?"

"She's white."

"Last seen?"

"Yesterday. Around five o'clock."

He lifted an eyebrow at her but kept writing. "Family?"

"None that I know of. She lives over in the Harmony Mission building. At least she did."

He stopped writing. "With the missionaries? The ones that run the Sunday schools for the children down in Public Square? Huh. This friend of yours doesn't exactly sound like our killer's taste. What makes you suspect she's missing?"

"I heard a woman screamin' down in the lower levels under the building. Something awful is happening over there. They have these prison cells in the basement, and I heard her screamin' up through the drain."

He lifted a skeptical eyebrow. "Prison cells?"

"Yeah. He said they were from the Civil War." She could tell by the angle of his eyes he didn't believe her. "Alls I know is that holy roller stripped me down and locked me in one of 'em."

The word *stripped* caught his attention. The detective pressed his lips together and shook his head as though arguing with himself. "Have you looked for her today?"

"No. I—I can't go back there."

"Well, I can't go chasing after a girl that ain't even missing, now can I? In case you hadn't noticed, we're conducting a serious homicide investigation, miss. If you're really concerned for your friend, I suggest we go on over there and check it out."

Grumbling his impatience under his breath, he marched up the hill and headed down West 5th Street. Ethel trailed behind, debating whether she should just run the other direction. The terrified look on Mary Alice's face as Wenger had led Ethel away kept her walking. The stupid girl had risked everything to help a good-for-nothing whore. She owed her something in return.

The gun on the detective's hip gave her courage as they approached the main entrance to the enormous building on West 7th. The words *The Harmony Mission Press* were embossed on the iron gate.

The detective walked right into the front office, with Ethel trailing in his shadow. The stone-faced schoolmarm Sister Frances was seated at the reception desk. "Welcome and God bless. Can I help you?"

"Good afternoon. I'm Detective Martin with the Cleveland Police Department. We were looking for a worker of yours. A Mary Alice?"

"Good heavens!" The woman clutched at her throat. "Is something wrong?"

"We just a have a few questions we'd like to ask if we may. It's a technicality really. Won't take but a moment. May we speak with her?"

"Of course." The shriveled woman's eyes shifted to Ethel's face and lingered there for a moment. "I'll go get her."

CHAPTER 35

"This was a bad idea," Ethel whispered more to herself than Detective Martin. She shifted her weight in her ill-fitting pumps and turned around in the cramped reception lobby of the Harmony Mission, debating whether or not to run. Sister Frances had recognized her face, she was sure of it.

The detective glanced from Ethel's worried mug down to his pocket watch.

A minute later, the door into the factory swung back open. Sister Frances led Mary Alice through it by the hand. The younger woman startled at the sight of Ethel standing in the lobby. Surprise twisted into horror as her eyes dropped from Ethel's face to her exposed cleavage and high heels, but she kept her mouth shut.

The relief Ethel felt at the sight of the girl standing there in one piece was short-lived. If Mary Alice wasn't in hot water before, she certainly was now that Sister Frances could clearly see that her "cousin Hattie" wasn't one of them at all.

"Here we are," Sister Frances declared with a tight smile.

"Are you Mary Alice?" the detective asked the girl in the plain blue dress and work boots.

"Yes." Her voice didn't waver, but Ethel could hear the terror in it. "Can I help you?"

"My name is Detective Martin, I'm investigating a series of homicides." It was clearly a rehearsed script. "Can either of you ladies tell me if any persons have gone missing from this establishment in the last six months?"

"As a matter of fact, yes," Sister Frances said without missing a beat.

The detective looked up from his notepad.

The old woman's eyes bent toward Ethel with a look of sympathy and concern. "Mary Alice's cousin Hattie went missing last night, but I see you've found her."

Detective Martin raised his eyebrows at Ethel.

"We've been terribly worried about her, disturbed as she is," the old woman continued.

Ethel opened her mouth to protest, but one look at Mary Alice's constricted face clamped it shut.

"Disturbed?" the detective asked.

"I'm afraid years of vice have bent the poor thing's mind. For days she didn't talk at all and then yesterday she just started cursing like a woman possessed." The old woman put a hand to her chest. "It troubles my heart, trying to fathom what the poor girl has been through, living on the streets. You can only imagine how hard it's been on the family. After months of looking, Mary Alice finally found her on a street corner, reeling drunk. We've been trying to help poor Hattie find her way back to the Lord, Officer."

Ethel's mouth fell open and gaped at Mary Alice. The girl kept her eyes on her feet. Ethel considered correcting the old bat, but thought better of it. If that's the story Mary Alice had to tell to survive, she wasn't about to shoot the poor girl in the foot.

"Is this true?" The detective swung his skeptical gaze back to Ethel.

She didn't dare answer, hoping he'd take her silence for what it was worth.

"Is this the Mary Alice you were concerned about?" the detective pressed.

"Yes, sir." Ethel nodded.

He jotted a few more notes, then paused and glanced through a few pages. He turned his attention back to the old crone. "I understand you have some underground rooms. Rooms near the sewer lines?"

The old woman's face screwed up into a question mark. "I'm sorry. I'm not sure what you mean."

"This woman claims she was held against her will in an underground cell."

The old woman shook her head sadly at Ethel. "Poor girl. Becoming sober can give some poor souls fits. They can't tell the difference between fantasy and reality. I believe some call it the DTs?"

Ethel gawked at the guileless-looking old woman standing there lying like a professional, radiating such sincerity and genuine concern it was almost believable. Ethel scanned the crone's eyes for smug victory as the cop took his notes and found nothing there but pity. Maybe it wasn't an act. Maybe Sister Frances didn't know the truth. Brother Wenger had dragged her down into the bowels of the building alone, after all. Ethel turned her gaze to Mary Alice, wondering if she knew what had really happened, but the poor girl seemed afraid to even look up.

The detective nodded and threw Ethel another glance. Only this time it was full of suspicion. Still he decided to follow the lead. "If it's all the same to you, do you mind if I take a look in your basement?"

"By all means, Officer." Sister Frances held out her hands in welcome. "We are happy to do anything we can to help. Come with me."

The sister paraded the odd group through the door down a long corridor toward the dining hall.

"What would you like to see first?" she called over the metallic clang and stomp of the printing presses below their feet. They walked past a team of young women scrubbing the floor. Each of the four sisters stopped brushing the boards to gawk at the detective and Ethel in her low-cut dress. "Back to work, ladies," Sister Frances sang out. "The Lord abhors idle hands."

They went back to scrubbing, but Ethel could see the whispers passing between them.

"I'd like the young lady here to show me where she believes she was held," the detective announced. He turned to Ethel and said, "Lead the way."

She bit her lip and headed out the far door where Brother Wenger had led her the night before. Down the narrow corridor they all went. The roar of the presses faded with each step along with Ethel's memory of her march to the gallows. After three turns and one narrow courtyard, it was gone.

Ethel turned around in a circle, racking her brain for the right path, but all the doors looked the same. "This place is a maze," she muttered and turned her helpless eyes to Mary Alice, but the girl just shook her head. She tried one door and found a staircase leading up and not down. Another door led to a broom closet. "I can't remember." She shook her head, ready to scream.

Detective Martin was losing patience. "Forgive me, Sister . . . Frances, was it? Is there a lower level near here?"

Sister Frances paused a moment to think and said, "I believe we're over the boiler room. Follow me."

She led them down another narrow hallway to a shortened door. It looked like the one Brother Wenger had pushed Ethel through, and her heart leapt with hope. It opened into a narrow stairwell that led down. The chill of the basement hit them all in the face as they climbed single file down into the lower level. A giant coal closet opened to their left through a cast iron door. Idle bricked-in furnaces lined the wall to their right. None of it was familiar.

A smallish door sat at the far end. Ethel walked the twenty feet over to it and pushed it open. It was another staircase leading up. Desperate, she climbed up and emerged in the loading dock where the farm workers had been dropped off the day before.

"This isn't the place," Ethel said as she climbed back down, shaking her head.

"Well, this is the lowest part of this wing." Sister Frances eased the door shut and held up her hands. "I'm sorry. I don't know of any other basements below this part of the building, but you are welcome to keep looking."

The odd company climbed the staircase back out of the boiler room and into the loading dock. Detective Martin brushed the coal dust off of his suit and straightened his hat. He scanned the plump, healthy faces of the young women sunning themselves on the benches out in the courtyard. "I'm afraid this is all I have time for today. I may take you up on the offer, though, when things settle down a bit, if that's alright."

"Of course, Officer. We're happy to help." Sister Frances gave him a little bow and led them all back to the reception desk.

Standing at the door, the detective tipped his hat at Sisters Mary Alice and Frances. "Thank you kindly for your cooperation. I apologize for the inconvenience."

"There was no inconvenience, Officer. We are all God's servants here. We'll be praying for you and your investigation this evening."

"Thank you. We'll take all the help we can get." With that he headed out the door.

"Wait!" Ethel called after him and ran to catch up. "That's it? That's all you're gonna do?"

The detective put his notebook in his pocket and rubbed his forehead. "Do you know how many crank leads we get each day on this case? Over a hundred. Do you think I have time to chase down a hundred dead ends each day?"

"This isn't a crank lead!" She slammed her shoe into the brick pavement. "I heard a woman screaming like a stuck pig last night. I heard two drunks dump a body."

He straightened his hat to leave. "I'm sorry, but those ladies in there aren't wrong. I can spot a drunk at ten paces, Ethel or Hattie or whatever your name is. Your lips are stained red, for Christ's sake. Now I'm not gonna go around chasing the phantoms in your head."

Useless words tumbled through her brain as she grasped at anything that might make him change his mind. The drainpipe, the door, the honeycombs full of old bones, the little girl's voice in the dark, the root cellar . . .

"There's a house! An abandoned house around the corner. It connects to the room I saw. Through the root cellar. I swear. I'll show you."

The detective held up a hand. "I got to go find a couple more divers and a half dozen men so we can track down leads on the actual dead body we found today. You do yourself a favor and go sober up. There's some good women in there that just want to help you. I suggest you let them."

Tears of frustration burned the corners of her eyes. "You can't just leave."

The detective shook his head. "I catch you walkin' the streets again, I'll run you in. Understand? I don't want to have to go fishin' you out of the river too."

CHAPTER 36

"Ambrosia! Wait!" Mary Alice shouted after her as Ethel turned down College Avenue.

Ethel kept walking. "Go away, Mary Alice. Go back to your sisters and tell 'em your drunk cousin is a lost cause."

"I'm sorry. I didn't know what else to do." She jogged up beside Ethel and put a hand on her arm.

Ethel shrugged it off and turned her fury on the nitwit. "I thought they killed you! I thought they chopped you up into pieces and threw you in the Goddamn river!"

"What?" Mary Alice's eyes grew wide.

The frightened doe routine didn't work on Ethel. She stepped right up into her pathetic little face. "You knew where he took me, didn't you? You knew all along and you didn't say a word. You let me stand in there like a lost drunk, and now the detective doesn't believe a word I say. Thanks to you, I'm some crazed wino who imagined the whole damned thing!"

"No!" Mary Alice shook her head. "I swear I didn't know a thing."

"Are you telling me Brother Wenger never dragged you down into his little dungeon to exorcise your demons?"

She shook her head vehemently.

"How'd you get the scars, Mary Alice?"

The girl shrank away. "Scars?"

"The scars on your back? Did Brother Wenger do that to you?"

"No." Mary Alice's eyes circled the street as though searching for a way out of the conversation.

"Who did that to you then? The reverend? Sister Frances? Who?" Ethel grabbed the girl's arm to keep her from running back to the factory and lowered her voice. "You can tell me. If they're hurting you, you don't have to go back."

"No. It's not what you think. Brother Milton is a kind man. They took me in and gave me a home and a life. All they want is for me to do God's work. I knew when I heard the call, I knew I would have to answer."

"Is it God's work to beat you? Was that your call? That's crazy, Mary Alice. You don't deserve that. No one does."

"You don't understand. I swear they didn't hurt me."

"Then who did? Some of those marks were fresh."

Mary Alice's eyes fell to her feet.

"Fine. Don't tell me. But something's goin' on in there. I heard the screaming, dammit. Brother Wenger is up to somethin', and I'm going to find out what it is." Ethel dropped the girl's arm and headed up the street toward the abandoned house.

"No one has seen him," Mary Alice called after her.

Ethel stopped walking and turned around.

"He never came back after he reported you missing. He wasn't at lunch this afternoon. Please. What happened?"

"He stripped me naked and pressed a Bible to my head for starters. Sound familiar? Isn't that the sort of thing your 'brothers' in the Lord like to do as penance?"

"No." Mary Alice shook her head. "They make us kneel on sticks and pray for forgiveness . . . or fast until we can see clearly."

"What exactly do you know about Brother Wenger?" Ethel leaned in. "How long has he been working with the dear reverend?"

"I don't know. Maybe a year, I guess. He came over from the Brethren in Lancaster. At least . . . that's what he said."

"Do you believe him?"

"I don't know. The rumor among the sisters is that Brother Milton broke from the Brethren and the Mennonite Conference years ago. He didn't like having to ask permission to do God's will. It's not so unusual. People break away for all sorts of reasons. My reverend back home felt that the elders were getting too lenient, so he decided to go back to the Old World traditions. They didn't approve of women answering a call to services. Especially not to a city mission like this."

"So you broke away from them?" Ethel raised an eyebrow.

"Everyone has to find their own way to serve God. This is the road I was called to."

Ethel shook her head a little. "So if he broke away, why did the reverend accept Brother Wenger?"

Mary Alice just threw up her hands. "He didn't explain it to me. That's Brother Milton's prerogative."

"You must know something. The devil whispers among us, remember?" Ethel hissed, recalling Milton's scolding that first night. "What does the devil say?"

"Just that . . ." Mary Alice tried to seal her lips as though against a flood.

Ethel rattled her arm. "Just what?"

"He had a wife a while back, and she died."

"How?" Ethel glared at her until the dam burst.

"I heard she got sick. Sister Dagna knows the family back in Lancaster. Folks thought the wife was bewitched. She'd have horrible fits. The devil himself was shaking her like a leaf. Dagna heard tell that one of the fits killed her."

"That's awful." Ethel could picture Wenger pinning his poor wife to the floor and attempting to exorcise her devils. She could see his hands around her neck.

"Truly . . . rumor has it he was so desperate he even tried an old powwow to save her."

"A what?"

"A powwow. Old country folk magic. People over on the farms relied on it for years. They brought it across the ocean along with the songs. My grannie used to work a spell to cure most anything. Croup. Turned milk. Gangrene. That was before the Brethren decided it was the devil's work."

Oh, for the love of God. "So Brother Wenger believes in folk magic?"

Mary Alice nodded emphatically. "Lots of folks still do. You ever have a lucky rabbit's foot or hung a horseshoe over a door? Ever knock on wood?"

Wenger's hot breath had steamed her face as he had tried to work some sort of magic spell on her, pinning her shoulders down with his knees. "So people say he does the devil's work?"

"Maybe some do."

"And that's how he ended up here." Ethel was losing patience. "Does he like to strip all the girls naked and try to work his magic?"

Mary Alice flushed at this. "No. I'm sure I would've heard about that."

"Is he the one I heard having his fun with one of you girls? Banging the floorboards over my head the other night?"

"No. I—uh." Her eyes darted down the street as though someone might be watching. "I think one of the girls might be courting Brother Bertram. At least that's the rumor . . . but we'd never say anything. Not until Brother Milton blessed the wedding."

Brother Bertram. She could see him holding the bleeding pig, ready to spill its guts while Wenger cut it through. She could see him holding a terrified girl. Ethel tried to picture the two men walking across the courtyard that night. It could've been him, she decided, but none of the little secrets hidden behind the walls of the Harmony Press explained the screams she'd heard coming up through the drain. She studied Mary Alice's pleading eyes and decided there was nothing else the poor girl could tell her.

"Go back to your good reverend, Mary Alice. Tell 'em I wasn't ready to answer God's call just yet. You tried your best to convince me, but I'm in the grips of the devil or whatever it is you people say. Just stay away from Wenger, okay? Don't let him lock you up."

"Do you think he has something to do with the murder that detective was talking about?" The girl's eyes swelled.

"I don't know . . . If you get scared, go to the police. They'll believe you. You're not a drunk whore like me."

"What are you going to do?"

Ethel opened her mouth to answer but was interrupted by the sight of Sister Frances storming up the street to where they were standing. "Sister Mary Alice! There you are. You left your post in the bindery unattended."

"I'm sorry." The girl bowed her head to prove it, then gave Ethel a pleading look. "Are you sure you won't come back with me?"

Ethel shook her head. "Take care of yourself."

Mary Alice pressed her lips into a worried smile that seemed to wish her well, then took off down the street at a steady trot back to her station in the Lord's work. Sister Frances let her pass and turned to Ethel.

"Sister Hattie." The old woman sized her up once again and gave her a prim nod. "I hope you were satisfied with your search of our facilities today?"

Ethel rolled her eyes and turned to go.

"I trust that we won't have any further outbursts or inquiries from you then. I'm sorry you did not find your calling among the Harmony

Mission, but God works in mysterious ways. I do hope we'll see you in our Sunday school classes this summer."

Ethel waved a hand at the old bat and headed up the street.

"It's never too late to take Jesus into your heart, dear," she called after her. "We are all sinners before the Lord until the day His mighty river washes away our earthly transgressions and lifts us up anew." She sounded eager to see the flood.

A severed leg floated up through the murky waters of Ethel's mind. The killer liked to throw the bodies in the water, she realized, a reverse baptism at the end of life. She glanced up at the half-burnt house, the one with a bleeding star on the door. The little girl might still be somewhere inside.

"You'll be in my prayers, Hattie," Sister Frances said before giving up.

Ethel muttered under her breath. "Thanks, sister. I'm gonna need it."

75 SILVER SHIRTS RALLY
DOWNTOWN

Last night, seventy-five men and a few women participated in a revival of activity here of the Silver Shirts, an American "constructive Christian" organization, by hearing the address by Ray Zachary of Asheville, N.C., speaker for the movement . . .

Chief targets of Zachary's two-hour exhortation to his audience to "help return this Christian country to a Christian government" were President Roosevelt, Communism, which he linked with the Washington administration, and "international Jewish financiers."

—*Cleveland Plain Dealer*, September 13, 1938, p. 3

CHAPTER 37

April 9, 1999

Glass jars of lead pellets and gray gunpowder lined the top shelf. The bottom shelf was empty, except for a large black leather binder. Kris pulled it out and slapped it down onto the steel counter next to the shell press. She glanced over at Jimmy and flipped the book open.

A yellowed newspaper clipping from the *Wapakoneta Daily* had been pasted to the first page. The headline hit Kris right in the gut— *LOCAL WOMAN KILLED IN CAR CRASH.* The large photograph splashed across the page showed a sedan upside down in a ditch. A cloud of smoke trailed up into the sky, and two firemen stood at the edge of the road. The date below the banner read June 18, 1985.

"That was my mom," Kris whispered.

Jimmy didn't say a word as his eyes skimmed the article.

Her father had underlined several phrases in blue ink. *The engine fire burned for over an hour . . . identified by her husband, Alfred Wiley, age 40 . . . exact cause of accident is still under investigation . . . have not ruled out intoxication . . . pending completion of the autopsy.*

Kris turned the page to find a second article published weeks later. It was much smaller than the first, without the flashy headline. In small print it read, *Area Woman's Death Alcohol Related*. The only words underlined in the two inches of type were *toxicology report*. Her mother's obituary had been pasted next to the article. It began with a smaller, grainier version of the portrait her father kept by his bed and the caption *Rachael (Froehlich) Wiley*.

The sound of Jimmy's voice cut through the mildew and dust hanging under the quiet hum of the fluorescent light. "Is that your mom's maiden name? Froehlich?"

Kris blinked the fog from her eyes. "Uh, yeah. It is."

"I'm sorry . . . I mean, I'm sorry she died."

"It was a long time ago." It was true, but a heavy weight settled onto her shoulders with the revelation that her mother had been drunk. She turned the page to find half a newspaper page pasted sideways. It was an inside page of the *Cleveland Plain Dealer* dated April 8, 1980. An article had been circled in red ink, and her breath caught at the headline—*MAN'S HEADLESS BODY FOUND NEAR TRACKS*. Jimmy's dreadlocks brushed her shoulder as he leaned in for a closer look.

> *Lakewood police are attempting to learn the identity of the body of a decapitated white man found next to the Conrail railroad tracks at 6:55 a.m. yesterday . . .*

Kris's eyes jumped between the lines. "You don't think?"

"I know this case." Jimmy tapped the paper. "It's all over the discussion boards. Yeah. It could be them."

They turned the page and then another. More clippings of headless bodies found in Pittsburgh, Cincinnati, and Indiana followed. Some were marked with underlines, some were just circled.

HEADLESS TORSO FOUND

*Barrington Hills, Ill. (AP)—The headless torso of a man—
the fifth dismembered body found in 16 months in sub-
urban Chicago—had lain in tall grass for about 24 hours
before it was found, a police official said.*

As they flipped through the stories, Kris began to count. There
were more than twenty. She backed away from the book, letting
Jimmy take over.

"I haven't heard of half of these," he mused. "Looks like your dad's
been at this for years. He must've really been on to something. Man,
I wish I could talk to him . . ." His voice trailed off, probably out of
respect for Kris, but she wasn't listening.

All she could see was the faded photograph of her mother's smoking car. She could hear the crunch of metal and smell the gasoline
spilled over the ground. Her mother had been trapped inside as it
burned. Her father had never told her the whole story. The car burning. Her being drunk when it happened.

She heard Jimmy's voice through her muddy thoughts. "Does
your pops have a computer?"

"What?"

"A computer? Does he have one?"

"I don't think so. Maybe at work. Why?"

"You said the guy that went looking for your dad was a David
Hohman, right?"

"Did I?" Kris couldn't remember, but she must've. "Yeah, that was
his name. Do you know him?"

"Not personally, but I've been thinking about it." He paused as
though he wanted to let it go at that, until she looked at him. "It's just
that there's a guy on the discussion boards that goes by DHOH."

She stared at him a beat. "Yeah. I know. I've seen him there too . . . Why didn't you mention him before?"

"I don't know. You were upset." Jimmy flipped open another page in the binder. *MURDER VICTIM NOT YET IDENTIFIED*, a headline screamed. "I don't know this DHOH guy or anything. No one uses their real name online, but I was thinkin' . . . that might've been how they met."

"Yeah." She narrowed her eyes at him. His murder room flashed in her mind along with nagging questions she wasn't sure she wanted answered. *How obsessed with the Torso Killer are you, Jimmy? Were you on the night Lowjack broadcast my dad's police file?* But she didn't remember seeing a computer in his squatter's lair. "Maybe. Do you, uh . . . go online a lot?"

"A bit." He almost seemed sheepish. Maybe it was because she was glaring at him with accusation.

She looked up at the cobwebbed ceiling and reminded herself that Jimmy had been nothing but kind to her. "Who are these people?" she muttered to herself.

"Just people," he answered. "A lot of them are looking for missing relatives. I mean . . . why did your dad collect all these articles?"

She just shook her head.

"Torsokillers.com is a pretty big group. There's a few more out there—nottinghillkiller.com, coldcasework.com. DHOH posted on all of them. He claimed to be some sort of ex-cop, but that could be bullshit. He liked to give everybody his professional opinion on their missing persons. He was obsessed with the Torso Killer. Definitely a Cleveland guy."

"And my dad met him online." It made sense, she supposed. But the feeling she was missing something nagged at her.

"DHOH said he freelanced as a private investigator. Maybe your dad contacted him about all of this." He tapped the scrapbook.

"Or maybe he suspected Hohman was the killer." She turned the idea over in her mind again, looking for cracks. "Mel said the guy wasn't friendly and he'd come looking for my dad right before he vanished."

Jimmy nodded as if to say it wasn't a totally crazy idea. "But there was more than one killer, Kris."

Kris swallowed hard at the thought of her father alone in the woods with a murdering cult. She tried to clear it away with facts. "Someone's been destroying the official records. Someone's trying to cover something up. Maybe this DHOH is just covering his tracks. That David Hohman guy used to hang out at the county archives. They told me about him."

"Maybe." Jimmy studied her pale face in the flickering fluorescent light. He leafed through the clippings again. "The only one that doesn't fit is the one about your mom. It was a car crash, not a murder. Any idea why he'd put that one in here?"

The memory of the car felt like cement in her chest. Its passenger door had been torn off. The paint was scraped off in metal stripes and blackened with soot. A tow truck pulled it out of a deep ditch by the side of an empty field. Kris watched it through the window of her father's backseat. He'd left her alone in his truck. He was on his knees in the middle of the road. Somewhere in her distant memory, she could still smell the smoke.

"Maybe it wasn't an accident. Maybe he thought . . ." Jimmy's voice faded as he looked at her. "Hey. You okay?"

She shook her head. After the accident, her father had never said a word about it. The tools and knives and bullets and cobwebs crowded in around her under the cold lights. *Maybe it wasn't an accident?*

Jimmy gave her shoulder a squeeze. "I could tell you more if I could just get to a computer."

"What the hell does a computer have to do with any of this?" She grabbed the metal counter to steady the room. "It was an accident!

You saw the article. She was drunk! She got drunk and left me! I saw the wreck . . . Careless idiots die in car accidents every day! Not everything is about a psycho killer! For Christ's sake . . ."

Jimmy softened his eyes and voice and cupped her ashen face. "I know that. But your dad put those articles about your mom in this book with the others. Don't you think that means something?"

"Maybe it doesn't mean *anything*!" She realized she was screaming and forced herself to breathe. After counting to five, she said in a lower voice, "So what are you saying? You think the whole car accident was some sort of elaborate cover-up? And that he talked to this David Hohman or DHOH or whatever the hell his name is about it?"

"Maybe. I don't know. That's why I need to get online. We need to find this DHOH guy and find out. I mean, it couldn't hurt, right?"

"Why the hell would anybody kill my mom?" Kris demanded, no longer caring if she was loud. "She was just a mom!"

"Hey. Take it easy. C'mon. Let's get out of here and talk." Jimmy led her by the arm out of the workroom, through the mesh bags of duck decoys, and back toward the stairs. "Your mother's maiden name was Froehlich, right?"

"Yeah, so?" She wrested her arm free and climbed the steps back up into the kitchen on her own.

"Isn't that Jewish?"

"What?" Kris frowned at him, realizing where he was going with this line of questioning and not liking it one bit. "I don't know. Maybe? Can you tell by a last name?"

"Yeah. Some people can. Green, Goldberg, Epstein—Jewish names can be just as easy to spot as Italian ones."

"Okay. So?" She knew the answer before he said it.

"So maybe somebody didn't like that. Your dad marrying a Jew."

Her grandparents sat like sentries on folding chairs in the back of her mind. "You mean the Silver Shirts."

"He had their weird gang sign tattooed on him, right?"

"No. Not really. It was more of a . . . scar."

"Okay, so maybe some Silver Shirts or whoever gave it to him. Either way, they would've hated your mom, right?"

Kris pictured her father's wide-open smile and the way he'd wrap an arm around her little shoulders during the ball games on TV. She shook her head. "But he wasn't one of them. There's no way."

"You sure? People change, you know. He went to Vietnam, right?" She nodded. "Airborne."

"Right. Death from above . . ." Jimmy thought on it for a moment. "Maybe blowin' people up changed him. War does some funny things to you, from what I've heard anyway. He talk about it much?"

"No." Kris sank down onto her father's ugly plaid couch and put her head in her hands. His shotgun still lay in pieces on the coffee table like he was getting ready for a hunting trip. She pictured him in the tattoo artist's chair, trying to cover up his past with ink. "So he fell in love with my mom . . . who you think was Jewish . . . and then they killed her?"

"Who knows? But maybe that's what he was afraid of. I mean, look at where he decided to live." Jimmy motioned to the empty fields surrounding her dad's house. "The Unabomber could live out here. It's the perfect place to disappear."

Kris had seen the tiny house and empty fields through Jimmy's eyes the moment they had driven up. It looked like a redneck bunker—a bunker full of guns. Her father's family never came to visit, and Ben was his only friend. The grandmother she remembered could barely look Kris in the eyes. Her un-blue eyes with her un-blond hair. Kris and her dad had been living on an island. "But who cares about being Jewish anymore? This is the '90s. The Holocaust was like fifty years ago. The war is over."

"You don't go online much, do you?" Jimmy plunked down next to her and took her silence as his answer. "The war never ended. There are Nazis and lunatics all over this country. Literally thousands of people think the world is coming to an end in a couple of months. The big millennium and the prophecy of Nostradamus and all that. Y2K. Whatever you want to call it. Dozens of chat rooms are out there discussing the second coming of Christ. The end of days. People really believe this shit. These people really believe that the devil is out there walking among us. And some of them crackers think the devil is Jewish. And some think it's black folks like me. Shit, some woman put her baby in the oven last week, sayin' it was possessed. It's a fucked up world out there."

Kris held up a hand to stop the stream of horrifying nonsense coming out of his mouth and tried to acknowledge the truth of what he was saying. *These people are real. Nazis are real. I might even be related to some of them.*

"Wait." She wiped an escaped tear and forced herself to track back through their conversation. So many pieces were still missing, and everything that came out of his mouth seemed absurd. People didn't get *murdered.* They died of heart attacks and in car accidents. Murder only happened to the not-quite-real people on the news. People from inner-city slums and foreign countries. "I don't get it. I really don't. I mean . . . if this David Hohman really wanted to find my dad—if they knew each other somehow—why would he give Mel at the diner a fake business card? How do we know he isn't just some sick stalker?"

"I don't. I never met the guy. DHOH is just an avatar. He could be anybody. Can I see the card?"

"It's back at my place."

Jimmy glanced up toward the kitchen. "It's after ten. We can't head back now . . . You still want to go to the morgue tomorrow?"

The photographs of severed arms and legs flipped through her mind in a broken filmstrip, stopping on the schematic diagram stitched with red dotted lines, separating the parts of the victim into cuts of meat. She'd never seen a dead body before. The closest thing had been the deer her father shot every winter. He'd hang the carcass from a rafter tie in the garage. She'd run past it into the house, not wanting to look at the body dangling there from its front hooves while her father peeled off its skin. Its guts would be hollowed out, leaving nothing but a wood stick holding open its ribcage, the white bones sticky with dried blood. A loud buzzing filled her ears. She shook her head and mouthed the words, *I don't know*, not trusting her voice.

"You're tired." He wrapped an arm around her and rubbed her shoulder. "C'mon. Let's get you to bed."

Jimmy led her back down the hall to her bedroom. Alarm bells went off in her head as he settled down on the mattress next to her. She shrugged off the arm draping around her and slid away from him. "It's okay. I'm fine."

"I know." He cracked a half smile and let his eyes circle her soccer trophies, lingering on her teddy bear. "We should probably get some sleep. Tomorrow's gonna be rough."

"Yeah. You're probably right. I, uh . . ." She glanced around the room uncomfortably, searching for a place to put him.

"Hey. Don't worry about me . . . I'll go find a couch."

She hugged her knees and glanced over at the window where Troy liked to crawl in. She got up and closed the curtains. The dead quiet outside reminded her how far away the nearest neighbors were. It would be easy for a crazed serial killer to break in without any of them hearing a thing. "I don't know if I can sleep. It's kind of creepy thinking someone could be out there."

The hint of a smile pulled at his lips. "Do you want me to stay?"

"Yes . . . No. I don't know." Tears burned at the corners of her eyes again. "I just want to wake up. I want to wake up from this nightmare and for everything . . . to be okay."

"Hey. I know." He folded his arms around her. "None of this is your fault."

She buried her head into his chest, despite her misgivings. The tears escaped in thin streams and then torrents. Her father. The racist brand someone had given him. How he'd loved her mother despite his parents. Despite his scar. Her mother's car burning up in the crash. He'd been all alone. She'd left him alone. Jimmy was wrong. It was her fault. All the terrible guilt she'd been holding spilled out of her, soaking his shirt. She'd even been happy for a moment . . . thinking she was free. *Ungrateful. Rotten. Whore.*

Warm hands rubbed her back, then handed her some tissues from the side of the bed. "I'll stay, okay?" He pulled back the covers and got in next to her. His wet shirt came off and dropped to the floor. "We'll just sleep. Nothing funny, I promise."

Her head felt both weighed down and lightened by her crying jag. The burning incense aroma of his skin filled in the empty spaces where her thoughts had washed out. She laid her head on his bare chest and let him wrap an arm around her. The heat of him warmed her shivering bones until her mind went blissfully blank.

"Just go to sleep, Kris. I got you." He stroked her hair and kissed the top of her head. His voice faded away. "Nothin's gonna happen, okay? Nobody's gonna get you . . ."

CHAPTER 38

"Kritter? Wake up, girl." A hand shook her shoulder. "We need to talk."

Kris lurched up to see Deputy Sheriff Ben Weber standing over her in uniform. "Ben?" Her bleary eyes darted back down to the bed. Faint early morning light filtered in under her curtains, casting a pale glow onto her rumpled sheets. Jimmy was gone. She shook the sleep from her head, wondering if she'd been dreaming. But the empty spot next to her was still warm. "What are you doing here?"

"Got your message. I'm glad you finally came to your senses. I'll go make you some tea." He lumbered out of the room and into the hall.

Kris pulled herself out of bed and scanned the room. "Jimmy?" she whispered.

There was no answer. His tear-soaked Bob Marley T-shirt lay crumpled on the ground.

Out in the hall, Ben's voice continued, "Awful sorry to barge in on you like this, but I've been worried sick about you, kiddo. I was headin' out to Cleveland to arrest you and drag your butt back home."

She forced her feet to the open door. "You were?"

His ruddy face looked haggard and pale as he nodded. "They finished the autopsy last night . . . They're ruling it a homicide."

"A homicide," she repeated. She had known from the moment Ben had showed her the plastic bags filled with clothes, but the air still fell out of the room. *They killed him.*

"Hard to believe it could happen here." Ben shook his head. "I'm so sorry, Kritter."

She pressed her back to the wall, seeing the police schematic of a body cut limb from limb with red ink. All of her blood pulled back to her heart. "But the DNA test isn't even in yet. Is it?"

"No." Ben hesitated in the hall next to her father's ransacked bedroom, oblivious to the mess she'd made. He pressed his lips into a pained line, then said, "I hate to say it, hon, but I put that test in to ease your mind, not because I believed it would make a damned bit of difference. The coroner already signed off on the ID after confirmation from me, Al's boss at the train yard, and Mel . . . We need to get you down to the station to process the paperwork. Your dad doesn't belong in that meat locker. He wanted to be cremated, right?"

His words registered in her ears out of order. *Paperwork. Station. Meat locker . . . Homicide.* A loud buzz hummed through her empty veins. Her legs dropped out from under her.

"I have to . . . I have to use the bathroom," she choked out. Holding on to the wall, she found her way to the tiny tiled room and shut the door.

She turned on the water in the sink and sank down to her knees. *He's dead. Oh, God, he's dead. Someone killed him.* The thought swung in and out of her mind in slow motion, spiraling through her. Down, down, down.

She pressed her forehead to the cold floor tiles. The Nazi pictures in Madame Mimi's tattoo book flipped through her field of vision along with the headlines in her father's scrapbook. *HEADLESS BODY FOUND.*

It was another Torso Murder. That's why he had the library books, she realized. He'd figured out the truth about them. *That's why they killed him.*

Her eyes darted around the bathroom as she realized she had no proof of any of it. Ben wouldn't understand about Madame Mimi. He'd call her a con artist. There was no possible way her father's murder had anything to do with what had happened back in Cleveland sixty years ago. He wouldn't understand about Jimmy. He'd think he was just a hoodlum. All he would see were his skin color and the drugs in his backpack.

Footsteps shook the floorboards from the kitchen back down the hallway. A knock hit the door. "Kritter, hon? I know this is tough, but we should just get this over with." Ben's voice filtered in from the other side of the hollow door.

"I—I'm not ready yet. Uh." *Jimmy.* "Why don't you go on without me? I'll meet you there."

"Don't be silly, girl. I'm not letting you go in there alone. You hear?" She could hear Ben shift his weight and stifle an impatient sigh. "Take all the time you need. You want that tea?"

"No." She wrenched open the door. "I don't want tea! Can't we . . . Do we have to do this today? It's all so . . . rushed. I can't even think straight right now."

"C'mon. Let's talk this through, kiddo." He grabbed her by the hand and led her down the hall to the kitchen table. "I know it's hard, don't think I don't. But this is what needs to be done."

Kris sat down, trying to sort through the million voices chattering through her head. *Pull yourself together, dammit! You know he's right, Kris,* her father bellowed at her. He was drowned out by the sound of the little girl inside her wailing for her father. *They killed him!*

Ben settled into the seat across from hers and picked up her hand. "Now what can I do to help?"

"I—I don't know," she whispered. *They killed him. They killed him.* "Who did it, Ben? Who are they?"

Ben's shoulders sagged. "It's an ongoing investigation, kiddo. I wish I knew."

"But why? Why would they kill him? You must know something. You two were best friends. Did he owe somebody money? Did he get himself mixed up with something? Did he say anything to you?"

"No." He shook his head, defeated. "I wish he had. Your dad wasn't one to air his problems. He was private like that . . . We can talk about all this on the way."

"Wait." She held up her hand. "If somebody killed him, doesn't that mean the killer is still out there? What if . . ." She stopped short of telling him about the mark on her door. He'd put her under house arrest.

"Well, I didn't want to say so out loud and worry you, but that's one of the reasons I was ready to drag you back home. You shouldn't be stuck in that city alone right now."

Kris nodded, but the knot in her stomach tightened. "What about that man David Hohman? He came looking for Dad at Shirlene's a while back. Mel gave me his card, but the address on it was wrong." She explained her trip to the county archives and the missing files. "It seems like this Torso Killer has something to do with all this."

"Now wait one damned minute."

Ignoring him, she pushed herself up from the table and gathered the library books out of her backpack on the kitchen floor. Jimmy had left the scrapbook on the counter. She plopped them all down in front of Ben. "Look at all these books I found in his bedroom! Look at this scrapbook we found downstairs in his workshop! This can't just be a coincidence."

Ben's eyes darted from the books on the table up to her face. He looked as though he'd just swallowed fire. "You went looking for him? Have you lost your damned mind? We don't have time for these games! *This is a police investigation!*"

Kris quaked at the look in his eyes but was too far gone to take any of it back. "He's my dad! What else was I supposed to do? Don't you think there's some sort of connection with all of this? Who is David Hohman?"

He grabbed her wrist and squeezed. "Did you talk to this David character?"

"No." She tried to pull her arm back but couldn't. "Ben, you're hurting me."

He didn't let go. "I need you to think real hard, Kris. Did you talk to this guy? Did you see him?"

She shook her head.

"Good." He must've noticed the stricken look on her face and released his grip. "I'm sorry, Krit. You're not the only one feeling the strain here."

She took a step back from him. "I know. It's just . . ."

"No. I shouldn't have lost my temper. You don't need that. I just never dreamed something like this . . ." He rubbed the anger from his face, and his shoulders slumped.

"I know." And she did. Her eyes darted down the hall. *Where's Jimmy?* she wondered, relieved he'd been smart enough to hide. Ben would've had a fit if he'd found a man in her bed, just on principle.

"Lookit. Let's just get this over with. Okay?"

No. The feeling that something was very wrong itched up her spine. There was something she was missing. Something he wasn't telling her. Her eyes fell on the scrapbook. "Did—uh—did my dad ever mention his suspicions to you that my mother . . . that it wasn't an accident?"

"What?" Ben's face went slack. "What are you talking about?"

"He put the articles about her in here." She flipped open the scrapbook to the first page. "See? And then there's nothing but murders after that. It's like . . . he thought they were connected somehow."

The color rose back up his neck as she talked. His eyes narrowed and flashed with an array of barely stifled emotions. *Anger? Surprise? Utter exasperation?* He wiped a hand across his face before she could decide. She could hear the strain in his voice as he carefully chose his words. "I can't imagine how hard this all has been on you, kiddo. But you're chasing ghosts. Your mother . . ." He stopped the next words with his teeth.

"What about her?" Kris leaned in to get Ben to look her in the eye. His face flushed again and he looked out the back window into the dormant cornfield instead.

"She was a good woman, but she messed up. And she messed up your dad pretty good too, her dyin' like that. I don't know what was going on with this book. And dammit, I don't care." He turned to her, no longer concealing his anger at her meddling. "What you really need to focus on is getting through this and leave the detective work to the police. Alright? This is a homicide investigation. Not a game."

She forced herself to nod and held her tongue. Eighteen years of living with her father had taught her when to keep her thoughts to herself. They'd also taught her how to leverage being a helpless female. "I'm sure you're right, Ben. Would it . . . would it be okay if I took a minute to pull myself together?" She let loose a few tears that had pooled behind her eyes. She glanced down the hallway to her room again and then to the basement door. Jimmy was still hiding somewhere, and the way Ben had reacted to her questions bothered her. She was in no rush to make her father's death official. Even if it was the right thing to do. "I can't go in there like this. I need to shower. I need some time. Can I meet you there in an hour?"

He appraised her up and down, debating with himself. "I don't like leaving you here."

"I need some time to process all of this," she pleaded, turning her teary eyes up to his. "Please? I don't . . . I really don't want to cry in front of everyone."

He squeezed her shoulder like an uncle would. "Okay. One hour."

CHAPTER 39

Kris teetered on numb legs down the hall back to her bedroom once Ben's cruiser pulled out of the driveway. She turned a circle in her room, stopping in front of her shotgun leaning up against the door-jamb. "What the hell am I going to do?"

"About what?" a voice whispered back.

She spun around to see Jimmy sliding out from under the bed, half-naked and covered in dust bunnies. "What the hell are you doing under there?" she asked. "Were you there the whole time?"

Jimmy brushed himself off and shrugged. "I heard the front door open. This is not a town where I wanna get caught in bed with a white girl. They'd probably string me up and burn a cross about it."

She wanted to protest but couldn't help but see his point. She could count the number of black people she knew in Cridersville on one hand. She supposed she'd feel nervous too. "Did he see you?"

"I don't think so." He picked his Bob Marley T-shirt up off the floor and pulled it on. Her tears hadn't even left a mark. "So you goin' down to the morgue?"

"I don't know." *The morgue.* Plastic bags of evidence were lined up on a table in her head, but this time they were filled with pieces of him.

She shook her head and bit back another round of tears. "He's . . . they say he's . . ."

"I know . . . I heard him." Jimmy's eyes hurt for her.

"He didn't believe me about the Torso Killer. He didn't even listen. And now . . . maybe they're still out there . . . And I can't go home." The red star painted over her door left no doubt. It wasn't safe. "My life is over."

Jimmy wrapped an arm around her and held her to his chest. "We'll figure it out. You could stay here and take care of things for a while. I'll hitch a ride back and find this David Hohman."

The warm smell of him stopped the room from shaking. Despite all the red flags, she didn't want him to leave. "But what if it isn't him? What if he doesn't know a thing about it?" She pulled away from Jimmy, frantic and lost. "What if we never know—"

A hard knock on the door cut her words short. "You expecting someone?" Jimmy whispered.

She shook her head.

A second later, the front door sprung open. "Kris?" a familiar voice called.

"Shit. I cannot believe he's here," she hissed.

"Who?" Jimmy whispered back.

"Oh, nobody. Just this guy I was supposed to marry."

Troy's voice boomed from inside the living room. "Kritter? You here?"

Jimmy nudged her.

"Yeah?" Her voice came out as a croak. She swallowed and called louder, "Yeah. I'll be right out."

Jimmy grabbed his backpack and planted a kiss on her cheek. "I better get the fuck out of here. You gonna be okay?"

"Yeah. He's harmless. Don't go. Just give me a minute to get rid of him."

Troy was standing in her kitchen with his head in the fridge. He popped up at the sound of her footsteps with one of her father's beers in his hand.

"Uh. Hi. Troy," she said, wiping her face clean of tears and other signs of weakness. "What are you doing here?"

"I saw your car out front and I figured you could use a friend."

She glanced at the clock on the stove. "It's 7:00 a.m."

He shrugged and popped open the can of beer. "Ben gave me a ring. He didn't think it'd be such a good idea you goin' down to the morgue all by yourself. He asked me to come check on you."

Ben must have radioed it in the second he left the house. *That figures.* "That was very sweet of you both, but I'm fine. I just need some time to get my head together. Alone." She went to open the door for him to leave, but he caught her by the arm.

"Hey, it's been a long time. I've been worried about you." His blue eyes radiated genuine concern. "Aren't we even friends anymore?"

Kris rolled her eyes and rubbed her forehead. They had never been friends. But she could tell he wasn't going to leave without a long talk. Jimmy couldn't hide in her closet forever. "Yeah. Sure. Just sit down and give me a minute . . . I just woke up."

She waded back down the hall to the bathroom and turned on the water. With the stream running, she crept into her bedroom and shut the door.

"Jimmy?" she whispered.

There was no answer. Her curtain wafted up as a cool breeze cut through the room. The window was open and he'd gone. Just as well, she told herself, but her heart sank anyway. He'd left without even saying goodbye.

Kris slipped back down the hall to the bathroom and turned off the water. The house fell strangely silent. The wall clock ticked in the living room. The compressor of the refrigerator kicked on. She could feel Troy's patience running out somewhere in the living room. It was just the two of them.

On her way back down the hall, glimpsing the mess of her father's bedroom through the open slant of the door stopped her in her tracks. The sheets lay in a heap on the bed. Piles of clothes were scattered across the floor. Her mother's picture was the only thing in its proper place on the nightstand. Her dark, smiling eyes watched Kris from behind the frame. Pins pulled back her curly black hair. Rachael Froehlich was beautiful. Kris picked up the frame and sank onto the bed, staring at the face of a woman she never knew. A woman that had killed herself drunk driving. *She messed up. And she messed up your dad pretty good too.*

"What the hell happened in here?" a voice boomed from the doorway.

Kris dropped the picture on the floor. "Troy! You nearly gave me a heart attack!"

"Jesus, Krit! What'd you do?" He grabbed her by the arm and dragged her out of the room. "Do you have any respect at all? Your dad would be furious!"

She wrenched her arm free and barked back, "Shut up, Troy! This has nothing to do with you. You know what? I don't feel like catching up right now, okay? I appreciate you coming by, but I need you to leave." She stormed to the front door and flung it open.

"You don't know what the hell you need!" He half laughed and slammed the door shut. "You're in way over your head, and this tough-girl routine is total bullshit. I mean, you up and leave town after hearing your dad was killed. You leave him in the morgue to rot? What the hell's the matter with you, Krit? Do you have any idea what you're putting us all through with these games?"

She gaped at him. "What I'm putting *you* through?"

"This isn't funny. Your dad is lying in a Goddamn freezer! How could you just leave him there?" He glared at her the way a father glares at a child who has just broken a lamp.

"What the hell business is it of yours? He's *my* father and you have nothing to do with it!" she shouted back. "Now get the hell out of my house!"

"This isn't *your* house. You moved out, remember?" He threw his hands up at the ceiling and paced the floor. After regaining his composure, he softened his voice, cupped her face in his hands. "Baby. Why won't you let me help you? I know you're hurting. You don't have to go through this alone."

"Ugh. I can't do this with you now. I can't, Troy. I appreciate your concern, but we broke up. Remember? If you won't leave, I will." She pushed her way past him and into the kitchen. The spot on the counter where she'd left her car keys was bare. "Where are my keys?"

"I can't let you do this." Troy walked up behind her, shaking his head. "I can't let you run away from this again. You're going down to the county morgue with me and getting this dealt with, and that's final."

The fatherly bite in his voice sent a rage through her. "Back off, Troy!" Kris shouted even though he was right. She should go and sign Ben's papers declaring her father dead. *Murdered.* She should make arrangements for a funeral. *But the killer is still out there.* "I'm fine! I'll take care of it. Just give me back my keys."

"No. I'm going with you." Troy folded his arms across his chest and put his giant body between her and the front door. "I owe it to Al to make sure this gets done right."

"Oh, fuck you, Troy! I'm not your girlfriend. I'm not your daughter, and I hate to break it to you, but Al's not your father! Just give me my Goddamn keys!" Kris held out her hand.

"Do you hear yourself? You're not okay, Kris. You sound like you've lost your mind. I am not letting you out of my sight. I promised Al I'd look after you, and that's what I'm going to do."

"What do you mean you 'promised Al'? When?"

He grinned, reveling in the fact that he knew something she didn't. "When you were off messing up your life in Cleveland, that's when. We saw each other all the time. Hunting trips. Fishing trips. Shit, I knew him a hell of a lot better than you did." His eyes wandered down her body like he owned it. "Whether you like it or not, I'm the only family you've got left."

That was it.

"You are *not* my family!" She shoved him hard with both hands. "I am not yours to keep! I don't even like you!"

She went to shove him again, but he grabbed her wrists. Holding her like a vise, he dragged her across the room, pushed her against the refrigerator, and smashed her lips with a kiss.

"I know you didn't mean all that. You're just hurting, Kris. I'm hurting too. You just need something to get you through this." He smothered any answer with his mouth. His enormous football player's frame crushed against her. He kissed her neck. "I'm here. I'm here now. I love you."

"Stop . . . Troy . . . Get off of me!" She could barely get any words out with him pressed against her. She hit and scratched and tried to kick, but he had her pinned. He outweighed her by over a hundred pounds. His giant hands pulled up her shirt.

"No!" she screamed and bit his ear hard enough to draw blood.

"Ahh!" He stepped back, clutching the side of his head. Before she could even scream, he slapped her to the ground. "Dammit, Kris! See? See what you make me do?"

As she struggled to gather her limbs, he scooped her up off the floor and cradled the flashing pain of her face in his hands. "Why? Why did you do that?"

Kris pulled her feet back under her, balled up a fist, and cracked him square in the jaw. *"Get your hands off me!"*

His head snapped back, and she grabbed the side of the counter. The knife block was just a foot away. She reached for it, but his hand wrenched her shoulder around. The room spun with it until all she could see was him.

"Why are you doing this to us?" He blinked the murder out of his eyes and wrapped his anaconda arms around her. "You need to just settle down and think about this, baby. We're meant to be together. He promised me we'd be together."

The ratchet of a shotgun somewhere behind them sent a jolt up Troy's back.

"Hands up, motherfucker!" a voice barked. It was Jimmy.

Kris went limp. *Thank God.*

Troy pushed her into the wall, then pinned her with his back as he turned to face the gun. "Hey. Take it easy, friend. What, ah . . . what can I do for you?"

"You can let her go, OJ."

Kris shoved the off-balance football hero away from her and squirmed out from the wall.

Jimmy glanced at her throbbing cheek. "You okay?"

She nodded, knowing full well she wasn't.

"Kris. You know this guy?" Troy shot her with his eyes and grabbed her arm, yanking her back.

A shotgun blast splintered the ceiling. Kris hit the floor with a yelp.

"Step. The. Fuck. Off!" Jimmy's eyes flashed rage. For a fleeting second, he looked like a crazed killer. Kris shrank from him in disbelief.

"Okay, man. Okay." Troy put up his shaking hands, his face freezing into a cringe.

Jimmy nudged Kris with his foot, not taking his hands off the gun. "Let's go."

She wobbled to her feet, cheeks flushed with adrenaline and terror. The sight of Troy shitting his pants at gunpoint was cold comfort. "Troy!"

He winced at her.

"Give me my fucking keys!"

DERELICTS WORRY AS CITY
PLANS TO BURN SHANTYTOWN

They were getting ready at noon today to set fire to a little village at the foot of Commercial Hill, just about 10 minutes' walk from the Terminal Tower. And in cells at Central Police Station were 38 men, most of them unwashed, unshaved and red-eyed from too much cheap whisky, to whom the fire will represent real tragedy.

—*Cleveland Press*, August 18, 1938, p. 1

CHAPTER 40

April 8, 1938

A dark red star marked the broken back door where Ethel had emerged naked the night before—one crooked square shifted on top of another, a circle of triangles around a crooked center.

Ethel waded through the overgrown grass past broken fencing, discarded burlap bags, and a bent bicycle wheel. The yards on either side were well kept and trimmed as if to compensate for the abandoned eyesore between them.

The windows above the shameful yard were mostly boarded along the first floor. The second-floor window sash hung open from a broken frame. Faded wood siding had been scorched black along one side, no doubt an attempt to pay off the mortgage with arson the year the market crashed.

The neighbors' curtains were drawn on every window facing the half-burnt house. The backyards were all empty. Ethel took in a breath and opened the splintered back door.

The kitchen and living room looked much the way she'd left them the night before. The hard soles of her shoes clapped slowly across the floor as she picked her way through piles of wadded newspapers and torn clothes to the staircase leading up to the second floor. Light leaked in through the staggered boards nailed across the windows, casting slashing stripes onto the walls. The smell of rotting food and stale sweat steeped the air. A dark black stain splattered over the floorboards of what was once a living room. *Blood?*

"Hello?" she whispered up from the foot of the stairs. "Johnnie?"

There was no answer.

She climbed the stairs one at a time, not fully trusting the wood as it creaked and groaned under her weight. A cool breeze whistled in through the open window as she reached the top. The landing opened into what would have been a child's bedroom. The flowered wallpaper now curled up at the edges. A small collection of cast-off dolls scattered about the floor. One was missing an arm. One was missing both legs. A ceramic head without a body sat on the floor as though buried in the sand. A thin crack ran down her porcelain face. Ethel's first thought at seeing the sad toys was *Johnnie.* But the girl was nowhere to be seen. A headless doll sat under the window.

Outside the broken glass, the sun had dropped lower in the sky. The five-story brick wall of the Harmony Mission loomed darkly on the other side of the fence. The windows along the top of the factory were all empty.

Ethel opened the small closet to see two dresses hanging from hooks. They looked about the right size to fit a nine-year-old. Another door sat closed on the other side of the stair landing facing the front of the house. Holding her breath, she swung it open.

A foul vapor of whiskey and vomit hit her face in the wake of the door. Holding her hand up to her nose, she squinted into the dark room. Boards covered the window. A humongous heap of old rags sat in the middle of the room. It was breathing.

Ethel backed out of the doorway and down the stairs. The enormous person passed out above her grunted and thumped the ceiling as she scrambled through the living room to the back door. She stopped at the basement stairs. "Johnnie?" she called down into the dark, no longer bothering to whisper, knowing the drunk upstairs was too far gone to catch her.

She waited long enough to hear another thump and a groan somewhere upstairs and headed out the door. The overgrown backyard ended in an alley running past the Harmony Mission building. Ethel gauged the twenty-foot distance between the factory and the house where she'd emerged the night before. Somewhere below her feet sat an underground tomb full of bones. Brother Wenger could be down there now, looking for her. If she was going to stop the sick bastard before he found another victim to dump in the river, she needed a plan.

"I'm no hero," she whispered to herself. "What the hell am I gonna do about it?" She wasn't a cop or even a reliable witness. She was nothing but a busted whore. Sister Frances had let her go with the detective watching, but she doubted she'd be so lucky the next time. She hugged herself, knowing she'd be better off just catching out on a train. She could head to Chicago behind One-Armed Willie and—

A flicker of movement caught the corner of her eye. A shadow darted between the houses a half block away on the other side of the gutter they called Thurman Avenue. Tiny one-floor cottages dotted the narrow brick street. The overcrowded houses sat between boarded-up arson attempts and scrub brush lawns littered with broken toys, but nothing was moving.

Ethel almost turned away, but a black mark on one of the little houses stopped her from across the street. It was another star. Someone had nailed a board across the door, telling her the house had been condemned. The partially covered star looked eerily like the one on the door behind her. She crept up the alley toward it.

Thurman Avenue sat empty. It stretched down past the Harmony Mission building, and Ethel glanced furtively up at the loading dock before crossing the narrow brick road to the marked house. The yards sat empty as she slipped between two cottages, out of view of the street. The back door of the condemned house hung half-open.

"Johnnie?" she called softly through the open door. She stepped inside and called again. "Johnnie? You there?"

The boards nailed over the front windows blocked out most of the light. The kitchen had been stripped clean of even the curtains. Dust and dead flies littered the windowsills. A dark brown water stain spread out over the middle of the floor. Above it, a meat hook had been drilled through the ceiling. It reminded her of Wenger's pig hanging from its hooves. Ethel's eyes drifted from the giant metal hook to the stain on the floor.

A floorboard creaked behind her. Ethel spun to see a small dark-skinned girl with a mat of black hair standing sullen in the doorway. She jumped a little despite herself. "Oh. Hi." Ethel forced a smile. "Johnnie?"

The girl didn't answer. She shrank from the door as though she were about to run.

"It's okay. I'm not going to hurt you. Do you remember me? You helped me find my way out of . . . that dark place?"

The girl gave the slightest nod.

"What are you doing in here?"

She didn't answer.

"What, uh . . . what happened here?" Ethel asked and pointed to the hook in the ceiling.

Johnnie just stared.

"Did you . . . did you see what happened?"

The girl nodded.

Ethel swallowed, picturing the pig spilling its insides out on the ground. "Something bad? Did the bad people come and . . . did they hurt someone?"

Johnnie shrank further into the corner, avoiding eye contact.

"Did you live here?"

She shook her head.

"It's okay. You can tell me about it. I won't get mad. I won't tell anyone. You found this house empty, right? Were you staying here all by yourself?"

She shook her head again and whispered, "My mom."

"Your mom was with you?" Ethel nodded to encourage the girl to keep talking while a rotten feeling crawled into her gut. Johnnie's mother clearly wasn't with her anymore. She glanced up at the meat hook. "Did somebody find you here?"

Johnnie just stared at the stain on the floor. Then Ethel remembered what she'd said in the dark. *I don't let people see me.*

"They found your mom? Did they find her here and think she was alone?" The stain spread out over the floor to the bottoms of Ethel's feet, and her stomach sank like a stone. Only one black woman had been killed by the Butcher, and that woman had been her friend. She shook her head, searching for another explanation, but couldn't stop herself from asking, "Was your mama's name Rose? Rose Wallace?"

Johnnie's startled eyes were her answer.

"I knew her." Ethel hung her head. "I'm so sorry, Johnnie . . . We've been looking for you ever since she disappeared." Her eyes circled the house and then scanned the street. They were on the wrong side of the river in a decidedly white part of town. "What the hell were the two of you doin' out here?"

Johnnie just stared at the floor, mute.

"Was she tryin' to find work?" Ethel crouched down to the little girl's level. "Was she runnin' from someone?"

"She heard 'em talkin'," Johnnie whispered.

"What'd she hear?"

"She heard 'em talkin' 'bout the dead bodies down in the Run."

"What'd they say?"

"They said it was too dangerous leavin' the hands and the heads. She heard them fightin' over how best to do it. One wanted to keep the heads."

"Did she say who?"

Johnnie just shook her head. "They was white men."

"Did she tell anybody?"

The girl nodded. "She talked to a policeman. He said we was in danger. He tol' us to hide here and wait."

Ethel sucked in a breath and looked back up at the hook in the ceiling. The cop had sent them right into a trap. "What was his name? Merylo or Martin? Either of those sound familiar?"

Johnnie shook her head. "Kessler."

"Did he come back here? Did he come here with the bad people?"

"I don't know. They had no faces. They just hung her . . ." The girl gazed at the hook in the ceiling with the empty eyes of a corpse.

Ethel touched the cheek of the poor little thing. "You shouldn't be in here, you know. We should find a better place for you."

She turned her dead brown eyes to Ethel and asked, "Where?"

"Do you have a grandma? Or an aunt? Or anybody nearby?" Rose had a husband once, but Ethel had never met him. If she remembered right, the husband didn't have much to do with this last baby.

The girl shook her head.

"Well, shit. I dunno." Ethel had nothing. No home. No education. No prospects. No faith in the prison-style orphanages. "Tell you what. You help me figure this thing out, and I'll . . . I'll help you figure out where to go. Deal?"

The girl just stared with those empty eyes.

"Okay. How many of them were there? Do you know?"

Johnnie shook her head. "Down in the dead place, lots of voices be talkin'. They say prayers and talk to demons . . . sometimes they light them on fire."

Ethel winced. *Down in the dead place.* The caverns under the Harmony Mission reeked of sewage and something worse—the smell of burning hair. She could feel Wenger straddling her naked body and pressing his Bible to her forehead. *Would he have taken a match to me?*

Johnnie gazed blankly at the spot on the floor. "When they was done, they took her away."

"Where did they take her?"

"They packed her up like food. In grain sacks. They rolled a barrel down the street like it was cider."

Ethel swallowed hard and looked up at the hook, seeing Brothers Bertram and Wenger bleeding her like a pig. "Where did they go?"

"Over there." Johnnie pointed at the front wall out into the street.

Ethel brushed the poor girl's cheek. "Will you show me?"

Johnnie led her out the back door and up the side of the house. She eyed both ends of the narrow street before darting across the brick pavement to the alley behind the Harmony Mission. The back side of the burnt-out bungalow sat five doors down. The blood-red star on the broken door faced the bricks of the factory. Straight ahead was the boarded-up hardware store with a blank sign out front. The cellar entrance was covered with weathered shed doors slanting out of the ground. The latch was padlocked.

"They went down there."

Ethel scanned the yards between the cellar doors back to the marked house and up at the tall brick wall of the factory behind her. She grabbed the young girl by the hand and walked her behind the houses until she'd come to the broken back door that led down to the dead place. The drunk on the second floor gave her pause. "Johnnie, do you know who's sleeping upstairs?"

"It's just Hortie." She shrugged.

"You afraid of Hortie?"

Johnnie shook her head.

"Okay. I want you to go inside and stay out of sight. Don't tell any-body what you told me, understand? The police are not your friends. We don't know which ones we can trust, so don't trust any of 'em."

Johnnie nodded in agreement.

"Don't tell anyone who your mother was. Not a soul. Not ever. Just say you don't remember. Can you do that? Just lock her away in here." Ethel patted the girl's bony chest. "If I don't come back for you by tomorrow, get as far away from here as you can. Catch out on a train. You hear?"

A small tear fell down the little thing's cheek.

"You're a strong girl. If you made it this far all by yourself, ain't nothin' can touch you, got me?" Ethel gripped Johnnie's shoulders hard, knowing all too well what was waiting for the girl out there in the world. "You do what you gotta do to get by, okay? That's what your mama would want. You're gonna be fine." It was a lie. Neither of them would ever be fine. Not in this world. Everyone knew the police could be bought, the mob owned half of 'em, but the idea that they were caught up in this . . .

"What you gonna do?" the girl whispered.

Ethel knew she should jump a train with Johnnie and get the hell out of town, but every town was the same town and she'd never done the right thing in her life. Not since her brother died anyway, and she learned that there was no justice in this world. No right. No wrong. Just kill or be killed, and she'd be damned if she let them get away with this. She'd be damned either way.

She gave the girl a pained smile. "I'm going to kill the bastards that took your mom."

CHAPTER 41

"Rickey!" Ethel hissed up the side of the bridge abutment. She climbed up the rubble slope to the concrete piers looking out over the city from under the shadow of the Lorain-Carnegie Bridge.

He didn't answer.

"Rickey!" she said louder, risking being heard by some other vagrant holed up in one of the scrap-metal shanties that dotted the tall grasses all the way down to the river. "Sugar, I got some hooch for you!"

A face peeked out from the web of a giant steel girder. "Dirty Bedsheets, is that you?" A large pair of high heels emerged from the cover of the riveted steel plates and dropped down to the concrete. The beam of a flashlight blinded her while he checked her face and then clicked it off. He straightened his wine-colored evening dress and sauntered over. "That better not be some old rotgut."

"It's Canadian." She waggled the bottle at him. It had taken a hard half hour with the bartender in the alley behind McGinty's.

"To what do I owe this pleasure?" He cocked an eyebrow and held out a delicate hand.

She put the bottle in it. "I need somethin'."

"Don't we all?" He carefully inspected the label before unscrewing the cap and taking a healthy swig. "Hoo! That is nice. What is it you think I can do for you, darlin'?"

"I need a gun."

He raised a pencil-thin eyebrow and took another drink.

"And that flashlight."

"Then I sure as hell hope you have more to trade than this measly little bottle, sweetness." He handed the bottle back to her and waved his hand at her like she must be crazy.

"I know who killed Rose Wallace."

This got his attention. "And how's that?"

"I found the empty house where they did her. She heard somethin' she wasn't supposed to. A cop calling himself Kessler told her to hide out and wait. That night they came for her and hung her up from a meat hook."

Rickey let out a low whistle.

"They found her body right around here. Ain't that right?"

"Yep. In a nasty burlap sack right down there. Soaked her in lime until there was nothin' but bone left." He grabbed the bottle back and took another drink. "Them cops have been tryin' to pin that one on me ever since. Me and Rose was friends . . . How'd you find out where they did her?"

"It doesn't matter." She shot him a look. If he really knew Rose, he knew about Johnnie.

He seemed to read her mind but just nodded. "Can you name names?"

"Besides Kessler? No. Not yet. But I think I know where they're gonna be."

"And you think a little gun is going to do the job? Shit, you are a nutter. If they got cops on the payroll, you haven't got a chance."

"Maybe not, but how long can this keep goin' before you and me end up swinging from a meat hook too?" Ethel hissed. "These people, whoever they are, they're cowards. They figure if they kill nothin' but passed-out drunks and working girls, no one will care. No one will fight back. They have no idea who they're messin' with now!"

Rickey flashed an amused grin. "So if I give you a gun and this light . . . you're gonna go in and kill them all?"

Ethel shrugged. "Maybe I just need to kill one. Someone's got to be in charge of all this, right?"

"And what's gonna happen to me when they find you floatin' in the river? What's gonna happen when they find my gun on your body? How long before they come for me?"

She held up a hand. "I get caught, I don't know you."

"Shit, honey. You don't know me now. I am not looking to be a hero in your little crusade." He turned away, shaking his head.

"What about Rose?"

"Rose is dead, honey. There's nothing I can do about that."

"Aren't you tired of all this? Business around here's dried up. Nobody wants to pay top dollar for a throw when it might cost 'em their head. Coppers keep huntin' you like a dog. Do you really think it's gonna stop?"

Rickey looked her dead in the eye. "No. I don't . . . but there'll always be a reason for the folks up there to lock us up. Torso Killer or not, I am not wanted here. And neither are you. They only want us in the dark when no one's lookin', and then when they're finished with us, we're supposed to disappear. We're ghosts to them. They'd rather we all got cut up and thrown in the damn river just so they wouldn't have to look at us in the daylight."

Ethel nodded in agreement. "If we want the killings to stop, we have to stop them ourselves."

Rickey held her murderous gaze for a moment, then stared out over the tall buildings on the other side of the river. "We won't win. Even if you kill every single one of them, we won't . . . We never do."

"They slaughtered her like an animal, Rickey. They turned her into meat."

"But isn't that what we are to them? Meat?" He threw up his hands at her and sauntered back to his hideaway under the bridge. He wasn't going to help her.

Ethel wiped away a tear with angry hands and looked down into the river. Somewhere below the depths lay parts of a girl, butchered into pieces small enough to carry home from the market. It would be her one day. If not from the knife of the Butcher, from the wear and tear of scraping by on her knees, bouncing from one hellhole to another, until they were all through with her. Ethel could already feel the weight of the water over her head. She felt herself sinking to the bottom of the river with the pieces of that poor girl. She could see the muted glow of the city lights floating high above the murky sewage and the runoff from the slaughterhouses.

She took several shaking steps down the slope. Rickey's voice stopped her.

"I got this little beauty hot off an armed robbery." He was holding a pistol with a worn handle. "I believe they used it to kill a cop, so be sure to lose it when you're done."

She took the pistol from him and tested the weight of it in her hand. He placed the flashlight in the other.

"Thanks, Rickey. I won't forget this."

He flashed her a grin. "You bet your ass you're gonna forget it, 'cause I know for certain that I've never seen you before in my life."

She nodded.

"Where'd you find the piece?" he asked, testing her.

"In an abandoned house down on Thurman. It was lying in a puddle of blood."

"You know how to use that thing?"

Ethel turned it over in her hand. The last time she'd held a gun, she'd ended up in the Mansfield workhouse for two years. She could still feel the kick of it and smell the gunpowder after it went off. She could still see her landlord's face as he fell back into a puddle of his own blood and hear her brother screaming tears in the corner as they took her away in handcuffs. She never saw either one of them again. The bastard died in the hospital three weeks later, and her little brother was shipped downstate to an orphanage for disturbed children. The court ruled it aggravated manslaughter instead of murder out of horror for what the man had done to the ten-year-old boy. None of the jurors seemed all that concerned about what he'd done to her. The light sentence was her only consolation. Her brother killed himself six months before her release. "Yeah," she whispered. "Yeah, I do."

Rickey held her eye for a beat, then turned to the skyline. He drew in a long, deep breath. "Don't matter anyway. One of my boys down at the Second District tells me they're raiding the jungles tonight, and they are arresting *everybody*. Eliot Ness himself has sworn to catch this Butcher, and after the body they found today, he is out of time. I'm catching out. If you have any sense at all, you'll do the same."

Ethel scanned the skyline. "Where will you go?"

"Anywhere but here, sugar. That's the benefit of being a ghost, ain't it? You can vanish and no one"—he shot her a pointed look—"will ever find you."

She shrugged off his warning and cocked a grin. "But you're forgetting the other benefit of being a ghost."

"Really, darlin'? What's that?" He smiled back.

"No one ever sees you coming."

CHAPTER 42

It was almost midnight when Ethel returned to the house where she'd left Johnnie. The mountain of a drunk the girl called Hortie lay snoring on the torn sofa in the living room with an empty bottle on the floor. Ethel scanned the room for signs of Johnnie, knowing she was there somewhere, hiding.

"Johnnie," she whispered. "Stay here. Go to sleep. I'll be back in a little while."

She crept down the basement stairs to the root cellar with the pistol hidden in the hem of her skirt and the heavy metal flashlight in her hand. At the bottom of the narrow ladder, the hole in the root cellar wall was just where she'd left it. She wriggled her way into the narrow tunnel connecting the abandoned house to the catacombs below the Harmony Mission presses.

As her head emerged from the long, narrow tomb, she heard a voice. Ethel clicked off the yellow beam of her flashlight and listened.

". . . 'save me from all them that persecute me, and deliver me. Lest he tear my soul like a lion, rending it in pieces, while there is none to deliver.'" It was a young woman's voice. She was weeping.

Ethel pulled herself out of the narrow tunnel and crept toward the faint glow of candlelight at the far end of the hall lined with crypts.

"'Oh, Lord my God, if I have done this; if there be iniquity in my hands, if I have rewarded evil unto him that was at peace with me.'" The voice stopped and sobbed. Under it a low shushing sound paused, then started up again. "'Let the enemy persecute my soul and take it; yea, let him tread down my life upon the earth . . .'"

As Ethel approached the corner, the light grew brighter. She pulled the gun from the hem of her skirts and pressed her back to the wall. After two harried breaths, she risked a look.

A woman was crouched on her knees with her back to the room and a scrub brush in her hand. The brush dipped into a bucket and went back to scouring the stone floor. The water was stained red. An enormous wooden cross hung from the wall over the woman's head. The life-sized crucifix had been mounted upside down.

The woman stopped scrubbing and shook with another sob. "'Oh, let the wickedness of the wicked come to an end, but establish the just . . . ,'" she wailed. "'My defense is of God, which saveth the upright in heart. God judgeth the righteous, and God is angry with the wicked every day . . . every day.'"

Ethel scanned the empty room. A metal table sat against the sidewall with a collection of large medical knives laid out according to size. The largest looked like a meat cleaver. The crying woman's prayers echoed off the stone walls, and her head was bowed down to the tops of her red-stained hands.

Ethel pointed the gun straight at the woman's back and stepped out from her corner. "Where are they?" she demanded. "Where are the rest of them?"

The woman turned, and the brush in her hands hit the ground with a hollow *clack*. The front of her plain blue dress was stained purple. A bruise darkened one of her swollen eyes. "Ambrosia? Is that you?" she squeaked.

Ethel lowered the gun. "Mary Alice? What are you doing down here? Sweet Jesus. What did they do to you do?"

Red marks darkened the poor girl's neck as though she'd been choked. Her face had gone hollow and pale.

"They were so angry you left. Why? Why did you come back?" Fresh tears spilled down the poor girl's face.

Ethel crouched down beside her. "Who did this to you? Was it Wenger? Where is he?"

Mary Alice turned her shaking red hands over. Her eyes drifted up to the inverted cross.

Ethel followed her eyes, then darted back to the bloody bucket. "Is he dead? Who killed him? You have to tell me, Mary Alice. Who is doing this?"

The girl's eyes darted around the empty room, and she shook her head.

"It's okay. You can tell me. Is it Reverend Milton?"

"No . . . no it's . . ." Her voice dropped below a whisper. "It's the Legion."

"The what?" Ethel hissed. "Who are they?"

Mary Alice shrank into herself and began to tremble. "They're everywhere, listening. You shouldn't be here."

"We have to get you out of here. C'mon. Let's get you up." Ethel stood and pulled the dazed girl up by the arms. She nearly slumped right back over. Ethel grabbed her by the hand and waist and led her back down the dark hallway toward the passage to the root cellar. "We have to get you to the detective. He'll listen to you. You're a real person to them. An honest person. You need to tell them what you saw."

As the hall grew darker, Ethel grew less certain which of the catacombs led back out. She glanced over her shoulder at Mary Alice's pale face then the empty corridor before pulling the flashlight out of her cleavage and clicking it on. She shined the light into full and empty graves, crouching as she went. "Don't worry," she whispered, letting go of Mary Alice to search. "There's a way out. I just have to find it."

"Jesus, I beg thee to walk these steps with me," Mary Alice whispered. "To guide my head. To guide my hand. Jesus, be with me."

"Here!" Ethel shined her light into an empty tomb. "It's right h—"

A hard crack to the back of Ethel's head knocked the words from her mouth. A flash of white blinded her as the room crashed to the floor.

BLAMES SLAYING ON
FREIGHT RIDER

A murderer who rides freight trains and is a pervert was responsible for the killing of the victim found in "Murder Swamp" near New Castle, Pa., and for at least several of the Cleveland torso murders, Police Detective Peter Merylo said yesterday upon his return from the Pennsylvania city with the other Cleveland officers sent there to seek possible links with torso cases here.

—*Cleveland Plain Dealer*, October 16, 1939, p. 3

CHAPTER 43

April 10, 1999

"Oh, God! Oh, God! Where are we going?" Kris's hands were shaking so hard she could barely grip the wheel as they went careening down West Hume Road.

"Pull in there." Jimmy pointed to Shirlene's Diner. The breakfast crowd was thin that morning. "We have to ditch this car. Pull up in the back."

"Okay." Kris brought the Jeep to a rumbling stop next to the grease trap behind the dumpster and out of sight of the restaurant windows and road. "What do you mean we have to ditch the car?"

"I just pointed a fucking shotgun at a white boy. The second we left the house, he called the cops. I guarantee it. And I'm pretty sure he left out the part where he smacked you around. They're gonna be lookin' for us." Jimmy took off his shirt and began wiping down the car door handle and dashboard. "They're probably setting roadblocks now."

Kris frowned at him cleaning the steering wheel while the word *fingerprints* slowly formed in her head. In the rearview mirror, she could see the bruise on her cheek forming where Troy had smacked her. It would be so much easier for Ben to believe Jimmy had done it. "He'll say you kidnapped me. Oh, shit! What are we gonna do?"

Jimmy took in a slow breath and gazed out the window toward the train tracks on the other side of the chain-link fence at the back of the lot. Two dilapidated boxcars sat behind it above a ditch. "You get junk trains through here?"

"What's a junk train?" She followed his gaze out toward the tracks.

"Scrap metal, produce, livestock, that sort of thing. Or are they all tankers?"

"We get everything through here. It's a hub. Trains roll through every hour." She started to understand his thinking.

Jimmy nodded and opened the car door. "Let's hope you're right. I hear one coming."

"Where are we going?" Kris scrambled out after him.

"We gotta get back to Cleveland. They can't prove a thing if they can't ID me."

"They're going to find the car."

"It's not illegal to park here, is it?" Jimmy threw her bags over the chain-link fence and climbed up after them.

"No. But . . ." She stopped at the rusted links, debating what to do. An eighteen-wheeler roared past on the road out front, blind to them standing there in the shrubs. Ben would be furious with her. The entire town would be in an uproar. She could picture Troy loading up his truck with guns and tearing ass all the way to Cleveland.

"But nothing. We'll work it out, but we've got to move. Now."

Kris nodded and hopped the fence.

Jimmy picked up the bags and patted her shoulder. "It's not a felony to ditch a car. All they can give you for it is a ticket. You're a grown woman. You can leave town whenever you want to."

"But isn't it illegal to stow away on a train?"

"Not if you don't get caught." Jimmy led her over the tracks, eying both directions. A rusted boxcar leaned against an abutment with its door open. He grabbed her hand and dragged her across two sets of tracks and up into the open container. "This track doesn't look like it's even patrolled."

"How do you even know which train is going where?" Kris hissed and backed up into a corner of the steel box. It smelled of moss and old onions.

"Any train pointed east should hit Cleveland. All the major lines go through." Jimmy kept his eyes on the tracks. "Besides, there's signs."

"What do you mean 'signs'?"

"In the old days, hobos would tag trains and stops with glyphs. You know, marks to help each other." He pointed to the graffiti on the walls of the boxcar. The marks looked like nothing but a collection of scribbles to Kris. "See. This car came from Cleveland."

"What are you saying? Hobos spray-painted the car?"

"Nobody calls themselves 'hobos' anymore, but they still hop trains."

"Why?"

"Free ride mostly." Jimmy shrugged. "Smuggling . . ."

A police siren wailed somewhere in the distance, then faded. Kris followed it with her eyes, through the trees.

"Don't worry. The cops will keep themselves busy setting up roadblocks for the next hour if your friend back there sold the kidnapping story."

"It won't be long before someone notices the Jeep. It's a really small town." Kris bit her lip, wondering if Ben would guess where they'd gone, wondering if he'd ever speak to her again.

"Well, lucky for us, here comes the train."

Kris stopped pacing. A whistle blew in the distance and an almost imperceptible vibration hummed under her feet.

"Stay out of sight until the engine passes," Jimmy said and took up a watch in the shadow of the open door.

"How many times have you done this?" Kris asked. The vibration crept up her legs and the whistle blew again but louder. The Jeep sat across the train tracks on the other side of the fence, waiting for her to lose her nerve.

"A couple times. For research."

"Research?"

"The Torso Killers liked trains. They left bodies in train yards, in old boxcars like this one back in the '40s. The Nickel Plate Railroad passed right through Kingsbury Run where the first bodies were found. I think one of the killers owned a rail line." Jimmy almost had to shout over the roar of the engine as it rumbled closer. He pressed her to the side wall. "This looks promising."

Kris watched the huge black engine chug past the open door. The screech of its brakes split her ears. Smatterings of graffiti lumbered past along with a steady string of boxcars and flatbeds holding containers.

"This is it!" Jimmy slung her bags onto his shoulders. "They're slowing down to take the turn. We're gonna run for it."

He hopped three feet down onto the gravel berm and reached up for her hand. She scanned the endless chain of containers and open cars and then jumped. They took off running next to the train as the cars continued to slow. The thirty-degree bend in the tracks sat a quarter mile ahead. The engine had already disappeared around the turn. An open bin of scrap metal rattled past. Long patches of dried grass grabbed at her legs, threatening to pull her under as they ran after it.

"This one!" Jimmy hollered and reached up and grabbed a metal handle next to a sliding door. He hopped on to a narrow runner board and slid the metal panel open a foot. Once he'd tossed her bags inside, he held out a hand to pull her up. "C'mon! You can make it!"

Kris was losing her wind. She could feel the train slipping away and her legs going soft. The brakes were no longer screaming. The metal wheels turned faster and faster. Jimmy stretched out toward her, hanging dangerously low from the running board.

"Move that ass, Kris!" he barked, reaching for her. "Don't let 'em catch you. C'mon!"

She stretched out her arm as far as it would reach, and he caught her wrist. Her feet barely stayed under her at all as he hauled her up onto the running board and pushed her inside.

Kris went tumbling onto the floor, crashing into a wood crate. A sharp piece dug into her thigh. "Ouch!"

"Sorry about that." Jimmy slid the door closed all but an inch and collapsed onto the ground next to her. "Some rush, huh?"

Her heart pounded its way out of her chest as she struggled to catch her breath. She inspected the long scrape down her leg. "This is crazy!"

"Probably."

"What's even in here?" The freight car reeked of motor oil and wet paint.

"Who cares. It's ours. And nobody knows where we are at the moment. That's all that matters."

A nervous laugh escaped her lips. "That's all that matters? Are you nuts? They know where I live. Ben's not stupid. They'll probably be waiting for us at the train yard in Cleveland."

"I doubt it. Seems obvious to you and me, but it'd probably take 'em at least a few hours to find the car and half a day to question everybody at the diner back there. They'll be lookin' for a trucker that picked up a couple hitchhikers."

"They'll check my house."

"So what? You won't be there. They don't know where I live. They don't even know my name."

"I can't just hide and wait. My father's dead, and now you think my mom was murdered too and some maniac out there put a mark on my door . . . on me. And I've left everything a mess back there. I don't have anywhere left to go." Her body began to tremble as her adrenaline crashed.

"We'll figure it out, okay? We have to find David Hohman and find out what he knows. Your pop was killed for a reason, and you're not safe until we figure out what it was."

"And you think we can do that?" She stared out at the sliver of trees and sky rushing past the car.

"You got a better idea? You want to take your chances with ol' boy wifebeater back there?"

"No . . . I just—I need to talk to Ben." But Ben had sent Troy to her house. And he had acted so strange when she'd asked about her mother. *He'd been so angry.*

"You're gonna call your cop buddy when we get back. You're gonna explain how that hillbilly back there hit you, scared the shit out of you, and how you ditched the car, thinking he'd follow you. You're gonna file a restraining order, right?"

It all sounded right, but the last thing she wanted to do was talk with Ben. She turned to Jimmy and studied his face. The gun. The train. The way he thought to wipe away fingerprints. "What am I going to say about you?"

"Not a damn thing. There is no *me.*"

"He won't buy it. He's always trusted Troy. They'll be looking for blood." *Both of them.*

Jimmy chuckled. "And that is exactly why we're sitting on a train right now."

"I'm going to have to come up with something."

"Fine. Say we met at school. You hardly know me. You don't know where I live. I'll give you a name that they'll never pin back to me. If it gets too hot, I'll just take off for a while."

Kris rubbed her eyes, hoping to unearth some better plan, but came up empty. The boxcar swayed back and forth in a hypnotic rhythm, leaving her limp. She leaned her head against his shoulder and he wrapped an arm around her. She didn't want Jimmy to just disappear, but an uneasy feeling in her gut nagged at her. *What is it? Think.*

Closing her eyes, all she could see was Troy's hand slamming into her head. Her lids flew back open. The fight replayed before her eyes. Troy had said something utterly insane like, *He promised we'd be together.* She shuddered at how close she'd come to being his prisoner. *His victim.* There had been plenty of times he'd pressured her into sex, especially when she was younger, but the word *rape* had never crossed her mind. *He promised we'd be together.*

Who promised? she wondered. *Ben?* It was Ben that had called Troy and told him to take her to the morgue. It was Ben that had threatened to drag her back to Cridersville in handcuffs. It was Ben who was so desperate to have the paperwork done and her father's remains cremated. Ben was a police officer with access to criminal evidence. Her father had never told his own best friend, his only friend, about his research into the Torso Killer. *Why not?*

"You okay?" Jimmy asked.

"No," she muttered. "I'm not. I'm going crazy. I feel like I can't trust anyone anymore." She'd known Ben her entire life and now her paranoid delusions were turning him into a killer.

"Just breathe. I got you." He gave her a reassuring squeeze.

Outside the cracked door, the cornfields rushed by in a blur. Kris closed her eyes and tried to process everything that had happened since Ben had shaken her awake. Her mother's photo flitted in and out of her mind.

Jimmy kept chatting about hobos hopping trains as the metal tracks rumbled beneath them. All Kris could see was her mother's crumpled car sitting by the side of the road. She never saw the body pulled from the wreckage or laid out on a slab like a burnt mannequin or a gutted deer. At the funeral, they buried a tiny urn and a photograph. For years, Kris would find herself staring at the front door to the house, half expecting the woman to walk through it again one day.

The sway of the train and Jimmy's voice lulled her to an uneasy sleep. In her dream, she found herself running across a long field. Running toward a woman with open arms.

CHAPTER 44

The train rumbled to a stop on a siding. Jimmy nudged her shoulder, then pulled himself to his feet. Kris glanced at the gap opening between the door and sidewall to see a sliver of Cleveland's skyline hovering over the murky waters of the Cuyahoga River.

A blast of light hit her in the face as Jimmy slid open the door. He hopped down onto the gravel below. They had landed down in the industrial wasteland flanking the river with mountains of gravel and shipping cranes. A giant cargo ship sat tethered to the far side of the river, a metal city unto itself. It had probably come in through the channels and locks that connected Lake Erie to the ocean. A pair of dockworkers walked by only thirty feet away. One glanced up at her emerging from the boxcar. He shook his head at her and kept walking.

"C'mon!" Jimmy hissed. "Let's get outta here!"

Kris jumped down and followed him under the abutment of the Lorain-Carnegie Bridge. They'd landed on the west side of the river, five blocks north of Tremont. The sparse skyline of the city watched from the other side of the water as they picked their way across the stones. The snow had melted away, but the wind still had a bite to it. She shivered in the shadow of the bridge, gazing down into the river. More than one body had been found there.

Four blocks later, they stopped at the foot of Thurman Avenue. Two police cruisers sat parked outside her tiny rental. *Ben.* She slipped behind the vacant storefront on the corner with its newspapered windows and peeked out at the flashing lights.

"They didn't waste any time, did they?" Jimmy said from behind her. He grabbed her wrist and pulled her down the crossroad. "C'mon."

A block north on West 7th Street, the gate they'd used the night of Jimmy's party had been padlocked shut. Kris marveled to think that had only been three days earlier. Her feet slowed in protest as Jimmy led her up to the chained door. She wanted to go back three days. No, a week, or better yet, a year. Back to the last time she'd hugged her father.

"Don't worry," Jimmy said, tugging her along. "Just keep an eye out."

She turned away from the Harmony Press Building and gazed down the block toward Jefferson Avenue and the spot where she liked to park her car. Her rusted-out Jeep was still sitting next to Shirlene's grease trap 150 miles away. *This isn't my life.*

In quick order, Jimmy popped the lock, loosened the chain holding the gate shut, and then squeezed through the gap, pulling her two bags behind him. The slim line of her shotgun pointed at her through the canvas. Her feet followed him while her mind wandered back down Thurman Avenue to the spot where two police cruisers sat, waiting.

Would they arrest her? she wondered. There was no doubt in her mind that they'd arrest Jimmy. The look in Ben's eyes, sitting across from her at her father's table, kept her moving. They were the eyes of a stranger.

Jimmy led her through the narrow vaulted passage and into the gallows courtyard. The flashing police lights on Thurman bounced off the dark walls of the loading dock. Kris stared at them through the iron bars of the gate a hundred feet away.

"It's okay," he whispered, pulling her through the hobbit door into his wing of the building. "They don't know we're here."

Her eyes traced each door as they went. Dozens of rooms and closets. Dozens of dead ends. She couldn't keep track of them all as she followed Jimmy up and down crumbling steps and through the dark, narrow hallways. It was the perfect place to hide. Did her father come here to hide too? she wondered.

By the time they'd arrived back in his squatter's hovel, she felt sick. She collapsed onto Jimmy's bed with her head in her hands while he unlocked the closet door in the far corner. A computer made from cast-off parts sat in a nest of extension cords and cables. He pulled up a beanbag chair to a cracked computer monitor and began to type. The clacking of the keyboard pounded through the silence as Kris laid back against his pillows. She couldn't just hide there forever.

"Hey. I think I found somethin'."

Kris forced herself to sit up.

Jimmy motioned her over to his half-shattered computer screen. "Take a look at this. It's DHOH's last postings."

Kris stood over Jimmy's shoulder and read the orange text glowing on his monitor. The web address read, *www.torsokillers.com.* "Wait, I thought the page was down."

"This is just a screenshot. See the date?" The upper corner gave a date from a week earlier. *April 3.*

"A screenshot?"

"Yeah. One of the guys in the chat room records everything in case the government or the aliens or whoever he doesn't trust that day shuts it down. He's bat-shit crazy, but it comes in handy. Look."

Kris scanned through the lines of discussion that all seemed to revolve around a series of news clippings posted by DHOH. She scanned the grainy headlines and dates. There was one from February 1997 in Sacramento, California. *Body Found in Boxcar.* Another from 1995 in Pittsburgh, Pennsylvania. *Unidentified Man Found Dead.* There were over twenty similar stories. "They match the ones in my dad's scrapbook."

"He wasn't the only one collecting them. See?" Jimmy scrolled down to a discussion thread.

DHOH: All bodies found missing fingers and heads. All found in trains or train yards. Sound familiar?

DOLEZAL: Interesting. Any arrests?

DHOH: All unsolved. 54 dead between 1972 and 1999.

SSLDIDIT: Could be gangland hits. No head, no fingerprints, no ID.

DOLEZAL: Any connection between the bodies?

LOWJACK: What train lines?

Kris stopped reading and pointed at the screen. "I know that guy. That's the asshole that stole my dad's police report."

Jimmy raised both eyebrows and started to say something, but she interrupted by tapping on the computer screen.

"Look at this."

DHOH: All dead trains passed through Cleveland. All dead trains passed through Lima. All dead trains on the CDX scrap division.

Kris read *CDX* again and recoiled from the screen. "My dad worked for CDX Rail," she whispered. "Oh my God. He must've seen something."

"Maybe he did." Jimmy scrolled down farther. A new name popped up on the screen.

BOGIE: DHOH, any suspects?

DHOH: Working through usual checks. Employee records crossed with criminal records crossed with Torso Database. List getting shorter every day.

"What's the Torso Database?" Kris asked, pointing to the place on the screen.

"The Notting Hill Killers keep a database of known suspects in the Torso Murders, including Cleveland Nazis and members of the Silver Shirt Legion."

Kris nodded and went back to reading. Her eyes froze on the next line.

BOGIE: I may have something useful.

DHOH: What do you got?

BOGIE: Probably nothing. DHOH, do you know a good computer repair shop?

DHOH: Hardware trouble?

BOGIE: Getting glitchy. Interference on the dial-up.

DHOH: I'd find a local geek. Repair shops are full of idiots.

BOGIE: Not too much outside Lima. Maybe Shirlene's knows a guy.

DHOH: Good luck!

"There's nothin' after this." Jimmy tapped the screen. "The name Bogie mean anything to you?"

"Yeah. It's the name of my dad's favorite dog." Kris scanned through the lines of cryptic text again. "What do you think all this means?"

"These are public chat rooms. Anybody can be lurking and reading along, so there's a few code phrases you throw if you think you're being watched. Sayin' your computer is glitching out is one way to warn the others that lurkers are listening. Isn't Shirlene's the name of that diner?"

"Yeah, it is . . ." Kris read the sequence again. "He also let him know he was near Lima. When was this posted?"

"April 2."

"They found the body on April 6," she whispered.

Jimmy started typing again. The words blurred on the screen.

"I'm going to try to get DHOH to meet me tonight. He's been dark for days, but he never stays away long. He's more addicted to this shit than I am."

She watched as he typed, her anxiety growing. "But we don't know a thing about this guy . . . He could be the killer. He could be fishing around to see what people know about him."

"Or somebody was lurking and found your dad before they could meet." Jimmy turned his soft eyes up at her. "We have to try, right? I'll be careful."

"You'll be *careful*? People are dead, Jimmy! We need to call somebody. We need to call the police or the FBI. Somebody."

"We can't go to the cops just yet. Not until we know what the hell's going on, right? Once we go to them, you and me can't . . . I'm going to have to ghost out of here or they'll throw me in jail."

Kris frowned, knowing he might be right. Ben certainly wouldn't pay the online detective work any real attention. He wouldn't listen to her, and she wasn't convinced he could be trusted even if he did. "But you can't risk it. This guy went looking for my father right before he disappeared . . . I mean, isn't the idea of a psycho who idolizes a serial killer from the 1930s more believable than some elaborate conspiracy involving Nazis? C'mon. We have to call somebody."

"What makes you think we can trust the cops?" He raised an eyebrow at her. "There were lots of Silver Shirts on the force back in the day. Look."

Jimmy clicked over to a different screen and pulled up a spreadsheet full of names. He scrolled through the list. There was an entire section marked "Government Officials." Kris leaned in and scanned the list over his shoulder. "Where did you get all these?"

"Newspapers. Court records. A bunch of us have been adding to it over the years."

A name flew past that she recognized. "Wait. Go back," she whispered. The name Benjamin C. Weber glowed orange next to his address in Wapakoneta. She sank down onto the floor next to Jimmy, the blood draining from her head. "Why is Ben in here?"

He expanded the field next to Ben's name. It read, *Suspected recruit through Camp Kessler—Survival Camp for Boys. Arrested in 1979 in connection with the hanging of a black man. Never charged. Parents Bill and Linda Weber members of the Cleveland Bund.*

She sucked in a breath. Ben used to bounce her on his knee during football games on Sundays. "Oh my God. Is this real?"

"It wouldn't stand up in court or anything, but yeah. It's real." He looked over at her. "Your dad's friend?"

She nodded and grabbed the mouse from him and started scrolling through the list. The name Reinhardt appeared more than once. Troy's parents. She kept going until she stopped on the name Wiley.

"These are my grandparents."

"Yeah." Jimmy clicked on their names, expanding the cell. "Clyde and Marta Wiley owned a couple grocery stores and a butcher shop in Cleveland before the Depression. During the war, the feds were huntin' down Nazi sympathizers, and your pop's folks were wanted for questioning."

Kris scanned the text and startled at seeing her own name listed. It sat below her father's. She sat up with a jolt. "I'm in here. What the . . . Who put me in here? You?"

"But that's before I really knew you." He held up his hands in self-defense. "This is just a list of people with connections to the Silver Shirts, Kris. People like you and your dad. Not everyone in here is guilty."

Kris clicked on her own name. The database expanded to show the address of her rental along with her student ID for Cleveland State University. Her heart slowed to a crawl. "Who else has seen this?"

"Just the closed group. That's it."

"Was DHOH in that group?" The red painted star on her door blazed in her eyes. "Jesus, did you give him my fucking address?"

His chin dropped and he shook his head. "No. I don't think he'd—"

"How the hell do you know? Huh? You don't know a thing about him. I can't . . . I can't do this. I'm calling the police." She stood up and staggered out of the room in a daze. Troy, Ben, her father, all the names on the list spun through her head. Everyone was a suspect. Even her.

She stumbled out into the hallway, nearly running into Madame Mimi in her caftan.

"The police?" the old fortune-teller asked with a small shake of her head. *Poor thing,* it said. "I really don't think they'll be able to help. Do you?"

Kris could feel her studying the bruises on her face and turned away.

Mimi looked past her to Jimmy. He had stood up from the offending database. "How did it go in Cridersville?"

"Not so good."

Madame Mimi shot Kris a scolding look. "We're not here to hurt you, dear. The police out there have no idea what they're dealing with, and the ones who do can't be trusted."

"That's it!" Kris threw her hands up at the leaking ceiling and crumbling walls. "I can't stay here. I have to go talk to Ben."

Mimi put a thick hand on Kris's arm. "What do you even know about Benjamin Weber?"

"I know that he was my dad's best friend and he—he . . . God, I don't know anymore." It was the truth. Kris dropped her bags and staggered back to Jimmy's futon.

"Give us a chance to help, hon," Mimi said softly and turned to Jimmy. "Try to find out what you can. You were going to send a message to someone?"

"Yeah." Jimmy sat back down at his terminal and began typing.

Mimi settled her bulk onto the bed next to Kris and picked up her hand. "I know this has been hard on you. Coming to grips with the truth always is." She turned Kris's hand over and studied her palm, tracing the creases. "There are so many broken lines in your life. The biggest is still to come."

"Thanks, but I'll keep my broken lines to myself." Kris pulled her hand back and stood up. Jimmy was opening another screen. Her mouth fell open as she crept up behind him, watching him click the keys.

LOWJACK: DHOH you there? What happened in Cridersville?

Lowjack? "You're Lowjack?"

Jimmy stopped typing.

"You stole my father's police report." Kris gaped at him. "You broadcast it all over the Internet. Oh my God. I've told you everything and you . . ." She didn't finish. Instead, she grabbed her bags and ran.

CHAPTER 45

"Hey, Kris!" Jimmy called after her.

"Leave me alone!" she shouted, running down the stairs into the gallery.

He caught up to her in the hall outside, grabbing her by the shoulder. She spun and whacked him in the ribs with her softball bag and the shotgun buried inside it. He held up his hands. "Whoa! Easy with that thing."

"I can't. I can't trust you anymore. How could you keep something like that from me? I've got to get the hell out of this place." Tears streamed down her face.

He held out his arms to her. "I'm sorry, Kris. I tried to tell you. I swear. I just knew if I did, you'd never let me help you. I'm not the enemy here."

"Then who is? Huh?" She wiped her tears, sending a shot of pain through the bruise on her cheek. "I have to go to the police. I have to talk to Ben."

"You can't go to him. Do you know who filled out the police report for your mom's accident?" Jimmy grabbed her arm. "Do you?"

"What?" The hallway seemed to flip over. *What?*

"It was him. I looked into it after I met you, and I wasn't sure how you fit into all of this." Her mother's burning car clouded her field of vision. "I'm sorry, but I liked you. I wanted to know."

"What did you find?" she heard herself ask.

"Officer Benjamin Weber signed off on the police report after the accident. And there's some stuff that just don't look right on it. He left half the fields blank."

"So? What does that matter?" But she knew what he was saying. Ben was involved somehow. She had seen it written all over the deputy's face as he sat across from her at the table. Ben was hiding something.

Sirens wailed outside the building somewhere in the distance. Jimmy ignored them. "All I know is that someone put that mark on your door, and it wasn't me."

She narrowed her eyes at him. "But you lied to me. How the hell can I trust you now?"

"If I wanted to hurt you, I would've done it already. Right?" He took a step toward her and cupped her face with his gentle hands. He'd had plenty of chances. He'd lain next to her in bed the night before and hadn't laid a hand on her. "Maybe they noticed you poking around and asking questions about your dad. A lot of people got killed for less. Whoever it is, they sent you a message, Kris. I don't want you to be next."

She opened her mouth to say something, but the sirens outside were getting louder and rapidly multiplying.

Alarm shot through Jimmy's eyes as he pushed through a doorway into another room across the hall. She followed him to a window looking out over West 7th Street. Eight police cars were lined up outside the Harmony Mission Press. Two more blocked either end of the street. Ben's Auglaize County cruiser pulled up next to the Cleveland Police Department's. A paddy wagon sat at the far end of the block. Policemen in riot gear assembled outside the locked gate.

Jimmy pulled her away from the window. "Shit! Someone must've seen us."

An old man with a cane was standing across the street with two uniformed police officers. They were taking his statement.

A voice over a loudspeaker blared. "This is a police action. You are trespassing on private property. Come out with your hands up. Failure to cooperate will be seen as an act of aggression."

"See what happens when a white girl goes missin'? They bring a whole fucking army. C'mon. We gotta get out of here. Mimi? Let's go!"

Ben's voice came on the loudspeaker. "Kris, if you're in there, hold tight. We'll get you out!"

"Jimmy!" Kris planted her feet. "This is out of control. I should just go out there."

"And do what? Surrender?"

"What about the little girl and her mother? What about the old lady? Somebody might get hurt."

"Yeah. And it could be you. Now c'mon!"

Kris protested as he dragged her down the hall behind Mimi. "But the little girl!"

"They know the drill. We'll find 'em." Jimmy led them down the flight of stairs at the end of the hall and into another corridor.

Maurice the drunk poked his head out of his door. "We havin' a party?" he growled as they ran past.

"Yep. CPD's brought the wagon and everything," Jimmy called back.

"Shit." The drunk stumbled out into the hall after them.

Jimmy turned the corner and stopped at a narrow doorway. He flung it open. It was a broom closet complete with mop bucket.

"What are you doing?" Kris asked, short of breath from running. "We can't all fit in there."

"Nope." Jimmy pushed the mop bucket aside and pressed against the wood beadboard behind it. An eight-pointed star had been carved into the wood just like the one on the old lady's door. Kris's eyes widened as the wall panel popped open. "Everybody in."

Kris, Mimi, and Maurice all filed through the narrow opening and into a two-foot-wide corridor lined from floor to ceiling with strips of wood and plaster drippings. Jimmy followed them, closing both doors behind him. Pitch-black swallowed them whole until he clicked on his flashlight.

"Where are we?" Kris whispered.

"The people that built this place carved out all sorts of back entrances and private corridors. Even whole rooms you can't find unless you know where to look. C'mon. This way."

"But why would they do that?"

"Smuggling, storage, you name it. I found a stash of rifles and canned food in one of these rabbit holes once. I think some of the later architects had ties to the Legion. Did you see the star? It's the perfect plan really, hiding out in a Bible factory where no one even knows you're there."

"Won't they find us in here?"

"I don't see how. Not even the folks that ran the mission knew about these places. They're not on any of the blueprints. Shh!"

Everyone froze. On the other side of the wall, three pairs of boots stormed past.

"Did you hear that, Jenson?" a muffled voice asked. A second later the sound of a door being kicked in somewhere on the other side of the wall shook the dust from the air. "Police! If you're in there, come out slowly with your hands on your head!"

Kris tightened her grip on her shotgun and waited. The closet door slammed open four feet behind them.

A second voice barked, "Clear! You boys got anything down there?"

"All clear," came the muffled reply.

The first voice came back, "East wing, third floor clear, sir."

A crackled response answered through a radio. "Proceed to the fourth."

The boots and voices moved on.

Jimmy turned the flashlight back on the rest of them. "We have to get to the lower level."

"Y'all go ahead," Maurice rasped, blowing out a cloud of stale whiskey that nearly knocked Kris off her feet. "I'm gonna take a nap right here."

"Just keep it down, Moe." Jimmy stepped over him and pushed past the rest of them. "Follow me."

Kris and Mimi followed Jimmy down the narrow space between two walls about fifty feet into a bricked-in air shaft. A narrow steel stair cut through the landing. Kris stared up three stories through the dim light of a window high overhead. "Where are we now?"

"We're in the chimney chase. College Avenue is that way." Jimmy pointed at the brick wall below the window.

Outside, the police repeated their earlier announcement over a loudspeaker a block away. "This is the police. Come out with your hands up . . ."

Kris turned her worried eyes to Jimmy. "I should go. This is just . . ."

Mimi held up a hand to silence her. "Someone's coming."

A few moments later a door clicked open overhead followed by the beam of a flashlight. Kris's muscles tensed to run the other way as footsteps shook the narrow stairway. She took a step back into the wall chase and dropped her bags.

"Jimmy? That you?" a voice whispered from the floor above.

"Hey, Jill," Jimmy whispered back.

The little girl from the window appeared coming down the steps. A white woman with a gash on her forehead and bruises on her neck stayed close behind.

"You know Arlene and her girl, Starr?" Jill motioned to her companions.

Jimmy nodded at them. "Hey."

Kris gave the little girl a wave, wondering if she'd remember seeing her down in the courtyard. Starr didn't wave back, she just stared at her with flat eyes, waiting for something bad to happen. Up close, Arlene's pale face was a map of scars and bruises held taut by a ponytail of greasy blond hair.

On the floor above, a door crashed open a wall away. "You got anything down there?" a muffled voice shouted.

"All clear" came a response.

"Scattered like roaches, sir," a third voice answered.

"The exits are blocked, dammit! Where'd they all go?"

"Maybe there's another way out?"

"No shit, Jenson. You think that up all by yourself? . . . Looks like we got a real detective on our hands, fellas!"

No one laughed. More doors crashed open. The crackle of a radio scratched on and off. The angry sergeant barked more orders. "We're lookin' for rat holes, boys! Watch the roofs. Head to the lower levels."

Jimmy shot Jill a warning look. "We have to move. Now."

Jill led the way down the stair tower with Starr and Arlene behind her. Jimmy gave Kris a nudge toward the stairs. She stumbled down the steep steps after Arlene. The frazzled companions followed one another in single file down three flights of stairs. They'd gone down two levels before Kris realized she'd left her bags behind.

As the air around her grew thicker with damp and darkness, Kris wondered where the old woman with her pink curlers had gone. *Lost. Fallen. Arrested.* At the bottom of the steps, Jill's flashlight stopped moving for a moment, then disappeared around a corner. Kris nearly lost her footing in her own long shadow cast by Jimmy's light five steps up.

"Jill?" she whispered, feeling her way off the last step onto a dirt floor.

There was no answer.

"This way," Jimmy hissed, motioning with his light in the opposite direction.

"But . . . Jill went over there." In the yellow glow of the flashlight, Jimmy looked more and more like a criminal. *Lowjack.*

"I know you're conflicted, but you have to trust us, Kris," Madame Mimi whispered and then shut her eyes and listened. "We can't linger here. He's coming."

As Kris's eyes adjusted to the dark, she could see they were at a T-shaped junction with the route to the left leading farther into the building and the right leading away from it toward College Avenue. Jill and her group had headed left. Kris bit her lip.

Jimmy put a hand on her shoulder. "This is the way out."

"So why did Jill go the other way?" Kris ignored Madame Mimi standing with her arms out like a third-rate witch and searched Jimmy's dark eyes for reassurance. The yellow flashlight in his hand left them in unreadable shadows.

"There's lots of ways outta here. We can't all go the same way. It'll draw too much attention. We gotta scatter."

Kris found herself nodding. "Like roaches. Fine. But if you get me shot or arrested . . . I'm going to kill you."

He cracked a half grin. "Deal. C'mon."

They turned down the vaulted hall. After what felt like two city blocks, it dead-ended. "What the hell?" She glared at Jimmy.

He ignored her and squatted down to clear the dust off something on the ground. It was a manhole cover. He pried it up and shined his light down into the hole. The smell of rotting leaves and sewage hit her in the face as she crouched down next to him. It was a six-foot drop down to the bottom. Brown water trickled along the rounded floor.

"You've got to be kidding me! The sewer?" She backed away from the hole. "No way."

"You got a better plan?" he asked. He sat down, dropping his legs into the stink, and then the rest of him vanished too. "C'mon! It's not so bad," he called up from the dark. "It hasn't rained in over a week. I'll catch you."

Madame Mimi patted her arm with a sympathetic smile. "This is where I leave you."

"What do you mean? Where are you going?" Kris looked back the way they came. "You'll get caught."

"That's the plan." The old hippie shrugged. "They can't charge me with a thing. I'm a friend of Jill's. Besides, no one is looking for me, are they?"

"But won't they ask about . . . us?" Kris whimpered.

"About who? I've never seen either of you before in my life. I'm just an old stoned hippie. Right?" She winked at Kris's slack face and headed back down the corridor, chuckling. She tapped on the walls playfully. "I'm going to tie those boys up for hours. They'll be chasing their own tails."

Jimmy's voice echoed up out of the sewer. "You comin'?"

Kris gazed down at his face trapped in the festering tunnel. She turned back into the darkness where Mimi had disappeared without so much as a flashlight. She breathed in a prayer and put her feet in the hole.

"Don't worry, I'll catch you."

Her legs dangled down into the chill of the pipe, then her hips. Jimmy grabbed her waist and held her steady as the manhole swallowed the rest of her. He set her down gently onto the floor of the giant pipe, then stretched his arms up to pull the manhole cover back into place. The sound of the iron cover scraping across the floor over her head sent a shiver through her bones. It clunked into place, sealing her fate. She was trapped.

"What now?" she breathed, struggling to control the urge to scream.

Jimmy grabbed on to her hand and started walking.

The brick-lined pipe was barely taller than she was. Up ahead, a puddle of light streamed in. As they walked toward it, she could see it led to an open grate in the street. There was another one fifty feet away.

The police speakers boomed somewhere above them, echoing down the pipe to where they stood. "This is the police. We have reason to believe a hostage is being held against her will. Any failure to cooperate will be seen as an act of aggression. Come out with your hands up."

Jimmy trained his flashlight on her. "Hear that? You're a hostage."

"Shit. This is really bad. We should split up. If they find you with me . . ."

"Not gonna happen. C'mon." He turned and started walking again.

They passed under the catch basin and the static of a police radio. A faraway voice asked, "Car two, what's your twenty?" They were under West 7th Street.

She stopped a moment to get her bearings. "No. I'm serious. I can't let you get arrested." *And I have no idea where you're taking me or who you really are.*

He pointed the light at her. "Good. And I can't let you get killed. C'mon."

They followed the trickle of brown water past three more catch basins, stopping at each to listen. At the third, they heard the crackle of another police radio high overhead. A disembodied voice said, "Nope. No sign of them. How long we holding the block?"

The answer was lost in static.

"We must be at the end of West Seventh," Jimmy said, gazing up at the light coming in from the inlet. Ten feet ahead, the sewer pipe hit a vaulted junction. Water trickled in from the left and headed out a smaller pipe to the right. An eighteen-inch outlet continued straight ahead, several feet off the floor.

"What now?' Kris eyed the small outlet. There was no way she could crawl through.

"That's an overflow out to the river," Jimmy said, pointing to the narrow opening. "We need to get off this block and into a crowd of people. This way."

He led her to the left, opposite the flow of the water.

"Where does this one go?" she asked, trying to imagine the streets above them.

"North. We're heading to the Lorain-Carnegie Bridge. There's a street vault there."

"Wait. What? That's like a half mile away. Isn't it?"

"Yeah, but don't worry. Most of this line was abandoned years ago."

They passed another junction where the brown water flowed in and past their feet. A block later they ran into another vaulted junction, but this one was half-clogged with broken bricks, and a coral reef of unfinished concrete hung in a frozen wave between the fissures in the ceiling.

"This is where they sealed off an old line," Jimmy explained, climbing over and under the debris. The flashlight bobbed up and down as he went, throwing sinister shadows across the rounded walls of the pipe. True to his word, the floor of the giant pipe on the other side had run dry, leading them into utter darkness. There were no more catch basins to let in light and fresh air from the world above. Stagnant must and dust filled her lungs like fetid water. Half a block up, the gnarled, matted hair of tree roots hung in clumps. Jimmy pulled the roots aside like a gentleman opening a car door.

"How many times have you been in here?" she asked, climbing over a pile of bricks that had collapsed from the ceiling overhead. She reached up and touched the underside of newer pavement that had taken their place.

"A few." Jimmy turned the flashlight ahead, scouting for the next obstacle, leaving her in his shadow. "Lots of folks speculate that the Torso Killer used the sewer pipes to transport bodies down to the river."

"Is that true?" Kris stopped walking and scanned the brick floor and walls in the dim light.

"One of 'em might've. Like I said, there was more than one." He stopped at another outlet, a smaller pipe set two feet off the floor. "All of these outlets went down to the river. It wouldn't have been too hard to shove a body down, but the forensics don't support it. They figured the skin of the bodies or the burlap sacks holding 'em would've been scraped up. I think they used these pipes for other things."

"Like what?"

"Like the same thing we're doin' now—moving around the city unseen. There's miles and miles of these things, new and old."

They passed another junction that was sealed more neatly than the last but with an overhead chute covered by a manhole. A car rumbled over it, shaking the lid. Jill's voice came back to her in the rattle, and she remembered her in the courtyard, covering up a manhole. *I keep putting the cover back down, but they keep lifting it up.*

She stopped walking. "Jimmy?"

"Yeah."

"Does anyone else still use these pipes?"

"I dunno. Bums probably do. Street people are smarter than you think." He held up a hand. "You hear that?"

Kris froze and listened. "Dogs," she whispered.

The barking was faint at first. As they continued walking, it grew louder, and there was something about it that sounded wrong. Kris stopped and listened again. It was an echo. "Jimmy!" she hissed. "The dogs are in the pipes."

He froze for a second and his eyes grew wide. "Fuck!"

"We have to get out!"

The barking was getting closer. She could hear the echo split north and south, bouncing off each junction.

Jimmy grabbed her hand and started running. They scrambled over fallen bricks and half-caved sections. "There's an outlet a block ahead," he panted. "But no cover. We'd be stranded somewhere on the bluff like sitting ducks. We have to make it to the bridge."

Kris pumped her short legs hard to keep up with his long ones, leaving her brain three steps behind. The barking grew sharper. The dogs had made the turn and were heading up right behind them. As fast as Kris and Jimmy were running, they were no match for the speed of a dog, but they managed to stay ahead. The thought *They're on a leash* ran through her mind almost too fast to catch.

Swampy air burned in her lungs. Her head grew lighter on her shoulders. Jimmy dragged her up and over another pile of collapsed brick, but her foot caught and sent her tumbling.

"C'mon, get up!" He pulled her arm.

"No. You should go. Don't let them find you with me," she mumbled through a fog. She was breathing too hard.

Jimmy pulled her onto her feet. "We're almost there. Hold on."

She stumbled forward. The barking bounced off the walls all around her, shuddering through her head. *They're here. They're almost here.*

Jimmy let go of her arm at the next junction to climb a rusted metal ladder.

"Whoa. Easy, Gunner. Easy, boy. You got somethin'?" A familiar voice called out fifty feet behind her, "Kritter? That you down there?"

Kris slowed her feet. *Ben?*

Jimmy pulled at her shoulder. "Kris, c'mon!"

But she couldn't run anymore. She'd have to face Ben and the truth about her drunk mother and her father's terrible past. *Ben wouldn't hurt you,* her father's voice echoed from the back of her clouded mind. *You're like a daughter to him.* "Run, Jimmy!" she whispered. "Don't let him find you with me!"

A radio crackled behind her under the barking dogs. "I got her."

She dropped her hands to her knees and took in a labored breath. Sunlight burst into the pipe with the metal scrape of a manhole cover. It was quickly eclipsed by a hulking shadow. "Well look who it is," it said.

"Troy?" Her words were lost in the metallic *clunk* of steel hitting bone. Jimmy came crashing down off the ladder in a heap. *"J—!"*

A shot of pain exploded between her shoulder blades, buzzing white and blue until she dropped to the ground.

"Keep a watch, son." Ben's voice floated over her as her mind plummeted down a black hole. "We'd better wait till the other boys clear out."

SAYS PELLEY HAD PLANS
TO BE 'KING'

Blond Agent Tells Dies
of Silver Shirt Plot

Washington, April 2—(AP)—From the lips of a blond secret agent, Miss Dorothy Waring of New York—the Dies committee heard today that William Dudley Pelley had planned to use his Silver Legion to seize the United States government and make himself king.

At the same time, the committee received evidence that aides of the Asheville (N.C.) publisher had kept in close touch with a national guard officer at Detroit who trained Ku Klux Klan members for cavalry duty during "the coming turmoil."

—*Cleveland Plain Dealer*, April 3, 1940, p. 2

CHAPTER 46

April 9, 1938

Ethel heard purple voices. They garbled and hummed through fifty feet of water. Her lungs constricted under the flood. The weight of an ocean pressed against her skull. The voices swelled and crashed like waves.

"O Lord, bind this wicked soul with Thine hand." A deep voice echoed between Ethel's drowning ears. "Protect us as we endeavor to Thine will. In Jesus Christ's name, we pray."

She recoiled from it, trying to lift her hands to her aching head, but they didn't respond. Her arms wouldn't move.

Several voices answered from all sides, "Amen."

"All trespassers against Your house shall be bound by the power of God," the man proclaimed. His voice sounded familiar.

Ethel forced her eyelids open. A large shadow floated in front of her surrounded by a fiery glow.

"Keep these unclean spirits from our hearts and foul intentions from our minds, O Lord." The shadow split and moved.

"Amen." The other voices murmured at her feet. Ethel blinked her eyes while her head sank deeper under the phantom water.

"I awash my hands in innocence and go to your altar." The split shadow moved again.

Legs, Ethel realized, focusing her aching eyes. A pair of legs walked across the ceiling, hard black boots hitting the flat stones.

"Humbly I pray for the repentance of my enemies." It sounded like Brother Wenger.

Ethel craned her neck to see a huddled shadow clinging to the stones over her head. It was a woman on her knees, bowed in prayer. On the ceiling.

"Mary Alice?" Ethel called out through the water in a choked slur of rasps and coughs. "Mary Alice . . . *Run!*"

The woman gazed at her from her upside-down perch. "Amen," she said again.

The inverted man walked up beside Mary Alice and patted her on the shoulder. Ethel watched in horror as a man she vaguely recognized placed a hand on the girl's head and reached the other down to the floor. "Lord bless Your humble servant Sister Mary Alice for being Your eyes, Your ears, and Your mighty hand when the devil was at our doorstep."

"Amen." The other voices answered, but Ethel couldn't take her eyes off the girl she'd found beaten and scrubbing blood off the floor. Her friend. The charitable Christian that took in the poor and fed them and—

"Ah, I see our guest has risen to join us." Another man's legs slowly approached Ethel's head as his body folded into a crouch on the ceiling. He gave her an inverted smile that sent a shudder through her. As her flesh chilled at the sight of him, she realized she was naked. "I remember you." He brushed her cheek with the back of his hand. She struggled to pull away from his touch but couldn't move. "You had a boy. Shame he didn't make it. I never forget a face . . . as much as I might like to."

She blinked at him as his face floated back down toward her feet. He had stood over her bed after they'd cut her baby out. *Infections set in so easy with working girls like you,* he'd said. Even through the fog of morphine, she'd heard the clinical disgust in his voice as she'd wept.

Try to be thankful I saved your life. Although I do suppose some might argue I've done you a disservice.

The doctor walked across the ceiling to a metal table upside down in the corner. He was wearing a long black apron. Ethel blinked at it as he picked up one of the larger knives, and realized it was the same table she'd seen earlier. It had been sitting on the floor next to—

"Brothers and sisters, we are at war," Brother Wenger announced while the doctor lifted the knife between both hands. "A plague has taken hold of our cities. A plague of sin. Murderers, thieves, and harlots walk our streets. Satan's soldiers are massing together against us. Our only hope is to fight back in God's name."

A murmur of agreement answered him.

"The only hope to save this poor lost soul before us is to guide her back into the grace of God. We must help her atone for her sins. In Leviticus, He tells us, 'For the life of a creature is in the blood, and I have given it to you to make atonement for yourselves on the altar; it is the blood that makes atonement for one's life.'"

Ethel barely registered his words as panic shrieked between her ears. Looking down at herself, she discovered why she couldn't move and why the world had inverted. They'd lashed her naked body to the wooden cross to be crucified, upside down.

"Ambrosia." Wenger turned his voice toward her. "I'm going to need you to repeat after me. Have mercy upon me, O God."

Ethel's eyes bulged from her head as she craned her neck to look around the room. All her blood pooled in her skull, her lungs collapsed into her throat. The place where Mary Alice had been kneeling was now taken by a small figure in a white shroud with only small holes cut for its eyes. Five more hooded figures stood next to it. Johnnie's voice whispered in her ear, *They had no faces.* Their hands were clasped before them in prayer.

A piercing pain in her right leg ripped everything else out of her head. Ethel screamed. Warm liquid dripped up her thigh.

"I said, repeat after me," Wenger barked. "Have mercy upon me, O God."

Ethel's voice shook. "Have mercy, O God."

"Good. Let us continue . . . According to Thy loving kindness, according unto the multitude of Thy tender mercies, blot out my transgressions.'"

The words tumbled out of her trembling mouth in an incoherent chorus.

"Wash me thoroughly from mine iniquity, and cleanse me from my sin."

As Ethel forced the words out, she felt something warm and wet on her feet. A hooded figure was at her side, scrubbing her raw skin with a sponge. It was wearing a black apron.

Wenger kept going as the hooded doctor washed her. "For I acknowledge my transgressions, and my sin is ever before me."

"For I acknowledge . . ."

Ethel lost track of the call and answers as she hung there with thoughts screaming through her flooded head. *They hung Rose just like this. They're going to bleed me out. They'll cut my throat and then pull me to pieces.*

Then Brother Wenger's voice changed its cadence. "Ambrosia, before God and these witnesses, do you take Jesus Christ as your Lord and Savior."

There was only one correct answer. "I do. Please . . . Let me go."

"Do you repent the sin of fornication?"

"Yes. I'm sorry. Please. God . . ."

A sharp pain pierced her arm. "Do you repent the sin of blasphemy?"

"I do. Christ, I do." Ethel turned to the six hooded figures standing like a choir. "Mary Alice! You can't let them do this. Help me!"

A cold steel blade dragged across her stomach not far from where the doctor had cut her four years earlier. "Do you repent the sins of self-gratification and deceit?"

Ethel let out a scream as the blade pressed deeper. Warm liquid dripped up her torso. Her head reeled out of her control.

"Enough," a deep voice spoke from under a hood. "Ask her about the revolution. Ask her before she fades. Where are they hiding their arsenal?"

The doctor pressed his wet blade to her throat. "Where are they stockpiling their weapons?"

"What?" Ethel croaked and stared up into the hood. The doctor's blue eyes glinted at her through the holes.

"We know their plan. They use human refuse like you as foot soldiers. You are the devil's hands. Where are your guns?"

Ethel just shook her head. It was madness.

"When will they attack?" the doctor pressed. His blade bit through her skin. Her flesh screamed.

"Maybe she doesn't know," a small voice whispered.

Mary Alice? Ethel craned her neck.

An upside-down figure held out a hand in appeal. "Perhaps she *is* only a whore."

The doctor straightened himself and strode back to his table of knives. He set down the bloody implement in his hand and considered another. "We are running out of time," he boomed. "The head of the Legion will be here in ten days, and we need answers."

"No need to despair." A woman's voice came from a far corner of the room. She was dressed in an expensive suit with a shroud of black lace draped over her face. A necklace with an elaborate eight-pointed star pendant hung from her neck. "Brother, let the blood tell us."

Wenger nodded his agreement and picked up the meat cleaver and Mary Alice's bucket. He dipped his hand in the pail, then dumped the blood-tinged water onto the floor.

With wet fingers, he drew a cross onto Ethel's forehead. "I baptize you in the name of the Father and the Son and the Holy Spirit. Amen."

"Amen," agreed the others.

The light of the candles danced on the blade of the knife in his other hand as he said, "May your immortal soul find its way home."

With that, he placed the bucket under her head and stood back up. He gripped the cleaver with both hands.

The woman in lace began to chant, "Three holy drops of blood are placed before the pail."

Drops of Ethel's blood streaming up her face hit the bottom of the bucket. *Tap. Tap. Tap.* Her screams came out as a broken siren, echoing up from the catacombs, echoing through the drain lines, *"Help! God, somebody help me!"*

The woman's voice droned on. "As surely as the Virgin was pure from all men, as surely shall no fire or truth pass out of this barrel . . ."

The doctor swung the knife with both hands to his shoulder.

". . . the Lord goeth before me."

"Help!" Ethel croaked, unable to muster a scream. She squeezed her eyes shut and made a silent wish for Johnnie. *Catch out on a train, sweet girl. Don't look back.*

"Hello?" a voice boomed from another room. "Hello? Who's down here? This is private property!"

The lights snuffed out in a plume of smoke. Ethel was certain that she'd imagined it, that her head had already been lopped off. The scuffle of feet and voices whispered above her as she felt her soul drop from her body on its way straight to hell, where it belonged. Her arms and legs collapsed to the floor with it.

A faraway angel called, "She's over here."

Ethel felt her body lift from the floor and cool air rush past her wet skin. *The devil has me in his arms.*

"Brother, I have found a lost soul."

A warm hand pressed to her cheek. "Sweet Lord in heaven. Sister Hattie? Is that you?" A shadow hovered over her in a wreath of glowing white.

Then the light blew out.

CHAPTER 47

Ethel woke to find herself lying in a bright white room. *I'm dead,* she thought, and the thought was a relief. It was all over.

But then she saw the bandages. Bandages were taped to her neck, her stomach, her leg. The moments before everything had gone black came rushing back in a jumble. Mary Alice's bruised face. The lady wrapped in lace. Blood running up her chest. The knife. The doctor. *Oh, God. The doctor.*

Ethel sat up and scanned the hard floor and wall of white curtains. *Where is he?*

They'd taken her to a hospital. The last time she'd been in an antiseptic bed like the one under her now, she'd just been cut open and roughly stitched back together by the same doctor with the black apron and smiling knife. He'd cut her baby out and told her it was dead.

Stifling a sob, she clutched her stomach only to find the fresh bandage. Was it the same hospital? she wondered, eyes darting from the floor to the ceiling. She had no idea. The memory of it smeared together in a cloud of morphine and tears she'd drunk so hard to forget.

The doctor might have been right down the hall, waiting to finish what he started.

The sound of approaching voices forced her head back down to the pillow. Let them think you're asleep, she told herself. It'll buy time. Ethel closed her eyes and took a silent inventory of herself. The cuts on her thigh and abdomen hurt but didn't ache deep down inside the way her stomach had after the baby. If she could sit up on her own, she could run.

"... do you think she'll be alright?" one of the voices asked. "The poor thing looked to be knocking on the good Lord's door when we found her."

"The doctor believes she'll pull through just fine." The curtain pulled back and Ethel could feel two sets of eyes on her still face. "I understand you knew her?"

"Yes. She joined our mission several days ago. She's a cousin of Sister Mary Alice."

"That's not what we have here." The sound of a page turning rustled the air. "According to her fingerprints, this here is Ethel Ann Harding, a known prostitute. She served a few years at the Mansfield workhouse for manslaughter. Says here she got into a scuffle with her pimp and shot him."

"Good heavens! I had no idea." Brother Milton's voice fell to a whisper. "There was a killer in our midst."

"Don't feel bad, Reverend. She's fooled plenty of folks before. Girls like this are always changing their names and worming their way back into the fringes of society. After they patch her up, she's heading back to the workhouse."

Ethel kept her face slack and her breathing even.

The reverend seemed distressed at this. "Why? What is her crime?"

"She's a derelict and a prostitute. No home. No family. We can't have her roaming our streets. Department's cracking down on these vagrants for public safety. With that mad killer on the loose, it'll probably save her life."

"You can't possibly agree with Eliot Ness's raids last night?"

"Something had to be done," the man argued. Ethel strained but didn't recognize his voice. "Those poor folks were sitting ducks, Reverend. How many more of them have to die?"

"Do you mind if I?"

"By all means."

A warm hand brushed her forehead. "Dear Lord, watch over Your daughter in her time of need. Speed her healing and mend her spirit. I pray You help this poor young woman find her way back into Your house. In Christ's name, amen."

"Amen, Reverend. Now I'm going to need to review your official statement before I finalize my report. Will you join me in the lobby?"

"Of course. I'm happy to help any way I can, Officer Kessler."

The curtain closed, and their footsteps carried the voices away. Ethel sat up again and strained to hear more. *The doctor believes she'll pull through just fine.* The thought of that madman sitting at her bedside while she slept sent a shudder through her. Then there was Officer Kessler's promise to help her back into the workhouse. She thought of Rose Wallace and her daughter. A cop by the name of Kessler had sent her into the house where they had killed her.

Lifting the bandages on her stomach and leg, Ethel studied the black catgut stitches lacing her skin together. The bleeding had stopped. She'd had enough brushes with a knife to know that the doctors had already done all they could do. They were just waiting for her to wake up, and she wasn't about to just lie there until they came for her.

She sat up. Her ankles were red and raw from the ropes. Her feet ached from being hung from the cross, but she forced them to bear her weight as she stood. She clutched the thin gown they'd given her to her chest and peeked out from behind the curtain at the foot of her bed. The ward was quiet except for two voices talking softly behind another curtain at the end of the row.

Two sets of doors led out of the ward at either end—one led to the brightly lit nurse's station and the other was dark. Ethel tiptoed in her bare feet toward the unlit doors, holding her breath the entire way. *They had no faces.* They could be anywhere. Mary Alice had warned her. *They're everywhere, listening.*

Her feet stopped moving as a wave of terror crashed over her. Or maybe it was the blood loss. She grabbed the nearest curtain to steady herself. *Mary Alice.* The girl had been there cleaning. Cleaning blood. With bruises on her face. Ethel reached up and felt the large lump on the back of her head where something hard had struck her. Mary Alice's tiny prayers echoed behind her. Ethel jerked around to stare at the empty hallway lined with white curtains. *Mary Alice.*

A small sob escaped from her lips as she pictured her friend with a rock in her hand. *Had it all been planned from the start? The free food, the warm bed, her wide and helpless eyes, the prayers?* Ethel's legs gave out and she crumpled to her knees.

A thin voice came from behind the curtain. "Are you alright, honey?"

Ethel didn't answer. She pulled herself back to her feet and forced them forward. The doctor would be coming for her any moment. The police would be coming. The killers could be anywhere. *It's the Legion.*

She pushed herself through the door and recounted everything she knew about them to keep her brain focused. The Legion included a policeman named Kessler, a doctor, a fancy woman in lace, Brother Wenger, Mary Alice, and God knew who else.

The dark doors led into a pale green stairwell. The hand-painted sign on one read, *Level 2.* All Ethel could read was the number, but she knew what it meant. She took the stairs down to the main floor and listened at the door before cracking it open.

A plain, beige service hallway stood empty behind it. It must lead out somewhere, she thought and stepped inside, scanning the walls for an exit. The door to the stairwell closed behind her. A pair of voices chatted merrily on the other side of the wall.

"Do you really think he'll ask me?" one chirped.

"Of course he will. You're a catch!" the other answered just on the other side of the door marked with more letters and the number *1*.

"Listen, I have to stop by my locker. I'll meet you there."

Ethel backed away from the approaching voices, grabbing the nearest doorknob and slipping inside a dark room. The door eased shut as another one swung open. The chipper nurse whistled to herself, and a door farther down the hall opened and closed.

Ethel released a breath only to inhale a rancid mix of urine and rotted food. She felt along the wall next to the doorjamb until she found a light switch. Flipping it on, she saw that she had landed in the room where they collected dirty laundry and cast-off clothes. Two large bins were filled with stained sheets. Another was filled with the flea-bitten street clothes of the patients. Ethel pulled a man's jacket off the top. It was stiff with dried blood.

The hospital gown they'd wrapped her in wouldn't get her out of the building unnoticed, she realized. Ethel stripped off the faded blue shroud and picked through the tattered clothing of the dispossessed and deceased until she found a dress with only a small gash in the side. She straightened her hair the best she could and picked a suitable hat and worn-down shoes out of metal bins.

Ethel stepped back out into the hall, debating which way to go.

A nurse emerged from another door and startled at the sight of Ethel standing there. "Excuse me, ma'am? Can I help you?"

"Oh, goodness . . . forgive me." Ethel forced a helpless smile as her mind raced for more words. "I must've . . . gotten lost. I was here visiting my niece." She folded her hands contritely at her throat to hide the bandages.

"It happens all the time. Are you looking for the lobby?"

Ethel nodded, avoiding the young woman's eye.

"You're almost there. Follow me." The nurse turned and headed down the long beige hall until they'd reached the door marked with a jumble of letters. She strained to remember if she'd heard the nurse's voice from behind one of the white hoods. The woman smiled warmly at her. *Is it a trap?*

The door opened into a brightly lit waiting room flanked by a long counter. Ethel could see the street outside the windows. She breathed in a small sigh and managed a thank-you.

As the door swung shut behind her, she saw Reverend Milton sitting in one of the chairs. He was talking to a man in a fedora. Ethel could spot a cop from across a room. The two men didn't notice her step into the lobby. A scattering of men and women held various ill-at-ease stances, waiting for a doctor to come and tell them the fate of a friend or family member.

Ethel kept her head down and slowly made her way to a spot near where the two men sat in deep conversation. The chair five feet away from them was empty, but Ethel forced herself to the window instead and gazed out at the street for a full minute before finding her way to the seat within earshot.

". . . exactly how that happened again?" The detective flipped open his notebook. Ethel stole a glance at his face, but she didn't recognize it.

"It happened just the way I told that other officer."

"That's fine. I'd just like to hear it again in your own words, Reverend." The policeman pulled out a worn pencil.

"Yes, of course, Officer. This evening I was working in the front office, going over the books, when this twig of a child rushed through the door. I let her know that the soup kitchen is open on Sundays."

"Did you get her name?"

"No. I did not."

"Can you describe her?"

"She was a Negro child about yea tall. Maybe seven years old, although it's really hard to tell with street children . . ."

Ethel picked up a pamphlet someone had left on the side table and pretended to read it.

"That sort of hardscrabble life stunts their growth, you know. No fathers or mothers looking after them, their numbers grow every day." The reverend let out a heavy sigh. "I pray for them all."

"Had you ever seen this particular girl before?"

"I can't say that I had."

"What happened next?"

"She wanted me to go down into the basement. I tried to explain that there are many basements at the Harmony Mission, but she was quite hysterical. She kept crying, 'They're killing her! They're killing her!'"

"So what did you do?"

"Naturally I went to telephone the police, but this made her even more hysterical. She grabbed my arm and tried to pull me away from my desk, which wouldn't do at all. She was practically speaking in tongues, the poor child. I set down the phone and urged her to calm herself. I suggested we take a moment to pray, and just like a spark, she lit straight out of the room."

"So she left?"

"No. She went tearing through the lobby and onto the press floor!"

"What did you do?"

"I followed her. We can't have a child running through the machinery. It's far too dangerous."

"Did you find her?"

"It wasn't easy. Our building is set on a very old site as you may well know. The factory was built in phases whenever the good Lord saw fit to provide the funding. It takes some getting used to. Our sisters say it takes at least a week to not get lost inside those walls. You can't blame the architects for the confusion; they did the best they could with what they had. We could only afford the ones just starting out. Several of them had emigrated from Russia, you know, after that Godless revolt overthrew them all."

Ethel thought of the men in the bar talking about the Russian Revolution. They were worried it would happen again.

The detective was losing patience. "So how did you find her then?"

"She kept calling for help. She'd pop up like a jackrabbit, then disappear again, always heading down deeper underground until we were in a part of the building I myself had never even seen. I had heard grumblings during some phases of the building project. Complaints of old cisterns and other buried anomalies under the ground. We never had the extra funds to remove them, so we simply instructed the masons to build around or on top of them. A hundred years ago, the city had seen fit to bury enormous pipes and water reservoirs, but I never imagined what else they might've buried. I was shocked by what we found."

"And what was that?" the detective asked.

"A tomb. Catacombs I guess you might call them. I would call it a mass grave."

The detective stopped writing.

The reverend held up a hand in his own defense. "Not anything recent, mind you. I'm no expert, but the bones looked very old to me. You know the oldest parts of the Harmony Mission were used as a hospital of sorts during the Civil War."

"And this is where the girl led you?"

"I believe so. It is easy to get turned around in the lower levels, but that is my guess."

"And you're saying this girl had never been inside the building before?"

"To the best of my knowledge, that is correct."

"So how did she know where to look?"

"I can only imagine. You know these children are like scattering mice, finding every nook and cranny. She must have found another way in. Through a sewer line perhaps?"

"So you followed her down into a mass grave. And what did you find there?"

"Our dear Brother Wenger was carrying Sister Hattie out of the tomb. He said he'd heard screams through the pipes."

"Was she responsive?"

"No."

"Was there anyone else present?"

"No. Brother Wenger said he'd dropped his lantern in shock. He didn't get a look at whoever attacked the poor lamb."

"It says here that the victim was found with lacerations on her neck, legs, and abdomen. Did you or Brother Wenger find a knife or other weapon on the scene?"

"No, we didn't, though I can't say we wasted time looking. Death was knocking on the poor girl's door."

"What did you do next?"

"We carried her out of course. Finding the way took some doing, but we eventually got back to my office and telephoned the police."

"And how long until Sergeants Wilks and Hohman arrived?"

"Maybe ten minutes."

"Did Ethel regain consciousness or speak during that time?"

"No. She didn't."

"What did you do during that time?"

"I covered her with a blanket and I prayed."

"There is no statement in the sergeant's report from this mysterious child. Can you explain that?"

"She'd gone."

"She'd gone," Officer Kessler repeated incredulously. "Where did she go?"

"Back from whence she came, I'd imagine."

The officer blew a stream of air out his nose. "When did you notice her missing?"

"Right after I found Brother Wenger holding Sister Hattie . . . or rather Ethel, according to your records there. When I turned to ask the girl what had happened, she was gone."

"So you're saying to me that a phantom of a girl just came into your office, led you to a crime scene, and vanished like smoke?"

"You don't believe me." The reverend sighed. "I suppose it does sound unbelievable, but I assure you, my son. It is the truth, so help me God."

The detective didn't speak for a minute as he appraised the man. Finally he said, resigned, "And you don't know how Ethel Harding got there or who assaulted her?"

"No, I certainly don't, but I pray for their souls."

"I understand Sergeants Wilks and Hohman then searched the premises and could not find any underground chambers or the mass graves you mention in your report."

"I'm afraid that is my fault. I attempted to retrace my steps with them, but after I got turned around once or twice, they decided to suspend the search . . . They said with no eyewitnesses that unless this turned into a homicide case, God forbid, it wasn't warranted."

"And this Brother Wenger? Did he assist them?"

"The poor brother was quite shaken. Quite a miracle he'd found her at all. He'd just returned from Lancaster . . ." The reverend went silent as though turning this piece of information over in his own head. Ethel stole a glance at the old man. Mary Alice had said Wenger had gone missing. "He refused to leave her side the whole way to the hospital. Of course, you are welcome to talk with him. Perhaps he could show you the way."

The detective closed his notebook and stuffed it into his pocket. "Anything else you'd like to share with me before I go question the victim, Reverend?"

"I have a question of my own, if you'd indulge me."

"Of course."

"This doesn't have anything to do with the body they found in the river the other day, does it?"

"Why would you think that?"

"Our Ethel was found cut up with a knife, the poor girl."

"We see it every day at the station. These are violent times, Reverend. Some say we're on the brink of a Godless revolt of our own."

Ethel's eyes widened at this. Any doubt that this police officer was the one who had sent Rose Wallace to the slaughter vanished.

"All the same, perhaps I should speak to that other detective. The one looking into the Torso Killings."

"Detective Merylo is still dragging the river. But I'll tell you what. I'll sit down with him and review this case in the morning. The Cleveland Police Department thanks you for your concern and cooperation, Reverend."

"God bless you, my son."

CHAPTER 48

Ethel followed Brother Milton out of the hospital, keeping a safe distance. The man walked at a leisurely pace, stopping to greet strangers on the street, crouching down to pat the heads of children and tell them about his Sunday school in the park. He stopped to speak with the flower merchant and the owner of the corner bakery. Each time he halted to speak to someone, Ethel turned to face the nearest shop window, feigning fascination with the local laundry rate schedule or the cost of tea.

She had to find some way to get the man alone and tell him all she knew. No detective would listen to her accuse his fellow police officers of a conspiracy. They'd sooner ship her back to the workhouse with all the other whores and bums. But if it came from a man of God, it would be like the gospel truth.

One block away from the Harmony Mission, a long green Cadillac pulled to a stop on the side of the road. Two men in expensive suits stepped out and approached the good reverend and shook his hand. After a few minutes of the usual pleasantries, Ethel watched in horror as they escorted Brother Milton into their car. She memorized the license plate as it pulled away. A bronze eight-pointed star had been fixed above the rear bumper. It matched the necklace the woman in lace had been wearing while Ethel had hung upside down.

It's the Legion. They're everywhere.

She started to run after it but stopped short. Drawing attention to herself wouldn't stop them. They were already gone. All she could do was wait for the reverend to come back. *If he ever does come back.* As she thought the words, she realized odds were good he wouldn't. She hung her head for the poor man. For all his lording over spinsters and keeping them under lock and key, he just might've been a good man. And if that was the case, he was as good as dead.

She had to find Johnnie. The sweet girl had saved her life. The poor reverend's words hung in her mind, *When I turned to ask the girl what had happened, she was gone.*

Ethel dragged herself down Thurman Avenue, debating what to do next. If she went to the police, they would simply arrest her. That or hand her over to the Legion. Her feet stopped outside the boarded-up cottage where Rose Wallace had died.

Ethel glanced over her shoulder, then went to the back of the house and opened the door. "Johnnie?" she whispered. "Are you in here?"

The menacing hook hung down from the ceiling. Directly below it, bloodstains radiated across the floor. *Rose.* Ethel felt the cut at the base of her throat and swallowed hard. The Legion would have figured out she'd escaped the hospital by now. They would be hearing the reverend's tale of the mysterious little Negro girl any minute. They'd be looking for them both.

"Johnnie!" she said louder. "We have to leave. We have to leave now. You can't stay here!"

There was no answer.

Ethel checked every room, but the girl wasn't there. She slipped back out behind the house and eyed both sides of the street. The windows of the Harmony Mission loomed over the west end. Somewhere inside, Mary Alice was no doubt on her knees, scrubbing away the blood and praying for God to cleanse away all her sins.

Ethel darted down the alley back to the other marked house, bigger and half-burnt. As she approached the familiar back door, something was wrong. Fresh boards had been nailed over the broken window, and the doorknob had been removed. Black paint marked a large X over the front door, and a padlock and latch had been installed that could only mean one thing. The house had been condemned. An official-looking piece of paper had been nailed to the doorjamb. Ethel scanned the street and saw four other black marks and notices. They'd all been raided.

"Shit!" she muttered to herself. She slumped onto the porch. Odds were good the police or fire marshal or whoever had come and found Hortie passed out drunk inside. If they hadn't found Johnnie, she could be anywhere.

She eyed the slanted shed doors sticking up out of the grass four houses away. They led down to the basement of the boarded-up hardware store. It was the spot where Johnnie had seen them dump Rose's body. *Was that how the bastards all got out when Brother Milton interrupted their little ceremony?*

She stood up and walked over to the weathered wood planks covering up a hole in the ground. A hole that must lead back to the catacombs. The back entrance into the empty store behind it stood unmolested. The inspectors had passed over the place, and she could guess why. *The Legion.* As she got closer, she could see the padlock to the cellar hanging open.

Someone was still inside.

Ethel froze and listened. All she could hear was the steady clang and hum of the mission presses churning deep inside the building behind her. She scanned the rubble lying in the yards until she found something useful. A rusted ax lodged in a rotting log sat ten paces away. Not taking her eyes off the cellar doors, she inched her way toward it. The ax pulled out of the bug-riddled wood with only the smallest jerk. She gave it a test swing. The handle and blade held together, weathered but solid.

The cellar doors didn't move.

A car rumbled by on the street out front. Ethel scanned the houses and yards for any sign of Johnnie as guilt twisted in her gut. The girl had saved her life, and she'd left the poor thing all alone.

Gripping the ax, she pulled open the cellar door.

A terrible smell wafted up from under the hardware store. Burnt hair and rancid meat. Her stomach heaved into her throat. She forced it back down and tightened her grip on the ax. She took the stone steps down into the dark cellar one at a time. Shelves lined the walls, stocked with large oil cans, wooden barrels, and plump burlap sacks. *They packed her up like food. In grain sacks.*

Ethel counted fifteen large oil cans and twenty burlap sacks. Photographs of Flo Polillo's butchered thighs and Rose's desiccated bones flickered through her head. The pieces had been found in burlap bags just like the ones lining the walls.

Outside, the street traffic beeped and bumped along, oblivious to the storeroom of dead bodies fifty feet away. Ethel risked another step inside. "Hello?" she whispered.

One of the burlap sacks moved.

Ethel startled, nearly dropping the ax onto the steps.

A muffled cry came from inside the bag. She scrambled down into the dank chill of the cellar and yanked it out from its shelf. She cut through the twine with the rusted blade until a nappy head of dark hair emerged.

"Johnnie!" she gasped, pulling the burlap from girl's ashen face. The girl's eyes were dilated black and rolled loosely in her head. Ethel gently batted the sides of Johnnie's face to bring her eyes back around. "What'd they give you? Was it a shot? Shake it off, girl. C'mon. We gotta get you out of here."

She pulled the slack girl to her feet, but the poor thing crumpled back to the ground.

"Johnnie!" She hoisted her up again. "We have to go."

"What—what are you doing here?" a weak voice asked from behind the stairs.

Ethel dropped Johnnie's arms and grabbed the ax. She swung the blade around, missing Mary Alice's stricken face by an inch. The pale girl stumbled back.

"You shouldn't be here." Mary Alice's eyes darted up toward the open shed doors. "They'll be back. They're coming back with the truck."

Ethel glared at the cowering girl she'd once considered a friend and righted the ax. "The truck?"

"Yes, we have to . . ." Mary Alice's hands motioned to the bags and cans and barrels.

"You have to what? Get rid of the bodies? How the hell could you do this, Mary Alice? How . . ." Ethel's mouth just hung open as words failed her.

"It is God's will." Mary Alice held out her empty hands in a plea. The bruises on her face and neck belied her conviction. She kept backing up. "He commands us to rid the world of these . . . abominations."

"Abominations?" Ethel followed her into the shadow under the stairs.

"Killers!" she whimpered. "Rapists and thieves—all of them. You've seen what men like Eddie Andrassy have done. All of the criminals we vanquished confessed on the cross! They molested women, and God knows how many boys. They were evil. All of them. The end of days is upon us, and we are making way. 'Behold, the day of the Lord comes, cruel, with wrath and fierce anger, to make the land a desolation and to destroy its sinners fr—'"

Ethel slapped Mary Alice hard enough to send her sprawling onto the dirt floor. "Wake up! You are not the Lord!"

Mary Alice pulled herself up by a stair tread. "The Lord's servants are many."

"Is that what you tell yourself? Was I evil too? I'm not a killer or a rapist! Am I?" The indignation sounded hollow even to her own ears. She'd murdered her landlord after he'd attacked her little brother. She'd managed to kill her own baby before it was even born by being such an unfit mother.

"You're a prostitute," Mary Alice hissed. "Revelations seventeen, 'And on her forehead was written a name of mystery: Babylon the great, mother of prostitutes and of earth's abominations.'"

An abomination. That's what she was. The ax hung limp from her hand as the weight of her sins pulled on her. "Is that why you killed Rose Wallace? Because she had to feed herself? Is that why you're ready to kill a little girl, for Christ's sake?"

Mary Alice's eyes fell to Johnnie crumpled on the floor as she inched her way to the foot of the stairs. "She was a thief. The devil's consort. And the blood of foul children can be telling . . ."

"The blood of *children*, Mary Alice?" Ethel gripped the ax in both hands and lunged forward. It didn't matter if she went straight to hell as long as she took Mary Alice with her. "What does all this murdering make you? A saint? But you're not a saint, are you? Who was the girl getting it upstairs the other night, Mary Alice? Huh? Was it you?"

The blood drained from the girl's face, leaving nothing but bruises as she shook her head. "The sins of the flesh must be exorcised. It is the blood that makes atonement . . ."

"Is that what he was doing? Bleeding you?" Ethel remembered the angry marks across Mary Alice's back. The grunts and whimpers she'd heard through her ceiling could have been a flogging. She could still feel Brother Wenger straddling her in the dark prison cell, fully erect with religious fervor. Exorcising her demons was like sex to him. And Mary Alice was his willing whore. "Did he beat the guilt out of you? Huh? Did he enjoy it? You're no better than me, are you, Mary Alice?"

"This is a war . . ." Mary Alice struggled for words, her eyes darting for an escape.

"Whose war?" Ethel narrowed her eyes and raised the ax to swing. "Whose? Brother Wenger's? The Legion's? Who are they? Who was the doctor? What's his name?"

Mary Alice stumbled back against the basement wall, opening and closing her mouth like a dry fish.

"Oh, come on now. How will the angels sing his praises if he doesn't have a name?"

"He'll kill me."

"That's funny. 'Cause I'm gonna kill you too." Ethel pressed the rusty blade into the fool's neck. "What's his Goddamned name?"

The wide-eyed girl swallowed and whispered, "Dr. Dietrich."

"Very good. And who was the high-society one all in lace?"

A trickle of blood trailed down Mary Alice's neck as Ethel pressed the blade deeper. "A—Adela Rae Wulf."

"Good girl." Ethel clubbed her with the butt of the ax, knocking her hard to the ground. She scooped Johnnie into her arms and mounted the stairs.

"Please. You don't understand." Mary Alice moaned from her heap on the dirt floor. "They'll kill me. They'll damn my soul."

"Well, then I guess you better do what you do best."

"What?"

Ethel slammed the cellar door and snapped the padlock shut before whispering between the boards, "Pray."

PELLEY FACES U.S. TRIAL IN INDIANA

Silver Shirt Chief Arraigned on Sedition Charge

New Haven, Conn., April 4—(AP)—William Dudley Pelley, anti-Semite publicist and advocate of totalitarianism for America, was arrested by FBI agents today on charges of sedition, waived examination and was held for trial in the United States District Court at Indianapolis.

—*Cleveland Plain Dealer*, April 4, 1942, p. 4A

CHAPTER 49

April 10, 1999

Kris woke to a cold, wet nose pressed to her cheek and hot breath panting in her ear. She opened her eyes to see a familiar ceiling overhead. It was the cracked plaster over her bed in Cleveland. A slimy tongue smeared across her cheek.

She jerked up to see the muzzle and front two paws of a golden retriever hanging on to the bed. The room pulsed with the pounding of her head. It weighed a hundred pounds. She squinted her swollen eyes through a tunnel of pain. "Gunner? Is that you?"

Her father's missing hunting dog wagged his tail furiously and prodded his wet nose under her hand.

She scratched the top of his head. "What are you doing here?" The graying snout of an aging Labrador popped up from the foot of the bed at the sound of her voice. "Bogie? How did you both get back?"

The last thing she could remember was running through the sewers. Dogs were chasing them. *Dogs.* She couldn't breathe. A blast of light had blinded her from above. And then—

Her eyes flew to the bedroom door. It was shut.

She bolted up out of bed but buckled to the floor as the blood rushed out of her pounding head. A dull ache like the punch of a fist radiated between her shoulders. She'd been stung by something. *The police raid . . . What happened to Jimmy?* She scanned the room, her head a lead balloon on her shoulders. There was no sign of Jimmy or Ben or her shotgun in the closet. Out her window she could see Ben's Auglaize County sheriff's cruiser parked on the street. Troy's pickup truck sat behind it.

"Oh, God," she whispered, pulling herself to her feet. Down the street the Harmony Mission building towered over the houses. The sky had grown dark, glowing yellow with the streetlights. The police sirens no longer blared. The clock on her bedside table read 9:30 p.m.

Gunner nuzzled his nose against her hand, demanding more scratches. She bent down to get a better look at him. Ben had said the dogs had been lost the day her father was killed, that they were out somewhere in the woods on their own, fighting for survival. She'd seen stray dogs wandering the streets of Tremont, and Gunner showed no signs of struggle. His face looked no worse for wear. No cuts or scrapes on his body. No broken claws. No scarring around his mouth.

"Who's been feeding you, boy?" She scratched behind his ears. His fur still smelled faintly of rotting leaves and sewage, as did her own hands. Her fingernails were black with dirt. In the back of her pounding head, she still heard barking. It had been Gunner and Bogie chasing them down in the sewers. They knew her scent. That's how Ben had found them. She leaned against the bed and reached up to feel the knot between her shoulders, aching like a tetanus vaccination. *Taser? Dart?*

Voices from the kitchen brought her back to her feet. She pressed her ear to the door.

"Is that really necessary?" It sounded like Ben.

"Was it necessary for this son of a bitch to pull a gun on me? Who knows what this animal did to our girl. I say we get real traditional with this piece of shit," a second voice seethed. She could tell from the venom it was Troy.

"But neighbors are still awake. It's too risky."

"Nah. You're not gonna make much noise, are you, boy?"

A muffled grunt barely made it through her bedroom door.

"What about Kris?" Ben said under his breath. She could hear him trying to keep his voice down, as if to protect her from the words. He'd shot her with something down in the sewer. He'd shot her and carried her out.

"We need to get her out of here," a third voice said softly. The sound of it sent a jolt through her heart. It was the voice of a ghost. "She can't have any part in this."

"Isn't it a bit late for that?" Troy hissed. The wet thump of a fist slamming into raw meat hit Kris in the ear. *Jimmy.*

She recoiled from the door. Hot tears spilled down her face. It was a dream. It had to be some sort of nightmare. Gunner cocked his head at her and whined. The wood floor creaked as she stumbled back from the voices, willing herself to fly away.

"She's up."

Scrambling to the edge of her bed, Kris searched the sheets until she found the knife she'd stashed there in a fit of panic the other night, never dreaming she'd actually need it. *This isn't happening,* she told herself as the door swung open.

"Hey, babe!" Troy flashed a manic grin from the doorway. "We've been so worried about you."

She shrank against the bed, sliding the cold blade between her waistband and the small of her back.

Troy grabbed her arm and dragged her from the bedroom and out into the kitchen. The first thing she saw was Jimmy bound and gagged in a heap on the floor. Naked. His beautiful dark skin marred with welts and bruises. Her insides fell out at the sight. Troy had to hoist her back onto her feet as the words *Oh, God! Oh, God!* sirened through her head.

The rest of the room registered in incoherent pieces. A heavy, squat figure in a police uniform standing over Jimmy. A giant steel hook bolted into the ceiling. A man seated at her kitchen table. Clean-shaven skin. Dyed black hair. Familiar blue eyes bent on her.

Troy forced her into a chair across the table from the stranger.

"Ah, Kris," the man said in her father's voice. "You should have just filled out the paperwork like you were told. Now look what you've done."

The sirens in her head went quiet.

"Dad?" she croaked. It wasn't him. It wasn't. But the eyes . . .

"Do you have any idea what I've gone through to keep you away from all this? Goddammit!" He slammed the table.

She flinched as though it were a slap.

"I was going to let you go. When will these stupid women learn to just mind their own business?" He looked to Ben, standing there with a gun on his hip, and shook his head sadly.

Kris gaped at Jimmy lying on the floor. "What have you done?" she whispered.

"What have I done?" he mocked her. "Christ, I should be asking you the same thing. What the hell were you thinking, sticking your nose in all of this? Poking around the archives? Asking questions in the chat rooms?"

Kris's eyes widened. *They're watching you.*

"This is no place for a girl. I did everything I could to keep you from it, but you just had to go lookin' for it, didn't you? You're just like your mother."

Kris's eyes circled the funhouse of horrors that her kitchen had become. Ben couldn't look her in the eye. A white hood lay on the kitchen counter. The words *Ku Klux Klan* skittered through her mind.

Her mismatched collection of knives had been laid out in perfect order on the kitchen table in front of her. Troy prodded the black man on the ground with his steel-toed boot.

Jimmy turned his swollen face up to hers. *Run!*

"But." She shook her head and forced herself to look at her father through the tears in her eyes. "You're not one of them. You tattooed over the brand. Your parents . . . they hated her . . . they hated me."

"They didn't have the stomach to properly hate anything. They didn't have the nerve to dirty their hands. They just wanted to sit back behind the scenes, the cowards. When Pelley went down, they all turned tail and ran." He waved his arm in disgust. "You don't get to sit at the table and eat the meat if you're not willing to go kill it yourself."

Kris knew the words well. She'd heard them every time she refused to pull the trigger. She turned to Ben. "You knew about this the whole time."

"I'm sorry, Krit," Ben said, putting his bulk between her and the front door. He gave her a sympathetic nod. "I always liked your mom, kiddo. Even if she was half-kike . . . I feel like I failed you both."

"You signed the accident report," she heard herself whisper from the recesses of a room deep inside where she'd barricaded herself. She turned back to her father. "What did you do to her?"

"I gave that woman every chance to get right with this world. I plucked her out of that clutch of Jews and tried to put her on the right side of things. I taught her everything. How to be a proper lady. How to be a mother. How to obey God's will . . ." The warped face of her father shook side to side in disgust. "I tried to save her from herself, but was she grateful?"

Flesh-and-blood memories of her mother had deserted her years ago, leaving nothing but pieces. Her small form perched on the edge of a bed. Sullen stares out the window. Her face buried in her hands. The soft warbling pitch of her crying. The gentle pained smile leaning over her bed. *Listen to your father, honey. Please don't make him angry, baby.* The fear in her eyes. Kris had always thought it was her fault for being a bad girl, but . . .

"You beat her," Kris said more to herself than to anyone else. She stared at him in disbelief. All the times she'd cowered in terror of his wrath, all the times he'd hit her in a rage came flooding back. All the ways she'd molded herself so that he would hug her instead. She'd managed to explain it away, that it was normal. Every kid got punished, right? As she blinked back fresh tears, she saw her mother's picture still sitting next to his bed. "Did you even love her at all?"

He just shook his head. "Love is a woman's game, Kris, you should know that by now. But I had such hopes for her. It was such a thrill wooing her, earning her trust, convincing her that I was the one, having her . . . But then, just like a woman, she let me down."

"You hunted her." She realized it as she said it. The picture was just a trophy, another deer head mounted on his wall. Nauseated, she shook away the thought, and DHOH's typed words jumbled together in her head. *All dead trains passed through Lima . . . All dead trains on the CDX scrap division . . . Fifty-four dead between 1972 and 1996.* Jimmy lying there naked on the floor. "It was you. You killed all those people. The scrapbook. They were all yours. And she found out . . ."

"She tried to take you away, Kris. My own flesh and blood." He gave her the helpless smile of a self-declared martyr. "I did it for you. I did it so you'd have a chance. And now look . . . I should've known better than to dirty my bloodlines."

The roar of adrenaline in her ears drowned out the words as the truth of it sunk in. For the first time, she could see it all clearly—the locked toolshed, the long hunting trips, her father sitting in the garage, washing the blood from his hands and boots. *It wasn't an animal's blood.* "How could you kill those people?"

The monster across the table tilted his head at her and spoke as though she were a little girl. "They weren't people, honey. Not like us. Look at the news. They tear each other apart every day like wild animals. They'd kill you same as look at you. Or rape you. Or drug you and steal you away into the disease-infested hell they make of this world. Take this animal here." It motioned to Jimmy on the ground. "What do you even know about him? Huh?"

"He's quite a catch, Kritter," Ben chimed in. He shook his head at her as though she'd failed a test. "We pulled a few prints from the house. His real name is James Howard Wills, and he's a convicted felon. Kid's got a rap sheet a mile long. Shoplifting. Drugs. Armed robbery. He's even wanted for questioning in a murder. Didya know all that?"

Kris felt the floor shift under her. *Jimmy? Murder?* He lay there bruised and beaten, pleading with his eyes. *No.*

"Do you really expect me to let this criminal near my baby girl? I shudder to think what he's done to you." The monster eyed her with disgust. *Whore.*

"No. He didn't do anything." All feeling drained from her limbs. Kris squeezed her eyes shut, hoping to disappear, but the thought of Jimmy forced them back open.

"I'm supposed to believe that he didn't lay a hand on you?" He motioned to Jimmy on the floor. "It's my job to protect you from the filth of this world."

She knew better than to argue with the man. He hated back talk, and she needed to keep him talking so she could think. *Be a little girl. Be his little girl.* "Then why did you die, Daddy? You left me alone . . ."

"What choice did I have?" The monster with her father's eyes smacked the table hard enough to make her jump again. "Our so-called government started asking questions. These Internet spies began poking around. That idiot Hohman found me at work. I couldn't just let them take me out and throw me in jail. What would that've done to you? No. I would never have left you like that."

He was pleading his case to her, she realized, working to turn her to his reason. She nodded slowly. "You killed him . . . You killed him and made everyone think what they found was you." His smug expression told her she was right. "But the tattoo . . ."

He cracked a sad smile. *Pity,* it said. "It helps to have friends with access to the files."

Ben.

"We had it all worked out. But then you started asking questions and refused to cooperate. Dammit, Kris! You don't know what's coming!"

"What's coming?" she whispered, quaking inside at his anger, at his insanity. She glanced up at Ben for help but knew she'd find none. Troy stood over Jimmy, hanging one arm from the giant hook in the ceiling in anticipation. The blade of the knife dug into the small of her back, but there were three of them. She needed more time.

"The illusion of this world is about to come crashing down, and we all have to be ready," the monster explained and gently picked up her hand across the table. "It's been predicted since the dawn of time. Jesus is coming back, girl. And he's coming for blood . . . When the grid goes down in eight months, all hell is gonna break loose. It won't matter who's alive or dead, but I'll be damned if I'll be locked in a cage to starve while the world outside burns."

"Jesus is coming back? What are you talking about? You don't even go to church!" She jerked away from him on reflex and immediately regretted it. She could tell by the way the flame went out of the monster's eyes that she'd blown it.

He shook his head in disgust, washing his hands of her for good. "My church is everywhere. Troy, get her out of here, son."

Troy let go of the meat hook and grabbed both of her shoulders hard enough to hurt. "Time to go, babe."

"Troy! How can you be a part of this?" she pleaded with him. The knife was lodged in her waistband, but her arms were pinned.

"You know your dad's always been like a father to me. He's taught me so many things." All their buddy-buddy hunting trips together took on a new color in her mind as he grinned. A chill ran through her. He intended to finish what he'd started back in Cridersville, and this time Jimmy wouldn't be able to stop him. She was his now.

She fought back a wave of panic and tried to focus. To keep talking. To keep him from dragging her to his truck. "You did it too . . . You helped kill those people."

Troy planted a wet kiss on her lips. "I did them a favor, babe. I saved them from themselves. Don't worry so much. I know we'll get through this thing together. Al's agreed to let me keep an eye on you from now on. I got a beautiful room all set for you. In time, you'll understand why all this was necessary."

Ben opened the door for them. The red eight-pointed star on the door swung into the house like an omen. If she let Troy drag her out, Jimmy was dead. She dug in her heels against the door frame and turned to the monster at the table. "*You* painted this, didn't you?"

"I thought you might come to your senses and come home. If you had, all of this"—he motioned to Jimmy and the knives—"wouldn't have been necessary."

She kept her knees locked. "You were here?"

"No need, kiddo." He waved a hand, reveling in his power. "We have many friends in this sewer of a city."

"The landlord," she whispered. The spying. The reports back home. "That's why you made me live here."

"The Legion is everywhere. We didn't die out, we went underground and splintered and spread like wildfire. Vietnam may have spawned the free-love movement, but it also trained a whole new generation of soldiers." He flashed a wry grin. *Death from above,* it said. "While those hippies were out marching for 'civil rights,' we were getting ready to cleanse the world."

Kris blinked her eyes clear and scrambled for something, anything to say. "If what you're doing is so good, why—why hide it? Why destroy the records? The archives?"

He raised his eyebrows. "Destroy them? Those are valuable historic documents! Do you know how hard we've been working to resurrect the sacred rituals? We've got scholars in our midst perfecting the true Holy Bible Hitler ordained . . ." The monster picked up one of the longest knives and spun the blade between his fingers and turned his eyes to Jimmy sprawled on the floor.

Tears blurred her vision. "No. You don't have to do this. I'll go with you . . . I will. I'll behave."

"I know you will, sweetie. But it's too late now. You're going to have to take responsibility for your mistakes. You should've just signed the papers like poor Ben here asked. You should've stayed in Cridersville where you belonged. You should've stayed far away from that animal over there. You left me no choice . . ." His eyebrows wrinkled into a frown. "Don't make it worse, sweetheart."

She strained against the crazed football player pinning down her arms, keeping her feet on the door frame. "You can't do this!" she squeaked.

The monster stood and motioned to Troy to set her down. The football player obeyed but kept a grip on her shoulders. A hand grabbed her chin. "I'm doing this for you."

"Bullshit," she whispered.

He wrenched her chin hard. "What did you just say to me?"

That got him. He hated nothing more than sass, and she needed him to stay focused on her, not Jimmy. Kris gathered her voice in her gut and belted right into his face, "*Bullshit!* All those people on the trains, Mom, Jimmy—you didn't do this for me. You did it for yourself. Because you're a *Sick. Twisted. Fuck!*"

The crack of his hand sent her sprawling out of Troy's grip and onto the floor. Her head hit the linoleum. Her vision exploded into red spots.

"Dammit, Kristin," he muttered. "You had a chance. You had a chance to be saved, but I'll be Goddamned if I let a filthy whore take the place of my daughter. Troy . . ."

The door slammed shut. Troy's boots shook the floorboard under her. Two pairs of hands grabbed the heap that was Jimmy and hauled him up by the ankles, twisting and bucking. After three attempts, they managed to get him hooked and left him dangling from his feet, naked.

Dazed, Kris picked up her bruised head. Headlights flashed under the blinds. The rumble of a car passed by on Thurman Avenue only a few feet away and kept going up the road. A pair of hands hauled her up off the floor. "Now you get to bear witness," her father's voice growled in her ear. He grabbed the back of her neck and jerked her to his side. The familiar smell of his aftershave made the room reel. *This isn't happening.*

"I know what I want to cut off first," Troy announced, picking the largest blade up from the table.

The monster wrested the cleaver from him. "You'll get your chance, but that's not how this is done. First you bleed him. Even the lowest creature deserves a humane death. It's what separates us from these animals."

The beast steadied the cleaver at Jimmy's throat with his other hand gripping Kris's neck. Both Ben's and Troy's eyes were trained on the kill as she grabbed the handle of her knife and pulled it from her waistband.

"Ben, will you say grace?"

Ben closed his eyes and said, "O Lord, we have brought this sinner forth on this altar to atone for his sins. We thank you for your teachings in the ways of the sacrifice. Leviticus tells us, 'The life of a creature is in the blood.'"

Both Troy and her father's voices repeated, "The life of a creature is in the blood."

"'And I have given it to you upon the altar to make atonement for your souls.'"

Gripping the knife, Kris felt her soul retreat. The beast holding her neck bowed its head low as it repeated the prayer. Watching herself through the murky waters separating her mind from the hell around her, she wondered if she'd have time to stick his throat before the other two realized what she'd done, if she'd have the strength the bury the knife to the hilt. Jimmy hung bleeding and bruised, his throat inches from the cleaver. Her mother's shattered car rolled over and over with the pounding pulse in her head, a fury rising to a deafening pitch. *He killed her,* it screamed. *He fucking killed her!*

Ben continued the prayer, "'It is the blood that makes atonement for the soul.'"

Jimmy's eyes darted to hers. He shook his head. *Don't.*

"It is the blood—"

The front door crashed open.

"Hey, Kris?" Her roommate, Pete, backed into the room, hauling his bike. "Say, what's with the spray paint? Has the landlord seen th—"

His voice cut out as he turned into the room and registered knife, victim, killers.

"Pete!" Kris shrieked. "Help!"

"Oh, shit!" he gasped. He threw his bike as the ex–football star lunged for him. Metal tubing and wheels knocked Troy back, and Pete took off running down the street.

"Dammit!" Ben unholstered his gun and took off after him.

"Police! *Help!*" Kris screeched out the open door.

Her father grabbed her by the mouth. "Troy," he barked. "Bring me that kid."

Troy grabbed the bike off the kitchen floor and headed out on it without so much as a word.

CHAPTER 50

The monster with her father's voice softly closed the door behind him, his hand still gripping her neck, dragging her like a bad dog. "I wouldn't worry about him. We have several friends in the area. That mark on your door is like a beacon . . . Word spreads fast."

Kris kept the knife hidden against her leg. She'd had an opening with his head down, but now she had his full attention. A trickle of blood leaked from her eyebrow where his blow had landed moments earlier. The pain throbbed.

"Dad," she pleaded, hoping to sway him now that it was just the two of them. "Please. This can't be right. You can't do this! Let him go! For me . . ."

His eyes lit at her and he bellowed, "Who the hell are *you* to tell *me* what I can and cannot do? This *is* for you!"

She shrank from the booming voice that had terrorized her as a child every time he had caught her stepping out of line. She'd always been afraid of him, she realized. Some part of her saw the murder behind his eyes, even when she was small. "You can't kill him," she whimpered. "It's wrong."

"I'll be the judge of what's right and wrong." The monster brushed her cheek the way a father might and shook his head. *Stupid little girl.*

"Is it wrong to kill the beast threatening your children? Is it wrong to kill a rapist? A drug dealer? A murderer?"

The killer's eyes shone with certainty. There would be no convincing him. Behind him, Jimmy thrashed and strained to break free. The seconds ticked by on the Elvis clock on the far wall. She said a silent prayer for Pete and tightened her grip on the knife.

"If he's a murderer, what are you?" she whispered.

He picked up the cleaver again. "I'm just a hunter, Kris. A hunter culling the herd."

"He's not a deer! His name is Jimmy!" She just needed to get close enough. He'd never suspect an attack from her. She couldn't even shoot a squirrel.

"Sweet girl, if he was a deer, at least he'd be useful. This one's nothing but a drain on society. This damned city's warped your senses, making you believe that we're all the same, that we're all equal. And now you're acting like you're in love with this animal. Are you?" he demanded, his eyes dilated with the bloodlust of a predator pinning its prey.

She shook her head and turned her flooded gaze to Jimmy. *I'm so sorry.*

"Look at me when I'm talking to you." The killer squeezed her neck, yanking her welling eyes to his. There was no trace of the father she knew in them. Her heart pounded against his grip.

Thump-ump.

Her trembling fingers squeezed the splintered handle of the knife, pressing the blade into her thigh to keep from letting it go. The killer dragged her toward his victim.

Thump-ump.

Jimmy hung there from his ankles. Kris could see his carcass dripping blood onto the garage floor, a wooden stick holding open his ribs, shaking gently while her father peeled off his skin.

Thump-ump.

"In the old days, we'd take the head while the animal's heart was still beating. They say the blood could tell the future if you knew how to ask it. Let's see, shall we?"

The killer's jugular pulsed inches from her nose. He lifted the cleaver to strike.

Thump—

Kris plunged her blade into the soft meat of the monster's neck.

A warm plume of blood erupted, splashing over her hand. Blurred colors and sounds burst. Arms flailing. Hands grasping. She heard herself screaming from a faraway room until he squeezed the noise out of her windpipe. She twisted the blade. His eyes bulged from his head, *Stop.* She twisted harder. His grip tightened on her throat, but she was beyond feeling.

She was gone.

A blast split the air. The monster blew into Kris, knocking her to the floor amid a muted chorus of shouts. The weight of him crushed the life out of her, blotting the light from the room. White flashed behind her eyes as her chest collapsed. Her fist held fast to the knife. *Die. Just die. Just die. Just*—

Air rushed back into her lungs like broken glass when someone pulled the bulk off of her. She rolled to her side, sucking dry sand until the thinnest thread of oxygen slipped through. A tinny ring in her ears mixed with the smoke and dust. She dragged herself away from it, retreating until she hit a wall, the knife still locked in her hand. Someone was calling her name, muddled and distant from somewhere underwater.

Jimmy's face appeared under the table, distorted with swelling and a broken nose. His bloody lips were moving as though he was shouting, but nothing was coming out. She just shook her head. He reached out his hands to grab her. She shrank away. *He's dead. He's come to take me with him.*

An old woman's withered face hovered several feet behind his, crowned with a pink curler and a puff of gray hair. The basement door was standing open.

Kris tried to speak but couldn't hear her own voice through the ringing in her ears.

Jimmy grabbed her by the front of her shirt and looked her dead in the eye. *We have to go.*

She nodded and let him pull her out from under the table. Blood and plaster dust lay exploded over the floor. Madame Mimi was standing at the basement door, clutching Kris's shotgun. She motioned Kris over. Flashing red and blue lights pulled up outside the kitchen window. Jimmy dragged her to the basement stairs.

Kris stopped to look back. Her father's body bled out over the floor, his hand lay inches from the cleaver. It wasn't him. The man that had raised her—the man that had kissed bruised knees and carried her on his shoulders—wasn't the killer lying dead in her kitchen. *Maybe he'd never existed at all.*

Two dogs crept out of the bedroom with their tails down. They stopped to sniff the body. Kris pressed her lips together and let out what she hoped was a whistle. The sound got lost in the high-pitched squeal between her ears, but Bogie and Gunner lifted their tails and ran to her.

A trembling hand gripped her shoulder. A voice finally cut through the ringing.

"Kris!" Jimmy shouted. "We have to go."

Kris blinked herself awake and nodded, the words *Go where?* not even registering. She herded the dogs down the steps after him and looked back one more time, expecting to see her father standing there in judgment of what she'd done, expecting to see him lunge at her with his knife. But her kill didn't move. Her first kill.

I finally did it, Dad. I pulled the trigger.

Another pair of flashing lights appeared outside her window. Any second, the police would burst through the door. They would arrest them and throw them into a dark cell for the rest of their lives.

"Kris!" Jimmy prodded.

She couldn't move. His blood soaked its way through her clothes down to her skin, still warm. The knife fluttered in her hand like a living thing. She hung there in the moment, dangling from the meat hook, her heart and guts carved out, a stick between her ribs, her own blood pooling out over the ground.

Then Jimmy pulled her down the steps and shut the basement door.

CHAPTER 51

The dark stain spread out over the underside of the floorboards over-head. The old woman in the pink curlers led Mimi and Jimmy past the abandoned stove and the dusty boxes scattered across the basement floor.

A hard knock pounded the front door above them.

Bogie and Gunner started barking. "Shh!" Kris pointed a stern finger at each of them, and they shut their muzzles and sat down.

"This is the police! Open up!"

Kris froze and listened. The old homeless woman shuffled across the floor to the storage closet in the corner. Her foot connected with the side of a box with an all-too-familiar *thump*. The sound of their basement ghost registered somewhere in Kris's ringing ears.

Another knock shook the wall above them. "Police! We're coming in!"

"Kris!" Jimmy grabbed her arm. "C'mon. We have to get out of here."

Out of here? Her eyes circled the basement walls as he pulled her into the tiny storeroom and shut the door. The muddy yellow glow of the streetlights above streamed in through a small dusty window. Spiderwebs hung in curtains from the rafters, and rusted paint cans sat four high on the floor. There was no sign of the old woman or Madame Mimi. They'd vanished through the hole in the floor.

Someone had built the house over a large well. A low ring of stone cut in half by the foundation wall. Dusty wood cover boards leaned against the stone wall in the shape of a half-moon. Candlelight flickered up through the cavern below.

A loud crash above them was followed by a rush of footsteps. "Police! Freeze!"

"Somebody get an ambulance!"

Bogie and Gunner began to yip. "Shh!" Kris hissed at them.

Jimmy shut the storage closet door and climbed halfway down into the well. Ladder? she wondered dully. "Give me the dogs."

Kris nudged Bogie and then Gunner whimpering down into the hole. A pair of boots came pounding down the basement steps on the other side of the door.

"Anybody down here?" a policeman called out. "If you can hear me, put the gun down and come out with your hands up!"

"Cover the back door!" another voice barked.

Kris looked down at herself covered in blood. The knife trembled in her hand. *I killed him. Oh, God, I really killed him.* She turned toward the police officer's voice in a trance.

"Kris!" Jimmy whispered up to her. "Come on!"

She peered down into the hole.

"Watch your step," he whispered, stepping off the wooden ladder leading down beneath the house.

Outside the closet door, she heard the policeman kicking his way through the piles of boxes.

"Kris!" A hand grabbed her ankle, pulling her toward the hole in the floor.

She stepped onto the ladder and slid the wood cover boards back into place over her head.

Clammy cold air drenched her wet skin as she stepped down onto soft dirt. The yellow light of a candle bounced off the stacked stones set in a wide ring around her. "Jimmy," she whispered, surveying the strange cellar. "Where are we?"

"I think it's an old cistern. Back when this was all farmland, they used them to store rainwater." He motioned her toward a two-foot hole in the wall before crawling inside it with the candle.

Kris climbed in after him. Pain registered in her knees as a mere curiosity, army-crawling across the uneven, damp fieldstones.

Talking seemed to soothe Jimmy's frayed nerves. His voice echoed back to where she lay the dark. "I'm guessing the bricklayers didn't know what to do when they found all this buried, so they just built around it. Or maybe the landowners liked the idea of leaving a few secret bunkers. You know the underground railroad had a big hub here in Cleveland."

"Where are we going?" she heard herself ask. "Shouldn't we talk to the police? What about Pete?" Somewhere inside she knew these were the right things to say, but she couldn't conjure a single emotion. *He's dead . . . Maybe I'm dead too.*

"Your buddy Ben *is* the police. Something tells me they'll be takin' his word over ours."

Kris and Jimmy crawled fifty feet across the mossy stones until they reached a larger cavern. Candlelight danced across the round fieldstones lining the walls. They had landed in a cave the size of a barn. Tree roots hung from the arched ceiling. Large stone pillars stood every ten feet like a forest of tree trunks holding them up. A series of black hieroglyphics marked the far wall next to a wood ladder where Madame Mimi and the little old lady stood waiting.

What the hell is this? Kris wondered, turning around.

Madame Mimi closed her eyes before answering, "The city built these caverns as rainwater reservoirs . . . It was before they put in the municipal water supply system in the 1850s." She tied a batik scarf into a skirt around Jimmy's naked waist. Black ink tattoos stretched across his back. Squinting, Kris could see a list of names and dates. She recognized them from his murder wall. He'd written the list of Torso Killer victims across his back. The word *unclaimed* carved over and over. She wanted to touch one, but her hand was covered in blood.

Something rustled at the far end.

Kris turned to see Bogie and Gunner rooting around in a pile of trash. She walked over to pull a piece of plastic from one of the dog's mouths only to find the wrappers from all the bagels and bologna Pete had stolen off her shelf in the fridge. *It wasn't Pete.* Her photograph of her father had been discarded with the trash. She lifted it off the ground.

"Did you take this from my room?" She turned to Jimmy. The bumps in the night, the stolen food, her missing picture all suddenly made sense. *Kid's got a rap sheet a mile long, kiddo.* "Have you been breaking into my house this whole time?"

He raised his eyebrows, offended.

"No. No, I'm afraid." The little old lady with the pink curlers shuffled over, her eyes glassy. "I'm afraid that was me."

"What?" Kris felt herself squeezing the knife in her hand. The old witch wandering around her house, eating her food, watching while she slept—the thought landed without a flutter of feeling. Dead numb, she asked, "Why would you do that?"

"I like to come and visit my ghosts from time to time. Don't you?" A crooked smile split the woman's face from ear to ear in the flickering candlelight.

"Ghosts?" Kris heard herself ask through the tinnitus left by the blast. It was like listening to someone else. "Whose ghost? Norma's?"

The smile shrank as the woman nodded and muttered to herself. "No. That's not really her name. I just thought . . . I thought she might come back."

"Who? Who is she?" Jimmy asked, intrigued. Maybe desperate.

"You know," the old woman chuckled. "I'm not even sure. She called herself Johnnie before we changed it. We had to, you know, after all that mess up there."

Madame Mimi touched the old woman's shoulder. "It was Rose's girl, wasn't it?"

She didn't answer, she just gazed up at the network of roots and stones overhead.

Kris turned to Jimmy. *Rose's girl. Jimmy's grandmother.* "Did you know about this?"

He shook his battered head.

She considered him for a moment, watching everything unfold from some place outside herself. *He's quite a catch, Kritter. He's even wanted for questioning in a murder case.* "Are you really wanted for murder?"

"Bein' wanted for murder and actually doing the murdering are two different things." Jimmy gave her a beaten smile. "There's a lot of ways for good folks to go to jail, and being black is one of them. They find us right now, I can tell you who's gonna serve time, and it ain't the white girl with the knife in her hand. Get me?"

She gazed down at the bloody knife. Her knuckles were white from gripping it so hard. *I'm the killer.*

"Kris, c'mon. It'll be okay. We'll figure it out." He crouched down next to her, making her realize she'd fallen to her knees. "You did what you had to do. You saved my life. That's gotta count for something. Right?"

She stared down at her blood-covered hands. They were her father's hands. "What if I'm like him?" Her voice sounded farther and farther away.

"You're no more a killer than I am. Sometimes you just do what has to be done. You want to know why I've got warrants? Because I loved my mom. I loved her every day she fell down drunk, every day she was too messed up to notice her boyfriend beatin' on me or how he'd turn her out to his friends. She still doesn't remember shooting the motherfucker. She still doesn't remember how I cleaned her up and got rid of the gun . . . but what else could I do?"

She looked up at him. "So they think *you* did it?"

He shrugged like it was nothing. "It was self-defense on her part, but no judge's gonna care what really happened. They'd just lock her up and throw away the key. Nothin' makes white folks feel safer than putting black folks in jail, so I took the gun and just fell off the grid. It wasn't hard . . . You'll see."

"But what if I don't want . . . to fall off the grid?"

"Maybe you won't have to, but we've got to contact somebody outside the good ol' boy network. We have no idea how many friends your dad's buddy has on the force. C'mon. Let's get you up." He pulled her to her feet.

We have several friends in the area. That mark on your door is like a beacon.

Kris shook off his voice and focused her eyes on Mimi and the old lady. "How did you find us?"

Mimi chuckled. "The Auglaize County sheriff's cruiser out front helped."

The old woman pointed a gnarled finger up another ladder and said, "This is the way out."

As they climbed up out of the dark, Kris felt a part of herself fall behind. The part that never got up off her kitchen floor. The part that never dreamed of killing anything. Maybe the most important part. Between her ribs, she felt nothing but a wooden stick.

A blast of cool air hit her in the face as Jimmy pushed a manhole cover up and out of the way. A minute later, Kris's head popped up through the round hole and into the courtyard outside Jimmy's stairwell. He pulled her up onto her feet. The antique bicycle was still chained to the stair railing. The windows where she'd seen the little girl with her puff of black hair wave down stood empty. Kris scanned them all while Jimmy and Mimi hoisted up the dogs and replaced the manhole cover. Looking for Ben. Looking for Troy. Looking for her father.

Jimmy led them down the empty corridors, past the kicked-in doorways left open during the raid. The sirens and pounding boots left a hollow silence in their wake. Motes of disturbed dust still hung in the air as the building settled back into a deep sleep. Jimmy stopped at an open broom closet. A familiar eight-pointed star marked the back wall. He pushed it open into a hidden room with a flowered couch and a broken window. None of the old lady's things had been disturbed. The cops hadn't even known the room was there. The only reason Kris found it the first time was the door had been standing open.

Kris stopped and ran her fingers over the star. It belonged to the Legion, and so did the room behind it.

"Make yourselves at home," the crone twittered and prodded her orange cat off the plastic-covered sofa. *We have several friends in the area.*

Gripping the knife, Kris sank down onto one of the cushions and stared at her blood-soaked shirt now cold and clammy against her skin. Sickened, she wanted to take it off but couldn't bear the thought of dragging it across her face and over her head.

"Here, honey. Let me help you with that." Madame Mimi tapped her shoulder and nudged her forward, pulling the dry back of the shirt up and over the top of her head. The woman wadded up the fabric and threw it into the corner, then plopped down next to her with her giant bag, pulling wet wipes and napkins out. She wiped off Kris's slack face and neck and said, "It's not your fault, Kris. None of it. No one gets to choose their family."

Kris recoiled from her. "Why are we here? This room? Is the old lady? Is she . . ." *Legion?*

"Heavens no!" Mimi gaped at her, catching her meaning. "Farthest thing from it. You're safe here . . . for now."

Grabbing the napkins herself, Kris scrubbed the red crust off her hands until the skin was raw. She held on to the knife just in case. The lady with the pink curlers had led Jimmy back into her bedroom, saying something about a telephone.

Old newspapers sat in a pile on the coffee table next to her. Kris scanned the grainy smudged print, desperate to focus on something, anything other than the hollow space between her ribs. One of the headlines was circled.

BELOVED HUSBAND AND DOCTOR FOUND DEAD, it read. She squinted her eyes at the smaller print.

> *Dr. Albert Dietrich was found dead in his office on August 22, 1938, due to an apparent overdose of morphine. County Coroner Samuel Gerber ruled the death a suicide despite the insistence of his family that he was not a regular user of the drug or prone to bouts of depression . . .*

There were several more circled headlines in the stack below it. Kris glanced over at Mimi, then stood up with the newspapers and walked into the bedroom. Jimmy sat hunched over an outdated phone book. A loose phone wire draped over the floor and out the small window.

The old lady sat perched on the edge of her flowered bed, watching Jimmy with glazed eyes. She wasn't all there.

"Who was Dr. Albert Dietrich?"

"Hmm?" she asked. Kris pointed to the newspaper in her hand, and the crone shrank as though the name weighed her down. "Oh, him."

"I know that name." Jimmy leaned over and scanned the article. "Dr. Dietrich was one of the leaders of the Cleveland Silver Shirt

Legion. Being a doctor makes him a great Torso Killer suspect. The
coroner's reports pointed to a killer with some medical knowledge.
They didn't think regular folks would know how to cut up a body
so well."

Kris handed him the paper and scanned the ones below it. A
Cleveland police officer named Marcus Kessler jumped off a bridge. A
prominent stockyard owner died of alcohol poisoning. The president
of one of the biggest railroad lines to run through Cleveland shot
himself. They had all died in the late 1930s and early 1940s. "They all
committed suicide," Kris said dully. It felt like sleepwalking. *Maybe
I'll wake up soon.*

"No shit?" Jimmy stood up to get a better look at the headlines
now covering the old woman's bed.

"Who were all these people?" Kris asked, eyes drifting from
one paper to the next. *ADELA RAE WULF MISSES TRIAL DATE,
ASSUMED MISSING.* She turned to the old lady at the edge of the
mattress. "Why do you have all these?"

The woman didn't answer.

Jimmy took another newspaper from Kris and flipped through
the pages. "I recognize a lot of these names from the Torso Database.
They're all suspected members of the Silver Shirt Legion. All except
this guy."

He showed Kris a small obituary that read, *Called Home:
Unitarian Minister William R. Milton, age 64, suffered an apparent
heart attack yesterday while walking near West Side Market. His body
was found behind one of the butcher stands . . .*

The crone just sat there staring at her hands.

Jimmy was too engrossed in this new cache of evidence to notice.
"This can't be a coincidence. Maybe somebody figured out who was
doing the killing. Or maybe someone inside the Silver Shirts decided
they were a risk and silenced them all. Man, they must've done

something to really piss somebody off because suicide's the worst death there is . . . you know, if you're one of them."

Kris turned to him. "It is?"

"Suicide's a mortal sin, if you believe in that kind of thing. You couldn't even get buried in a proper cemetery back then. You'd just be damned straight to hell. It's also more convenient for any police officers that wanted to avoid an embarrassing investigation. They're open and shut cases."

The old lady nodded in agreement.

Kris studied the woman's empty expression. "Who are you?"

"I'm not anybody anymore." The lady chuckled. "When you get this old, you just disappear."

Jimmy wasn't amused. "What's your name?"

"Oh, it's changed so many times over the years it doesn't really matter." The lady waved her hand like a name was a trifle.

"What do your friends call you?" he pressed.

"Nothin'. I haven't had a friend in ages." The old woman's eyes drooped, water pooling in her sagging lower lids.

Kris stared blankly at the newspapers piled on the bed. *BELOVED HUSBAND AND DOCTOR FOUND DEAD*, she read again and wondered what the newspapers would say tomorrow. *Beloved Father Gunned Down, Daughter Missing.* She shook the thought from her head and turned to the old woman. "What about Johnnie?"

"Have you seen her?" The crone grabbed her arm, eyes lit with hope. Or madness. "Dark skin, beautiful eyes? She'd be older now. Not as old as me, but old. She might be using a different name—Norma?"

Being touched sent shudders through Kris. She could still feel his hand squeezing her throat. She recoiled her arm and reflexively felt for the knife she'd left in the other room. The woman didn't seem to notice.

"We haven't seen Norma or Johnnie," Jimmy answered for her. "How long has she been gone?"

The crone shriveled with disappointment. "Years. I lost her years ago. She'd gotten herself another man, and one day she'd just . . . I did my best by her, I really did, but a girl needs a proper mother . . . needs so much more than what I could do."

"I'm sorry. I know it's tough . . . But you did okay. Some part of her made it out. It did . . . I think Johnnie was my grandmother." He patted the woman's hand.

She turned to him and studied his face as though for the first time. "You have her eyes! Those sad, haunted eyes. Oh, honey." She cupped his swollen face in her gnarled hands. "What happened to you?"

"I've had worse." Jimmy closed his heavy lids and nodded a moment. When he looked up, there were tears in them. "What did Johnnie call you?"

"Ethel." She bent her head as though she owed him an apology. "She used to call me Ethel."

"Why do you have all these old newspapers, Ethel?" Kris lifted a stack of yellowing newsprint.

Ethel looked up with a mournful grin, a pink curler dangling from five strands of hair. "Because I killed them, dear."

The answer should've been a shock, but Kris just felt herself nod. Her eyes dropped to her buzzing hands, her broken lifelines stained red with blood.

"We were right." Jimmy scanned the headlines again. "The Legion were the Torso Killers, weren't they?"

Ethel gave a faint smile. "Among other things."

"How'd you do it?"

"It wasn't so hard. No one ever expects to be killed, you know. They just go about their business, never suspecting that death might be waiting for them in their office or at the end of the bar." She folded her frail hands. "You just have to be patient."

Kris clasped her own stained palms together to steady the tremor in them and whispered, "But how could you do it? How could you live with yourself?"

"Someone had to stop them, Kris," Jimmy protested. "Merylo, Ness, the sheriff—none of them could build a case. These people were murderers . . ."

"Heh. So what does that make me? The hand of God?" Ethel shot Jimmy an amused glance and patted his arm like a grandmother. "The devil needs hands too, you know . . . Anyway, it don't matter much. I decided I don't believe in God. The devil, I'm not so sure, but I wasn't going to wait around for him to show up. That was my choice . . . and I've had to live with it every day since."

"Is that why you stayed here . . . like this?" Kris asked, scanning the water-stained walls. *Beloved Father Gunned Down, Daughter Missing.*

"I tried other cities, other names, other lives . . . but none of them fit worth a damn. I was never part of this 'society' of yours. Besides, all that killing takes something from you . . ." The woman let out a heavy sigh and turned her glassy eyes to the cracked window. "They never stopped, you know. Just when I thought I got 'em all, another body'd show up somewhere. Headless. Naked. Cut up. It made me crazy. Truly . . . They even locked me up for a bunch of years until the politicians closed the asylum. I got too old for anybody to care what I'd done. Got good dental for a while there, though . . ."

Kris gazed down her blood-splattered bra. "Are you sorry you did it?"

"I'm sorry about all sorts of things, but . . ." The old lady shrugged and patted Kris on the knee as though she understood the girl's pain. "Killin's just a part a human nature. I don't care what the preachers say. Push anyone far enough, take enough from 'em and . . . Don't matter anyway. I was damned from the start. If I had to go back, I'm sure I'd do it all again. I can't help what I am."

Kris wiped a stray tear. "What are you?"

"I'm a ghost, dear. Always been a ghost . . . just been waitin' here for one of 'em to come back to their altar and start up again. If I could just get one more, maybe . . ." Ethel's watery eyes circled her stark room, reeking of cat urine and mold. "I ain't afraid of 'em. Whatever's gonna be done to me got done years ago."

"But that can't be it! Can't you . . ." Kris felt a pang for the old woman. For herself. She grasped at the air. "I don't know, make it right somehow?"

"Right by who? God? Jesus? Santa Claus? Don't think I haven't tried, but none of that nonsense works if you don't believe in it . . . just a child tryin' to cast a magic spell. Nah. I'm biding my time here until hell or whatever you want to call it comes for me. Until then, I'm free." Ethel leveled her watery eyes at her.

Free. Gravity failed her. All the things that had tethered Kris to the earth fell away at the thought, and she began to drift. *He's gone. He's really gone.*

"Maybe you could make it right if you did something really good." Jimmy knelt on the ground next to the old woman, but he was staring at Kris.

Ethel shook her head. "The path to good was always closed to the likes of me, even when I went lookin' for it."

"I get you, I do." Jimmy nodded, reaching for Kris's hand, holding on to it, keeping her from hurtling off into space. "But maybe we've got a chance here to do somethin' . . . I don't know, worthy of redemption."

"Redemption?" Ethel laughed. "Oh, he's good, ladies. Isn't he . . . And I imagine this redemption's got somethin' to do with you?"

HEADLESS BODY OF
MAN IS FOUND

The headless body of a man, almost beyond the possibility of identification, was found yesterday afternoon on the westerly edge of the yards of the Norris Bros. Co. movers and erectors, 2139 Davenport Avenue N.E.

The torso, both arms and one leg were beneath a high pile of steel girders and hoisting machinery beams near the Lakeside Avenue side of the yards.

—*Cleveland Plain Dealer*, July 23, 1950, p. 1

CHAPTER 52

August 22, 1938

Dr. Dietrich came into the examination room with his head behind a clipboard, not even bothering to look up. "And how can we help you today, Miss—uh—can you please tell me your name?"

"Wallace. My name is Miss Wallace." Ethel's voice shook with adrenaline. Just being in the room with the doctor sent two thousand volts through her. *I should've taken another shot of whiskey.* She kept her head down below the brim of her hat. *I never forget a face,* he'd said. . . . *As much as I might like to.*

"Yes. Miss Wallace. What seems to be the trouble?"

"I'm afraid I might be . . ." She cleared her throat and gripped the gun hidden under the folds of her skirt in her sweating palm, afraid it might slip and go off. "In a family way."

"I see." Dr. Dietrich lowered himself onto a stool at the end of the exam table and flipped to a new page on his clipboard. He still hadn't looked at her. "And how late are we?"

"Two months." Her heart rate slowed to a slightly less suicidal pace. He didn't suspect a thing. The doctor sat in a white coat with nothing but a pen in his hand. In the cabinet behind him, there were only jars of cotton balls and swabs. None of the drawers held a knife or gun. She'd checked.

"And the father?"

"I—uh—I don't . . ." Ethel let her head sink lower and feigned tears. She remembered how much the doctor liked seeing his patients squirm. He liked shaming them, and Ethel was an expert at giving men what they liked. "I'm not looking to make anyone a father . . . I can't. I'm sorry, Doctor, I just . . . I don't know how this happened."

The doctor stopped writing and chuckled, quite pleased with his position in the matter. "I think we all know how this happened. Are you a mistress or a whore? Not that there's a significant difference between the two in my opinion, except for your ability to pay of course."

"He said he'd pay whatever you want." Ethel let her voice break. She felt the polished wood grip of the gun, wondering when the right moment would present itself. Part of her wanted to just shoot him in his smug face right then and there, but she needed to find out more about the Legion. She needed him to talk. "Please, Doctor . . . can you help me? I don't know what to do."

Her plea seemed to pique his interest. His tone changed ever so slightly, but Ethel could hear the predator in it. "How old are you?"

"Nineteen," she lied. The younger the better for men like Dietrich.

"Have you ever been diagnosed with a social disease?"

"I—I don't think so." She had him. She could see his posture shift with his intent. He stood and locked the examination room door. *So it is going to be* that *kind of exam.*

"Any sores? Discomfort urinating?" He set his clipboard and pen down on the counter.

Ethel forced herself to shrink and squirm for his amusement. "No."

"We're going to need you to remove your clothes, Miss Wallace." The doctor pulled the metal stirrups out of the exam table beneath her with two menacing clanks. "Let's see what sort of shape we're in."

404 D. M. PULLEY

"All of them?" she whimpered, debating whether to wait until his pants were around his ankles and he was hobbled.

"It's the only way to do a proper examination of your condition." His voice turned hard and impatient, perfectly practiced at frightening a desperate girl. "If you'd rather go see another physician, I'll bid you good day."

"No." She stood up from the table and made a show of her shame, head hung low. "Could you please . . . turn around?"

"Of course." He turned toward the wall, the power of his position thrilling him, his entire body taut with anticipation. Ethel stood up from the exam table and rustled her skirt as the doctor tapped his hard-soled shoes against the tiles. She trained the gun on the back of his head, hands trembling. "Will it hurt, Doctor? I'm awfully afraid of the pain."

He cocked his head to the side, and she could hear the amusement in his voice. "Of course not, Miss Wallace. If you'd like, I can administer morphine . . . or ether. It will just cost a little more."

Ethel pressed the cold barrel of her pistol to the nape of his neck and pulled back the hammer. The image of Johnnie drugged and bound in a basement nearly blinded her. "Did you charge the other girls for the morphine, you sick son of a bitch?"

He turned his head toward the sound and got a good look at her face. Recognition registered in his pale blue eyes. "What is this? How the hell did you get in h—?"

Ethel fired the gun over his shoulder. The bullet barely missed his nose before lodging itself in the bricks behind the plaster. The kick of it jumped up her arm, but she held steady. It felt good. Shooting a raping bastard like her landlord had been one of the most satisfying moments of her life.

Dietrich froze, bent in a half crouch, eyes stunned, his cheek flamed red with a gunpowder burn. He opened his mouth to speak but nothing came out. She held the gun to his head and considered pulling the trigger.

The doctor's office was in an old brick colonial a block off Central Avenue where gunshots weren't unusual and cops were slow to respond. No doubt someone had heard the shot, but odds were good it would go unreported. She'd slipped the receptionist ten dollars to take a long lunch and lock the door. From the looks of her, the poor girl would be happy to find the good doctor dead when she got back. He gaped at the locked door in dazed desperation.

"Nobody's coming, Doc. It's just you and me."

His gaze didn't waver, if he'd heard her at all. His ears were probably still ringing from the blast. Years on the street told her the shock wouldn't last. Nobody waited around after jumping a guy to see what might happen, they just snatched the fool's wallet and ran. And he outweighed her by fifty pounds. *Drop him fast.* She shoved his stunned carcass away from the wall and kicked him hard in the groin, as she'd done to many men in dark alleys. "You're keepin' your pants on today, Doc."

He doubled over onto the stool, toppling it to the ground. Ethel kept the barrel trained on him lying there wheezing, and started pulling open drawers, tossing gloves and metal instruments to the ground until she found what she was looking for. She slapped the wire and fabric ether mask onto the metal counter and grabbed a brown medicine jar out of the cabinet above. She popped the glass stopper and gave it a sniff. She knew the burning sweet smell all too well from the junkie doctors she'd met in the Run. It had come in handy more than once. Before the doctor's brain could track her, she'd doused the mask and pressed it to his crumpled face.

"Breathe nice and deep, Doc," she said, holding the barrel of the gun to his temple with her other hand, her knee on the side of his neck.

He struggled against the weight of her, gulping big breaths until the spark of panic in his eyes went dim. The ether hit and his muscles went limp. She eased her weight off him and pulled the mask once a heavy fog settled over his face.

She stood up, flushed with adrenaline. The doctor lay there in a stupor. The urge to strip him naked and gut him like a fish nearly overpowered her. She reared back and kicked him hard in the gut instead, again and again, growling every curse under the sun. His pig face by the side of the bed telling her the baby had *gone to a better place* replayed again and again. For all she knew, he'd killed it.

He let out a low groan with each blow but barely moved. It finally occurred to her that if she kept going, she'd kill him before she got what she wanted.

She hauled his dead weight up to sitting and slapped him in the face. "Hey, Doc! Wake up! We need to talk."

His voice came slipping out of his lips with a string of drool. "You don't . . . have the slightest idea . . . who you're dealing with."

"You're right. I don't. Tell me about the Legion. Who are they?"

He breathed out a woozy laugh. "They're everywhere."

"Who killed Rose Wallace?" she yelled in his ear.

"Who?" His eyes rolled wildly, pupils swollen.

She shoved her face into his warped field of vision, making him recoil. "Did you kill the black girl Rose Wallace?"

He shook his head. "I told them she was too dirty. That it wouldn't work, but her blood was so red . . . as red as the others."

Ethel grabbed him by the throat. "Who did you tell it wouldn't work? Who wanted her blood?"

His mouth hung slack, garbling his words. "The witch . . . Adela."

She loosened her grip. "Adela Rae Wulf?"

"She was the . . . demanded the bleeding ceremonies . . . it was all of her witchcraft nonsense . . . so could see through the underworld to the future, but I knew . . ." His head fell back against the wall.

Ethel grabbed him by the hair. "Who else was there?"

He didn't answer.

She banged the back of his head against the cabinets. "Who else?"

Dietrich blinked his eyes back open and startled at the sight of her. "What are you doing here? They'll kill you. You're . . . dead."

"Who? Who's going to kill me?" When he didn't answer, she tried a different tack. "Your friend Adela already told them everything."

"What?" The fear in his eyes told her she'd hit a nerve. He was too far gone to reason it out, she realized. He was in a blackout.

"Adela told everyone you're the Mad Butcher—the cops, the press." She watched the words sink in. Rich folks like Dietrich never faced justice in the real world, not unless they turned on each other. "They're comin' for you, Doc. They're going to give you the chair for all those people you did."

"No. It wasn't . . . ," he sputtered, his dilated eyes darting to the walls like a caged animal's. "It was the Legion. The Silver Shirts . . . they told me . . . it's the war."

The phone out in the reception area started to ring. The sound of it seemed to wake something up in the doctor, so she gave him another dose of ether.

"They're gonna put you on trial. How do you think the boss . . . what's his name?"

"Pelley," he breathed, drooling onto his shirt.

"Right. What do you think Pelley will do when he finds out you've been caught? Do you think he's gonna want you blabbing everything you know to the coppers?"

The color drained from his face. He gaped at her, dumbstruck. "No. It wasn't supposed to . . . like this . . . Pelley's armies . . . he promised me . . . promised a gov'n—ship . . . And now . . ."

"Now they're going to kill you." The helpless terror on his face sent a cold satisfaction through her. The bastard that had strung her up deserved to die pissing himself. "They're going to hang you from a meat hook and bleed you dry . . ."

"No . . . ," he wailed and heaved onto the floor. His body trembled in a cold sweat. "I'm not a dog! I'm a doctor for Christ's sake! A respected member of the com—ity. A pillar . . ."

"No. You're a killer . . . a sex maniac even. You stripped young hustlers like Eddie naked before cuttin' him up." Ethel stood up from the mess and considered whether she had the stomach to cut up the doctor like he deserved. Or she could shoot him. Outside, the street noises went about their business without a siren in earshot. Newspaper headlines reading *GOOD DOCTOR GUNNED DOWN* flashed through her mind. *No,* she decided angrily. *He must die in shame, an utter disgrace. A bum. A junkie.* "You know what they said down in the Run about the Butcher when they found those first two bodies? They said it must be a queer love triangle. You a swish, Doc?"

The doctor recoiled from the words in his ether fog and pulled at his hair. "No, no, no . . . that wasn't me . . . Those bastards . . . Woznick and Kessler wanted to make an example . . . The pimp fucked Woznick's wife."

Ethel made a mental note of the names and scanned the medicine cabinet. She grabbed a morphine vial, recognizing the label from her years hustling junkies. She found a hypodermic needle and filled it to the top. She pulled rubbing tubing from another drawer and hunkered down next to him on the ground. "How many cops are in the Legion?"

The doctor shook his head. "In Cleveland? Eleven? Twelve?"

"You're going to fry, Doc. All those cops against you? Judges too?"

The doctor nodded and then retched again onto the floor. "God . . . I can't . . . it's not me."

"I need their names."

"You stupid bitch," he mumbled, his head falling to his chest. "They're going to find you . . . The Legion is everywhere. New York, Detroit, Chicago, Los Angeles. They've got armies . . . Pelley will be king and you . . ." He let out an inebriated laugh.

Ethel slapped him hard and shoved the ether mask back over his face. "I need their names!"

A stream of garbled names poured out of the doctor's mouth as his eyes went out. The list went on and on. *They've got armies.* He slumped against the floor, unconscious. She had half a mind to let the Legion find him and do their worst, but then they'd know what he'd told her.

She rolled up the doctor's sleeve with the rubber tubing in her teeth and the gun next to her knee. Needle marks dotted his arm. *Good.* She tightened the tourniquet around his bicep and slapped his veins. "Don't worry, Doc. Lotsa folks kill themselves in times like these. You're goin' straight to hell either way."

He mumbled something into the floor. It sounded like "You're dead."

She checked the dosage again just to be sure. It was enough junk to kill two men. She sank the needle into a fat vein and pushed it home. She grabbed the handkerchief out of his pocket and cleaned her fingerprints from the syringe. Lifting his limp hand from the floor, she pressed it against the vial and plunger.

He shook a little as the enormous dose of morphine hit his bloodstream. A puddle of urine spread across the floor. She gazed into his eyes as they drifted back into his head. He deserved so much worse. "They can't kill me!" she spat at his still body. "I died years ago."

Ethel stood up and wiped all traces of herself from the office as she left the room. It wasn't perfect. The bullet hole in the wall. The powder burn. The bruises on his ribs. The receptionist. But something told her that the doctor's police friends would keep it quiet and avoid a big investigation. She decided it didn't really matter.

Across the street, Johnnie's legs swung back and forth from a park bench. "Is everything okay?" she asked as Ethel walked up.

"Yep. Everything's just fine, sugar."

"What we doin' now?"

"We're gonna go visit a lady that calls herself a witch." Ethel picked up the girl's hand and started walking, watching the street. "And then maybe we'll get some ice cream. You like ice cream?"

TORSO KILLER VICTIM COMES FORWARD

Religious Cult May Be Responsible for Murders

The Torso Murder investigation reopened today based on the sworn statement of an 84-year-old woman who claims to have escaped Cleveland's most notorious serial killer in 1938. Sources inside the FBI suggest a religious cult may be responsible for the brutal slaying of at least 11 victims between 1934 and 1938, and federal agents are investigating whether the recent shooting death of Alfred Wiley in Tremont is linked to similar cult activity. Material witnesses to Wednesday's shooting claim that a pseudo-religious white supremacist group was involved. The alleged crime ring has been implicated in a series of unsolved murders throughout Ohio, Illinois and Pennsylvania. Witnesses are reportedly being held in an undisclosed location and were not available for comment. Sources have confirmed that one of the initial suspects, Peter Davis, has been released from custody . . .

—*Cleveland Daily News*, May 8, 1999, p. 1

EPILOGUE

January 21, 2000

It wasn't her.

Passing by the shop window, she caught her own reflection in the glass. The sight stopped her cold. The girl was a stranger. Her cropped hair dyed black. Her small frame swallowed by an oversized hoodie. Her amber eyes nothing but a shadow under her pierced brow. A street artist. A punk. A pickpocket. A thief.

A killer.

She studied the specter of herself and lifted the camera hanging from her neck. The teeming streets of Mexico City bounced their vivid colors off the glass. In the frame, a tall, dark figure peeled away from the crowd, walking toward the girl reflected in the window. She watched him through the lens, her body braced with a fear she'd come to know like her own skin. *They found me.*

She closed her eyes and exhaled slowly, refusing to turn around. *Ben's still in custody. Troy hung himself in his cell. Still . . . don't look behind you.*

When she peered through the lens again, the man stood four steps away from the girl with the camera. His face distorted by light and shadow, he raised his hand—*Click.*

Click. Click.

It was a perfect shot for her growing collection. Two ghosts caught in the blur of the street. *A victim. A killer.*

"Hey," Jimmy asked from over her shoulder. He held out a foil-wrapped taco he'd bought for her. "You okay?"

She turned and flashed him a wary smile. "Yeah. Never better."

AUTHOR'S NOTES

The Unclaimed Victim is a work of historical fiction, and as such it contains several true events, places, and people that form the backdrop for a fictional story. It should be noted that the characters and the plot itself are all figments of the author's imagination. The Harmony Mission never existed; however, the story was inspired by a real building.

The following is an index of true events, places, and people that give historical context to the novel. Any characterization or dialogue involving any real persons are fabrications invented by the author to enhance the story.

Torso Killer—Police detectives and the Cuyahoga County coroner believed the severed remains of thirteen bodies found in and around Cleveland from 1934 to 1938 to all be victims of a serial killer. Dubbed by the newspapers as the "Torso Killer" and the "Mad Butcher of Kingsbury Run," the perpetrator was never officially identified, although many professional and amateur detectives have well-founded theories. There is no substantial evidence to support the theory of the killer's identity presented in this novel. Instead, this work of fiction is a thought experiment that explores the inconsistencies between the homicides and the possibility that more than one killer may have succeeded in getting away with murder.

Silver Shirt Legion—A secretive society known to be Nazi sympathizers and harsh critics of Communism was active in Cleveland from 1934 to 1939. The Silver Shirt Legion's leader, William Dudley Pelley, working out of Ashville, North Carolina, was tried for attempting to overthrow the government in 1940. He was arrested again for sedition in 1942 and sentenced to fifteen years. There is no direct evidence to suggest that Pelley or the Silver Shirts were involved in the Torso Murders; however, detectives did suspect at various points in their investigation that a cult may have been involved.

A reported leader of the Cleveland Silver Shirt Legion, Alice Tucker West, ran a finishing school and was rumored to dabble in witchcraft and the occult. Ms. West never became a suspect in the Torso Murders as far as the author is aware. However, detectives suspected that the occult may have been involved in the brutal beheadings and dismemberments of the victims.

Dr. Chester Doron was another reported leader of the Cleveland Legion. Dr. Doron never became a suspect in the Torso Murders as far as the author is aware. However, many doctors became prime suspects in the case over the years due to their knowledge of anatomy and the surgical techniques used to dismember the victims.

Tremont Place Lofts—The 178,000-square-foot building complex that currently houses the Tremont Place Lofts, located on West 7th Street in Tremont, inspired the labyrinthine Harmony Mission Press Building at the center of the novel. The author has been endlessly inspired and obsessed with its long and storied history that dates back to 1851.

Edward Andrassy—Identified in the canon of the Torso Killer as Victim No. 1, Edward Andrassy was a known criminal and a suspected pimp.

Detective Peter Merylo—Peter Merylo acted as the lead detective investigating the Torso Murders for many years and was known to disguise himself as a hobo and ride the rails in search of the killer. He continued to follow the cold case well into his retirement.

Eliot Ness—The famous Prohibition agent that took down Al Capone with his crew of "Untouchables" in Chicago served as safety director of Cleveland from 1935 to 1942. During his tenure, he publicly vowed to catch the Torso Killer, a promise he was never able to fulfill despite his best efforts and questionable methods. He allegedly kidnapped and illegally detained a suspect for questioning in May of 1938 but was unable to make a case. Daunted, Ness ordered the hobo jungles in Kingsbury Run and the Flats burned to the ground on August 18, 1938.

Flo Polillo—A known prostitute and alcoholic, Flo Polillo (Victim No. 3) was one of the few victims of the Torso Killer to ever be identified.

Dr. Francis Sweeney—Perhaps the best known of all the Torso Killer suspects, Dr. Francis Sweeney was an alcoholic who spent years in and out of psychiatric hospitals. It is widely assumed that Dr. Sweeney was the secret suspect that Eliot Ness allegedly kidnapped and illegally detained for questioning in May of 1938.

Rose Wallace—Torso Killer Victim No. 8 was tentatively identified through dental records as Rose Wallace. Rose was a known prostitute and had at least one child, a son that identified her remains. She was also the only African American victim of the killer.

Newspaper clippings—All newspaper article excerpts are authentic and true as cited in the novel except for the final excerpt from the *Cleveland Daily News*, which is fictional.

Many fine scholars, journalists, and detectives have studied the Torso Murders over the years, and I relied heavily on their research and hard work. Most notably, the following books gave me valuable insight into the history of the Torso Killer:

Badal, James Jessen. *In the Wake of the Butcher: Cleveland's Torso Murders, Authoritative Edition, Revised and Expanded.* Kent: Kent State University Press, 2014.

Bellamy, John Stark II. *The Maniac in the Bushes and More Tales of Cleveland Woe.* Cleveland: Gray and Company, 1997.

Bernhardt, William. *Nemesis: The Final Case of Eliot Ness, A Novel.* New York: Ballantine Books, 2009.

Martin, John Bartlow. *Butcher's Dozen and Other Murders.* New York: Harper & Brothers, 1950.

Nickel, Steven. *Torso: The Story of Eliot Ness and the Search for a Psychopathic Killer.* Winston-Salem: John F. Blair, 1989.

Ressler, Robert K., and Tom Shachtman. *Whoever Fights Monsters: My Twenty Years Tracking Serial Killers for the FBI.* New York: St. Martin's, 1992.

My research into the Cleveland Bund and the Silver Shirt Legion relied heavily on newspaper articles published in the *Cleveland Press* and the *Cleveland Plain Dealer* around the time the Torso Murders occurred (cited within the novel). In addition, the following book by a scholar at Cleveland State University provided valuable insight:

Cikraji, Michael. *The Cleveland Nazis: 1933–1945.* Cleveland: MSL Academic Endeavors, 2016. Available from http://engagedscholarship.csuohio.edu/msl_ae_ebooks/1. Accessed May 18, 2016.

The religious language and customs used in the story were largely inspired by my research into Mennonite and Unitarian missionaries active at the time the Torso Killer roamed the streets. Given the loose connections between the Silver Shirt Legion and the occult, I was also inspired by my research into German and Pennsylvania Dutch folk magic. Any errors or omissions are my own, and I sincerely apologize for each of them. This story is not intended to disparage or denigrate the cultural history, religious beliefs, or traditions of any person.

The biblical book of Psalms provided many of the incantations and prayers used throughout the story. In addition, the following books provided unique insights into spell casting, prayers, and customs during my research:

Hohman, John George. *Pow-Wows, or Long Lost Friend: A Collection of Mysterious and Invaluable Arts and Remedies, for Man as well as Animals.* Lexington: Wildside, 2016.

Stoltzfus, Louise. *Quiet Shouts: Stories of Lancaster Mennonite Women Leaders.* Scottsdale: Herald, 1999.

ACKNOWLEDGMENTS

It takes a village of friends, family, editors, and helpful civilians to make a historical novel like this one possible. Ty Harris, Claudia Madden, and the Tremont Place Lofts staff graciously allowed me to explore and sleep inside the building that inspired the story. Mary Maglicic offered her time and family records to give me insight into the secret life of the vacant building complex once owned by her brother Joe Scully. Dr. Judith Cetina at the Cuyahoga County Archives and Lynn Bycko and her staff at the Cleveland Press Collection were amazing resources for me as I researched the Torso Killer and the secretive Silver Shirt Legion. Cleveland author and Torso Killer expert James Badal graciously met me for coffee to discuss his work and the tenuous possibility that there was more than one killer.

Thank you, Jessica Tribble, Gracie Doyle, Faith Black Ross, Sarah Shaw, Laura Petrella, and all my friends at Thomas & Mercer and Amazon Publishing, for bringing *The Unclaimed Victim* into the world. I couldn't ask for a better team. From editing to cover design to marketing, you do it all so brilliantly.

I'd also like to thank my agent, Yishai Seidman, for giving me a new perspective on my writing and opening so many doors, and a hearty thanks to my friend James Renner for introducing us.

It should never go without saying that my family makes all this possible. I couldn't write a word without their amazing love and support. My fabulous sister, sister-in-law, mother, and mother-in-law give me invaluable advice and encouragement. My husband reads every draft I write, weathers every edit, and soothes every fit of doubt I bring to bed with me. My two sons cheer me on and do their best to keep the peace while Mommy is working, but more importantly, they keep my heart and mind open to endless possibilities.

ABOUT THE AUTHOR

D.M. Pulley lives just outside Cleveland, Ohio, with her husband, her two sons, and her dog. Before becoming a full-time writer, she worked as a Professional Engineer, rehabbing historic structures and conducting forensic investigations of building failures. Pulley's structural survey of a vacant building in Cleveland inspired her debut novel, *The Dead Key*, the winner of the 2014 Amazon Breakthrough Novel Award. She is also the author of *The Buried Book*.